WEDDING NIGHT

Daniella stared up at his shadowed face. She felt a dozen different fears, not the least of which was her body's reaction to Travis's touch. The tingling heat had started before she woke. How was she to stop it?

He loomed over her, the moonlight on the back of his head creating a silver halo effect. He was waiting for something from her. But what? What was she to do, to say, while his hands still caressed her? It felt good. Too good.

Then she realized something else. Of all the things she feared—saying or doing the wrong thing, feeling things she was sure good girls don't feel, being married to him, not being married to him, the mating act itself—she felt no fear of *him*. He hung over her in the dark, had total possession of her body; she lay helpless beneath him. Yet in her heart, she knew Travis would not hurt her.

So why was she hesitating? This was her chance to prove, to him and herself, that she could be his wife.

With her heart thundering in her ears, she looked steadily at him and whispered, "Yes."

BOOK YOUR PLACE ON OUR WEBSITE AND MAKE THE READING CONNECTION!

We've created a customized website just for our very special readers, where you can get the inside scoop on everything that's going on with Zebra, Pinnacle and Kensington books.

When you come online, you'll have the exciting opportunity to:

- View covers of upcoming books
- Read sample chapters
- Learn about our future publishing schedule (listed by publication month *and author*)
- Find out when your favorite authors will be visiting a city near you
- Search for and order backlist books from our online catalog
- Check out author bios and background information
- Send e-mail to your favorite authors
- Meet the Kensington staff online
- Join us in weekly chats with authors, readers and other guests
- Get writing guidelines
- AND MUCH MORE!

**Visit our website at
http://www.zebrabooks.com**

JANIS REAMS HUDSON

APACHE MAGIC

Zebra Books
Kensington Publishing Corp.

http://www.zebrabooks.com

ZEBRA BOOKS are published by

Kensington Publishing Corp.
850 Third Avenue
New York, NY 10022

First Printing: December, 1991
10 9 8 7 6 5 4 3 2

Printed in the United States of America

This book is dedicated to:

Louise Babcock, who first encouraged me to read a romance novel. Actually, she grew tired of listening to me complain about the office computer being down, slapped a copy of Johanna Lindsey's A PIRATE'S LOVE in my lap and said, "Shut up and read." It was my first romance, my first historical, and I've been hooked ever since. Hooked to the point of writing my own stories. Thanks, Lu—this one's for you!

and

To the Adamses, the Reamses, and the Hudsons, for all your encouragement and . . . well, for everything. Most especially to Ron, my own personal hero, for the freedom you gave me, your patience, your encouragement, and your unfailing support. (Thanks, too, for chapter one.) I love you.

Land of Magic

Raw

Unnamed,

Untamed.

Treasure lies

beneath the ground.

Death

and danger all around.

Cool mountain streams,

Dry desert sands.

What magnificence!

What splendor!

Arizona—

It lies there,

waiting

to test the strength

and will of man.

Prologue

In early February, 1861, Cochise declared war on all Americans, vowing no white man would ever see his face and live to tell about it.

Wednesday, February 20th, the four o'clock stage was an hour late at Apache Pass. Howard Blackwood, who expected his daughter, Daniella, on that stage, insisted that the Butterfield agent inform the army. The patrol from Fort Buchanan found what was left of the stage by following the buzzards.

All that was left of Blackwood's daughter was her luggage and one scuffed, dainty slipper. Daniella and two men were missing. The rest of the passengers and the driver were dead.

In his mind and in his heart, Blackwood buried his daughter. If she was still alive, she wouldn't be for long.

Three weeks later, Apaches struck another stage. This time there was a survivor—Travis Colton. But his ten-year-old son, Matt, was missing.

Unlike Blackwood, Colton would search until he found his child. He would bargain with the devil himself, or even Cochise, to get Matt back.

Chapter One

March 22, 1861
Self-Proclaimed Territory of Arizona

Texas Canyon was a perfect place for an ambush. From his vantage point in the rocks, Travis Colton watched the Apaches approach. They were still too far away for him to tell if they had his son.

That's it, you bastards, just keep coming.

It felt like years since he'd spotted the small group and positioned his men for ambush, but he knew from the shadow of the boulder beside him that it hadn't been more than an hour.

This wasn't a raiding party—he damn sure knew what one of those looked like, he thought, fingering the half-healed scar on his cheek. He and his son both knew, too well. Travis wrenched his mind away, back to the group of Apaches.

There were eight of them. Good. He and his men were an even match for them. If he could keep his element of surprise, he could finally accomplish what he hadn't been able to do so far. He wanted to take one of those savages alive, like they took Matt. Then he'd find out where his son was.

The Apaches wove their way through the scattered boulders below Travis's hiding place. *This way, you bastards. That's it, turn this way and just keep coming.* As if following his direc-

9

tions, the riders turned toward him, heading for the wide gap where he and his men lay hidden. He forced himself to relax. After crouching in one position for the last hour, the muscles in his legs ached. Rivulets of sweat trickled down his spine.

Finally the Apaches got close enough so he could pick out individuals. Six of the eight looked almost identical: bare-chested, wearing nothing more than loin cloths and tall moccasins, straight black hair hanging down across coppery shoulders. The seventh one was smaller and wore a blue shirt and floppy brown hat, undoubtedly plucked from the body of some luckless victim.

Travis wondered briefly where the smaller Apache had stolen that black horse with the white mane and tail and a white blaze between its eyes. It was finer than any range-bred mustang he'd ever seen.

A quick glance at the last rider brought a bitter taste to his mouth. There was no small, blond head among them. No Matt. Travis closed his eyes against the dark surge of hopelessness that threatened to consume him. *Matt, where are you?* But as he opened his eyes again and his gaze rested on the last of the group, he stiffened. No Indian he'd ever heard of had a bushy gray beard. It was a white man!

A strange mixture of desolation and excitement flooded Travis. He might not get Matt back today, but he could free the white man from his Apache captors. For once, he could do *something*.

Somewhere behind him in the rocks, a horse snorted. Travis flinched. In the clearing, one Apache raised his hand sharply. The others halted.

Travis ground his teeth to keep from cursing aloud. Damn that Quint. His orders were to keep the horses under control. And quiet. It was the only thing the fool had been hired for.

The Apaches sat unmoving, searching the rocks and scrub—looking directly at him. He had to steel himself to keep from moving into deeper cover. His only chance was to remain as still as the hot, motionless air. He realized he hadn't even breathed since the horse snorted. He forced

10

himself to exhale slowly as he racked his brain for his next move.

He had primed his men to hit the Apaches brutally, to rush them on his signal. They knew he only needed one alive. Only one to give him the information he *must* have. If Quint's carelessness with the horses cost Travis this chance to discover his son's whereabouts, Travis swore he'd strangle the son of a bitch. Slowly.

But here was another white captive. Surely his men had seen him. How would they react? And now they might not get a chance to act at all. *Damn it!*

The Apaches slowly but deliberately moved apart, making a more difficult target. Two of them stayed together, the white man and the smallest Apache. So, that was the one in charge of the captive. That was the one Travis wanted alive. The one who would tell him where Matt was.

As Travis watched, the Apaches moved even farther apart. He had to act and act now or miss his chance.

In one fluid motion he sprang to his feet, aimed his rifle, and opened his mouth to signal his men. A twig snapped beneath his feet with a crack as loud as a rifle shot. All that came out of his mouth was a gasp as a thousand needles of pain shot through him. One knee gave way, sending him crashing against the boulder. His legs had gone to sleep.

Instantly, as one, the Apaches whirled their mustangs and whipped them into a gallop. The floppy hat flew off the smallest warrior. Travis froze, forgetting all about the pain in his legs and the Apaches slipping from his grasp. From underneath the hat tumbled waist-length tresses of pure ebony. And from one temple, streaming across those glorious black curls, a streak of white. Stunned, Travis lowered his rifle to point at the ground.

My God, it's a girl. A white girl!

Chapter Two

Two days later the six Apaches, the gray-bearded white man, and the white girl with the streak in her hair reached their destination. The black and white mare shifted and snorted impatiently as the girl reined in on the hill overlooking her father's ranch. The girl, too, was impatient, but she curbed her eagerness and blinked back tears of relief in order to savor the scene before her. Home! Here she would be wrapped in her father's strong arms and the outside world could go away.

Daniella Blackwood closed her eyes and breathed in the sharp scent of sage. She felt like getting down and kissing the ground. Three years. She'd been gone a lifetime. Three years of freezing, snowy winters with bare-limbed trees. Three summers and springs of carefully tended lawns and parks in Boston's better neighborhoods. Three years of rigid, controlled society. Of fancy clothes, fancy balls, and fancy carriages. Of maids and butlers, grooms and gardeners.

A wry grin twisted her lips. Three years of corsets and petticoats and lace and ruffles. And Miss Whitfield's School for Young Ladies.

Three years. Three years and six weeks, counting the Apaches. She shivered in the warm afternoon sun.

The soft, gentle breeze tossed her long black and white hair into her face. With a trembling hand she brushed the curls back and took in the welcome sights of home. The cattle looked fat as they grazed on the lush natural grasses of the valley, and from Daniella's vantage point on the hill, she could see that the herd had increased in size while she'd been gone.

A pair of mallards flew overhead, angling toward the pond on the far side of the basin. Squawking and scolding, a blue jay chased a crow from the wild blueberry patch a few feet away. A squirrel skittered to a halt when it spied the horses, then ran back for cover, chattering all the way.

Dear God, I've missed it.

She almost pitied the people in Boston, crowded together in a noisy, smelly city. They thought this southern part of the Territory of New Mexico, particularly the area struggling to become the Territory of Arizona, was nothing but hot dry desert, populated with snakes, lizards, and savage Indians.

Here in her father's valley there were no deserts, and not too many snakes and lizards. But savage Indians? She shivered again as she glanced at her companions on this last leg of her trip home—one crazy old prospector and six Apache warriors. She had invited Tucker, but not the Apaches. They were her escort—to make certain she got home safely.

Safely. What irony.

When the stage in which she had traveled from St. Louis had neared Apache Pass, where her father was to meet her, the Apaches swooped down and killed nearly everyone on board. Daniella and two wounded men were taken into the mountains to Cochise's stronghold, leaving no survivors behind.

Daniella wrenched her thoughts away from what happened after that. It might haunt her dreams at night, but she'd be damned if she'd let it ruin her homecoming.

She'd been repeatedly assured that this last leg home would be easy and safe. Her escorts would see to it. But her escorts had been the problem. The six fierce-looking Apache warriors had drawn attention—unwanted attention—like manure draws flies. They'd drawn fire from two separate army patrols and a band of Mexican *banditos*. Then there was that business in Texas Canyon that first morning, when someone tried to ambush them.

But she was home now—safe. Papa would take care of her. He'd make the nightmares go away; he'd help her forget. She couldn't wait to see him!

"This is it, Tucker. We're home." She urged her mare down the hill, and the old man followed. The Apaches didn't.

All the way down the hill she worried about her appearance. Her father might not even recognize her, her skin was so brown and dry from a month in the sun. Her full red skirt, a gift from the Apaches, was hitched up so she could ride astride. It showed knee-high moccasins and a scandalous amount of tanned, bare thigh. Even the horse, another gift from the Apaches, would cause comment.

Then there was her hair. *Lord, how will I ever explain this damn streak?* She ground her teeth and wished desperately for her lost hat.

Her father and stepmother had sent her east to become a lady, but she didn't feel or look like one now, and doubted she ever would again. There were more important things in life than being a lady, she'd learned. Like surviving.

At the bottom of the hill she had to squint against the last rays of sunlight sinking below the dark purple silhouette of the Santa Catalina Mountains. The house, a sprawling whitewashed adobe with a red tiled roof, sat in cool shadow on the crest of a low rise.

As she drew close enough to recognize the two people out front, she read stunned disbelief on both faces. They'd probably given her up for dead after so much time. White women didn't survive long with Apaches.

She gripped the reins tighter. Terrible little images crept forward from the dark recesses of her mind, crawling, inching into her consciousness. Tears welled up in her eyes. She slammed the door on the terrifying memories of that first night with the Apaches. She couldn't let those thoughts get the upper hand. If they ever broke loose, she'd go crazy.

But she couldn't stop the tears.

"Papa!" she cried. She kicked her heels against the sides of her mare and raced past the barn to the house. The horse skidded to a halt on the hard-packed earth. Daniella jumped off, a cloud of dust swirling around her. She cried harder now, unable to control her sobs.

"Ella?" her father questioned tentatively. "Ella? My God, it can't be!" He took a hesitant step forward, his wide, disbelieving eyes locked on her hair.

Daniella threw herself at his broad chest and sobbed. "Papa! Papa!" She clung to him desperately, waiting for his loving arms to wrap around her and make her feel safe again.

Warm, strong hands grasped her shoulders, then thrust her backward, away from the comfort she craved.

"Ella!" Her father stared at her in disbelief.

She cried so hard she could only nod her head in response. When she did, she heard a high-pitched shriek from behind and turned in time to see her stepmother, Sylvia, collapse to the ground in a dead faint.

Howard Blackwood shoved his daughter aside and knelt to see to his wife. With tender, loving hands, he picked the woman up and carried her indoors.

Daniella was left standing in the dirt, alone.

Bewildered, crushed, Daniella quietly followed them into the house. Her father bellowed for the servants, and they came running from every direction to fuss over their mistress. As Daniella looked on, the ache in her chest threatening to suffocate her, she realized that aside from her father and stepmother, there wasn't a familiar face to be seen. Nor was there a single friendly smile in the group. Those few who looked at her at all did so with ill-disguised disgust.

Not caring in the least about the fate of her stepmother, Daniella let out a strangled cry and ran stumbling down the hall to her old room.

Even there things were different. None of her personal belongings were in evidence. The treasured dolls from her childhood, the colorful blanket her mother had helped her weave, the miniature portrait of her mother, all the personal things she'd left behind three years ago were gone.

Oh God, why is this happening? Where was her loving father? Where were the servants who'd been her friends? Where were the arms she needed to hold her, the shoulder

15

she needed to cry on, the love she needed to surround her and help her forget her shame?

In misery, Daniella Blackwood curled herself up into a tight little ball in the middle the bed that used to be hers and quietly, painfully, cried herself to sleep.

She woke sometime later to a knock on her door.

"Señorita?" a girl's voice called from the hall.

Daniella climbed stiffly from the bed and stumbled through the darkness to open the door. In the light from the hallway lantern a young, pretty, Mexican girl stared at her with wide eyes and gaping mouth.

One thing Daniella learned at Miss Whitfield's School for Young Ladies was if a servant didn't know her place, the servant should be put in her place, and swiftly. Daniella had scoffed at the attitude—the servants in her father's house were her friends. But none of the old servants had ever stared at her so rudely. She took Miss Whitfield's advice in hand.

"Don't stand there gawking. What do you want?" She bit back a laugh when the girl jumped as though burned.

But the young girl recovered quickly. She raised her chin and tried to look down her nose at Daniella, which, from her lesser height, left her staring at the floor. "Señor Blackwood says you are to join him in his study *immediatamente.*"

"Gracias," Daniella said with a regal nod any queen would envy—another of Miss Whitfield's lessons. "While I'm speaking with him, I'd like a tub and hot water for a bath brought to my room. A comb and brush, and some clean clothes, too." Without a backward glance, Daniella swept down the hall toward her father's study, inwardly cringing at her ragged appearance. No wonder the girl had gaped so. Daniella knew she'd never looked so unkempt in her life.

She took a deep breath and knocked on the study door. If Sylvia wasn't there to practice swooning every few minutes, maybe her father would welcome her the way she'd dreamed he would. With a hopeful smile she knocked again, then entered.

At last a room that still looked familiar, with books lining the back wall, two stuffed leather chairs facing the massive,

16

uncluttered desk, and the portrait of . . . portrait of—Sylvia!

Before she had time to feel hurt or angry over the replacement of her mother's portrait with one of her stepmother, Daniella realized either emotion would be unfair to Sylvia. What second wife wanted such a vivid, constant reminder of the first wife? In Sylvia's place, Daniella knew she would have done the same thing.

"You wanted to see me, Papa?" she asked quietly.

Her father didn't acknowledge her presence as he stood staring out the open window into the darkness, his broad back tense and forbidding. When he finally turned, his face was set in grim lines. Daniella swallowed nervously.

"That was an unforgivable thing you did this afternoon."

His cold, hard voice lashed out at her with a vicious intent and struck home swiftly. The blood drained from Daniella's face. "Wh-what do you mean?" she stammered. "What did I do?"

Howard turned his back on her again as if she hadn't spoken . . . as if she weren't even in the room.

"Papa, what did I do? All I did was come home!" she wailed.

Howard spun back around and glared at her, fists clenched against his thighs. "No decent white girl comes home after doing what you've been doing up in those mountains for an entire month with those goddamn, stinking, redskin bastards."

She'd never seen her father so angry. Some part of her mind registered that his face was beet red. When he clenched his jaws shut, the muscles in his cheeks quivered. As his words soaked in, she felt the blood rush back into her face, heating it. "What I've been doing?"

"Don't play innocent with me, missy. You can't tell me at least a dozen Apaches didn't crawl all over you while you were up there with them. How dare you set foot in this house after letting those gut-eaters have you!"

Bile rose to her throat. Her heart threatened to stop beating. *"Letting* them? You think I *let* them?" His cruelty and crudity stunned her. She felt herself blush again with shame

17

and humiliation. "Do you think I *wanted* them to touch me?" she raved. "I fought and fought, until I couldn't fight anymore, and still they had their way. I had no say—no way to stop them. It wasn't something I did! It was done *to* me! Papa, I'm your daughter! Don't be this way—please!" Tears streamed down her dirty cheeks, but she made no attempt to stop them.

"No!" he shouted. "You're no daughter of mine! My daughter didn't have hair like a—like a witch out of some storybook. My daughter was a good girl. She would have put a bullet in her own head before she let those bastards touch her."

Daniella reeled as though he'd doubled up his fist and hit her. "Papa, please! You don't mean that! You can't!"

"Get out. You're not my daughter. My daughter's dead. Killed when the Apaches attacked her stagecoach."

For one brief instant, which felt more like an entire lifetime, Daniella gaped at her father in horror and disbelief. His words beat against her, cut her, bruised her like hail from a summer storm. A choking cry escaped her throat. She ran from the room, trying to blot out his unbearable words. *You're not my daughter! . . . not my daughter! My daughter's dead. Dead. Dead.*

But in his eyes there had been another word—one he had not voiced. His eyes said *whore!*

She ran down the hall and outside into the night, sobbing, running until she stumbled and fell to the ground. The pain of his words crushed the breath from her lungs. Even the Apaches thought more of her than her own father did!

Daniella didn't know how long she'd lain on the ground, but cold started seeping into her bones. Was it the cold from the air and the ground, or the cold radiating from the lump of ice where her heart used to be? She didn't know. She didn't care. It settled in the pit of her stomach like a rock in a pond.

Footsteps approached in the darkness. Quickly she dried her tears and turned to face the intruder on her misery. It was Tucker. The old man had been in the Apache camp when the warriors brought her and the two men in that first night. The *shaman* later told her Tucker was an honored guest because he was crazy. Indians had strange customs, to her way of thinking. But Tucker wasn't crazy. He'd known most tribes refused to harm crazy people, so he'd pretended.

Daniella discovered Tucker's secret one night when he let slip with a few very sane, very vulgar words in English. The Apaches spoke their own language among themselves. They spoke Spanish for her benefit when they learned she understood it. But apparently none of them within earshot had understood English, or Tucker would have been a dead man that night.

He approached her now in the moonlight with a calm, sober look on his face. "You all right, girlie?"

"I don't think so." She didn't question why she felt comfortable with him, she just accepted it. "They don't want me, Tucker."

Tucker reached out a bony hand and patted her awkwardly on the shoulder. "Take it easy, girlie. I know. I was out back. The window was open."

Daniella groaned, mortified. He'd heard! He'd heard those horrible things her father said.

But what did it matter? He may have heard all that, but he'd seen worse. He'd *seen* what the Apaches did to her.

Yet somehow her father's words were worse—much worse than the other.

She dashed fresh tears from her face. "What am I going to do, Tucker? I can't stay here, but where can I go? How will I live?"

"Now don't be gittin' hasty, girlie," he said in his gravelly voice. "You cain't run off in the middle of the night like some dad-blamed thief. You didn't let them 'Pachees git the best of ya. You gonna let these people drag ya down after all you been through? You gotta stand up for yourself now, just like ya done up in them mountains."

"Oh, Tucker." She sighed. "I don't think I can fight them. I'm tired of fighting. It's too hard. It hurts too much."

"Where's all that spunk gone to?" Tucker demanded.

19

"These here folks ain't near as scary as them redskins. 'Cept maybe for that screechin' female what put on that show this afternoon."

Daniella couldn't restrain a smile at his description of Sylvia. "She's pretty scary all right. She's my stepmother. Ever since she first came here she's had one of those spells probably once a week, just to keep in practice. She's the one who made Papa send me back East. Said I needed to become a lady or no man would have me. Ha. Look at me. Some lady. No man will ever have me now, that's for sure."

"Don't be judgin' all men by your father, girlie. You might just find your rod's a tad short. Now, you gonna sit there all night afeelin' sorry for yourself, or are ya gonna gather up your wits and figure out what we're gonna do?"

"We?"

"I'll stick with ya, girlie, long as you want me around. Heckfire, I ain't got nothin' better to do, do I?"

"I hope not." Her loneliness eased a little at his words. At least somebody wasn't shunning her. "I think I'm going to need you around for a long time." Daniella rose on shaky legs and kissed his scraggly gray beard. "Thank you, Tucker." With lagging steps, she made her way back to the house.

Her bath water was still surprisingly hot, and she luxuriated in the first warm bath she'd experienced in weeks. She scrubbed herself from head to toe until her hair squeaked and her skin hurt, then donned a robe someone had left her and went out into the central courtyard to dry her hair.

This courtyard was one of the things she'd missed most while she'd been away. Oh, there were plenty of gardens, and even a few courtyards in Boston, but not like this one. The winters were too harsh in that city for a courtyard to serve as one of the main rooms of the house. She'd missed the free, open feeling of passing through the greenery and fragrant blossoms countless times during the day while crossing from one room to another. Now that she was no longer welcome in her own home, she knew she'd miss it again.

The evening chill sent her back inside while her hair was

still damp, so she sat in the middle of the bed, brushing her hair and thinking on Tucker's words.

He was right. If the Apaches couldn't bring her to her knees, why should she allow anyone else to try it? But God, how her father's words hurt.

Put it behind you. Close off that part of your life, the way you did when you left the Apache camp.

She would start a new life, that's what she'd do. *But how? Where?*

She fell asleep long before any answers came to her.

Then the nightmare started.

Screaming . . . pitiful whimpering, pleading moans, and pain-racked screaming pierced the night. Continuous, never-ending screaming.

Hands! Hands came at her, grabbing, hurting, trying to pull her limbs from her body.

Fire! A glowing stick! The sickening odor of burning flesh — her own flesh!

More screams.

A terrible weight pressed down on her, pounding her into the ground, thrusting again and again into her tormented flesh.

Hammering. Bright light. The screams grew louder, echoing all around her amid other voices. She thought she heard her father, but that was impossible. He was home, safe. In her madness she'd only conjured up his memory.

"Ella! Ella, wake up!"

"Daniella! Stop it this instant!"

Sylvia? It was just her imagination. Her stepmother wasn't really here either. Why did she sound so cold, so angry?

The screams intensified. Daniella bolted upright from her pillow. The screams were coming from her own throat! Terrified, stunned, she panted heavily and turned her wild-eyed stare on the faces around her.

"*¡Madre de Dios!*" Sylvia whispered as she backed toward the hall and crossed herself, a look of horror and revulsion distorting her face.

Papa was there too, his face unreadable.

21

Sylvia squared her shoulders and sneered. "She woke Ramón."

A commotion in the hall drew everyone's attention. As Daniella turned to face that direction, her eyes passed the mirror near the door. Her gaze froze. What she saw in the mirror was every bit as terrifying as the images in her nightmare. She screamed again. The face in the mirror screamed with her. It was a scream filled with horror.

"My word, Howard," Sylvia screeched. "She's lost her mind."

Tucker elbowed his way into the room. "Get outa here — all of you!"

Daniella kept screaming, her eyes riveted on the stranger in the mirror, while Tucker shoved out everyone else and closed the door. He placed himself in front of Daniella, blocking her view of the mirror.

"Girlie, girlie. Calm yourself . . . calm yourself." His low, quiet voice finally penetrated her shock. She dropped her head into her hands, and her screams turned into wrenching sobs. Tucker kept on in his soft, gravelly drawl until she quieted.

"That must have been some nightmare you had, kid."

With a shudder, Daniella wiped her face on the sleeve of her nightgown. She leaned back against the carved wooden headboard and took a deep, painful breath.

"That the first time you looked in the mirror?"

"Yes," she croaked, her lips quivering.

"But you knew what you'd see, didn't you?"

"Yes . . . but I was hoping—" Another sob shook her, cutting off her words.

"Hoping what?" he prodded.

"That it wouldn't be so bad," she wailed, tears streaming down her face again.

"And was it so bad?" the old man asked gently.

Daniella buried her face in her hands, unable to answer. It couldn't be much worse. Her own reflection terrified and sickened her.

"Come on, girlie. Stop that caterwaulin' and come over here." He tugged on her arm and pulled her out of bed, making her cross the room. He turned up the lantern so her reflection showed clearly. With a firm, calloused hand, he forced Daniella to look in the mirror.

Her face looked about the same as always, only darker after a full month in the sun. The deep tan made her pale blue eyes look even paler, and now they were red-rimmed and swollen from crying. The pert nose and full lips hadn't changed, except for the slight tear-induced puffiness.

With dread, Daniella slowly raised her eyes to the hair of the woman staring back at her. She lifted a trembling hand to touch the black curly locks that still reached to her waist. What caused her breath to catch was the two-inch-wide streak of pure white hair sprouting from her left temple.

She'd known it was there, had even seen it once, but her reflection then had been dim and distorted by the ripples in the pond near the Apache camp. When she'd bathed and dressed this evening, she'd purposely avoided the mirror. This was the first time she'd *really* seen it.

"What I see," Tucker said, "is a beautiful young woman. Heckfire, lots of folks have white in their hair. Look at me—mine's white all over."

Daniella took a deep breath and turned away. "All over is one thing. I'll bet I'm the only person around with striped hair. A few more inches up, and I'd look like a stinking polecat," she said with disgust.

Tucker cackled. "Maybe so, girlie, but I think it's what some folks would call 'striking.' Besides which, kid, it did get you out of that 'Pachee camp, and me right along with ya. Yup, the more I think about it, the more I like that stripe of yours."

"Well, it's sure going to cut down on my primping in front of mirrors from now on."

Tucker smiled with satisfaction. They talked for a few minutes, then he left for his bed of straw in the barn. He said he preferred it to sleeping in the house.

Daniella turned down the lantern, leaving a small glow to keep the darkness at bay, and crawled back into bed. Her eyes stayed open the rest of the night. As long as she didn't close her eyes, she couldn't dream. She could still remember, but waking memories could sometimes be shoved aside and blocked out. Nightmares couldn't. She stared wide-eyed at the lantern, struggling to keep the horrible images at bay.

Concentrate. Think about something else.

She tried to plan what to do with herself, since she obviously wasn't wanted in her father's home. Where could she go? Was there someplace she and Tucker could live? Hour after hour, she searched her mind for ideas, trying to come up with a plan. All she knew was she had to leave. But not immediately. Not until she had a place to go and everything she'd need to start a new life.

By the time the blackness beyond her window turned gray, she'd stared at the tiny lantern flame so long that her eyes refused to blink. It held her trapped in its spell, mesmerized her with its subtle sway and flicker. Then it broke loose from the wick and floated free to hover in the center of the room. There it grew and grew until it filled her vision.

She shivered. How odd. With a flame so large, she should feel heat, not this numbing coldness that surrounded her.

A pinpoint of black emerged from the center of the flame. It grew and shifted and tore itself in half to become two dark eyes. They lightened to brown and stared directly at her. Daniella shivered once more, but couldn't drag her gaze away from those eyes or the face forming around them.

It was him again — the man she'd seen before in the flames of the *shaman's* fire. *He's alive!* When she'd seen him that first time, she'd watched in horror as half his face was blown away by the Apache warrior who held the man's son. She'd thought he was dead.

She must be mad to be seeing faces in the night. Even madder to want to ease the suffering etched in cruel lines across the rugged, handsome apparition. His dark eyes beseeched her for help. Yet what help could she give a phantom?

Her hand trembled as she reached to smooth the furrowed brow. In that instant, the golden-haired man with the pleading eyes vanished. Daniella was left staring once again at the tiny lantern flame, shaken clear through to her soul.

Chapter Three

During the next few days the disturbing vision lost itself in Daniella's determination to leave home. Her father's open contempt was all the incentive she needed. Whenever she made the mistake of being in the same room with them, her father and stepmother talked around her as if she weren't there.

Each night Daniella suffered the same horror-filled dreams, until she gave up all efforts to sleep at night. Instead, she napped during the day. No bad dreams plagued her daytime sleep, and the vision of the golden-haired man didn't return.

The new routine gave her the freedom of the house at night. She began a thorough inspection of each room to locate items she might wish to take with her when she and Tucker left. She dared anyone to stop her from taking whatever she wanted from the house.

Through it all, Tucker was Daniella's rock. She hadn't told him about her vision, yet she told him everything else. Whenever she needed someone to talk with, he was there. When she needed advice, he was there. When she just wanted the company of another person, he was there. *Thank God for Tucker.*

If not for him, she didn't know what she'd have done. He became her confidant and best friend, her father, mother, and brother all rolled into one. He was her whole family now.

She said as much to him one day, and he scoffed. "Shoot, girlie, I'm jist an old man. I'll be yer friend, or whatever else ya want me to be. But I ain't never been no father. Leastwise, not that I know of," he added with a grin. " 'Sides. You still have a father. Two, if ya wanna count Cochise. I wouldn't be forgettin' him, girlie. Much as I hate to admit anything good about an Apache, he done right by ya."

"Yes," she said, "he did, didn't he." Then, with a shiver, she pushed all thoughts of Cochise and Apaches away. "But he's not the same as my real father." However, the man she called father wasn't the same as he used to be, either.

Daniella wanted to hate her stepmother for persuading her father to send her away three years ago, but somehow the emotion just wouldn't take hold. She realized that her present circumstance wasn't all Sylvia's fault. Howard Blackwood was a grown man, well able to make his own decisions. If he wanted his daughter home badly enough, Sylvia would never have been able to convince him to send her away.

No. It wasn't all Sylvia's fault. Daniella's father bore his share of the blame.

And me, too, Daniella finally admitted to herself. She hadn't exactly welcomed Sylvia with open arms when Howard had married her. Daniella had been only fourteen then, and jealous of the attention her father paid his new bride. She'd thought Sylvia was trying to take her mother's place, and no one had ever bothered to tell her differently.

They were all to blame, all three of them. Yet Daniella was the one who paid the highest price for their failure to become a family. She was the one without a home. Without a home, and running out of time.

She knew she'd delayed leaving long enough. Her father could barely stand the sight of her. Then there was Sylvia. The woman spent most of her time locked away in one of the spare bedrooms near the back of the house. No telling what she did in there. When she happened to venture out, she refused to so much as look at Daniella.

If nothing else, Sylvia's comment to Howard the morning after Daniella's third screaming nightmare was enough to send Daniella packing—if only she'd had someplace to go.

Daniella had been sitting in the courtyard, letting the morning sun ease the sharp pain in her head, residue from her nightmare, when her parents came out. She never knew if they saw her or not; she remembered nothing but Sylvia's voice, cold and hard and filled with hatred.

"It's got to stop, Howard. The girl has to go. Ramón is afraid to go to sleep at night for all the screaming that goes on around here. Your daughter is not the same girl who left here three years ago. The Apaches made her a whore. She is ruined. What chance will Ramón have at a normal life once our friends and neighbors learn what's happened to her? We'll all be scorned. She *must* go away."

Daniella shivered at the memory of the hatred in Sylvia's voice. And at her father's telling silence.

How dare Sylvia call her a whore. If the sounds coming from the master bedroom meant anything, Sylvia had been spreading herself beneath Daniella's father almost nightly — and apparently enjoying every minute of it.

From what little Daniella had learned on the subject in Boston, both from her grandmother and the gossip at school, nice girls — ladies — did not derive enjoyment from performing their wifely duties. That's why men used whores. For fun. But they never married them. They married ladies.

And she calls me a whore.

It was time to go. Past time. But where? The question had been bouncing off the walls of her mind for days. Where could she go?

Wandering around her father's study late that night, she noticed papers scattered across his usually immaculate desk. She carried the lantern over to investigate and discovered the deed to her late uncle's ranch.

Her pulse quickened; her hands trembled. *This is it! El Valle de Esperanza — The Valley of Hope. That's where I'll go!*

It was perfect. Even the name was perfect. Hope rose in her chest — hope for the future.

El Valle wasn't close enough to a town that she'd have to deal with strangers all the time, strangers who would undoubtedly stare at her hair and call her filthy names, yet it was close enough to Tucson that getting supplies wouldn't be a problem. Of course, running a ranch would be hard work, but the little valley was small enough that she felt confident she and Tucker could manage. If not, maybe they could hire help.

Plans and ideas ran through her mind so fast she had to sit and write them down so as not to forget them. The list of things she would need became much more definite than the vague ideas she'd had for days.

Uncle John died last summer of a heart attack. Would there be anything left in the small adobe house in the little valley, like furniture? She could find that out tomorrow. All she really had to do was get her father to deed the valley to her. He'd do it, too, just to be rid of her.

The next morning Daniella dragged Tucker along for moral support and joined the family for breakfast. The two were, as usual, ignored.

After several minutes of listening to her father and step-mother discuss what a beautiful day it was going to be, Daniella interrupted them. "I'll be leaving soon, Papa."

There was a long, tense silence while Howard studied his plate. He finally threw down his fork and took a deep breath.

"So be it," he said without looking at her.

"I want you to sign over the deed to El Valle to me."

He whipped his head around and gaped. "You want what?"

"There's no need to shout, Papa." Oh, she enjoyed this. "I believe you heard me."

"That is a very valuable piece of property. There's no way in hell I'm turning it over to an irresponsible young girl."

"It's a valuable piece of property only if used to its potential, and you aren't using it at all. And I'm not an irresponsible young girl. I'm your daughter, whether you care to admit it or not, and I know a lot about running a ranch. I learned from you, remember? Sign it over and I'll go there and never bother you again."

Howard stood so abruptly and with such force that he knocked his chair over, startling a squeak from Sylvia. He stormed out of the room. A moment later everyone in the house heard his study door slam. The dining room filled with silence. Finally Sylvia exited in a flurry of rustling silk, leaving Daniella and Tucker alone at the table.

After a moment Tucker chuckled. "You sure know how to stir up trouble, girlie. What if he don't sign?"

"Oh, he'll sign, all right," she said with a sneer. "He wants

28

me gone from here bad enough to do about anything. If he's reluctant, I'm sure Sylvia will talk him in to it."

Sylvia was back in a matter of minutes. She resumed her place at the table, a look of smug satisfaction on her face.

Daniella's stomach tightened with uncertainty. What if Sylvia convinced Howard not to sign? She might have, out of spite, simply because Daniella wanted the deed.

She felt her hands turn to ice. What if—

"Ramón, no!" The shriek came from the other end of the house, followed by the slamming of a door and, of all things, a childish giggle.

It was the third time Daniella had heard the name Ramón since she'd been home. Just who was he, anyway, and why hadn't she seen him?

Howard returned from his study, his mouth no more than a grim line in his harsh face. As he sat down, a small, brown-eyed boy of about two burst in from the other door, followed immediately by an overweight Mexican woman who wrung her hands and chewed on her lower lip.

"Madre! Padre!" the little boy cried.

Daniella felt like she'd been punched in the stomach. *Mother? Father?*

Howard and Sylvia stood at once and moved toward the boy. Sylvia reached him first and swept him up in her arms. She raised her head proudly and glared an unmistakable challenge at Daniella. "This is Ramón. I have given your father the son he has always wanted."

Daniella's lips formed a soundless "Oh," before they parted in a wide grin. "I have a brother? I have a brother! Hello, Ramón." She slid her chair back and stood, holding out her arms. "Will you come see me?"

Ramón widened his big brown eyes and smiled back at her. With chubby arms he reached out, but Sylvia tightened her hold on him and stepped back. "He's only your half brother, and he doesn't like strangers," she said sharply.

Daniella started to protest that she wasn't a stranger, she was the boy's sister. Something in Sylvia's eyes stopped her.

"Do you think I'd let a girl who whores for Apaches near my son?" Sylvia shrieked.

Ramón's lower lip trembled at his mother's tone. Sylvia thrust him into the arms of the fat servant and hissed, "This time do as you're told and keep him in his room."

Daniella gripped the edge of the table, her eyes locked on the tiny dark head as it disappeared through the doorway. *My God. A brother.* And they hadn't even told her. Hadn't planned to ever tell her. It wasn't fair!

Her nails dug gouges into the underside of the table. She forced herself to concentrate. She couldn't let them see her pain. Anger and contempt were all they deserved from her. With new resolve, she sat back down and centered her gaze on her father. "When I leave here I'll be taking my sheep. How many do I have these days, anyway?"

Howard looked away. Sylvia's jaw tensed and her eyes narrowed. When neither answered, Daniella prodded. "Well?"

"Well what?" Sylvia demanded.

"I asked about my sheep. How many are there?"

Sylvia screwed up her face as if she'd just smelled something rotten. Then slowly her expression changed to one of malicious delight. "Well, let me see." Her lips formed a perfect pout. One long, buffed nail tapped thoughtfully at a dusky cheek. "At last count I believe there were . . . none."

The words slipped right past Daniella for a moment, then whirled and struck her in the stomach. "I don't believe it," she said, coming slowly to her feet.

Sylvia dropped all pretense of cordiality. "Believe it!"

"Where are they? What happened to them?"

"Ha!" Sylvia tossed her head, carefully, so as not to disturb a single curl. "We sold them."

"You what?" Daniella shrieked.

"Sheep have no place in cattle country. They smell, they ruin the grass, and all they're good for is feeding the coyotes." Sylvia's voice rose in pitch and volume; her eyes glittered darkly. "We sold them the day you left for Boston. We got rid of all our troubles in one day. Except you had to come back, didn't you, and ruin everything. You've always ruined everything. When are you going to get out of here?"

Daniella's mind refused to believe her sheep were gone. "You didn't. Papa, you wouldn't. You wouldn't sell my sheep.

I know you wouldn't." Clenching her fists, she took a step toward Sylvia and glared. "Tell me where they are, Sylvia. Where are my sheep?"

Sylvia smirked. "Tell her, Howard. Tell her where her precious sheep are."

Daniella looked to her father. His gaze darted to Daniella, then away. A muscle ticked along his jaw.

Pain stabbed through her heart as she realized this final betrayal. She braced herself against it. "It's true then? You really sold them, Papa?" she asked in a voice so smooth she doubted it was hers.

"We sold them."

At his calm, matter-of-fact statement, pain and despair swept through her.

Her father watched her face and frowned. He took a step back from the heated glare she cast him. "Now Ella—"

"Don't you *now Ella* me," she hissed. "Damn you! Damn you both to hell. First you treat me like a leper for something that wasn't my fault, then you don't even bother to tell me I have a brother, and now you say you sold my sheep. You had no right! Those were *my* sheep, not yours. They were my mother's. She gave them to me when she was dying. She gave them to *me,* not you. You had no right!"

"Ella," her father said, glaring at her. "I'm sorry. Listen to me . . ."

She returned his glare. "Listen? That's all I've done since I've been home is listen. I'm sick to death of listening to you. As far as I'm concerned, Papa, you can go straight to hell, and you can take your wife with you. From this moment on, you're not my father."

Through a haze of red, Daniella shoved her way between her startled parents. Her father grabbed her arm and stopped her.

"Now see here, young lady, you can't talk—"

"Let go of my arm."

Responding unconsciously to the threat in her voice, Howard released her.

"I pity Ramón as he grows up," she told him coldly. "You've forgotten what little you ever knew about being a father.

I hope he isn't expecting any love or loyalty out of you."

With that, she hiked her skirt above her ankles and fled. Behind her she heard Tucker mumble as he left the house.

The surge of adrenaline that fortified her through this latest ordeal stayed with her. She marched into her room, slammed the door behind her, and started yanking off her clothes. She was through walking around like a whipped puppy, by God. She was through letting them belittle her and make her feel guilty for being alive.

She'd been captured and tormented by Apaches. And she'd survived it. Did that make her worth any less as a person? No, damn it, it didn't!

She threw her dress and petticoats to the floor, then dug through the bottom of the wardrobe and pulled out the old breeches and shirt she'd worn around the ranch before she'd been sent away. With muttered curses, she jerked the clothes on. After tugging on her tall, Apache moccasins, she flung the bedroom door open so hard it bounced off the wall and slammed shut behind her. With her back as stiff as a fence post, she marched down the hall and out of the house. Her stomach rumbled in protest; she hadn't eaten a bite of breakfast.

She shielded her eyes from the sun with a hand and scanned the men leaning against the corral fence. "Tucker!" she bellowed. He met her halfway. "Pick out the best draft horses and bring the sturdiest wagon up to the front of the house. We're getting the hell out of here."

The old man's bristly, gray beard split with a slow grin. "Whatever you say, girlie."

Daniella marched back into the house. She began a systematic raiding of every room, every closet. She hauled pots and pans, lanterns and candles, sheets and blankets, her mother's spinning wheel, and anything else she thought they might need, and piled them outside the front door. From there Tucker loaded them into the wagon. They didn't stop for dinner or darkness or anything. Not even to answer questions from the curious *vaqueros*.

It was late when she shoved open the door of her father's study without knocking and grabbed the brand new Spencer repeating rifle she'd sent him for Christmas from the rack on the wall. She'd heard one of the men say her father preferred his old Sharps anyway, and she needed a rifle. Might as well take the new one. She also grabbed a Colt Navy, a holster, and ammunition for both guns while Howard watched in stony silence.

Halfway to the door she stopped and spun back to his desk. "I want the money you got for my sheep."

Howard's face hardened. Without a word, he got up from his desk, moved his chair, flipped the heavy, wool rug beneath it aside, and opened the floor safe. The bag he retrieved and dropped onto the desk gave a satisfying *clink*. Next to it he tossed the deed to El Valle, his signature boldly scrawled across the bottom, her own name written in as the new owner.

Daniella grabbed the deed, hefted the coins, and gave her father a twisted smile. "Thank you. You're so good to me."

She had to unload several items to get to her trunk in the wagon bed. Beneath her clothes she stashed the bag of gold coins and the deed to her new property.

"Is that it?" Tucker asked, holding a lantern beside her.

Daniella ran down her mental list of things to take, then nodded. "That's it from the house. My mare and the two geldings to pull the wagon should be enough horses. We'll cut out a few head of cattle on the south range on our way to Fort Buchanan."

"Thought you said we was headed west. Fort's south."

"We're headed west, by way of the fort. We'll need supplies."

A moment later a rooster crowed, warning that dawn was near.

"Damn," Daniella said. "I nearly forgot the chickens."

"Chickens? You're taking chickens?"

"Well, you like fresh eggs, don't you?"

Tucker grinned again. "Sure do."

"Then let's go."

By the time they loaded the chickens and hitched the team to the wagon, the sky was turning pink over the Dragoon Mountains. A few minutes later, the faint pink turning to red streaks, Tucker slapped the reins against the horses' backs and the wagon pulled out. Harnesses jingled, wheels creaked, and the chickens, trapped in their crates on top of the supplies, squawked and shrieked in protest. Daniella, mounted on Blaze, rode beside the wagon. She didn't look back to see if anyone came out to watch them leave. She knew they wouldn't.

She didn't even look back for a final look at her home. It wasn't her home anymore.

The anger that had sustained her throughout the night faded, leaving her numb and exhausted.

Lord, how did all of this happen? Just a few short months ago she'd eagerly looked forward to coming home. Now here she was, leaving again, this time for good, and she was frightened. If it hadn't been for Tucker's level head she didn't know what she would have done these past few weeks.

Thank God for Tucker.

The urge to turn and take a final look was strong. So strong, she couldn't resist any longer. As her gaze swept over the whitewashed house one last time, a movement caught her eye. Heavy drapes at one of the windows parted. A face appeared, a tiny, dark face, nearly swallowed by huge, brown eyes. Ramón stared at her solemnly from his bedroom window.

Daniella's eyes misted over. He was a beautiful boy, her baby brother. Her arms ached to cuddle him close. She wondered if she'd ever see him again.

Now that his black-sheep sister was leaving, Ramón's life could get back to normal. "Good-bye, little brother," she whispered. Her farewell wave was not returned.

With a dull pain in her chest, Daniella squared her shoulders and faced the trail ahead. As Tucker would say, *Git on with it, girlie.*

Chapter Four

"Bein' followed."

"I noticed," Daniella said with a frown. She'd spotted To-más, Pecos, and Manuel, three of her father's *vaqueros,* shortly after leaving the house. She'd hoped they would have gone back by now. Why were they following? What would they do when they saw her cutting out the cattle she meant to take with her? Maybe they would turn back before she reached the south range.

They didn't. The south range spread out before her, the cattle grazing along the east edge near the river. Before Daniella could decide what to do, the three riders spurred their mounts and swung off across the range. A few minutes later they came thundering back over the new spring grass herding two dozen head of cattle. They fell in behind Daniella and Tucker, and Tomás rode forward.

"Tu padre, he say we ride with you to El Valle de Esperanza. See you get there safe. *Los ganados,"* he added, nodding toward the trailing cattle, "they are for you."

Daniella frowned, then shrugged. Maybe her father had a conscience after all. Maybe the men and the cattle were his way of salving it. She wouldn't mind a few extra guns along.

They nooned beside a shallow, rocky stream nestled between two low hills. A huge fist of sandstone thrust from the ground and provided a backdrop for the temporary campsite, with a single narrowleaf cottonwood offering scant protection from the glaring sun. Daniella had been awake all night for more nights than she cared to remember. She sat down against the rock, tugged her hat down tight, and fell asleep.

It seemed like only a minute later when Tucker prodded her awake. He handed her a cold biscuit and a cup of hot coffee. The coffee revived her. She was ready to go. The sooner she got to her new home, the better. But the horses needed a rest, especially Butch and Ben, the draft horses, so she didn't urge the men to hurry.

She leaned against the rock, forcing herself to relax, while the men finished their coffee and joked softly among themselves. Across the stream, a crow pecked at the remains of a dead lizard and paid the humans no mind. Then it squawked, and with a loud snap of wings, took off. An instant later, a flock of black-throated sparrows on the hillside flapped into the air.

Daniella pushed away from the rock and cocked her head. Around her, the men stiffened. Had the crow spooked the sparrows, or had something else spooked them all?

Manuel muttered a curse in Spanish, one she'd never quite been able to translate and thought she was better off not understanding. She followed his gaze as all four men rose to their feet. Her heart leapt to her throat. On the crest of the hill across the stream sat five mounted Apaches, three with lances held ready, two with rifles.

In the sudden stillness, a cow bawled to her calf. As if on signal, the Mexicans grabbed their guns. Tucker dove behind a rock. The Apaches raced down the hill shrieking their blood-curdling war cry.

The cry froze Daniella where she stood. The pounding of her heart was so loud it drowned out the thunder of hooves, the shots, the shouts. She couldn't move, couldn't think, could only remember another day, another group of Apaches on the attack.

A shot from one of the warriors whizzed past her shoulder. She jerked out of her trance. In an instant, she whipped the hat from her head and screamed in Apache, *"Duuda' duuda'! Bini'!"* No, no! Stop!

The first Apache at the creek jerked back on his reins so hard his mustang reared and danced on hind legs.

"Hold your fire," Tucker called to the Mexicans from where he crouched. "Stop your shootin', damn ya! The girl can get us outa this. Let her handle it."

The other Apaches joined the first one at the creek, ready to attack at any second, but holding off for now. All eyes centered on Daniella. The first Apache, the oldest of the group, signaled the others to wait while he crossed the stream.

Terror gripped Daniella as the warrior rode slowly toward her. Straight black hair fell down his back and across his bare shoulders. He was naked except for a breech cloth and high, curl-toed moccasins that reached his knees — moccasins just like the ones she wore.

Daniella clenched her teeth and fists to keep from shaking. The warrior's fathomless black eyes raked her from head to toe and settled on the white streak in her hair. Her scalp tingled.

He stopped a few feet away. The smell of sweaty horse and unwashed man nearly overwhelmed her. She stared straight into his eyes, refusing to allow her gaze to waver. Gradually, the hostility in his eyes faded.

But the fear in her soul didn't. She didn't know this man, nor any of his companions. They weren't from Cochise's band. Did they know who she was? Had word spread about Woman of Magic to other bands? Even if they knew she was Cochise's adopted daughter, would they care?

Images from another time and another Apache attack tore through her mind, dashing themselves against the barrier she'd erected, trying to free themselves to wreak havoc on her sanity. With determination, she shored up the crumbling mental wall and forced the memories back into their dark prison. Her mind focused instead on the sweat trickling down between her breasts and the fly buzzing around her head.

When the warrior snapped back on his reins, causing his horse to rear and paw the sky, Daniella jerked as if shot. With a shrill, ear-splitting cry, the Apache spun his mount around on its hind legs and splashed back across the stream. Amid whoops and cries of "Aiyee! Yip yip!" the Apaches thundered back over the hill in a swirl of dust.

As soon as they were out of sight, Daniella collapsed to her knees. Tucker was beside her at once, patting her shoulder with a hard, wrinkled hand. "Ya done good, girlie," he said hoarsely. "Real good."

Daniella squeezed her eyes shut and sucked in a deep breath, trying to escape the sight behind her trembling lids. The sight of the Apaches who'd just ridden away, and those others, weeks ago, who hadn't ridden away — at least, not without her.

She sniffed back the threatening tears and tossed her head in defiance. *I survived that, and I can surely survive this.* She turned around, then stiffened.

The three *vaqueros* stood side by side staring at her, mouths gaping. *"Madre de Dios,"* Pecos whispered. "If I had not seen it with my own eyes, I would not believe it."

"I did see it," Tomás claimed, "and I still don't believe it."

"El señor, he is not going to believe it either."

The urge to run and hide was strong, but Daniella fought it.

"It was her hair," Pecos said. "Something about the streak in her hair made them back off."

Daniella gritted her teeth and strode to her horse. "Mount up," she ordered. "We're wasting time." With her hair tucked back up inside her hat, she swung into the saddle and rode out.

Several hours later, the easy rhythm of the mare had nearly put Daniella to sleep. When Fort Buchanan came into view she jerked herself awake. She'd need her wits about her for this.

It wasn't much to look at, as far as forts went, but it was the closest military establishment and supply center around. Unlike other forts she'd seen, Fort Buchanan had no protective wall surrounding it. It consisted of a parade ground, which to her knowledge had never witnessed anything resembling a parade, bordered on three sides by adobe buildings and corrals. Adobe was the standard building material in these parts; even the corral fences were made of it.

Daniella had been here several times in the past with her father when he came to trade at the post. She steeled herself, hoping she wouldn't see any familiar faces. The last thing she wanted right now was to run into anyone she knew. As Tucker drew in on the reins to halt the wagon in front of the trading post, she helped herd the cattle into the corral. Afterward, she headed toward Tucker and the sutler's store.

As Daniella dismounted beside the store, Blaze shook her head and knocked Daniella's hat off. Long black and white curls tumbled free. The soldiers, in various stages of work, stopped what they were doing and stared in awe, first at the sight of a girl dressed in breeches, but mostly at the band of white hair flashing in the sun.

"Lieutenant Lord, come quick! You gotta see this!"

Daniella braced herself against the curious, rude stares, but no one made a move toward her. She led her horse to the water trough and tried to ignore the soldiers.

"That's her! The one the Apaches call 'Woman of Magic.' I heard about her from one of the scouts. Nobody else could have hair like that, with a horse to match."

Daniella stood rooted to the spot. She was grateful that band of Apaches earlier had heard of her, but she could have done without the notoriety at the fort.

"You men! Get back to your duties!" a lieutenant ordered. When the men had scattered to their various posts, he turned toward Daniella. "Good afternoon, ma'am," he said, tipping his hat. His smile did not quite reach his eyes. "I'm Lieutenant Lord. May I be of service?"

"Good afternoon, Lieutenant." She didn't like the way his gaze traveled over her body, as if he could see through her clothes. She wished she had disregarded the heat and worn her poncho.

"Are you from around here?" Lord asked. His eyes kept straying from her face to her hair.

"Yes, I am." She read the question, the expectation in his eyes. He was waiting for her to introduce herself. If he wanted to know who she was, he'd have to come out and ask.

"Forgive by boldness, ma'am, but I thought I knew everyone in this area, yet I have no recollection of ever having met you, and I doubt that's something I would have forgotten." He looked at her expectantly.

"You are quite right, Lieutenant—we've never met." He was practically glowering at her now, and she had to struggle

39

to keep from laughing. Deciding she had teased him enough, she quickly grew tired of the game. "I'm Daniella Blackwood."

"Miss Blackwood, it's a pleasure to meet you." He smiled with satisfaction, then frowned. "Pardon me, but we heard you were taken captive by Apaches."

"Yes, Lieutenant, that's true." She tried to keep her face and voice expressionless, but her heart pounded in her chest. Would he scorn her as her father had done?

"I wonder, Miss Blackwood, if you could take a moment of your time to come inside and answer a few questions."

He asked politely enough, but she didn't feel comfortable with the look in his eyes. "What kinds of questions, Lieutenant?" She made no move to cross the dusty parade ground toward the building he indicated.

"I was wondering if you could perhaps aid us in locating Cochise's stronghold. We've been hunting him in the hills since he escaped from Apache Pass back in February."

"Ah, yes. Apache Pass," she said. "That was when one of your officers invited Cochise in, then arrested him for stealing cattle from a ranch two hundred miles away. Just why is it the army believes Cochise would go that far from his usual territory to steal a few cattle, when cattle are scattered all over the area? Did it ever occur to anyone it could have been someone else?"

Even though his own warriors had nearly killed her, she owed Cochise her life. She couldn't betray him; he was the closest thing to a father she had now, since her own had rejected her. Besides, she knew Cochise was innocent, at least of the charges the army had made, and there was something about this lieutenant she just didn't like.

"It was Apaches, all right," he said. "There was never any doubt about that. Several people saw them."

"Apaches. So that means it was Cochise? Do you have any idea how many different bands of Apaches live in this territory? It could have been the Membrenos, the Coyoteros, the Aravaipas, the Pinaleros, or anyone."

"If Cochise is so innocent, why did he run?" Lord asked with a smirk.

"What would you do if you walked under a flag of truce and

40

someone slapped a pair of iron shackles on your wrists? Stand around calmly and chat about the weather?"

Lord's jaw tightened and his eyes narrowed. "We aren't talking about me, Miss Blackwood. We're talking about Cochise—a ruthless killer. If what I've heard about you is true, I'd think you'd be eager to see him caught and punished. All you have to do is tell us where he is."

"I'm afraid I can't help you. It's true I was at his camp, but I have absolutely no idea how to find the place again. I'm sorry."

Daniella wasn't used to telling such bald lies. She knew she could find the stronghold again, and she certainly wasn't sorry to deny her help. Lying seemed easier than trying to explain why she would never help the army find Cochise.

According to most people's standards, Lord was right—she should hate the Apaches. But she didn't. In the first place, she hadn't been attacked by all Apaches, only by a few Chiricahua. Those few she did hate, with all her being. But she found it impossible to hate Cochise or his entire band because of what a handful of drunken warriors did to her.

She'd been taught all her life that Apaches were nasty, dirty murderers, and were to be hated with a vengeance. But once she'd been accepted by them, she'd been confronted with many warm and caring people. At first she'd feared and hated them all, but not for long. It just wasn't in her to condemn an entire race of people for the crimes of a few.

Daniella knew she wasn't the only white woman who'd been captured. But she was one of the very few who had survived, and to her knowledge, she was the only one to go free.

These attacks were all part of the Apaches' war against the whites. She abhorred the fact that they made war on women and children. But the war itself—how could she blame them for fighting for their freedom and their land? Land that had belonged to them for centuries?

"Are you certain, Miss Blackwood?" Lord asked impatiently. A muscle in his jaw ticked.

Daniella bristled at his tone. Even if she hated Cochise, she wouldn't talk. She wouldn't turn her worst enemy over to this toad! "Yes, Lieutenant, I'm certain. I'd help you if I could, but I can't." She was tired of trying to remain pleasant. A

41

sound in the background caught her attention. "Excuse me, but do I hear sheep?"

"Yes, ma'am, I'm afraid you do," he answered after a short hesitation. "I don't mean to be a bore about this, but you're obviously the one the Apaches call 'Woman of Magic.' Could it be you're just trying to protect Cochise, Miss Blackwood?"

The red, white and blue flag snapped on top of its pole in the stiff afternoon breeze, echoing Daniella's agitation. "You're quite correct, Lieutenant. You are becoming a bore. I repeat—I have nothing to tell you. Now if you'll excuse me, I have supplies to purchase." Daniella spun on her heel and stormed off toward Tucker, who had been watching the whole episode from the sutler's doorway.

They purchased flour, sugar, salt, coffee, ammunition, and everything else they felt they might need to see them through the next several months.

"I understand you have some sheep here," Daniella commented with a polite smile, trying to hide her excitement.

"Yes, ma'am, I'm afraid we do. If we don't find someone to take them off our hands soon, we're going to be eating lamb chops around this place for the rest of the year. And none of us are that fond of lamb chops." Major Caldwell, who ran the trading post, spat in disgust.

"How much do you want for them?" she asked eagerly.

Tucker groaned and rolled his eyes.

The price the major quoted was high. Undaunted, Daniella said she'd take them. She got a grin out of Tucker when she charged all their purchases, including the sheep, to her father.

Major Caldwell led them to a brush corral behind his building to inspect the sheep, and Daniella agreed they were a good looking lot, all two dozen of them. She smirked at the makeshift brush enclosure. The sheep were eating their fence.

"Who is that?" she asked, indicating a man in civilian clothes lounging in the shadows, fondling a dog. Something about the picture he and his dog made tugged at her.

"That's Simon. He was left here with the sheep . . . him and that dog. Simon doesn't say much. He's not exactly all there, if you know what I mean, Miss."

"What do you mean, he was left here?" she asked.

"About a month ago somebody brought these sheep in, those two mules," he said, pointing to the back of the brush corral, "and Simon and his dog. This was all that was left from a small ranch somewhere over near Tubac after an Apache raid. He's been taking care of the sheep ever since he was brought in."

"But if they're his sheep, why am I buying them from you?"

"Didn't say they were his sheep. He just takes care of them, that's all."

Daniella walked toward Simon. The closer she got, the bigger he looked. He stood well over six feet, had shoulders as broad as a mountain, and not one ounce of flab or fat apparent. He looked just about as movable as a mountain, too.

When she got a good look at his face she was too surprised to offer him more than a slight nod. He couldn't have been more than sixteen. His big brown eyes reminded her of a doe's eyes, gentle and sad, but his smile was open and friendly.

She wrinkled her nose and bit back a grin. If the major hadn't told her this boy took care of the sheep, she'd have known anyway, by the smell of him.

His open, friendly looks called to something inside her. "Hello, Simon. My name's Daniella. I understand you've been taking care of these sheep. Is that right?"

He nodded yes to her question, but didn't speak.

"Do the sheep belong to you?"

The smile on his face faded. He lowered his gaze and scuffed the worn toe of his boot along the ground. She took that as a "No."

"I just bought them from Major Caldwell. What will you do now? Do you have anyplace to go?"

Distress covered the boy's face and tears filled his eyes. His reaction upset her. He looked out lovingly over the sheep for a moment, then took in a deep breath and let it out slowly. When he turned to walk away, she saw moisture on his cheeks.

Daniella reacted without thought. "Simon, wait." She reached out and touched his arm. "Would you like to go with us and take care of the sheep for me?"

The big giant turned back toward her with a look of cautious hope on his face. "Really?"

43

He hadn't spoken the word aloud, but Daniella heard it, just the same. "Really." She nodded vigorously.

Simon looked at her with gratitude shining in his eyes, as though she'd just given him the world. Daniella had the uncomfortable feeling she'd just gained a willing slave.

She escorted him to the store and introduced him to Tucker. The old man looked skeptically at the size of the young giant, then added enough provisions to accommodate two extra people.

Tucker saw to the loading of the wagon and made certain everything was secure. Simon and his dog herded the sheep and mules out of the corral, and Daniella and the *vaqueros* followed with the cattle. She felt Lieutenant Lord's malevolent stare boring into the back of her head. She resisted the urge to turn around and look at him.

She wanted nothing more than to get out of this place. She wanted no more of these soldiers, Lt. Lord in particular. There was still daylight left, and she didn't intend to waste a bit of it. She and her party headed back north, the way they'd come, then swung slightly west toward their new home.

Daniella felt good. She had two dozen head of cattle, supplies to last for months, and an armed escort who, since the incident at noon with the Apaches, now regarded her with something approaching awe. She'd escaped the probing questions and thinly veiled accusations of Lieutenant Lord. And she had her sheep. And Simon.

A roadrunner sprinted alongside the wagon for several yards before it darted back into the brush.

Daniella smiled. Things didn't look half bad.

"I guess you know, girlie," Tucker said a moment later, "your old man's gonna have a fit when he finds out you charged all this stuff to him—especially them damn sheep."

Her good mood slipped a notch. "He sure is," she said bitterly. "But he'll probably consider it a small price to pay to be rid of me."

Chapter Five

When they stopped to camp that night, Daniella saw to her horse, but let the *vaqueros* handle the cattle and the cooking. Simon and his dog took care of the sheep. She kept to herself at the edge of camp. After a while, Tucker brought her a plate of beans and cup of coffee and sat down beside her.

"You doin' all right, girlie?"

She gave him a little half-smile. "I'll manage." She took a sip of coffee and asked, "How do you feel about farming and ranching for a living?"

"Reckon I can stand it awhile."

Daniella laughed. "You don't have to, you know. I want you to stay with me, but I don't want you to feel you have to. I'll manage if you want to go off on your own."

"Now just where is it you think I might wanna be goin'?"

"I don't know. Prospecting, maybe? That's what you were doing before the Apaches captured you, wasn't it?"

He took a swallow of coffee then chuckled. "I may be old, girlie, but I ain't no fool. If you don't mind my company, I'll just stick with you. Thataway I can keep my scalp. You're my protection, whether you realize it or not."

"Apaches don't take scalps. At least, not usually."

"Yeah, well, I don't aim for mine to be one of the few."

"Then you think they won't bother us? Today wasn't just a freak thing?"

"They won't bother *you*. If I'm with you, then they probably won't bother me either. That's the way I see it. Besides, I'm

45

gittin' too old to be traipsin' around ascratchin' rocks."

"Scratching rocks?"

"Yeah—that's what them 'Pachees say. Rock scratcher. That's a prospector."

They shared a companionable silence, and Daniella sat staring into the fire several feet away. What Tucker said about the Apaches not bothering her was probably true, especially if today was any indication. She hadn't known those warriors, but they had recognized her.

The Apaches had explained to her the first morning after her capture, after a night of horrifying abuse and brutality, that sometime during the night Yúúsń, the Great Spirit, had visited her. That's how she got the streak in her hair, according to their *shaman*, Dee-O-Det. He said Yúúsń honored her for her bravery and courage, and her fierce determination to live.

During the next few weeks, the Apaches treated her like a long lost daughter, with affection and respect, whether she wanted it or not. There'd even been a formal ceremony making her Cochise's adopted daughter. It had been hard for her to reconcile those warm, generous people with the ones who'd tortured and beaten her that first night, but they were the same people. At least, they were from the same band of Chiricahua. She wondered what her fate would have been if Cochise had been in camp when her captors first brought her in. Maybe her captors wouldn't have done what they did. But what if he hadn't come at all, she thought with a shudder.

Daniella forced the thoughts away and took a last sip of coffee as she listened to the howling of a nearby coyote. What if's were a waste of time. Nothing could change what happened to her that night.

The coyote howled again. The night was full of sounds. Frogs set up a chorus that rose and fell, sometimes soft, sometimes deafening. Cattle lowed. The sheep were quiet, but the horses stomped and snorted occasionally, and an owl hooted. A moment later its mate answered. From far off in the distance came the scream of a mountain lion. Daniella shuddered, hoping the cat stayed away.

The dancing flames of Pecos's cook fire flared before her eyes, flickering, rearranging themselves, shifting, changing,

46

leaping, until a face formed, the face of the golden-haired man, and suddenly she knew he wasn't a phantom. He was real. He might be only an apparition in the flames here and now, but somehow, somewhere, this man existed. She could see his lips moving, but couldn't hear the words. All she knew was he was suffering. His misery was so real she could feel it.

His coffee-colored eyes were full of pain. One cheek was swollen with an angry-looking wound. Strong white teeth clenched tight in frustration, and deep furrows lined his brow. Once more she had a strong desire to reach out and smooth those lines away. She longed to comfort him in some way. He looked directly into her eyes, and something deep inside her moved.

A gust of wind shifted the face, blew it away, leaving nothing but the dancing flames. She blinked her eyes and shook her head. Her breath came in short gasps. Perspiration covered her face in spite of the night's coolness.

Beside her, Tucker leaned forward and watched her keenly. "What's wrong, girlie? What do ya see?"

"I don't know," she whispered. "I only know he's real, and he's alive."

"Who's alive?"

"I don't know. But I've seen him before. Twice."

"And?"

She shuddered at the memory. "The first time was just like this. I was staring into the fire, and there he was . . . right there, in the flames." She stared at the fire, mesmerized by the orange tongues dancing with the sparks and shadows.

"He was on the stage," she continued, her voice almost a whisper as she recalled the scene. "His son was with him. They were attacked. A warrior dragged the boy away and shot the man. It looked like . . ." She had to swallow before going on. "Like half his face was blown away."

"You saw all that while lookin' at a campfire?"

Daniella nodded again, her eyes still glued to the flames.

"Then what happened?"

Her brow furrowed in confusion. "I . . . I blinked, and he disappeared. There was nothing left but the fire. When I looked up, Dee-O-Det was there."

47

"Heh!" Tucker twisted at the waist and spat into the bushes. "Bet that old buzzard had plenty to say about it."

She shook her head, not raising her eyes. "He didn't say a word. Just looked at me. For a long time. Then he nodded, almost like he was pleased, and left." She threw her head back and took a deep breath as she looked at the stars. "It happened again the first night at Papa's. Am I going crazy, Tucker?"

"No, girlie, I don't think you're going crazy. But I'm beginning to think maybe them 'Pachees was right—maybe their Great Spirit did visit ya."

With that, Tucker spread his bedroll out a few feet away and lay down. A few short minutes later, his soft snores joined the other night sounds.

Daniella was too shaken to sleep. Where did her visions come from? Why did she feel some sort of connection with the man and his son? Where was the boy now? The questions buzzed around in her head until the sky lightened. Dawn came, but no answers.

They crested the ridge forming the southwest boundary of Daniella's new property just before sunset the next day. The valley ran east and west, with a small stream running from the high, east end, down the center of the valley. The dying rays of the sun reflected off the small adobe ranch house at the high end, making it glow in welcome for its new occupants. The land sloped gently down from the house to the small stream. The whole valley, a half-mile wide and just under a mile long, was ringed on all sides by the rugged foothills of the Santa Catalina Mountains.

"El Valle de Esperanza," she whispered. The Valley of Hope.

It was a peaceful valley, with lush native grass, a few cottonwoods and cedars along the stream, an oak or two, some juniper and mesquite, and the peach trees her uncle had planted years ago. An industrious woodpecker worked somewhere near, tapping away at a tree. Clumps of ocotillo, Mexican goldpoppies, and yellow brittle-brush, sage, and greasewood grew randomly across the overgrown pastures. And scattered everywhere, a full compliment of yuccas and cacti: prickly pear, barrel cactus, chollas of all sizes.

A feeling of calm settled over Daniella. The land seemed to welcome her, reaching out to protect her from pain. She was going to be happy here. After three years in Boston, even the cactus looked friendly.

"Smoke."

"What?" Daniella asked, turning to Tucker.

"I smell smoke."

Daniella sniffed the wind. At first there was nothing, then came a hint of burning mesquite. Alarmed, she stood in her stirrups and scanned the valley again. "Damn," she muttered. There it was, a thin trail of smoke coming from the chimney. Her chimney. She narrowed her eyes. "Someone's in my house. Tomás, Pecos, come with me."

She kicked Blaze into a gallop and thundered up the valley toward the little adobe house. Her house. Her house with a stranger in it. The hat flew off her head and she ignored it. She reached beneath her right thigh and slid the Spencer from its scabbard. No squatter was taking over her land.

The noise of their approach finally alerted whoever was in the house, for as she and the two *vaqueros* skidded to a halt, the front door flew open. A big, barrel-chested man stepped out.

He ran a huge hand through his shaggy red hair, then scratched at his equally shaggy, equally red beard. "Howdy." His grin revealed yellowed front teeth, the bottom half of one chipped off. "Welcome. I just put the coffee on."

"Who are you?" Daniella demanded, the Spencer resting across her thighs.

"Wow! Ain't you a looker. Name's Crane, ma'am. Billy Joe Crane. Step down and sit a spell."

"What are you doing on this land?"

Crane's eyes narrowed. "Well, now, don't rightly see's how that's any of your business, but I happen to live here. Fact is, I've lived here for years."

"Is that so?" Daniella leaned down against the saddle horn and glared at him. "For years? My, my. That's a little confusing, since this was my uncle's ranch until six months ago. Now it's mine. You're trespassing, Mr. Crane. We both know it."

"Jist who the hell do you think you are, Missy?" Crane demanded, waving his beefy arms in the air. "You cain't go callin' a fella a trespasser and git away with it. I ask ya, jist who the hell do you think you are?"

Daniella calmly lifted the Spencer and aimed it at his chest. "I'm the one who's running you off my land. Get out. Now."

The man stood there, his thumbs hooked through overstrained suspenders, and glared at her.

"I said *now*, Mr. Crane," Daniella added softly.

She never knew if it was her tone of voice, the Spencer, or the two armed, mean-looking *vaqueros* at her side, but Crane muttered a curse and stepped back through the door. She half expected him to come out shooting, or not come out at all. But a moment later he appeared with bulging saddlebags thrown over his massive shoulder.

She motioned for Tomás and Pecos to follow him to the corral, while she dismounted and went in the house. A sneer of disgust curled her lips. It was a pig sty. Dirt and leaves covered the floor and most of the furniture. The fireplace was filled with ashes and Lord-only-knew what else. Dried bits of food littered the table, some looking like they'd been stuck there for years. The whole place smelled like something she'd rather not identify. It would take days to clean it up.

By the time she walked back outside, Crane had saddled his horse and was trying to get his ladened pack mule to follow him out of the corral. The animal refused to budge. Tomás and Pecos laughed out loud and Daniella choked back a giggle as the giant man pulled on the mule's lead rope with all his weight, to no avail. Crane finally dropped the rope and stomped around behind the animal and gave it a push. The mule objected and lashed out with a sharp hoof.

Crane quickly dodged, then cursed. He left the mule and went inside the shed next to the barn. *How odd*, Daniella thought, eyeing the load on the mule's back. It was prospecting gear. What would anyone be prospecting for in this valley? Uncle John had never mentioned finding a hint of silver or gold on his ranch.

When Crane came out of the shed, he carried a hefty chunk of firewood. Puzzled, Daniella watched him walk up to the mule's head, then club the beast right between the eyes.

Daniella gasped in outrage and sprinted toward the corral, cocking her rifle as she ran. At the sound, Crane spun to face her, the firewood raised in his hand as if he thought it could ward off a bullet.

"You hit that mule again, mister, it'll be the last thing you do."

Crane sniffed and growled, "I'll treat my mule any way I damn well please."

"Not on my land you won't. Now mount up and ride out, before I change my mind and shoot you where you stand."

Crane hesitated, weighing his odds. Just then Tucker, Manuel, and the cattle arrived, followed by Simon and the sheep. Crane swallowed whatever he'd been about to say. With a snarl, he pitched the chunk of wood aside, grabbed the mule's lead, and mounted up. When he spurred his horse, the mule followed.

As he rode past Daniella, he glared at her with cold gray eyes. "You and me's not finished, gal. You haven't heard the last of Billy Joe Crane."

Daniella returned his glare. "Let me give you a warning, Mr. Crane. If you ever set foot in this valley again, I'll shoot you on sight."

Chapter Six

It was late—after midnight. Travis Colton sank down onto the soft leather sofa in his study with a weary sigh. His head fell back and his eyes slid shut. At the gentle nudge on his shoulder a moment later, he opened his eyes and took the drink his father held out.

"Anything?" Jason Colton asked his son.

"Not a goddamn thing," Travis said with disgust. "It's as if he's just disappeared. None of the army's scouts have spotted him, or even heard about him. Neither has anyone else."

At thirty years of age, Travis Colton had never felt so helpless, so frustrated, or so scared in his life. It was already May, and Matt had been missing since February. Missing. Stolen by Apaches right off the stagecoach near Apache Pass. Was Matt still alive after all this time? Travis forced the question away. Of course he was still alive. He had to be. *Dear God, he just had to be.*

He took a sip of whiskey and felt it burn a path down his dry throat. He closed his eyes again in exhaustion, and remembered. In December he'd received a letter from his late wife's father. The old man was sick and dying, and wanted to see his grandson one last time. Unable to deny the man's request, Travis had taken Matt east and spent a few weeks with the boy's maternal grandfather. The trip had gone well. The weeks they'd spent with the old man seemed to cheer him somewhat, and Matt's grandfather was in good spirits when they left him.

When Travis and Matt were almost home, disaster struck.

Apaches, disaster—they were the same in Travis's mind. Warriors swooped down on the unsuspecting stage, shot everyone on board, and took Matt. They even took the team of horses. When the army found the stage the next day, Travis was the only one left alive.

He didn't remember how they got him home. He only remembered waking up in his own bed several days later, the pain in his face nearly unbearable. Just the memory of it made the scar on his cheek throb. He took another healthy swallow of whiskey.

He'd awakened that morning to learn Matt had not been rescued. As soon as he'd been able, he'd hit the trail and started searching. Day after day he and his men rode the hills and valleys for any sign of a small white boy in the company of Apaches. They'd run into a few small hunting parties and one raiding party, but there was never a sign of Matt. Neither Travis nor the army had been able to capture any of the Apaches alive for questioning.

He and his men had been staying out on the trail until their supplies ran out, then they would return home to rest a day or two, load up with fresh supplies, and change horses. This last time out they'd been gone three weeks, and still no trace of Matt.

"Did you make it by Fort Buchanan again on your way home?" Jason's deep voice interrupted Travis's memories, which was just as well, for they weren't particularly pleasant.

"Yes, for all the good it did me. Damn that Lieutenant Lord. He's nothing but a puffed-up jackass," Travis said fiercely.

"What'd he say this time?"

"Oh, just the usual. You know—finding Matt is the army's business, and I'm just getting in the way. Hell. Benito talked to some of the troopers and found out their patrols haven't been more than ten miles from the fort in weeks. They've had their scouts out though. Their best guess is that Matt's in Cochise's stronghold, in which case they can't touch him, or won't."

"How soon are you going out again?"

"Two or three days, as soon as the men rest up a bit." Travis never gave a thought to his own need for rest. His only concern, which drove all other thoughts from his mind, was to find Matt. Find him and bring him home. Nothing else mattered.

"You fire Quint?" Jason asked.

"Didn't have to. He quit."

Travis downed the rest of his whiskey, then pushed himself up from the sofa and trudged down the hall to his room.

Two doors away, Carmen Martinez tiptoed softly across the hardwood floor and pressed her ear to her door. If her *dueña*, *Tia* Maria, wouldn't snore so loudly, Carmen could hear better. Still, she heard all she needed to hear—the closing of Travis's bedroom door.

He's home. Carmen's heart pounded with anticipation. Three weeks he'd been gone. Her breath came rapidly when she remembered the last time Travis had been gone that long. Oh! Such a night they'd had when he came home. He'd been wild with despair and frustration, and his lovemaking was savage, nearly brutal, as if to punish them both for his inability to find his son.

She wished he would give up his futile search for the boy, except she realized that when he was in a good mood, as he'd been before his trip to New Orleans, he wasn't nearly so exciting in bed. She liked him the way he'd become since then—wild, untameable, sometimes cruel. But having him once or twice every few weeks wasn't enough. She wanted him every night, and she'd have him, too, she vowed silently.

The rhythm of the snores behind her remained constant as Carmen quietly opened the door and crept down the dark hall to Travis's room. *Tia* Maria never woke up during the night. She had no idea her niece had been sleeping with the handsome, blond American for the past several months.

But just to be on the safe side, Carmen vowed to move into a room of her own soon.

Without knocking, she entered Travis's room and found him sitting on the edge of the bed, elbows on knees, head in his hands.

"Mi querido," she cried, dashing to his side and throwing her arms around his neck. "You did not find him? Was there no

54

word? No word at all?"

"None," Travis answered dully, ignoring the soft red lips pressed against his neck and the purposeful brush of her breasts against his arm. He wasn't in the mood for her games tonight.

Christ. What was she still doing here, anyway? More to the point, how the hell did he ever get tangled up with such a grasping, shrewish bitch in the first place?

Ah, yes, he thought. *Now I remember. My brain was between my legs that night for sure.*

Travis and Jason had been at Lucien Renard's ranch down near the border when Pete Kitchen, across the river at El Potrero, invited everyone to his place. Pete's wife, *Doña* Rosa, was entertaining visiting relatives with a grand fiesta. That's when Travis met the beautiful, dark-eyed Carmen, whose black eyes had issued a most blatant invitation. Of course, there was a definite lack of privacy at the time, so Travis hadn't been too surprised when she accepted the invitation, which he'd never extended, to visit the Triple C.

The next morning, Carmen and her *dueña,* Maria Francesca Vargas, had met him beside his wagon, their luggage packed and ready to go.

Her first night at the Triple C, Carmen slipped into his bed after the house was quiet and delivered what her body and eyes had promised.

Unfortunately, Carmen turned out to be like most of the other women Travis had ever known. She talked constantly of clothes, jewels, and traveling, all of which she wanted in greater quantity. She was heavy-handed with the servants, never lifted a finger to help anyone, and pouted if she didn't get her own way.

Travis had grown bored with her in no time at all. Months ago, before he and Matt left on their trip, Travis had told Carmen it was over between them. When he'd come to after the army brought him home, he'd been more than irritated to find her still hanging around. Since then he'd paid little attention to her, except for his last visit home a few weeks ago. He winced when he remembered that night, what little of it he could remember.

He'd come home, headed straight for the liquor cabinet, and gotten blind, stinking drunk. Then, as now, Carmen had crept into his room and flaunted herself, letting the straps of her transparent negligee fall until the gown caught on the dark tips of her breasts, threatening to reveal all if she so much as breathed. She hadn't bothered with breathing. She simply shrugged her shoulders and sent the wispy material to the floor.

He wasn't certain what happened after that, except they had both been savage and wild, tearing at each other in a lust-filled frenzy born of frustration. He'd known from the first Carmen liked her men to play rough, but he'd had no idea how rough until that night. He'd taken all his frustrations out on her, and she'd loved every minute of it. The next morning they were both covered with bruises, scratches, and bite marks. Her dark eyes had glowed with pleasure, and she'd licked her lips in anticipation of more. All Travis had felt that morning was disgust—with her and with himself.

Tonight, three weeks later, he knew she was back for more, and he didn't want any part of her. He was every bit as frustrated as he'd been the last time, but tonight he was sober. Her wet lips sucking on his throat filled him with loathing instead of desire. He pushed her away.

Carmen, who reminded him more each day of a cat with sharp claws only temporarily sheathed, rubbed her lush curves against him.

"Oh, Travis, don't you see how hopeless it is?" She bit the side of his neck none to gently, then rushed on before he could interrupt. "I know you love your son, *querido*, but he is gone. He is lost to you forever. The Apaches will never release him, if he's even still alive. Let go, Travis. Let go of the past. I can give you more sons to ease your heart. Let me, Travis. Let me love you."

Travis couldn't believe it. Give up? More sons? The bitch was out of her mind! He stood abruptly. She tumbled to the floor with a cry of dismay.

Carmen looked up into his face and gasped. One glimpse into those cold brown eyes and she knew she'd made a mistake. The muscle ticking in his jaw warned of an impending explosion, as did the throbbing red scar on his cheek. This was not the kind of explosion she'd been hoping for. Her mind scurried in all directions trying to find a way out of the tangle she'd created.

"Travis, I didn't mean—"

"The hell you didn't. Get out. Get out before I break your disgusting little neck."

Carmen swallowed heavily, deciding she'd better do as he said. Tomorrow he'd be calmer, and by then she'd have thought of something to make him believe he'd simply misunderstood her.

Under other circumstances, his violent anger would have fascinated her. Even now she felt the flames of desire licking hot and fierce in her belly. But she'd erred in trying to get him to forget his son. The boy was everything to him.

Soon, Travis would realize on his own that he'd never see Matt again, then Carmen intended to step in and fill the void in his life. No interfering little brat was going to get in her way. It was ridiculous that Matt should be more of a hindrance to her since his capture than he'd ever been before. But she'd find a way around that. Oh, yes, she certainly would.

Chapter Seven

Daniella pulled Blaze to a halt at the hitching rail in front of the sprawling adobe ranch house. Her little home in the valley would probably fit in one small corner of this house.

She had left home scarcely two hours ago, not knowing where she was headed, only certain that the golden-haired man in her visions was somewhere near. She'd seen him again last night, had seen how tired and miserable he was. She'd even heard his voice this time, calling out to Matt, the boy who'd been torn from his side months ago — his son.

Next Daniella had seen the boy, Matt, inside a wickiup at Cochise's stronghold, the same place she had been. Then it came to her — that was the Chiricahua winter stronghold. Winter was long past; they'd be leaving soon. She knew she could get the boy back, but time was running out.

She had scribbled a brief note to Tucker, afraid to wake him for fear he'd try to stop her. God knew this was the most foolhardy thing she'd done yet, going after a man she didn't know, who was searching for a boy she didn't know. The man was going to think she was absolutely crazy.

She wasn't ready for this. She and Tucker and Simon had only been at their new home for a few weeks now, and she was still unable to sleep at night. The three of them had settled into an easy routine of hard work and good companionship. They repaired the barn roof, cleared out and planted the garden, gave the house a thorough cleaning, and started repairs on the split-rail fence that divided the valley into three separate pastures.

It was really starting to feel like home. She wasn't ready to

58

leave it. But she could no more ignore the plea she saw in the young boy's eyes in her vision than she could stop the sun from rising. He thought his father was dead, but he had an air of expectancy about him, as though he knew someone would come for him. She just couldn't let him down. Besides, she knew she was the only one who could get him free. His father, the golden-haired man, would never find him on his own.

As she dismounted her nerves stretched taut. How was she going to explain this to these people? Was the boy's father really here? Tucker would definitely not have approved of this scheme. She was glad she left him a note instead of waking him. Now that she thought about it, however, she realized she didn't even know if Tucker could read. Too late to worry about it now.

With trembling fingers, Daniella raised the brass knocker on the solid oak door and banged it against the wood several times. She hadn't seen a living soul since she rode up, and the sun was well over the horizon. What if no one was here? There should have been ranch hands out working by this time on a spread this size. Where was everyone?

The door before her swung inward, and Daniella was left staring at a broad chest covered in blue cotton. Her gaze traveled up until she met a pair of curious brown eyes. The man before her looked about fifty years old, his blond hair streaked with silver. He looked like the man in her vision, but this couldn't be him—the man before her was too old.

"Good morning," he said pleasantly. "What may I do for you?" He took in her appearance in one glance, eyeing the poncho, the hat, the breeches, and the moccasins, then his face went carefully blank.

But not before Daniella saw his expression. She cringed. She'd seen vagrants in the alleys of Boston dressed better than she was. With a deep breath, she pushed the thoughts aside. It was time to get down to business.

"You're not . . . Matt's father, are you?" she asked.

The man's eyes lit with interest. "I'm his grandfather. What do you know about Matt?" he asked cautiously.

Daniella took a deep breath to steady her nerves, then blurted out, "I know where he is."

The man paused only a second before grabbing her by the hand and dragging her inside. "Travis!" he bellowed. "Travis!"

A moment later he stopped abruptly. Daniella ran smack into his back. When she righted herself, her gaze immediately settled on the man seated at the table eating his breakfast. She sucked in her breath sharply. It was him! The man in her visions! Their eyes met, and locked. Something indefinable passed between them. Each read the acknowledgment of it in the other's eyes.

"Travis, this . . ." The older man's eyes traveled down Daniella once more, taking in the way the poncho did *not* hang straight down in front of her. She felt like a mare being inspected for possible purchase. Would he check her teeth next? "This girl says she knows where Matt is."

Travis felt his breath leave his lungs. Those eyes! Sweet Jesus. It was like looking into the other half of his own soul, looking into those eyes. He mentally shook himself. Ridiculous, he thought.

In weeks past, he never dreamed he'd have to force himself to remember Matt, but that's exactly what he had to do now. The very idea infuriated him. It only seemed proper to place the blame for his rage on this girl in boys' clothes. "Tell me what you know and how you know it," he demanded.

The girl took a deep breath. "I know Matt is with an Apache family, in Cochise's winter stronghold," she said. "But not for long. They'll move to the summer location soon. Matt thinks you're dead. I can get him back, but we have to leave now before they move their camp, or I won't be able to find them. Will you come with me?"

Travis shook his head and laughed. "Sure, honey, I'll come with you. We'll just waltz right into ol' Cochise's camp and he'll hand Matt over like we're old pals."

The girl's eyes narrowed. Her chin jutted out stubbornly. "You have it all correct except for one thing."

"Oh?" Travis bit the inside of his cheek to keep from smiling at her nerve. She was a cool one. "What part wasn't correct?"

"I'm *not* your honey," she hissed. "The sooner we get that straight, the better we'll get along."

"What makes you think we need to get along at all?"

"Well, I suppose that was a little presumptuous on my part. I'm going to get your son back, and I assumed you'd want to come with me. If you'd rather stay here, that's up to you. I'll let you explain to Matt why a stranger brought him home instead of his own father."

Travis would have laughed out loud at her audacity if they hadn't been talking about Matt. His head spun with questions. "Who are you? How do you know anything about Matt?"

"My name is Daniella Blackwood, and aside from your being Matt's father, I don't know who you are either, except this man, who I assume is your father, called you Travis."

"This is ridiculous," Travis exclaimed. "Are you telling me you don't know my name? How did you know where to find me?"

"Look," she said urgently. "If you don't want to tell me your last name, that's fine. But I swear I can get your son back. Will you come with me?"

"No," he said flatly.

She blinked at him in surprise. "Why?"

Where did she get her nerve, Travis wondered. *What's she after?* "Who put you up to this?" he growled. "If this is supposed to be some sort of joke, I don't think it's funny."

"Do you see me laughing?" she demanded. "It's not a joke. I do know where Matt is, and I can get him back for you."

"How do you know where he is?" Travis demanded.

The girl closed her eyes and took a deep breath. A moment later she pierced him with her blue-eyed gaze. "I know where he is the same way I knew how to find you. The same way I know how you got that scar on your face."

Travis resisted the urge to touch his cheek.

"You were on the stage, on your way home, when you were attacked," she added.

"Hell, everybody in the territory knows that."

"Does everybody in the territory know that just before it happened, you were tickling your son, and both of you were laughing?"

Travis felt the blood drain from his face. He stared at her in awe. How could she know those things, unless she'd seen

61

Matt, talked to him? It couldn't be, but just maybe . . .
"What did you say your name was?"

The girl squared her shoulders and looked him straight in the eye. "Daniella Blackwood."

Something tightened in his chest. He swallowed heavily, then whispered, "Take off your hat."

For a brief second he saw panic flash across her eyes. Her hand shook when she pulled off the hat. Long black and white curls fell down her back and over her shoulders.

"Goddamn," Travis muttered. He sat forward in his chair and clenched his fists. It was her—the girl he almost shot that day at the ambush. "You're the one I . . . the one Lord told me about." What was it Lord had said? Something about . . . magic. Woman of Magic . . . that's what the Apaches called her.

The girl sneered at him. "If you mean Lieutenant Lord at Fort Buchanan, I can imagine what he had to say about me."

A wry grin twisted Travis's lips. "Well, let's just say you're not exactly one of his favorite people."

"The feeling is mutual, I assure you."

"If you don't like the good lieutenant, I suppose that's one point in your favor," Travis said with a smirk.

"How very kind of you," she replied with exaggerated sweetness.

"He said I'd be wasting my time talking to you because you didn't know anything about Matt, and if you did, you're too cozy with the Apaches to help me."

"Had he bothered to ask me about Matt, I couldn't have told him anything, because at the time, I didn't know where your son was. Now I do."

"Why are you so willing to help me?"

"I'm not helping you. I'm helping Matt. But we're wasting valuable time. We need to leave immediately."

Travis leaned back in his chair and folded his arms across his chest. "In the first place, Miss Blackwood, I haven't said I'd go anywhere with you at all. In the second place, we just got in late last night. My men need a couple days' rest before I can ask them to head out again."

"Your men won't be going with us. I can't take an entire

group of strangers into Cochise's camp. It will have to be just the two of us."

"*Dios!*"

The girl glanced toward Carmen, apparently only just then aware someone else was in the room. He could almost read her thoughts as she eyed Carmen's yellow satin gown and gripped the frayed edge of her own dirty poncho. Carmen stared at the girl's hair with horror and revulsion. Daniella blushed fiery red from the neck up.

"This is the most preposterous thing I've ever heard," Carmen exclaimed. "*Querido,* you can't possibly believe a word this . . . this *puta* says. I've seen her kind before. You get out on the trail somewhere, alone in the wilderness, just the two of you, and before you know it her father shows up with a shotgun, and *poof!* The next thing you know, you are married. It is the only way a girl like her can get a husband."

The room grew silent as all eyes once again turned to Daniella.

"Well," Travis drawled. "Is that what this is all about? Are you simply out to trap a husband?" Lord had said the girl would never catch a husband after spending all that time with the Apaches. Who'd have her? A shudder ran through him. He'd been trapped that way once in his life, but never again, by God.

Daniella returned his stare coldly. "I assumed you were already married. Most men with children are."

"My wife died several years ago," he said. "Does that mean you're not after a husband? I thought all females were after a husband." He let his gaze flick briefly to Carmen. That one was definitely after a husband.

"Not this female. Do you know how I got this?" Daniella hissed, pointing to the white streak in her hair.

Travis indeed had no idea. But he did have a very good idea of what must have happened to her at the hands of the Apaches, and he felt uncomfortable with the subject. He didn't particularly want to embarrass the poor girl, although why he should concern himself with her feelings was beyond him. He shrugged carelessly and said, "No."

He watched her clench her hands into tight fists until her

knuckles turned white. "Let's just say I'm most definitely not after a husband. In fact, the next man who even touches me will find his throat slit before he knows what's happened."

Travis looked into her pale blue eyes and knew it was no idle threat. His gaze skimmed over her again and picked out things he hadn't noticed before, like the bowie knife sticking out of the top of her knee-high moccasin, and the telltale bulge on one thigh. She had a holster strapped to that thigh, and the holster wasn't empty. The look in her eyes said she knew how to use both the knife and the pistol.

"That's something I'll take your promise on right now," she said. "We'll be alone on the trail together for some time. I don't care if I fall off my horse and get bit by a rattler, you've got to promise right now you won't touch me, even accidentally, or I go without you."

Travis almost felt like laughing, except the girl was so serious. Was she crazy or something? He wasn't the type to go for young girls, and this one couldn't be a day over sixteen. But still, he felt like needling her. "What makes you think my promise is worth anything?" he asked.

"I just know it is, that's all."

Odd. As prickly as she acted, she didn't seem like the type to give her trust blindly. "Besides," Travis went on. "I haven't said I'd go."

"Will you?" she asked.

Travis just stared at her, trying to think. None of this made any sense. Still, the rumors, that streak in her hair . . . Hell, he'd seen her with Apaches himself. "When's the last time you saw Matt?" he asked abruptly.

"I've never seen him," she said hesitantly. "At least, not the way you mean."

"You must have seen him, talked to him, to know what we were doing on that stage. What do you mean you've never seen him?" *Jesus*. She had to be the most infuriating female he'd ever met. When she didn't answer, only looked down at her entwined fingers with a deep frown, Travis felt his temper rise. "If you haven't seen him, then you don't really know where he is, do you? You're just guessing, aren't you? Answer me, damn it!"

"Travis, I think—"

"Stay out of it, Dad. Let her explain herself, if she can."

"I can explain," Daniella said softly. She raised her eyes to Travis. Her expression turned defiant. "But you're not going to like it, and you probably won't believe me."

"You're probably right. Try me anyway."

She paused a moment and licked her lips in a nervous gesture. "I know where Matt is the same way I know that last night, late, you sat on the edge of your bed with tears in your eyes and cried out your son's name."

"Sweet Jesus, you were here? In this house? I don't believe it. You're guessing again."

"No," the girl cried, her cheeks blazing. "I wasn't here, and I'm not guessing. That's what I'm trying to tell you. I wasn't here, but I saw you anyway. I've seen Matt, too, the same way. I . . . I have . . . visions."

In the total silence that followed, Travis could do nothing but stare. Did she really expect anyone to believe her?

"I'm leaving now," she told him softly. "I'm going to get your son. I'm going to bring him home. I can't wait any longer. Are you coming with me or not?"

"Goddamn it, girl," Travis roared, slamming his fist down on the table. "You expect me to just get up and walk out with you after the line of shit you just handed me?"

The girl sucked in her breath sharply and squinted her eyes. She sauntered toward him, slowly. "Which *shit* is that? The shit about my knowing where your son is? Or that I can get him back for you? Or that this isn't some elaborate plan of mine to catch a husband? Or the fact that I've never seen Matt, but I know he's got freckles across his nose and a loose front tooth? Which *shit* don't you believe?"

Damn, Travis thought with sudden awareness. *I think I'm beginning to believe every bit of it. Shit.*

But even if he never believed her, if there was the smallest chance she could lead him to Matt, he had to take it. Even if he ended up smack in the middle of Cochise's stronghold. There was no place on earth he wouldn't go to find Matt.

The girl spun on her heel and stalked toward the door, hands clenched at her sides.

"Wait!" Travis called.

She stopped and looked at him over her shoulder, her eyebrows raised in question, lips firmly sealed.

"I'll get my gear," Travis said.

She studied him gravely for a moment, then nodded. "There are a few things we have to get straight before we leave."

"All right." He fought a sudden grin. "I promise I won't touch you, even if you fall off your horse and get bit by a rattler."

"Thank you," she answered. "Since we'll be traveling together, would it be considered prying if I asked your name?"

Jason let out a whoop of laughter. Travis glared first at his father, then at her. "Colton. Travis Colton."

"Thank you, Mr. Colton. Besides the promise you've already given me, there are two others I'd like you to make."

"What now?"

"Since I'm the only one of us who knows where we're going, we go where I say, when I say, with no arguments."

"Fair enough," he replied. "And the other?"

"When we're around any Apaches, you must do exactly as I say, immediately, with no questions."

It galled him to have to take orders from a girl, but he didn't see any way around it. She was possibly the only chance he had of finding Matt. *If* she was telling the truth. He studied her for a long moment, then nodded. "Agreed."

Chapter Eight

Travis was ready to ride in a matter of minutes. "Which way, Miss Blackwood?"

The girl stuffed her hair back inside her hat and stared off toward the horizon. Without a word, she kicked her mare into a mile-eating gallop, heading southeast. She set the pace, and it was a fast one. They rode hard across rugged land, following the foothills of the Santa Catalina Mountains. They crossed acres of natural pastures of lush green grass, scaring up several deer and jackrabbits hidden in the tall forage, as well as a few longhorn. The grasslands occasionally gave way to rocky, cactus-studded terrain, forcing the two to slow their pace for a time.

Travis studied Daniella out the corner of his eye. He'd never seen anyone like her. She looked about sixteen, except when he looked into her eyes. Those were the strangest, most captivating eyes he'd ever seen. Their pale blue shade reminded him of the morning sky, or perhaps a robin's egg; their directness fascinated him. But they also looked weary, and sad. Old, as though she'd seen things other people could only guess at. He loved her eyes.

And that hair! He had heard about her last week at Fort Buchanan. The soldiers talked about how she saved herself and her *vaqueros* from Apache warriors simply by standing still and looking at the Indians. Magic? Probably not. That hair would make her instantly recognizable, and he'd seen her with Apaches himself. They knew her. She didn't need magic.

Right now the only magic he wanted her to perform was

to make that damn hat disappear so he could see all that black and white hair tumbling down to her waist again. He shifted his weight in the saddle, not at all sure he should be having such thoughts.

When he first saw that white streak of hair, he knew there was much more to her story than he had been told. For some reason, he believed she really could find his son. And if she could, he'd give her anything she wanted, even though she said she wanted nothing but to find Matt. What a fairy tale. He'd never met a woman yet who didn't want something—usually the moon, at the very last.

They stopped in the early afternoon to rest and water the horses, and Travis was further amazed by his companion when she sat on the ground, leaned back against a boulder and fell instantly asleep. He took a strip of jerky from his saddlebag, picked out his own boulder, and sat down to study her more closely.

He'd never seen a girl in men's breeches before, and found himself wishing she would take off that poncho, which covered her loosely from neck to knees, so he could see the shape of her. He couldn't even see her throat or that bandanna she wore wrapped around it. What was she like, he wondered as he sat looking at the delicate features of her face. She had taken off her hat when she sat down, and he decided he liked the look of that white streak in her hair.

Travis smiled to himself and looked over at Daniella's mare. The markings were extraordinary. Was the horse her idea of a joke? Not that the animal was funny looking—far from it. But the similarity of coloring between horse and rider could not be a coincidence. Had someone chosen the horse especially for her? Her father, maybe? He knew she didn't have a husband—besides, she didn't look old enough to be married. And no husband would let a wife as pretty as this girl go riding through the wilderness with another man. Neither, for that matter, would a father. All his speculations only led to more questions.

The mare snorted and pawed the ground, then Travis's big buckskin stallion did the same, as if answering. Travis watched in bemusement as the black horse with the strange white markings walked over and nudged the sleeping girl. Daniella came instantly awake.

They started out again, and Travis noticed she didn't put her hat back on. He was glad. They rode hard and fast for the rest of the day, pushing their horses to the limit, slowing only when the terrain forced them to, stopping only when necessary for the sake of their mounts.

The sun beat down on them. The hot air sucked up every ounce of moisture it could find. Travis knew Daniella must be nearly roasting in that damn poncho, yet she seemed un-affected by its weight and the heat it trapped beneath its folds. She rode with her back straight and her head high. Her stamina amazed him. Many men he knew would have been falling out of their saddles by now; he nearly was.

When it got too dark to ride safely, they halted for the night. They made camp in the shelter of some huge boulders beside a small stream, about halfway through the pass between the Santa Catalina and the Santa Rita Mountains. They had made good time today, but Travis still didn't know exactly where they were going. She hadn't said. In fact, she hadn't said anything at all since they left his house. He'd never met a woman before who didn't talk constantly.

Travis pursed his lips in a soundless whistle. The girl had picked a good place to camp, unsaddled her own horse and rubbed it down, and had coffee brewing over a fire faster than any two men could have done. His fascination grew by the minute.

Daniella chewed on a piece of jerky and felt Travis's eyes boring into her, trying to strip away all her secrets. It un-nerved her. "Coffee's ready," she said in an attempt to dis-tract him.

"Smells like it."

After taking the proffered tin cup, he sat down a few feet away and kept staring at her. It was all she could do to keep from squirming in agitation. Was that a blush she felt stain-ing her cheeks, or just the heat from the fire? She frantically searched her mind for some safe topic of conversation to oc-

69

cupy him, and came up with absolutely nothing. They ate in silence, his eyes riveted on her.

Halfway through the meal, she started to fidget. She couldn't take any more. "You're staring, Mr. Colton."

"What? Oh, sorry." He shook his head. "You're a unique experience for me."

"How's that?" she asked without thinking, then cringed inwardly, not really wanting to hear his answer after all.

"I've never seen a girl like you before. You wear men's breeches, Indian moccasins—Apache, from the look of them. You wear a pistol on your hip and a knife at your knee, and you look like you probably know how to use them. You carry a brand new Spencer repeating rifle on your saddle, a gun so new I only saw my first one a few weeks ago. You ride astride, like a man, and from what I've seen today, I'd guess you could ride most men right into the ground. You lift that saddle with an ease that seems impossible for someone your size—you look like a stiff breeze would blow you away. You have the stamina, and probably the ability, of a seasoned ranch hand, but you're not one." He paused and smiled slightly.

"You're a very attractive young woman. Your refined speech tells me you've been well-educated, probably at one of the better schools back East, yet you're obviously at home in this rough territory. You claim you have visions, and you make one hell of a mean pot of coffee. That's enough to make any man stare."

Daniella was dumbfounded. She sat perched with her tin cup halfway to her lips, returning his bold gaze. It sounded like he was actually . . . complimenting her . . . sort of. She lowered her eyes in confusion. "I-Is . . . the c-coffee too strong?" she stammered, unable to think of anything else to say.

Travis threw his head back and the sound of his laughter filled the night. "No," he said when he could talk again. "The coffee's perfect." His eyes glowed warmer than the coals in the fire before he looked away and sighed. "I've embarrassed you, and I didn't mean to. I'm sorry."

She glanced at him once, then looked away and frowned. She shook so hard, coffee sloshed over the rim of her cup. She set the cup on the ground and clasped her hands together.

"Where do you live?"

She was concentrating so hard on hiding her nervousness, and trying to understand exactly why she was so nervous in the first place, that his voice startled her. Even though she was reluctant to talk about herself and reveal too much, she felt relieved at the abrupt change of topic. "A couple of hours northeast of you, at El Valle de Esperanza."

"John's place? You must be a relative of his."

"He was my uncle."

"John Blackwood was a good neighbor. We miss him. I thought he left his property to his brother, Howard."

"You know Howard Blackwood?" she asked hesitantly.

"Dad knows him pretty well. I've only met him once or twice. I've heard, though, that he's pretty tightfisted. How did you ever get that property from him? Dad tried to buy it last fall, but Howard wouldn't hear of selling it."

"I bargained for it."

"You what? I don't get it."

"I offered him something he wanted very much, in exchange for the deed." Daniella cringed. She'd made it sound like . . . like she'd offered him . . . *that*.

According to the expression on his face, that was precisely what Travis thought. "Oh really?" His gaze swept over her. "Wonder what that could have been."

She took in his narrowed, speculative gaze and knew he thought the worst. To not answer would only be to confirm his suspicions. She didn't want him to think that of her. To tell him the truth would undoubtedly bring more questions, but she could get around those.

"My absence from his home," she answered bluntly.

"Your absence?" The way he raised one golden eyebrow, as if he had a right to an explanation, made her want to scream.

She took a deep breath to control the urge. "Look," she

said briskly. "I was up all night last night, and you didn't get much sleep either. We've got two or three more hard days of travel ahead of us. I suggest we turn in."

She stretched out on her bedroll with her back to him and listened to his every movement. The rough wool blanket scratched her cheek. A stick made a lumpy ridge beneath the blanket at her hip, but she refused to move. Would he stay on his own side of the fire? Would he keep his promise not to touch her? Damn. What was she doing here in the middle of nowhere with this stranger?

But, deep down, she wasn't really afraid of him. It was a peculiar feeling, this trust in him that came from nowhere, yet trust him she did.

Soon she heard the sound of his deep, even breathing, mingled with the shrill chirrup of crickets and the raucous, undulating drone of a hundred cicadas.

She tried to shake off the low mood brought on by the mention of her father. She was glad she hadn't admitted her relationship to Howard Blackwood. If anyone were to ask him about her, he'd probably swear he'd never heard of her anyway.

As her thoughts rolled on, her body began to relax more and more. It was not her intention to fall asleep, but she'd only had one short nap in the past two days. She was out before she realized she was even sleepy.

Travis dozed, but jerked awake sometime in the middle of the night and reached for his rifle out of sheer reflex. The fire was no more than a few glowing embers, but the quarter moon was bright enough to light the clearing amply. Everything looked all right. The horses dozed where they stood.

Then he heard it again—a deep moan. It was the girl! He threw back his blanket and raced to her side. "Daniella," he called softly, dropping to his knees beside her thrashing form. Her face contorted in a soundless scream; her hands, doubled into small fists, struck out at some unseen terror. Moonlight highlighted the white hair at her left temple.

"No!" she cried. "Noooo!"

He reached out and shook her by the shoulders to bring her out of the nightmare.

His touch brought her upright like a loaded spring, and she fought him with all her strength.

"Daniella!" Travis said firmly, trying to dodge the blows pounding his head and shoulders. "It's me—Travis. Wake up, Daniella!"

His words had no effect at all. She shrieked and scratched and clawed at him. "No! Get away!" she screamed between sobs. "Stop! *¡Alto! ¡Alto!*"

Travis tried to still her hands, but she yanked loose and dug a deep gouge in the side of his neck with her nails. He swore and backed out of range of those sharp claws.

In that instant she came sharply awake. She looked up at him, her eyes wide and frightened. With a jerk, she scrambled to her knees and backed away until she ran up against her grounded saddle at the head of her bedroll. Her breath came in great rasping sobs; moonlight traced the pattern of tears down her cheeks.

"Are you all right?" he asked.

She sagged, apparently recognizing his voice, and nodded. Travis reached out a hand toward her. She went rigid and slapped his hand away. "No!" she hissed. "Don't touch me!"

He froze. Her words of that morning rang in his ears. *I don't care if I fall off my horse and get bit by a rattler. You must promise not to touch me.* He also remembered Lieutenant Lord's words: *She was captured by the Apaches. Spent over a month with them. Wonder how she liked it?*

Travis slowly lowered his hand. "I'm sorry. I didn't mean to scare you." She didn't respond; she just stared at him. Her entire, rigid body radiated fear, a fear so great he could feel it. He spoke softly. "You were having a bad dream. You spoke Spanish."

She panted heavily. "Did I?" The pulse at the base of her throat fluttered like butterfly wings.

"Apaches speak Spanish, don't they?" he asked softly.

"Sometimes," she whispered with a nervous lick at her lips.

"You . . . you were captured, weren't you? Is that what your nightmare was about? Is that why you're afraid to let me touch you? You think I'm going to hurt you?" How could she think he would ever hurt her? Then it dawned on him. "It's not just me, is it? I can see it in your eyes. You're afraid to let anyone touch you. You're terrified of all men, aren't you?"

His heart went out to this slender young girl who was so petrified with fear. No girl should have that much pain and terror in her eyes. He watched as slowly, ever so slowly, sanity crept back across her face.

"Christ, Daniella, what did those bastards do to you, to make you so afraid?" It was the wrong thing to ask. He knew it even as the words left his mouth.

All expression left her face; she wore a mask cold as stone. "Use your imagination, Mr. Colton," she hissed, her eyes shooting daggers at him in the moonlight. "You're a smart man—I'm sure you'll figure it out." The cold lash of her voice struck him. He knew he deserved it for such a thoughtless question. "But do us both a favor, mister," she went on. "Do your thinking on the other side of the fire. About five miles on the other side, preferably."

Travis rose slowly, his eyes sweeping over her crouched figure, briefly noting she had been sleeping in her poncho. "I'm not a molester of girls, or women, Miss Blackwood, and I don't appreciate being treated like one." He walked around the dying embers of the fire and lowered himself to his bedroll, disgusted with himself for handling the situation awkwardly.

Daniella sat up and rekindled the fire, refusing to raise her eyes to see whether or not Travis was sleeping. She sat with crossed legs and leaned her elbows on her knees, thinking what a mess her life was in.

If she had remained in Boston, as her grandparents had urged, she'd be safe right now. Her life wouldn't be in ruins. But when the states in the South started leaving the Union, the talk of war had convinced her to go home while she still could.

She tossed another stick in the fire and wondered if fighting had broken out yet. If it had, would Miss Whitfield close her School for Young Ladies? Would Daniella's grandparents be safe? Would any of the young men she knew take up arms against the Rebels?

All the young men she had picnicked with and gone to parties with paled next to the man on the other side of the fire. Travis Colton was one of the best-looking men she had ever seen, in spite of the scar on his cheek. And he was all man, unlike those boys in Boston with their frilly shirts, fancy cravats and silk hats. Travis was big and rugged and sturdy, with muscles that rippled beneath the fabric of his clothes.

Daniella felt herself blush at the very idea of noticing a man's muscles. She must have been studying him more closely than she realized to have noticed such a thing.

Perhaps in a different time and place, under different circumstances, he might have noticed her as a woman. She might have had a chance to gain at least his friendship, if not more. But in reality, he would never be attracted to her now, and she didn't want him to be. She had nothing to offer him, or any other man. Just a ruined reputation, a soiled body that shrank away from being touched, and nightmares.

One corner of her mouth twitched slightly as Tucker's voice floated through her mind. *There you go again, girlie, afeelin' sorry for yourself. Snap out of it. There's people alots worse off than you, and don't you forget it.* Whatever would she do without Tucker?

Travis woke when the sky was barely gray. Without a word, they shared a breakfast of more dried beef and the cold, leftover biscuits he'd brought from home.

Daniella went into the bushes to relieve herself. When she returned, Travis had taken off his shirt and was shaving in a mirror propped on a tree branch. She tried not to notice how broad his shoulders were, or how smooth his golden

75

skin looked. She concentrated on packing up their gear, but every now and then her eyes strayed to that huge expanse of bare skin across his back, and the lean waist, which tapered down to narrow hips bound up snugly in his dusty trousers.

Her gaze traveled back up and was trapped by his reflection in the mirror. She was held captive by the tiny gold flecks dancing mischievously in his deep brown eyes. He moved slightly, and her gaze was drawn to the deep gash down the side of his neck, now encrusted with dried blood. Her eyes widened. She remembered flailing her arms wildly last night and striking something. This morning there had been dried blood beneath her fingernails.

"Did . . . did I do that?"

"What, this?" he asked, indicating his neck. "It's nothing. Don't worry about it."

She hadn't meant to hurt him, to mark him like that, but at the time, he'd been all mixed up inside her nightmare. "I—I've got some salve, for cuts and such. Would you . . . let me put some on it?" After the way she acted last night, she was surprised and relieved when he eagerly nodded his permission.

She dug a rag from her saddlebag and wet it with water from her canteen. When she turned back and faced him her palms grew suddenly damp, and it had nothing to do with the wet rag she held. It had to do with the man before her. If his bare back fascinated her, it was nothing to what the up-close view of his naked chest did.

Golden curls formed a vee over the perfect sculpture of rugged muscles and tanned flesh. His stomach was flat and hard.

While she stared, he sucked in his breath. His pants dropped a notch, revealing a narrow strip of white skin.

She jerked her eyes away and felt a blush sting her cheeks. She cleared her throat and centered her gaze on his scratched neck. Touching him nowhere else but there, she proceeded to clean the dried blood away.

Her gaze strayed briefly to his chest again, wondering if that mat of curls was soft and silky, or wiry and crisp.

What a stupid thing to wonder, she thought, forcing herself to concentrate on her task. Unconsciously, she rubbed harder with the rag.

"Ouch!" Travis cried. "Easy, there, girl. Leave me a little skin, please."

"Sorry," Daniella mumbled, completely unrepentant. "If you'd told me about this last night, it would have been much easier on you. It's your own fault for ignoring it. I'm almost through." She finished cleaning the scratch, then took a tin of salve from her saddlebag and applied its contents liberally. "There."

"Thank you. But last night I was under the distinct impression you didn't want to be touched," he reminded her.

Daniella bristled at his tone. "That's right. I still don't. This isn't the same thing. This time I'm touching you. Anyway," she continued, "About last night." She lost her bravado, and the words stuck in her throat. She forced herself to go on. "I — I'm sorry about last night, Mr. Colton. I didn't mean to wake you, or . . . scratch you. I'll try not to let it happen again." The words came hard, and her downcast eyes focused on the loose gravel at her feet; she couldn't face him.

"Look at me, Daniella." Travis waited while her eyes traveled slowly, hesitantly, up his chest. He could almost feel those eyes touching him. Finally she met his gaze. She licked her lips nervously. He had to force his eyes away from her tongue and her moist lips.

He cleared his throat. "In the first place, I seriously doubt you had that nightmare on purpose, just to wake me up, so forget it. In the second place, my name is Travis. You keep calling me Mr. Colton, I'm liable to break my neck looking around for my father. And in the third place, the only thing in the world I was trying to do last night was help you. You have nothing to fear from me."

"I realize that," she said softly.

Travis tore his gaze away from her and shrugged into his shirt. There were so many more things he wanted to know about her. As he fastened the buttons, he kept his voice deceptively casual. "Do you have nights like that often?"

She took a slow, deep breath, then let it out. "I normally wouldn't answer a question like that, Mr. Colton—"

"Travis."

"Travis," she acknowledged. "But it's likely your son may suffer similar problems when he gets home, so you should know what to expect. Since he's been with the Apaches this long, he's undoubtedly seen some pretty terrible things. They don't shield their children from life, or death, or anything in between. In answer to your question, the only time I have nightmares is when I happen to fall asleep at night, so no, it doesn't happen often. I usually sleep during the day." Her words were clipped and curt, as though by keeping the feeling from her voice, she could keep the memories locked away.

"Is there anything I can do to make it easier? For Matt, I mean," he added quickly.

"Just hold him, tell him he's safe, that you'll take care of him." She blinked as her eyes filled with sudden moisture.

"Is that all it takes?" he murmured, taking a step closer.

She backed away slightly and turned her head. "Believe me, the support of his family, his father's love, will make all the difference in the world."

"And where is your family, Daniella Blackwood?" he asked quietly, confused by the ache he felt for her. "Why are you out here in the middle of nowhere with a man you're afraid of, instead of nestled snugly in the bosom of your loved ones?"

Every drop of color drained from her face, leaving her so pale he feared she might faint. Instead, she turned away abruptly and began saddling her mare. "To coin a popular phrase, Mr. Colton, 'we're burning daylight.' Let's ride."

And ride they did. This second day on the trail was at least as grueling as the first had been. This time, when they rested the horses and Daniella slept, Travis was tempted to let her sleep for a few hours. The dark circles under her eyes told him she needed it. But if he let her sleep, it would just take them that much longer to get to Matt, and Matt

78

was waiting.

It startled and hurt him to realize that aside from setting out on this trip with the sole purpose of finding Matt, he really hadn't thought much about his son in the past thirty-six hours. All his thoughts had been centering on Daniella Blackwood. It made him feel guilty, like he was somehow cheating Matt, which was, of course, ridiculous. If Daniella was telling the truth, Travis was doing everything possible to reclaim his son by riding wherever she led.

Was she telling the truth? The only thing he really cared about was that she could take him to Matt, and then get them all away from Cochise in one piece. Nothing else mattered.

And if she wasn't telling the truth? Well, it was like she said—he'll only lose a few days. He certainly hadn't been making any headway on his own. So, if she was lying . . . if she was lying . . . if she was lying, he'd damn well break her neck!

Somehow, during the course of Daniella's short nap, Travis had swung from feeling sorry for her to wanting to strangle her. Before he could decide which end of the scale was the most reasonable, the black and white mare nudged Daniella awake.

That night when they made camp they were both too tired to talk. Later, when Travis slept, Daniella was afraid to move—she might wake him. She was afraid to sit still—she might fall asleep. In the end she gave up worrying about him and concentrated on keeping herself awake. She did wake him once when, for lack of anything to occupy her mind or hands, she decided to clean her rifle and pistol. The flickering firelight wasn't exactly adequate, but she didn't care; she had all night. At the first metallic click of the cylinder of her pistol, Travis bolted upright, rifle in hand, and nearly shot her.

"Christ Almighty, girl! What in the hell do you think you're doing? I could have killed you!"

After an instant of paralyzing fright, Daniella forced herself to relax and concentrate on what she was doing. "So I noticed," she said tartly. "I'm only cleaning my gun. Go back to sleep."

"It's the middle of the goddamn night." He put his rifle down and glared at her. "Why the hell are you doing it now?"

"Because I've never mastered the art of doing it while I'm riding. Go back to sleep. I'll wake you just before sunup."

"You planning on staying awake all night?"

"Yes, if you must know. And unless you're planning the same, I suggest you stop badgering me and go back to sleep."

"Badgering you!"

"Mr. Colton—"

"Travis!" he shouted. "Goddamnit, girl, my name is Travis!"

"I do believe, *Travis*, that you swear more than any man I've ever met." For an otherwise seemingly stable man, he sure was easy to rile, she thought.

"And if I had a bottle of whiskey, I'd probably start drinking more than any man you've ever met, too," he growled. "You just have that effect on me, *Miss Blackwood*."

"Good night, *Travis*," she sang sweetly.

His only answer as he turned his back and settled down into his bedroll was an angry snort.

On the third day they cut through Texas Canyon and turned south along the west edge of Sulphur Springs Valley. Late in the afternoon, Daniella swung due west. The Dragoon Mountains loomed before them in all their rocky, rugged splendor. Daniella led the way toward the harshest, most inhospitable part of them.

"Sweet Jesus," Travis murmured. Before him lay a section of the Dragoons that appeared to be solid rock, punctuated by cliffs and crevices and outcroppings. "No wonder the army's never found Cochise yet. Is there a passage?"

"I know the way, but before we go in we need to talk."

"About what?" he asked impatiently. They were so close!

He didn't want to stop. He wanted to get to Matt. To get him away from here.

"I know you don't have any use for Apaches. I can't blame you. But if we're to get your son back, you're going to have to put on some show of politeness."

"Meaning?"

"Meaning we're not going to just ride in and demand they hand Matt over. The matter will probably have to go before the council for a vote."

"I thought you said you could get him free. Now you tell me they're going to *vote* on it? When did the Apache nation become a democracy?"

"I *can* get him free, Travis, if you'll just stay calm, do what I say, and don't go off half-cocked. The Chiricahua admire courage. They'll respect you for riding in alone."

"What do you mean, alone?" he demanded. "Where are you going to be? This whole thing was your idea."

"I'll be with you, but to them, I'm one of The People. I'm a member of the tribe."

Travis was bewildered. "What are you talking about? How can you be a member? Is it because they took you captive?"

"Only indirectly," she replied. "I was adopted into this band by Cochise himself. That's why I know they'll listen to me, and they'll let you talk. You do speak Spanish, don't you?"

"Yes."

"Good. I don't know you very well, but I think you're an honest man. In case I'm wrong, I'll warn you, the *Chidikáágu'*, as the Chiricahua call themselves, don't tolerate deceit of any kind. They're a very, very honest, honorable people, despite what you may think."

"How can you—"

Daniella raised her hand to stop him. "We'll get into that some other time. All you need to do for now is follow me into these rocks. When we dismount at camp, take off your gunbelt and hand it to the nearest woman."

"You expect me to walk unarmed through a bunch of

81

Apaches, the very ones who stole Matt and left me for dead? You've got to be kidding!"

"I'm not kidding! What good will your gun do you, except get you killed? There are over a hundred people in this band, Travis. You threaten any single one of them, and you're a dead man. Nothing I say or do will be able to save you."

Travis studied her face carefully, weighing her words in his mind. She was right—a gun wouldn't do him much good. Better to do it her way. Either way, he stood a good chance of being dead this time tomorrow. "All right." He gave her a curt nod. "Let's go."

Daniella returned his stare for a long moment, then answered his nod. She took off her hat and shook out her hair. The bright spring sun bounced off the white streak, flashing her identity to any who might be watching.

They rode their horses at a slow walk up an indiscernible trail through winding, twisting rock. The canyon was so narrow a dozen men strategically placed along its rim could hold off thousands of invaders. Travis's nerves were stretched taut. He held his breath, waiting for the whine of a bullet or the hiss of an arrow, but none came.

Daniella, too, was nervous, but for a different reason. They crossed the same winding trickle of a stream a half-dozen times. The lookouts should have hailed them by now. She searched the edge of the rim above for a flash of sunlight on metal, or a movement, but saw nothing. Of course, if the guards didn't want to be seen, she'd never spot them. But they knew her. There was no reason for them to hide. Something was wrong. Very wrong. She felt it in her bones.

They broke through the rock into a dark, shaded oak grove, and Daniella drew her horse to a standstill. She cocked her head and frowned.

"What is it?" Travis asked, his voice tense and strained.

Daniella simply shook her head in response, unable to voice her fear, and started her horse forward. When they emerged from the trees, she uttered a cry of protest at what lay before them.

82

Chapter Nine

Emptiness! Trampled grass and footpaths, a bubbling spring, huge boulders, scattered shade trees, dead campfires. No horses, no wickiups, no barking dogs. No laughter, no people.

"Damn, damn, *damn!*" she cried. She beat her fist against her saddle horn in frustration.

Travis's sharp eyes picked out the cold ashes of many fires, the narrow trails leading in all directions, and the bare ground trampled by dozens of feet. He glared at her, accusation and anger plain in his eyes.

The man she knew, the one in her visions, the one she'd ridden the trail with for the past three days, was gone. In his place rode a hard-eyed stranger. A dangerous beast who looked ready to pounce and rip her to shreds in an instant. Even his voice was different when he said, "Is this supposed to be some sort of joke, *Miss Blackwood?*"

"No!"

"This is our destination, isn't it? *Where is my son?*" he bellowed.

"Matt was here! They must have left for their summer stronghold the day we left your ranch."

Something, either her words or her tone, triggered a response. The dangerous beast calmed, then disappeared, leaving Travis Colton in its place. He was still angry, but he was at least recognizable as the man she knew.

"Well, you're in charge," he said, a note of sarcasm entering his voice. "Do we follow them?"

"Follow them how?" she wailed. "They left the same way we came in—it's the only entrance I know of. There were no tracks. There's nothing to follow."

His eyes narrowed while contemplating her. "You mean to tell me you don't know where they've gone? We just busted our asses for three days for nothing? You can't find my son? Answer me, damn you!"

"I don't mean any such thing!" she shouted back. Then, taking a deep breath, she went on more calmly. "We'll find him. I swear it. It's just going to take a little longer than I thought, that's all."

"How do we find him if you don't know where they've taken him?"

"First of all, we stop shouting at each other so I can think. We might as well stay the night here. Not many places are safer."

Travis gritted his teeth and pointed across the clearing. "That looks like a good spot there, next to that split pine."

Daniella shuddered and refused to look where he pointed. She'd never sleep there! "No," she said emphatically. "We'll camp here." She picked a spot as far away as she could get from the jagged stump and twin halves of the pine.

By the time full darkness fell they had already eaten and were sitting across the fire from each other, not speaking. The sound of water gently trickling down the rocky streambed would have soothed her, if she'd let it. Instead, she racked her brain for any scrap of information she could recall about where Cochise and his band spent their summer months. All she knew was it was a few days away, somewhere to the southeast, high in the pine-covered mountains of the next range. Not much to go on. The best they could do was head in that general direction and hope the trail guards spotted them. She should tell Travis what little she knew, but his countenance was still too forbidding.

"You think I tricked you, led you here on some wild goose chase, don't you?"

Travis glared at her for a moment, then let out a weary, disgusted sigh. "I don't know. Did you?"

"No, Travis, I didn't. I know they were here the night before I came to your ranch."

"What makes you so sure?"

"Because that's when I saw Matt, and he was here. When I see something, it's never in the past or the future. I see it as it happens, in the present. At least, I always have before."

"You mean you didn't just make that up the other day? You really do have . . . visions?"

"Incredible as it sounds, yes, I do."

They stared at each other a long moment, then the peace of the evening shattered.

In the blink of an eye, an arrow shot from out of nowhere and twanged into the ground mere inches from Travis's feet. Reflex action brought him instantly to a crouch, pistol drawn and cocked. But even his split-second response wasn't fast enough. He and Daniella were already surrounded by a half-dozen Apache warriors, some with arrows strung, bows pulled taut, others with rifles aimed and cocked, each one ready to deliver instant death.

Daniella saw it all in slow motion through glazed eyes. The arrow before her still quivered in the firelight, and suddenly other arrows flashed through her mind. Arrows thudding into the stagecoach that day; the arrow protruding from the chest of the man in the opposite seat; the arrow sticking out of the driver's back as he tumbled from his perch to the ground. She felt the scream rising in her throat, and she was paralyzed with overwhelming fear. *Not now!* her mind screamed. *You go crazy now and they'll kill you both!*

"*Ahagahe!*" she raged in Apache. *Yúútatske'! Dánánal'ázhi!*" As she cursed the warriors in their own language, all arrows and guns swung from Travis toward her. Her heart shot into her throat.

A tall, older Apache stepped from the shadows. He stood a full head taller than Travis's six feet. Daniella dug her nails into her palms. There was only one Apache she'd ever heard of who was that tall, and he hated whites worse than Cochise did. The small, square-cut sombrero tied to his huge head, as well as the bright red shirt he wore, confirmed his identity.

"Travis, put your pistol away." Daniella spoke in Spanish, so

85

the others could understand. Her eyes stayed locked on the tall Indian before her.

"As soon as they lower their weapons," Travis replied tersely in Spanish.

The tall man, leader of this group of warriors, made a motion with his hand. Arrows and rifles were lowered to point at the ground, bow strings and trigger fingers relaxed. Travis put his gun back in his holster, but didn't seem to relax so much as a single muscle.

"How is it that a white woman speaks our language?" the tall Apache demanded in his native tongue.

Daniella swallowed. *"Por favor,* I don't know much, only a few words and phrases, Mon-ache," she answered in Spanish.

The Apache also switched to Spanish. "You know enough to insult and curse brave fighting men. Where did you learn these words? How come you to know this place, and my name?"

Cochise's words rang in her ears. *Never show fear to an enemy, unless it be to your advantage.* Consciously, she straightened her spine and squared her shoulders, looking the fierce Apache directly in the eye.

"I learned both from your son-in-law, Cochise, leader of the *Chidikáágu';* husband of your daughter, Nali-Kay-deya; father of your grandson, Naiche."

A low muttering spread throughout the warriors as they gaped at her in wonder and disbelief. Another half-dozen men stepped from the surrounding shadows and gathered close. Two came forward and stood on either side of their chief. One looked a few years older than Travis, with narrow, cunning black eyes and a thin, cruel mouth. The other was even older than his chief, but much shorter than the rest of the men. His shoulders stooped. Squinty, twinkling eyes, thick lips, and miles of wrinkles gave him a comical look that was surely deceptive.

"Who are you, to know such things?" Mon-ache demanded.

"I am called Woman of Magic," Daniella stated, somewhat surprised at the pride she heard in her own voice. "I am the adopted daughter of Cochise."

"She lies, I say!" The warrior with the thin lips glared at her.

He took a menacing step forward and rested his hand on the hilt of his knife.

Daniella's first impulse was to back away, but she didn't. She forced herself to stand her ground and return his glare. "Who are you to call a *Chidikáágu* a liar?" she questioned hotly.

"I am Golthlay. Apache warrior." He strutted before her arrogantly, pounding his chest with a fist. "The Mexicans call me Geronimo."

"Sorry," she answered with a shrug. "Never heard of you."

"Cochise would never take a white-woman as his daughter," Golthlay said firmly. Then an evil grin split his thin lips. He took another step forward. "His slave, maybe, or his whore, but never his daughter." His hand shot out and grabbed her breast through her poncho.

Daniella reacted with sheer, blind reflex. Her left arm came up on the inside of his and knocked his hand away, while her right hand clawed toward his face. "Don't touch me!" she screamed into his stunned face.

A dark, bronze arm clamped around her waist from behind and lifted her off the ground. Deep laughter rang in her ears. "I'll help you, Golthlay!" her captor yelled.

Daniella screamed. She reached for the top of her moccasin. Beneath the loose folds of her poncho she withdrew her long bowie knife. The blade flashed once in the firelight. The man holding her dropped her to the ground, blood streaming from the long cut down his naked thigh.

Daniella sprang to her feet and crouched before Golthlay, ignoring the wounded man behind her. The other men started moving in slowly, muttering, but Mon-ache motioned them back.

"You still want to touch me, you son of a dog?" Daniella hissed at Golthlay. She held her knife slightly in front of her and to the side, not like an hysterical female, but like an experienced knife fighter. Cochise had taught her well.

Travis tensed to lunge forward, but found himself seized by both arms. A knife flashed at his throat. A harsh voice whispered in his ear, *"¡Alto!"*

Damn that girl! She was going to get herself killed. Then it would be his turn. Only he knew he wouldn't die as swiftly as she would. He might last two or three days before these blood-thirsty gut-eaters let him die. They were masters at keeping their victims alive. He willed her to drop the knife.

She didn't.

"I'm not going to touch you," Golthlay said with a growl. "I'm going to kill you." He drew his own blade from his belt.

"You mean you're going to try," Daniella taunted. She saw surprise register in his eyes.

They circled each other, Daniella wary, alert, terrified and trying not to show it; Golthlay sure, cocky, angry.

"You need a man to teach you some manners, woman. Now I know you lie. Cochise would take a whip to a daughter who acted like you."

"Is that so?" She refused to back away. "What do you suppose he'd do to the man who grabbed his daughter, threatened her, called her a liar and a whore? Are you a fool? Who do you think gave me this knife and taught me how to use it?"

A shadow of doubt flickered across Golthlay's dark eyes, then disappeared. He feinted to his right, then lunged left. Daniella twisted away. His knife tangled in her flying poncho. While he tried to free it, her blade flashed out and left a narrow stream of red along his forearm. Golthlay jerked his knife free of its trap and howled with rage. In his eyes, Daniella saw death—her death.

Never let an enemy see your fear unless it be to your advantage. Use every weapon at your disposal. A woman can get away with more than a man can. Never, ever try to fight fair. Never let him see your fear, unless it be to your advantage.

Golthlay swung closer, the muscles in his neck and shoulders standing out in rage. His mouth was no more than a grim slash above his chin. Daniella's fear threatened to overwhelm her.

. . . unless it be to your advantage.

Suddenly she darted sideways and threw herself to the ground in a crouch. She wailed loudly. Great wrenching sobs racked her body. She covered her head with both arms. "Don't hurt me!" she begged. *"Por Dios,* please don't hurt me!"

Golthlay stared at her cringing figure for a stunned second, then threw back his head and roared with laughter. He sheathed his knife and turned in a circle with his arms raised in victory before his comrades.

Others joined in his laughter. Travis breathed a sigh of relief for this short reprieve, however temporary it might be.

It was very temporary indeed. Relief died in his chest when he spied the tall one she'd called Mon-ache watching her with narrowed, speculative eyes. Mon-ache was not laughing with the others.

Daniella forced herself to breath deeply between sobs, waiting . . . waiting for her chance. Almost! Golthlay stood there laughing, turning, arms in the air. *A little more. Turn a little more.* She couldn't rush it. *Wait. Wait,* she cautioned herself. Blood pounded in her ears. *Almost . . . another step . . . one more . . . just one more step, you ugly—* There. *Now!*

She sprang from the ground, her tears dry, and caught him behind the knees with her shoulder. The force and surprise of the blow tumbled Golthlay over her shoulder. He landed with an audible thud on his back, the wind knocked out of him.

Without pausing, Daniella spun around and landed forcefully on top of him, one knee in his stomach, the other pressed firmly against his throat. The ten-inch blade of her bowie knife gleamed viciously as it flipped his breech cloth aside and poised between his out flung legs.

Golthlay's eyes nearly bulged out of his head, as much from surprise and lack of air as from the feel of cold steel at his crotch. He heaved beneath her. She pressed the blade more firmly against him. He froze in place.

"Touch me again, you stinking bastard," she told him, "and you'll be weaving baskets with the women the rest of your unhappy life!"

Golthlay emitted a gurgling, gasping sound. By the time Daniella sprang away, his face was nearly black with blood and rage and lack of air. He rose to his feet, his warrior's dignity in ashes at having been defeated by a woman.

Mon-ache stepped forward and slapped the younger man on the back in friendly fashion. "Come, Golthlay, do not be troubled at being bested by a woman. Woman of Magic must have great powers. I think no man could crush her." Under his breath, but loud enough for Daniella to hear, he added, "Do

89

not make things worse, my friend, for I believe she speaks the truth, and you know Cochise will hear of this."

Golthlay glared his hatred at Daniella. She met his gaze briefly, then stepped forward and lowered her eyes. She knew she had to do something to cool him off. Despite the terror still choking her, her voice was calm, yet strong enough to carry across the clearing.

"Golthlay, I am sorry for this trouble between us. I understand your doubts about who I am, and I don't blame you for not believing me. As for the other, I ask you not to take it personally. I . . . I don't like to be touched. It was only a reflex that made me pull my knife. I would do the same if you were my best friend, before I even knew what I was doing."

She swallowed heavily and went on. "I have embarrassed you before your friends and your chief, and I have offended you. For this, I ask your forgiveness." She stood silently, eyes downcast, trying to keep from shaking visibly, waiting for his response.

After a long moment, Golthlay signaled, and Travis was brought to him and released. "Did you ever touch her?" Golthlay asked him.

Travis somehow managed to act a lot calmer than he felt. He couldn't believe what he'd just seen with his own eyes. A beautiful young white woman, no bigger than a mite, could not possibly have defeated a seasoned Apache warrior in a knife fight, no matter what tricks she used. Yet it had happened.

"White man! Did you ever touch her?"

Golthlay's harsh tone brought Travis back to the present. "Once," he stated.

"And did she take her knife to you?"

Travis tried to relax, sensing the crisis was over. "She couldn't reach her knife, thank God," he answered with a half-grin for her. He pulled back his collar and displayed the long, angry looking gash on his neck. "Otherwise, I'd be dead."

Golthlay looked at Travis's wound a moment, then threw his head back again and laughed in appreciation. *"Nzhú!"* he cried. "I am satisfied. Let us drink now—talk tomorrow!"

Daniella looked ready to faint, but managed a shaky smile.

Whiskey bottles appeared and the warriors got down to some serious drinking. Travis took a swallow from a proffered bottle, then extended it toward Daniella. She shook her head in refusal.

"Drink it," Travis ordered in English. "Before you collapse."

Daniella's hand shook visibly when she tilted the bottle to her lips, but Travis seemed to be the only one to notice. She took only a small sip, but still she choked and sputtered as the fiery rotgut burned its way down her throat and stole the breath from her lungs.

Mon-ache reminded his men they were to get an early start in the morning, then turned back in time to see Daniella wheezing from the effects of the whiskey.

"Supplies intended for a cantina in Fronteras. You like?" he asked.

Daniella coughed and sputtered; tears streamed down her face. "It's awful!" she exclaimed.

Mon-ache laughed, then took a long pull from his own bottle. "Come, daughter of Cochise, introduce me to this man."

"Of course," she said, handing the bottle back to Travis. "This is Travis Colton, my . . . friend and neighbor. I brought him here to see his son, who is with Cochise's people, but we were too late.

"Travis, this is Mon-ache, chief of the Membrenos Apaches, and war chief of all the Apache nations. He's also known as Mangas Coloradas — Red Sleeves."

Travis did his best to hide his surprise. Mangas Coloradas had an even worse reputation than Cochise for being a bloodthirsty savage. Surely there was a reason for that reputation, yet here the man stood, drinking whiskey with him like they were old friends. Whether it was "magic" or just plain luck that Travis and Daniella were still alive, Travis didn't care. He just hoped that whatever it was, it held long enough to get them out of there in one piece.

When Mon-ache learned they wished to find Cochise, he offered to lead them there, as he was going there himself. "Right now," the tall chief said, "I must collect what is left of the whiskey. My men love drinking the white man's poison. So do I. But it is sometimes hard to know when to stop. If I let them have their way, *jigunaa'áí*, the sun, will be halfway across the sky tomorrow before any of them wake, and then they would spend the next hour trying to drink the stream dry. Better to listen to their grumbles tonight, than their moans tomorrow."

When everyone finally bedded down, the Apaches gave Daniella and Travis plenty of room and did not intrude on their privacy. Soon the clearing was filled with the sounds of enthusiastic snoring from the half-drunken warriors.

Now that it was all over, the danger past, Daniella lay with her back to the fire and shook uncontrollably. From his position across the fire, Travis saw the violent tremors shuddering down her frame and swore softly. He yanked up his blanket and spread it next to hers.

She rolled to face him. "What are you doing?" she asked, her eyes wary, body tense.

"Relax. I just thought you might like a little company. I don't bite, and I won't touch." He lay down a couple of feet away from her and propped his head on his hand. "I want to, though," he added after a moment.

"Want to what?"

"Touch you," he answered softly. "But don't worry, I won't. Besides, I can't make up my mind whether I should kiss you for keeping us alive, or turn you over my knee and beat you for nearly getting yourself killed tonight. Are you all right?"

Daniella closed her eyes and trembled visibly. "Ask me again, in about ten years."

Travis lay back and gazed at the stars, so big and bright he should have been able to reach out and touch them. But they were like Daniella—out of reach, not to be touched.

"Yes, sir," he said out loud to himself. "She has visions, she brews a mean pot of coffee, and she wields a knife better than an Apache warrior." He rolled his head over lazily and gazed at her familiar features. "I've never met a woman like you in my life." He considered his choice of words and smiled to himself. He'd stopped thinking of her as a girl sometime during the past few days, and started seeing her as a woman. A unique, special woman. One of a kind.

"Is that supposed to be a compliment?" she asked with a choked laugh.

"Yes ma'am, Miss Daniella Blackwood, Woman of Magic, it certainly is." A slow, devastating grin spread across his face.

Daniella thought in that moment that he must be the most handsome man in the world. His eyes sent messages to hers, sparking a warm glow, wiping out the terror of the last hour. Her own tentative smile spread her lips. "Then, Mr. Travis Colton, Yellow Hair, I thank you."

"Yellow Hair?"

"That's what some of them are calling you."

"Does that mean if I fall asleep, I won't wake up in the morning with my throat slit?"

Her smile faded. "We're safe now. They won't harm us."

"I know that," he answered seriously. "Thanks to you. I think you must be the bravest person in the world."

"Brave! I was scared to death, and you know it. I was terrified. I still am."

Without moving closer, Travis laid his hand palm up near her face. "I know," he whispered. "Maybe we'd both feel better if you'd take my hand, just for a little while."

Daniella's breath came in nervous little gasps. His hand, just inches away, was large, and tanned, and inviting. His warm, brown eyes implored her to reach out to him, to take what he offered. It would be so easy. All she had to do was move her fingers a few inches, and she'd be touching him. Touching another human being. One who offered his comfort, his understanding, his strength, all things she needed so badly and hadn't had in so long.

Her fingers jerked once, then slid slowly across the narrow space between their hands. To her, that six-inch span of blanket was a wide, deep chasm, and she felt perched on its edge. If she made that terrifying leap to the other side, where his hand lay waiting, would he be there? Would he hang on to her? Or was he just a phantom, someone she'd dreamed up in her desperate need to touch another person? Her fingers moved forward another inch.

Travis held his breath, his eyes on her face, as she stared at his hand. At the first tentative touch of her fingers, his heart began pounding furiously. When her palm slid across his, he wrapped his fingers gently around hers and let out his breath. It was a tiny hand, delicate and fragile despite the small callouses he felt along the pads at the base of her fingers. Yet this was the same hand that only a short time ago had gripped the hilt of a knife with such deadly intent and skill. What strength lay within these fragile bones?

He savored the feel of her while his mouth twisted ironically. He should be worrying that they were completely surrounded by cutthroat Apache murderers. Instead, he lay there thinking about how badly he wanted to slip his arms around Daniella and pull her close against his chest. He wanted to taste those soft, trembling lips and teach her she had nothing to fear from him. He wanted to bury his face in her hair and feel her run her fingers through his.

Travis forced himself to relax and resist his urges. He was a man used to taking what he wanted, but this time, with this woman, it was different. For the first time in years he found himself considering the future, not just his immediate desires. He would go slowly, take his time, and gain her trust. Then, well, who knew what would happen once she trusted him.

When his bronze fingers closed over hers, Daniella breathed in deeply. His hand was so strong and sturdy, she could feel the comfort of his strength. Her eyes slid shut and she slipped into a deep, dreamless sleep.

Chapter Ten

At dawn the next day they rode out, Daniella, Travis, fifteen Apache warriors, and twenty-two stolen pack mules laden with stolen goods. Around midmorning two riders dropped back behind the others. One was Golthlay. The other was Nana, the short, wrinkled old man who had stood at the right hand of his chief last night, the same as he'd done for many years. Nana had seen more than sixty winters and had been fighting to rid his homeland of intruders for as long as he could remember. He could out ride, out fight, and out last any man half his age, Just as his chief, Mon-ache, could.

For most of his life, Nana had fought against the Spanish-speaking Mexicans. Recent years had seen the white Americans as enemies of his people. Now he hated all whites and Mexicans, and vowed to kill as many as he could. He did not trust the two whites presently among them.

"You don't really believe Cochise would have adopted an American woman, do you?" Nana asked Golthlay, careful to keep his voice from carrying. "I have never trusted *Los Goddammies,* and I don't trust these two now."

"You forget, Nana, how much Cochise trusted his old *shaman,* Nocholo, who was *shaman* before Dee-O-Det. When the first white-eyes came here and trapped the beaver in our mountain streams, Nocholo counseled Cochise to trust them. After all, weren't these white men always fighting the Mexicans, the same as we were? And from the white-eyes we get the iron-that-shoots so we can kill more Mexicans. Cochise has

95

only recently learned to hate the *'indaa,* these white enemies."

"Then you believe the girl?"

"I believe her. How else could she know of that place we just came from?"

"She and the Yellow Hair could have found it by accident."

Golthlay snorted. "You know that is nearly impossible. Besides, she knew too many other things. In any case, we will learn the truth when we reach Cochise's main *rancheria.*"

"I say we should kill them both!" Nana urged. "How else will you get even with her for what she did to you last night?"

Golthlay smiled grimly at the old man. "Do not worry, my friend." His black eyes gleamed evilly. "If she is who she claims to be, I have the perfect way to make her pay. Soon she will be begging me to touch her."

"Take care, Golthlay," his old friend warned. "If Cochise really has adopted her, he will protect her in all ways. So will his band. This you must know."

"Yes, but you forget—his oldest son, Tahza, already has his eye on my sister, Nod-ah-Sti, and intends to offer for her as soon as she reaches womanhood. I am almost like one of the family. There is much Cochise would do for the future brother-in-law of his firstborn son."

Nana resisted the urge to snort his disgust. Golthlay was a brave, fierce fighter, but when not fighting, he sometimes turned into a self-important fool. Cochise was a great man. A man who never put himself in another's debt. The chief of the Chúk'ánéné would feel no obligation to favor a young hothead like Golthlay.

Of course, Nana wasn't about to speak his thoughts aloud—that would be rude. But he would listen and remember. Perhaps, if the white girl calling herself Woman of Magic spoke the truth, Nana would be able to warn Cochise of Golthlay's scheme.

"What are you planning?" he asked.

"You will know soon enough, for I will need your help when the time comes." Golthlay smiled mysteriously, then kicked his mustang into a gallop to rejoin his chief at the head of the column. Nana followed swiftly.

When they rode past Travis and Daniella, Golthlay still

wore his mysterious smile. He looked steadily at Daniella for a moment, then laughed before he and Nana rode on.

Travis's hands tightened on the reins. "I'm not exactly comfortable being constantly surrounded by Apaches," he admitted. "But those two make me wish I had eyes in the back of my head."

"To Apaches, raiding and killing enemies is exciting," Daniella said. "It's something they're *supposed* to do. It's their way of life. But a few of them—I've heard Mon-ache is one—they really, truly hate their enemies. As though it's personal. And then, Apaches are just like any other people. Some individuals are just plain mean. That, I believe, is Golthlay's problem. But then, I'm just guessing."

"And Cochise? He enjoys killing his enemies?"

"I don't know if 'enjoy' is the right word, but he kills them. If he didn't, his warriors wouldn't follow him, and they *all* follow him. I've heard that when Mon-ache dies, all his followers, all the Apache tribes, will follow Cochise."

"So why would he adopt a white woman into his family?"

Daniella's eyes darkened, then darted away. "It's . . . a long story," she said in clipped tones.

"I've got all day," he said easily, trying to maintain the friendliness they'd been sharing since they broke camp.

Daniella looked at him again, then lowered her gaze to the trail. "Don't worry," she said with a sigh. "I'm sure you'll hear all the gory details when we get where we're going."

She, too, remembered this morning. She woke to a gentle squeezing on her fingers and was at first startled, then embarrassed to find her hand still resting in his. The rough sleepiness of his voice when he'd said good morning still sent her pulse racing when she thought of it. There had been a new easiness between them all day.

Yet she knew it couldn't last. Soon he would remember who and what she was. What he hadn't already guessed, he would hear around the campfires at the *rancheria*. Then he would withdraw from her and shut her out of his life. If her own father could disown her, then this man beside her, who made her ache with a longing she'd never known, would not want anything more to do with her once he had his son back.

97

She barely knew him at all, yet the thought of how he would shun her sent a coldness creeping through her. She shivered beneath the folds of her poncho.

It took them two and a half days to reach the Chúk'ánéné summer stronghold. By the time they arrived, mid-afternoon of the third day, Daniella was ready to drop. She hadn't slept at all the past two nights, and there had been few opportunities for napping.

The *rancheria* was nestled high in the cool, pine-covered mountains south of the towering rock formations south of Apache Pass. There were natural pastures for the cattle and horses, and cool mountain streams provided a continuous supply of fresh water. Dogs barked and children shrieked and jumped aside when the riders thundered into the compound, Mon-ache's warriors shouting and calling out greetings to friends. Dozens of wickiups, looking like so many grass domes, were grouped in every direction, each one with its opening facing east, so everyone could view the rising sun and pray. The tantalizing aroma of roasting meat mingled with wood smoke and drifted on the cool breeze.

A tall man shouldered his way through the gathering crowd. He stood a head taller than those around him, and was nearly as tall as Mon-ache. His long black hair hung below his shoulders, and his keen dark eyes searched the newcomers, for word had been brought to him by the trail guards that there was a special visitor among this group. When his eyes found Daniella, a soft welcoming smile curved his lips.

"Jeeke'!" he cried. "Daughter!"

Daniella slid from the saddle and did something she never dreamed she'd do — she fell gratefully into the arms of Cochise, war chief of the Chiricahua Apaches. *"Shitaa,"* she murmured against his chest. "Father."

He was the only father who would acknowledge her now. Never had she thought to be so glad to see him. He welcomed her as her own father hadn't. He would take care of her, keep her safe. She could stop worrying, for now, about the sly, speculative glances cast her way for the past two days by Golthlay.

She could stop fearing the warriors would change their minds and kill Travis and her.

Cochise stepped back and held her at arm's length. "You look terrible," he stated bluntly. "What is the trouble?"

Daniela shook her head in denial. "There is no trouble, Cochise. I'm just tired, that's all."

Out of the corner of her eye she saw Golthlay flash her a look of warning. He needn't have bothered. She had no intention of talking about the trouble between them the night they met.

"Come and rest, then," Cochise suggested. "This one said you would come." He nodded toward Dee-O-Det, the old *shaman,* Daniella's friend. "He had a wickiup prepared for you. Tonight we will have a fiesta to welcome you back among us, and to welcome our brothers from the west who brought you to us."

Daniella smiled her thanks. "I've brought someone with me, *shitaa."* She motioned Travis forward. She noted with relief that he had already unstrapped his gunbelt and handed it to Nali-Kay-deya, Cochise's wife, who had come to greet her father, Mon-ache. "This is my friend and neighbor, Travis Colton. Travis, this is Cochise, my . . . father. Cochise, I've brought him here to find *biye'."*

"His son?" Cochise repeated.

" *'Au, shitaa.* When your men took the boy from the stage last winter, they must have thought Travis was dead. I've assured him you're not the kind of man who would keep a young boy away from his father, even though you've been accused of it before."

Cochise eyed the white man sharply, then turned his gaze on his *shaman.* "You knew of this?"

"I knew Woman of Magic was coming—I told you that," Dee-O-Det answered calmly.

"That's not what I meant, old man, and you know it."

Travis shot Daniella a worried, questioning look. She shook her head. She had no idea what was going on.

"Did you know the boy had a father?" Cochise demanded.

There was no need to specify which boy. Even though she'd never come face to face with Matt before, Daniella knew the resemblance between father and son was too striking to leave room for doubt. But Cochise had forgotten one thing: it never paid to lose his temper with his *shaman*. If he had noticed the gleam in the old man's eye he would have been warned.

"But my chief, everyone has a father."

"Bah! I should have known better than to expect a straight answer from you." Cochise glared at the old man.

Dee-O-Det shook his gray head and cackled. "Welcome, child," he said to Daniella.

"Thank you, Dee-O-Det." She kissed his wrinkled cheek. The *shaman* let out a wild Apache war whoop, bringing raucous laughter from those present. He jumped into a crazy, comical dance and circled Daniella before coming to a halt before her. *"Taeh!* Kiss me again, girl, and I might die from too much excitement!"

"Stop trying to court my daughter, old man, and let her get some rest. You'll need your wits about you if you intend to call a council meeting to discuss this new development before the feasting begins. Go with him, child," Cochise said to Daniella in a somewhat softer tone than he'd used on Dee-O-Det. "I will see to our guest."

Daniella gave Travis what she hoped was a reassuring smile, and left the center of camp with Dee-O-Det.

The old *shaman* patted Daniella's shoulder with his gnarled, wrinkled hand. "Do not worry. Your man will be seen to."

"He's not my man. You know better than that. He's just a friend who needed my help."

"Ah, but his eyes say he would like to be your man."

Her heart gave a funny little leap. She chose to ignore it. "Is that the *shaman* talking, or just a well-meaning friend who is sticking his nose where it doesn't belong?" she teased.

"Aiyee! Everyone is touchy today. Cochise is in a temper. Tonight he will waste good food on his sour stomach, then he will have a belly ache. He will blame me, a humble *shaman,* and demand a cure from me."

"And why is Cochise in a temper?" she asked seriously. "He was fine until I mentioned the boy. Something's wrong, isn't it? Is the boy all right?"

"Trust me, child. Everything will be fine. You will see."

100

"But can't you tell me what's going on?"

"All in good time, child. I will send someone when the council meets. Until then, rest."

Chapter Eleven

Travis had been toured around the *rancheria*, noting the various familiar brands on some of the horses and cattle. (It looked like Howard Blackwood needed to double his guard.)

To his stunned amazement, he'd been treated with utmost courtesy all afternoon. But no one had mentioned Matt. He learned quickly that his son was a forbidden subject until the council meeting. No one would even admit Matt was here. And he hadn't been allowed to wander around on his own for even a minute.

It was dark when Daniella joined him and the others at the council fire. A space was reserved for her at Dee-O-Det's right. Travis was seated to the *shaman's* left. The other council members fanned out in both directions, forming a large half circle at the fire. Directly opposite Dee-O-Det sat Cochise.

Travis was relieved to learn the meeting would be conducted in Spanish for his benefit.

When all were seated, Cochise rose with deliberate slowness. The long fringe on his ceremonial buckskin *jaqueta* shimmered with his movements, each string tipped with a silver bead or turquoise spangle. On his left breast was a gold cross, the ends of its arms bent at right angles. On the right was a similar design worked in silver, inlaid with turquoise and mother-of-pearl. Around his neck he wore what the *shaman* said was the badge of the High Chief of the Chiricahua, a thunderbird emblem made of turquoise.

Cochise began to speak, and Travis felt the sheer power and magnetism of the man.

"When winter walked the land, before this Season of Little Leaves, a white captive was brought to us by our warriors. She was treated as any other hated white captive. Tortured, used, beaten, left to die beneath the limbs of the sacred pine. Several commented that night on the courage and determination of this captive, and that it was a shame such a brave woman had to be white, and therefore would die. We have not seen much bravery from her kind."

The war chief's dark, glittering eyes settled on Travis. Travis worked at keeping his expression as blank as possible, refusing to respond to the deliberate taunt. The Apache could take pot shots at white men's bravery all night for all Travis cared. Until Travis had Matt safely away, there was no way in hell he'd take such bait.

"During the night, while she lay waiting to go to Big Sleep," Cochise said, "a miracle occurred. Yúúsń, in His great wisdom, asked the thunderbird to send a bolt of white light from the sky, and He placed it in her hair so all who looked upon her would know her as a Woman of Magic. It was a great sign from the Spirit World, for when the white light in her hair touched the ancient pine, the tree exploded with a tremendous crash. Even now it lays on the ground, split in half by the mighty thunderbird of Yúúsń and His chosen one, Woman of Magic."

No wonder she hadn't wanted to camp there!

"Our *shaman* spoke of protecting her, teaching her our ways, learning from her the ways of the white man. So I, Cochise, chief of the Chúk'ánéné, formally adopted her as my daughter, making her one of us. She left us to return to her white family, but was cast out by them."

Travis glanced sharply at Daniella. Her head jerked up and her mouth flew open.

"Now she has come back to us," Cochise continued. "She brings us a most serious request, of which she will now speak."

Cochise sat on the ground. Daniella stood, took a deep

breath, and unclenched her small fists. Travis could almost feel her trying to relax. What courage it must take for her to come back to these people, to stand before them with her head up, shoulders back, after what they did to her. When she spoke, her voice was calm.

"In the days just before I left the Chúk'ánéné to return to my first father, I looked into the flames and saw a face." Travis listened intently as she told of seeing him shot and Matt taken. She told of the other times she had seen Travis in the flames, and of her last vision, of Matt with the Chúk'ánéné in their winter stronghold.

Travis's eyes scanned the dark faces around the fire. Some looked skeptical, others impressed. But most of them stared at her with expressionless black eyes as she went on speaking.

"This man, Travis Colton, whom some call Yellow Hair, walked today, weaponless, among people who nearly killed him, left him for dead, and took his son. People who consider themselves his enemies. I ask you to think of the courage it takes for a man to walk freely into the enemy camp, not knowing if he will even live long enough to voice his request. It is not a common thing for a man to do. I ask that you honor his bravery by allowing him to take his son home."

She closed her eyes briefly and took a slow, deep breath.

"Right now you are angry with the white men, and your anger is just and reasonable. But do not blame all white men for the misdeeds of a few. Someday you will grow tired of hating and fighting and watching your young men die in battle. Some day you will want peace. But the road to peace will not be easy. It must be taken one step at a time, and may take many seasons. Take that first step now, with this white man. Let him see that the Chúk'ánéné are a generous people, and word will spread of your kindness to him."

Daniella crossed her feet and sank to the ground.

"Peace! Bah!"

Travis felt every muscle in his body tighten. He scanned the council, but couldn't tell who had spoken.

104

Across the fire, Cochise rose again and fixed his steady gaze on the second man from his right.

"Woman of Magic speaks with much wisdom for one so young," he said. "What she asks, that a boy be returned to his father, should be a simple thing." He looked at the *shaman*. "But in this case, it is not so simple."

Travis tensed with dread. Cochise sat and nodded to another man, a powerfully built, middle-aged warrior seated near Daniella. The Apache rose and studied Travis with wary eyes. Then he addressed the council.

"I am Hal-Say, son of Baishan. I am known to you as being strong of arm and brave in battle. I had two sons. They were strong and fine. They rode into battle together with courage in their hearts and were slain by the Ñaakaiye, the hated Mexicans. My wife and I cut off our hair, painted our faces black, and mourned our loss. For many moons we lived in sorrow, with no children in our wickiup.

"Then a white boy was brought into our midst. He was alone in the world, thinking his father had gone to Big Sleep, as our sons had gone. Huera and I took him in and shared our wickiup with him. After a time, we grew to love this boy, whom we called Little Bear, and adopted him as our son. Some objected, wanting the boy for themselves, but we defied them." Hal-Say paused and settled his gaze on Travis.

"I look at this white man tonight, and I know he is the sire of Little Bear. But he is a young man. He can have more sons. My wife and I have already lost two sons. I fear Huera will die of a broken spirit if we now lose Little Bear."

Travis listened, stunned. Daniella had seemed so positive there would be no problem. She obviously hadn't known about this complication. The anxious look on her face now filled him with cold foreboding.

Dee-O-Det motioned for Travis to rise and speak. Travis came to his feet slowly and studied the faces around him. Apaches. Every man here—and for miles around—was his hated, sworn enemy. In the past months these men and others like them had stolen horses and cattle, killed his friends, his neighbors, terrorized the entire territory.

He knew without a doubt that they hated whites every bit as much as whites hated them.

So why was he still alive, standing here among them, treated like a guest? Why were they willing to let him speak?

Magic. Or a miracle.

Daniella.

She was the reason he was still alive. She was the reason he was so close to Matt right now that he could feel his son's presence.

He gazed at her face, golden in the firelight. She met his look for a long moment. When she nodded, he turned away and faced the council.

"I am Travis Colton. Last winter the stage my son, Matt, and I were traveling in was attacked. I was wounded." He touched his fingers to his cheek. "When I came to, my son was gone. I am not interested in who did this, or why. I'm only interested in getting my son back.

"And he is *my* son," he said directly to Hal-Say. "I held him when he was a baby, I changed his diapers, I steadied his first shaky steps, and listened to his first words. His mother died when he was a few weeks old, so I did these things alone.

"If you tell him I'm alive, he'll want to come home with me. If you don't tell him, and deny me my son, then one day he'll learn the truth. And when he does, he'll hate you for keeping it from him, Hal-Say. I don't think you want that.

"In any case," Travis went on, his voice tinged with hardness. "I came here to get my son. I will not leave without him."

Perhaps it wasn't the wisest thing to do, Travis thought as he sat down. He wasn't in any position to threaten or demand. But Daniella said these people appreciated honesty, and anger and determination were his honest feelings.

Next to him, Dee-O-Det rose. "I wish to address this council," the old man said. "Not as your spokesman, but as your *shaman*." He paused, waiting for the council's approval.

"When *ha'*, winter, walked the land, our brother the *shash* sought his den, as he always does when the cold comes. He lay down to sleep, and to wait for Yúúsń to speak to him. When spring came, the Season of Little Leaves, the bear awoke and left his cave. He found me in the woods and told me many things."

The old man waved a gnarled hand toward Daniella. "He told me that although Woman of Magic had left the Chúk'ánéné, she would return many times to walk among us."

With his other hand, the *shaman* motioned toward Travis. "He told me Little Bear's father lived, and this white man would be a true friend to our people. Our brother the bear said if the boy leaves here with his first father, the boy, too, will return to us many times, just as will Woman of Magic."

When the old man finished, Cochise led Daniella and Travis away from the council fire to the small family cooking fire before his own wickiups. Cochise sat on a blanket and began sharpening the knife he wore at his waist. Daniella knelt next to him, her eyes glued to his actions. The smooth, shiny steel caught and reflected the firelight as Cochise rubbed it across the sharpening stone.

Travis paced. And worried. And waited. If he was home, a good, stiff shot of whiskey might ease the wait and soothe his nerves.

He tried to cheer himself. They'd come this far . . . all the way to Cochise's summer stronghold. And they'd made it in one piece. He was a white man, standing where, most likely, no white man had ever stood, and he was alive. The council had listened to him. The *shaman* spoke in his favor. Daniella spoke in his favor. And Cochise no longer seemed angry over Travis's presence.

There was no telling how many miles he paced during the next two hours. He wasn't aware of time passing. It wasn't passing at all, he was certain. It was standing still. It would never move forward again. Hadn't he already spent his entire life pacing before this same fire, with the scraping of steel against rock grinding his nerves into dust?

He stopped when a small child teetered across his path, stumbled, and fell. A woman rushed over and swooped the child up, casting a look of pure hatred at Travis.

He wasn't surprised. What surprised him was that they hadn't all been looking at him like that for the entire day. Why wait till now to show their hatred?

He must have spoken his thoughts aloud, for Daniella answered him. "The feasting has to wait until the council has voted. The woman blames you for the delay."

Travis whirled on Daniella. "Well, what's taking so goddamn long?"

She swallowed at the fierce look he shot her.

The question uppermost in both their minds was one neither of them would voice. What if it all went wrong? What if the council voted that Hal-Say keep Matt? What would happen to Travis? What would he do? What would they do to him?

Suddenly, out of the darkness, Hal-Say appeared. He stopped and looked at Travis, his expression unreadable. After a brief moment he walked on.

The man would make a great poker player, Travis thought. Not one hint of the council's decision showed on the bronze face.

Dee-O-Det walked up then, a similar expressionless look about him. Judging by the wrinkles on the ancient face, Travis was ready to swear the *shaman* was older than God Himself. Then the old man grinned. "Come, my friends!" he cried. "Let us feast and celebrate! When bellies are full, Hal-Say and Huera will bring Little Bear to you, Travis Colton."

Travis felt his knees weaken with relief. He closed his eyes and offered up a prayer of thanks for this miracle. When he opened his eyes, Daniella was there, grinning at him. Without thinking, Travis matched her grin. With a shout of joy, he picked her up and hugged her tightly, then spun her around in circles.

Daniella was so pleased for Travis that she forgot to be afraid of him. It wasn't until he released her that she realized he was the first man, aside from Cochise, Dee-O-Det, and Tucker, to put his arms around her without threat of violence since she'd returned to the territory. She thought to herself, *Dear God, but that felt good!* Then she blushed in confusion over the direction her thoughts were taking. She lowered her gaze and missed the knowing look that passed between Cochise and Dee-O-Det.

Travis had never seen so many fires or so much food in one place in his life. Cochise and Daniella led Travis to a small clearing in the forest near the center of the compound. It was surrounded by wickiups, and there were two fires going, each roasting an entire deer. But judging from the number of people gathered, there would barely be enough to go around.

Travis began to get some idea of why the Apaches raided so often. It must take a lot to feed and clothe this many people. And of all the Chiricahua he'd seen today, not one of them appeared to suffer the affects of overeating; they were all lean and trim.

There was, however, plenty of *tiswin* to go around. Travis was introduced to the homemade brew while he ate. It was, without a doubt, the vilest tasting stuff he'd ever sampled. Thicker than cold molasses, it went down slow and tasted like pure yeast. He passed up the chance to refill his gourd.

But the doe they ate was delicious. The entrails cavity was stuffed with onions, garlic, potatoes, pinto beans, and corn. Travis couldn't help wondering which farms and supply trains had unwillingly provided the vegetables.

By the time they'd eaten their fill, the celebration was in full swing and *tiswin* flowed freely. Mon-ache even donated his stolen whiskey to the cause. Cochise motioned for Daniella and Travis to follow him. He led them away from the crowd, back to Daniella's wickiup.

"You two have shared a campfire on the trail for many days. Will you mind sharing a wickiup while you are with us? I'm afraid there are no others available." Cochise looked at Travis expectantly.

Travis was about to voice his agreement when Daniella shrieked in rage.

"*Shitaa!* If you're trying to be funny, it isn't working! And if you're trying to deceive our guest, to trick him, then I am ashamed of you."

Cochise looked wounded.

"I've already been accused once of trying to trap him. How dare you suggest such a thing?"

"Daniella," Travis interrupted, confused by her objection. "It's no big deal. We can sleep on opposite sides of the wickiup, just like we slept on opposite sides of the campfire. I don't mind."

"You see, daughter? He does not mind."

"Of course he doesn't mind," Daniella hissed irritably. "That's because he doesn't realize we could sleep a mile apart, or sit up and talk all night, but if we spent the night together under the same roof, we'd be married."

A funny feeling stirred in Travis's gut. "Married?"

"As married as if we stood before a preacher in church— to them. I swear, Travis," she said earnestly. "I had nothing to do with this. Sometimes Cochise takes his role as father a bit too seriously." She glared at Cochise. "He'd like to marry me off so someone else will have to worry about me. He doesn't think I can take care of myself."

Cochise shrugged and grinned. "A man must do what he must."

At that point Travis lost track of the conversation. There were only a few people around in that part of the camp. He spotted Hal-Say walking slowly toward them with a woman at his side, but Travis's gaze riveted on the young boy walking between the two.

Matt!

Travis rapidly blinked the moisture from his eyes. The child before him was taller than he'd been last winter, his hair was longer, and all he wore was a breech cloth and a pair of knee-high moccasins, but it was unmistakably, miraculously, Matt.

"Dad!"

110

"Matt!" Travis dropped to his knees and Matt hurled himself into his father's outstretched arms, his face lit with joy.

"Dad! Dad! I thought you were dead!" His voice shook and ended with a slight sob.

"It's okay now, Matt. I'm here. I've come to take you home." Travis squeezed his eyes shut, blocking out everything but the feel of his son in his arms.

"Oh yes, Dad! Yes!"

Daniella couldn't keep her tears from falling as she witnessed a father's deep love for his child. This was exactly how she had pictured her own homecoming. But Travis Colton and Howard Blackwood were two entirely different men. The pain of that difference nearly choked the breath from her.

She had to get away. Watching Travis and his son as they clung to each other in joy and love left her with an emptiness inside, the likes of which she'd never felt before. It was as if she'd just discovered a jagged hole in the fabric of her life — a hole she thought was closed off and sealed months ago. But this hole was larger, colder, emptier than the old one. This one contained only deep, profound blackness, and she felt herself slipping into its depths. If she ever fell into that emptiness, that great nothingness, she would die.

Daniella backed away, wanting to leave camp, to escape and seek solitude, as a wounded animal might seek a hiding place where it could lick its wounds in peace and privacy, there to heal, or die. She needed to be alone to fight the terrible void threatening to engulf her.

Travis held his son with all the strength he possessed. His face twisted in a grimace of pain and joy — pain at all he and Matt had suffered during their separation, and joy, such joy as he had never known before, at being able to simply hold his son in his arms again.

There had been many dark, lonely nights when he'd feared Matt was lost to him forever. Never before had he known such despair and helplessness. But there had always been that tiny spark of hope — hope that if he searched long enough and hard enough, he would one day find his son. Travis's father and the people at the Triple C had encouraged him during the long months of searching, keeping his hope alive.

Only Carmen had tried to get him to give up. Why he ever got mixed up with her was a mystery to him. Perhaps his loneliness had finally gotten the best of him. He thought he had already learned to stay away from women. That lesson had been pounded into his head by Julia. How could he have forgotten that to trust a woman, to believe he could find happiness in a pair of scheming, deceiving, feminine arms, was like trying to share a den with a rattlesnake?

He was letting his bitterness rule him and he knew it. Carmen couldn't help being selfish—it was just her nature. She had probably never matured, emotionally, past the age of five. He didn't care. She meant nothing to him anyway. And Julia—well, she had done one good thing before she died, God rest her troubled soul. She had given him Matt. Matt was worth any amount of pain he may have suffered by being married to her.

Travis felt his son shudder against him and jerked his mind back to the present. He stroked the boy's hair and back, murmuring soothing words in an effort to ease the storm of emotions raging within them both.

Out of the corner of his eye he saw Daniella backing away. He turned slightly toward her, with Matt still clinging to him, and wondered at the pain he saw in her face. Her pale blue eyes were deep pools of misery. Wet trails of tears glistened on her cheeks, leaving clean streaks through the day's dust and grime.

Here was a woman with enough compassion to shed tears for someone other than herself. As he reached a hand out for her, needing to touch her, he acknowledged that without Daniella he probably would never have found Matt. He ached with the need to pull her into his embrace, to hold her as he held Matt, to share this moment with her, to somehow express his boundless gratitude for this most precious gift she had given him.

Through the haze of her tears Daniella saw Travis reach out to her, saw the tenderness mixed with something else she didn't recognize expressed in his deep brown eyes, and she panicked. If he touched her, she'd crumble. She would fall to the ground and shatter into a million pieces.

"No!" she whispered fiercely, fighting the sob she felt rising in her throat. "No!" She saw a look of bewilderment cross his face as she stumbled away. She clamped her hand over her mouth to hold back the wail of pain threatening to erupt, and ran away from Travis, away from the Apaches, away from the warm fire. She had to be alone—*had* to be!

Cochise saw her pain and misery and motioned for Travis to let her go. Through the scouts at the white man's fort he had heard of her father's rejection. This reunion between the man and his son must have reopened old wounds. He idly wondered if Woman of Magic would mind too much if he lifted her father's scalp. But no, that would not be such a good idea. The spirit of the person scalped always became a part of the warrior who took the scalp. Cochise did not think he would like to have such an unfeeling spirit as part of himself. Then there was the four-day purification ceremony he would have to undergo after taking a scalp. No, he really didn't have the time for that. Scalping wasn't something his people usually did.

But an anthill . . . I could stake him out . . . perhaps a few cactus spines under his fingernails . . . or a wet strap of green rawhide around his forehead on a hot, sunny day . . . such possibilities! I must give it some thought. And the thought he gave to it brought a wistful smile to his face.

Daniella slowed her headlong flight when she reached the edge of the forest. The thick stand of pines blocked out the light from the campfires, as well as the silver moonlight flickering in and out of the small scattering of clouds in the dark night sky.

In the blackness engulfing her she struck her shin against something hard and uttered a pain-filled oath. Bending down carefully, she explored with her hands and felt the rough bark of a fallen tree. She sank down on it, folding her arms tightly against her stomach, rocking back and forth in a useless effort to suppress the agony welling up inside her.

She squeezed her eyes shut, trying to block out the images racing through her mind, but the faces only became clearer, the memories keener, the pain sharper. Her father, thrusting her aside; Travis holding her hand in the night; Travis holding his son; Travis reaching out toward her, longing mingled with tenderness and gratitude in his eyes; Travis; Travis; Travis.

Stop it! It was her father's comfort she longed for. Wasn't it?

But Daniella had always been brutally honest, with herself as well as with others. Here in the darkness and solitude of the forest she was forced to admit it wasn't her father she cried for at all. It was Travis. She wanted him to hold her again, as he had earlier. She wanted him to hold her and comfort her as he held and comforted his son, telling her everything would be all right, telling her he loved her.

Those last words rumbled through her mind like a roll of thunder. Her tears dried up instantly.

"Fool!" she hissed to herself.

He only came with her on this trip as a last desperate effort to find his son. He was polite and friendly because he wanted her help. That's all! And now maybe he would even be grateful—but nothing more.

Good heavens. She'd only known the man a few days, and here she was fantasizing about him. *Fool! Shameful, hopeless fool.* Was she so desperate for affection that she could imagine a man like Travis Colton would ever love her?

And what about her feelings for him? Why did her stomach go all fluttery every time he looked at her? Did her blood really heat up whenever she got the chance to watch the play of muscles across his shoulders or along his thighs? God, she was confused.

His ruggedness, his strength, his very masculinity both attracted and frightened her. She wanted to feel the warmth and safety she knew she'd find in his arms. She could even

114

imagine what it might be like if he kissed her, although she'd never been kissed before. But no man, least of all one as totally male as Travis Colton, would ever settle for hugs and kisses—that much she knew about men.

And hugs and kisses were all she would ever have to offer. She would never willingly let a man do to her what the Apaches did that night of her capture. If that was the way of things between men and women, and if women were supposed to accept it, then Daniella knew she would spend the rest of her life alone. No man would ever touch her again—not like that—not ever again like that.

She threw her head back and took in a deep breath, savoring the sweet fragrance of damp earth and pine needles. What was the point in all this soul-searching anyway? Travis would never want a woman who was thought of as a whore by every white man in the territory.

With a ragged laugh she slid from the log to the ground. Loved and abandoned in less than an hour—at least in her own mind. She drew her poncho close around her for warmth, having no intention of going back to camp that night. She wasn't ready to face Travis or anyone else. After her imaginings of the past hour, she needed time to regain her equilibrium. Her secret longings had no place in reality, and must remain hidden if not destroyed.

The night sounds of frogs and crickets filled the air. Daniella concentrated on them, drawing comfort from the knowledge that even frogs and crickets cried out in search of a mate. She wasn't alone after all.

"Why does Woman of Magic hide in the forest like a frightened child, while the rest of The People celebrate her homecoming?"

Daniella shrieked and jumped to her feet at the sound of the deep, guttural voice so close behind her. As she whirled to face one of the demons from her nightmares, she slipped the thong from her Colt's hammer and drew the heavy pistol from her holster. "Get away from me," she warned.

"What is this?" Loco demanded, arms spread wide. "You still fear me?"

"I don't fear you, I *hate* you." Not for her life would she admit her fear of this warrior who'd slung her belly-down across his mount and carried her away from the stage. And not for her life would she let him near enough to touch her again.

"Because I am the one who brought you here?" he asked. "Because I was the first to have you? You were our enemy then. Now you are one of us. You have nothing to fear from me. I'm the one who should be angry with you."

"And just why is that?" He took a step closer, and she cocked the Colt. He halted in mid stride. A shaft of moonlight through the dense pine needles highlighted the anger in his fierce, dark face.

"Because of you, I have no wife. Klea took offense that I spent on you what she considered hers. When I woke that next morning, all my belongings were piled outside her wickiup. She won't even let me near my own children. Tahnito and Alope are forbidden to speak to me! You cost me my wife—you will take her place. You cost me my children—you will give me more. I will deliver ponies to Cochise in the morning."

Daniella gaped at him, stunned. He actually thought she would consent to marry him? What colossal conceit!

He moved closer.

"Take another step toward me, you stinking *gusano,* and you won't live till morning."

Loco paused. "You are new to our ways, so I will forgive you for calling me a worm. We do not consider it polite to call each other names. We also do not kill one another. It is forbidden."

"You're right, of course," Daniella said, allowing a false smile to curve her lips. "I won't kill you." She lowered the pistol from his chest and took aim on the center of his breech cloth. "But you may wish I had."

Loco sucked in his breath. "Woman, you are crazy! When you are my wife, such behavior will not be tolerated."

"I will never be your wife," she spat.

As Loco turned back toward camp, he said, "We shall see, woman, we shall see."

When he was gone, Daniella sank to her knees, her hand shaking so badly it took three tries to get the Colt back in its holster. God, how she hated that bastard. His face brought back every horrifying memory of that night.

She rose again on trembling legs and made her way deeper into the forest.

Chapter Twelve

"Yellow Hair Colton."

When Cochise's low voice called his name from outside the wickiup, Travis sat up, instantly alert. Matt was asleep, but Travis had rested with one ear open, hoping to hear Daniella come for her bedroll. Cochise's coming to him in the middle of the night put all his senses on alert. It could only mean trouble. "What is it?" he asked tensely.

Cochise entered the wickiup and crouched near the opening. The darkness was so thick Travis could barely make out the Apache's outline in the doorway.

"I need a favor, Yellow Hair."

"What's wrong?"

"Nothing . . . yet," Cochise said. "In the morning someone will find Woman of Magic and tell her you wish to leave as soon as possible. You must get her away from here. Not at first light, but no later than midmorning."

"What's happened?"

"Old Nana has asked me to hunt with him at dawn. The *tiswin* loosened many tongues tonight, including Golthlay's."

At the mention of that name Travis tensed. "What about Golthlay?"

"For some reason, I believe he has decided my white daughter will be his next wife."

Wife! Daniella, married to that . . . that . . . ? Unthinkable! So that's what Golthlay was up to. That's how he planned to get even. Marry her, and he could do whatever he wanted with her.

118

"Nana must be acting as the go-between," Cochise continued. "I think tomorrow he will offer for Woman of Magic on behalf of Golthlay. If she is here, I will be forced to repeat the offer to her. She will refuse, I know, and that is her right. But it will cause trouble. Did something happen between them on the trail, Yellow Hair?"

"I don't think she intended you to hear about it," Travis said slowly. "But I think you need to know." So Travis told him everything about the night he and Daniella met Monache and his warriors, and the sly looks and smirks Daniella had been receiving since.

"Ah, that girl! She is something, is she not?" Cochise said, teeth gleaming in the darkness. "So then, from what you say, I would guess her refusal of Golthlay's offer will not be a polite one. And that will cause trouble. First, between the two of them. Then Golthlay will expect me to persuade her. I will not, and there will be trouble between him and me. If one of us does not back down, and neither of us will, the trouble may extend to involve more and more of our people."

Cochise paused and sighed, then went on. "The days when we could fight amongst ourselves, Chidikáágu' against Membrenos, Pinals against Mashgalén, or Mescaleros, as you call them, Coyoteros against Arivaipas, those days are gone. We cannot afford to live the old ways. We must join together or lose our homeland.

"You must get Woman of Magic away from here before Nana and I return from the hunt. Will you do this thing for me? For her? For all our people?"

"Of course," Travis stated. "But she won't want to leave without telling you good-bye," he warned.

"You must convince her. Dee-O-Det will help you."

Travis took a deep breath. There was bound to be trouble, no matter what happened. But far better for her to be angry with him than to have her publicly humiliate Golthlay again. That one would kill her the first chance he got. "All right. I'll get her out of here by midmorning, even if I have to drag her."

Laughter rumbled deep in Cochise's chest. "For your sake, white man, I hope it does not come to that."

"So do I," Travis said with feeling. "So do I."

"I have another request, one perhaps not so easy for you to accomplish."

"What is it?"

"I ask that you remember how you felt when you could not find your son. There are those among us now who feel the same. A few days ago, two of our young boys were separated from a hunting party and have not been seen since. If you hear of them, or see them, I ask your help in sending them home to their families."

Travis was deeply moved that this fierce Apache chief would humble himself on behalf of two young boys, to ask a white man for help. If Travis found the boys and sent them home, would they grow up to one day attack his ranch, or his neighbor's ranch, or some unsuspecting stage?

Then he looked over at Matt and recalled the frustration, the terror of not knowing where his son was for all those weeks.

"I'll do what I can," he said.

"*Bueno.*" As Cochise turned to leave, he paused. "There is one thing more I would say to you, Yellow Hair, and that is this. You and your son, Little Bear, are welcome among the Chúk'ánéné at any time. I hope you will come back when we have more time to talk, you and I. I know Hal-Say and Huera will always welcome Little Bear in their wickiup, and in their hearts. His leaving will be hard on them."

"*Gracias,* Cochise. Matt and I have already talked about that. He would like to come back occasionally. He's grown quite fond of them, especially of Huera. He's never had a mother before."

"You should do something about that, white man. I happen to have an adopted daughter you might be interested in, but she is valuable to me. I would expect many horses to ease my loss." The Apache chief's teeth flashed briefly in the darkness as he grinned.

"Is that a fact?" Travis asked, amused.

"Good night, Yellow Hair," Cochise said with a chuckle. "I wish you fruitful work."

His "work," getting Daniella to leave by midmorning, turned out to be much easier than he had anticipated. He hadn't needed to do more than say he was ready to go home. Apparently the old *shaman* was quite adept at handling situations like this, for Travis, Matt, and Daniella walked casually away from the compound without telling anyone they were leaving and met Dee-O-Det on the other side of a thick stand of pines. There he had their horses, saddled, loaded and waiting. Travis's gunbelt hung from his saddle horn.

In addition to Daniella's mare and Travis's stallion, there was a beautiful red and white pinto pony. Matt recognized his bow and quiver tied on behind the saddle. Dee-O-Det explained that the pony was Matt's, a gift from Hal-Say. The boy was thrilled—he'd certainly never expected anything like this. But he was disappointed at not being allowed to go back and thank Hal-Say. Dee-O-Det assured Matt that he would personally deliver the message of thanks for him.

"This, too, is for you, Little Bear." The old man handed Matt what looked like a powder horn, except it had an extra hole, this one in the side, near the base. "It is from Cochise. You blow through here," he pointed to the tip, "and move your finger over this hole, like so." He showed Matt how to cover only part of the side hole.

"Is it some kind of signal?" Matt asked.

The wrinkled old face split in a grin. "Very good. Yes. It is a signal horn. When you come back to us, blow on this and we will know a special friend is coming."

Travis fought down the surge of jealousy over his son's receiving such gifts from other men. He owed Hal-Say, Huera, and Cochise a great deal—more than he could hope to repay. Jealousy made him feel small.

Last night Travis had learned that Apache law states the

spoils of war belong to the entire tribe. Matt had been a "spoil of war." If Hal-Say had not gone before the council and received permission to adopt Matt, the boy would have become a slave, led around on a leash, forced to fight the dogs for a scrap of food. Yes, Travis owed Matt's "other parents" a great deal.

He was glad he'd gone to see them this morning, to tell them Matt would come back to visit. Their profound gratitude made him see just how much they cared for Matt. But it bothered Travis more than a little to realize how fond Matt was of them. His son was establishing relationships outside the bounds of his immediate family. He was growing up.

Oh, Matt, Travis cried out silentiy. *Don't grow away from me. Don't grow up too fast.*

"Well, old man," Daniella said to Dee-O-Det from atop her horse. "Can I assume that sometime today Travis will explain to me just what this is all about?" She bit the inside of her mouth to keep from demanding an explanation then and there.

"What what is all about?" the *shaman* asked. He was the picture of innocence.

"Humph!" she said. "I've never seen anyone so glad to be rid of another person as you are me."

"My child," he protested. "You are imagining things."

"I don't think so. But I must admit—at least it was all done politely. What was it you said? Something about it being a perfect day for traveling? And then there was that bit about how rude it would be of me to make Travis stay, when he was ready to leave."

Pounding hoofbeats brought Daniella's head around sharply. It was seventeen-year-old Tahza, Cochise's oldest son. His presence here meant things must be serious, for Tahza never had much to do with her. "Good morning, brother," she greeted. "Let me guess. You're here to show us the fastest way out of the mountains, and probably to reassure me, as your mother did earlier, that *shitaa* would feel terrible if his simple hunting trip caused me to delay my

122

departure."

Tahza's black eyes bored into her. He nodded once, hesitantly.

"What is going on around here?" she demanded.

"*Núúghuyáhah* — go on!" Dee-O-Det commanded. "Tonight, as you eat the dried venison I placed in your packs, Yellow Hair Colton will explain. I have also loaded extra blankets. You will need them on these cool nights, with no fire to warm you."

"No fire?" she repeated stupidly. This was much more serious than she had imagined. The caution meant someone might be following them.

"No fires until you pass the place where we spend our winters. Ride swiftly, my friends."

They rode as swiftly as the narrow mountain trails allowed, with Tahza leading the way.

That first night at camp, with no fire, Travis told Daniella of his visit from Cochise. She sat up all night thinking about what he said. Initially she was outraged that Golthlay should have such nerve. Then she felt hurt that Cochise believed she would cause trouble. But she realized Travis was right in one respect. Golthlay would think it a good way to get even. He probably thought he could take her back to his own *rancheria,* away from her powerful adoptive family, and make her pay for humiliating him.

But then, Golthlay didn't know her very well, and Cochise, it seemed, did. There would most definitely have been trouble. If she had somehow ended up married to Golthlay, she would have slit his throat the first night, if he didn't slit hers first.

She wondered if Cochise had also learned that Loco planned to offer for her, too.

The night wind swallowed up her soft sigh. Cochise's way was best, after all. If she simply disappeared from the stronghold, she would never receive Golthlay's or Loco's offer.

The next day Tahza gave them the explanation planned regarding her swift departure. He would first escort them out of the mountains, then return to the stronghold. That would take five or six days. Meanwhile, Tesal-Bestinay, Tahza's mother, would inform Cochise upon his return from the hunt that Tahza had taken the three whites exploring. No doubt they would return tomorrow, or surely the day after, she would say.

When Tahza finally returned, alone, he would tell his father that they had intended to be back by the second day, but that Little Bear had fallen ill. Yellow Hair insisted on taking his son home, and Woman of Magic had gone with him.

Someone, probably Golthlay, would surely ask what had taken Tahza so long to get home. He would say that the stupid white man was afraid he would get lost, and insisted Tahza lead them out of the mountains.

"After all," Tahza said innocently to Travis's groan, "everyone knows a white man cannot even follow his hand in front of his face."

"I think I hear the words of a *shaman* somewhere in that last part," Daniella said, not trying to hide her sarcasm.

Tahza hooted with laughter. "He said you would blame him for that. But you are right, sister. That part was his idea."

Travis pursed his lips in chagrin. "You tell him I owe him one for that, Tahza."

"What does this mean, owe him one? One what?"

"It means," Daniella explained, "Yellow Hair Colton plans to get even with our *shaman* for the slur cast on his character."

As Tahza thought this over, they made their way toward a second cold, dark night. Having only had brief snatches of sleep for the past several days, Daniella couldn't stay awake as she huddled beneath her blanket for warmth. After a few hours of restless slumber, the nightmares returned.

A few feet away, Travis came awake. This time he knew what was wrong. He crept to her side and trapped her arms

124

beneath her blanket. "Daniella," he whispered in her ear. "Wake up, Daniella. You're having a dream. It's only a dream, love. It's all right. Wake up now."

Finally her eyes opened. She gasped for breath and struggled to free her trapped arms.

"It's all right, Daniella. Just be still. Everything's okay."

"T-Travis?"

"It's me, love. I'm here . . . you're safe."

Daniella took in great gulps of cool night air. She couldn't move her arms! She was trapped! "Let go of me!" she gasped in panic.

"Are you awake now?" he asked, holding on to her firmly.

"I-I'm awake. L-Let go of me, p-please."

Slowly, Travis released her and leaned away. She threw back the blanket and scrambled to her knees, then turned and doubled over, pressing her heated face against the cool, smooth leather seat of her saddle at the head of her bedroll. She sucked clean night air into her lungs. When she exhaled, her whole body shuddered violently.

God, the nightmare had seemed so real. In fact, she thought, it wasn't even a dream—it was a memory. A black, terrifying memory that held her in its grip and refused to set her free. She opened her eyes wide, searching the darkness to reassure herself of where she was. She sensed Travis's presence close beside her and felt a little safer, but also a little threatened.

"Daniella," he murmured quietly. "I won't hurt you, you know that. But I'm going to touch you."

"No!" she gasped, too shaken and weak to move. "Don't, please."

"Yes," he insisted. "I'm going to touch you and hold you, do for you what you told me to do for Matt. I can't let you go through this alone."

Travis reached beneath her poncho and placed his palm on the small of her back. Daniella flinched and whimpered. She didn't want to be afraid of him, but she was.

It took her a long moment to realize the warm, firm hand on her back didn't hurt, didn't threaten. It massaged gently

125

up and dawn her spine, spreading a tingling warmth in its wake.

Somehow Travis shifted around, and Daniella found herself lying against his hard, wide chest while he leaned back against her saddle. She uttered a murmur of protest, but his arms beneath her poncho held her firmly in place.

"Hush, love," he whispered. "Just relax and let me hold you. You've done so much for me. Let me help you now. Let me hold you and keep the bad dreams away for a while."

His hands stroked her through the thin cotton of her shirt, warming her, relaxing her. She could no longer find the strength, or the will, to protest. She couldn't believe how good it felt to have him touch her and hold her this way. Her head fit perfectly into the hollow of his shoulder. She'd never felt so safe in her life.

He knew what the Apaches had done to her, yet instead of scorn and contempt, he offered her comfort and tenderness. She knew it was only his way of thanking her for taking him to his son, but she didn't care. If she never saw him again, it would still be worth this one night in his arms.

She relaxed against him, and soon her breathing was deep and even. Travis frowned at the thinness of her frame. He'd never seen her without the damn poncho, but now his fingers could trace her delicate rib cage. When he spanned her waist with both hands, his fingers met.

This trip had been hard on her. Surely at home she slept more and ate real meals. What kind of a woman gave up the comfort of her home, unasked, to help a total stranger? The journey so far had been grueling, the food scarce, her sleep practically nonexistent, and at one point, they'd both come uncomfortably close to being killed, yet not once had she complained.

She was extremely independent, as hard as nails, at home in the wilderness, and at ease with a bowie knife in her hand.

That was by day. By night she was a frightened child. Somewhere in between those two extremes must be the real

126

Daniella. That was the woman he was determined to know.

A few hours later, before the sky even hinted at dawn, Daniella came awake with a start. Immediately, Travis's arms tightened around her.

"Ssh," he whispered. "It's all right."

When she realized where she was, she relaxed again against his broad chest. After a moment, she tried to rise.

"Be still, love. It's early. Go back to sleep," he murmured. He'd lain awake all night savoring the feel of her in his arms.

"Let me up, Travis," she urged.

"No. Go back to sleep. I'll wake you later." He didn't want to let her go. She wasn't likely to slip back into his arms anytime soon. That much he knew. He wanted to hang on to her as long as possible.

"Travis, let me go," Daniella insisted. "If Tahza wakes up and finds us like this, there may not be a shotgun wedding, like you feared, but there would certainly be a bow-and-arrow one."

And a young girl like you wouldn't want to find herself tied to a thirty-year-old man like me, he thought with surprising bitterness.

What the hell was the matter with him, anyway? He didn't want to get married any more than she did. He'd been married once. That was more than enough for any man. He'd learned his lesson, hadn't he?

Besides, what did he really know about Daniella Blackwood? The girl had quite a few more problems than he was prepared to deal with, not the least of which was her fear of men. The only reason she was in his arms right now was because she had temporarily found something she feared even more than she feared him. He sighed deeply and released her.

To Daniella's mind, she mentioned the word "wedding" and instantly found herself alone on her blanket. *So much for knights in shining armor,* she thought with disgust. She'd been right about him all along. He didn't want "tainted goods" any more than the next man did.

Across the small clearing, Tahza watched through narrowed eyes as the Yellow Hair returned to his own bedroll. *Interesting,* he thought. *Yes,* shitaa *will find this very interesting.*

Chapter Thirteen

The morning of the fourth day, Tahza left to return to the stronghold. Travis stared thoughtfully at the youth's retreating figure. His troubled frown stayed with him while they started down out of the mountains.

"Something wrong?" Daniella finally asked.

Travis looked at her for a moment, then at Matt. He shrugged and returned his gaze to her. "I liked him," he admitted.

"Who?"

"Tahza."

"So what's wrong with that?" Matt wanted to know.

"I don't know," Travis said, troubled. "I liked Cochise, too, and Dee-O-Det. I even liked Hal-Say and Huera, Matt, and I know you like them. You probably have quite a few friends back there." His eyes shifted back to Daniella. "And you have what amounts to a whole family. Yet they've done something to each of us that should make us hate them. Instead, we make friends."

He shrugged again, not sure if he was saying what he meant. "I guess it boils down to individuals," he reasoned. "I'm sure if I'd known which ones attacked our stage I wouldn't have liked them, but then for all I know, I could have sat beside them and never known."

Daniella was quiet for a moment, then said, "I know what you mean. They're supposed to be our enemies, yet we like them. At least some of them. Not very popular in this territory."

129

"Well, I hope you didn't eat with the one called Loco," Matt said heatedly.

Daniella stiffened. The dark face of the one Matt mentioned rose up before her, vicious, menacing. She pictured him as he appeared in her nightmares, cradling his bleeding hand against his chest, his other hand reaching toward the fire. She pictured him as he was the other night, looming over her in the dark forest, talking of marriage.

"Daniella?" Travis questioned. Then more sharply, "Daniella."

"What? I—I'm sorry. I guess I wasn't listening." She forced the pictures to the back of her mind, knowing full well Loco's face would escape again to haunt her in the dark.

"Who is this Loco?" Travis looked from Daniella to Matt.

"He's the one who shot you and took me," Matt said with emotion. "He put a slave leash on my neck, and he didn't want Hal-Say to adopt me. I hate him!"

Daniella stared straight ahead, her back rigid, trying to keep her mind a blank.

"Do you know him?" Travis asked her.

Instead of answering, she kicked her horse into a gallop and raced ahead. She couldn't stand to hear any more. She couldn't answer any more questions.

Matt turned solemn eyes on his father. "I think she knows him, Dad."

Travis was shocked by his son's eyes. They were so old! Too old for a ten-year-old. They'd seen too much for one so young. They were like Daniella's eyes. *Dear Lord, what has he seen to make him look so ancient?* Travis shied from the answer. He didn't want to know; still, he was afraid he already knew.

They reached the lowlands, and the noon sun beat down with oppressive heat. Daniella realized with a start that she'd been concentrating so hard on keeping her mind blank that she hadn't even felt the dampness of her own sweat beneath the oven-like folds of her poncho. She was glad when Travis suggested they stop to water and rest the horses. As soon as she'd seen to her mare, Daniella reached for the bottom hem of her poncho and peeled it off over her head. The slight breeze felt cool as it penetrated the thin fabric of her shirt.

Travis eagerly watched her remove the heavy garment, like a boy might watch his Christmas present being un-wrapped. When she turned her profile to him and threw back her shoulders, taking in a deep breath, his mouth went dry. Her shirt was stretched tight across generous breasts, and the breeze cooled her skin until her nipples puckered beneath the thin, worn fabric. He swallowed heavily and nearly choked. If she breathed any deeper, at least one but-ton would succumb to the stress. He almost groaned aloud when he remembered from the night he'd held her that she wore nothing beneath that shirt.

He watched as she shook out her poncho, folded it, then knelt in the shade of an enormous cottonwood and bent for-ward to brush some twigs away. Her hair slid sideways as she moved, exposing her back and hips, which happened to be pointing at Travis. He tried to maintain an outward ap-pearance of calm while his pulse pounded in his ears. He drank in the first sight of her slim back and trim waist. He'd felt them in the darkness, but he'd never seen her without the poncho. Dampness gathered on his palms, which yearned to fit themselves over the soft curves of her but-tocks, outlined perfectly by her breeches.

She placed her folded poncho at the base of the tree to use as a pillow, then lay down on her side with her back to him. He'd seen her nap this way several times before, but this time was different. This time he felt a hardening in his loins and had to fight the urge to lay down beside her and press himself against her softness.

Damn! What was he thinking? She wasn't much more than a girl. She didn't need a man his age in her life, he

131

reminded himself. But still, he couldn't deny any longer how much he wanted her. He wanted her with an intensity he hadn't felt in years.

Forget it, man. Even if he could get past all her defenses, when she found out she had nothing to fear from him she'd probably show her true colors and turn as cold and grasping as the other women he'd known.

He waited for Blaze to nudge Daniella awake. Once on the trail again, he watched the girl sway in the saddle. She looked numb with exhaustion. When he finally called a halt late in the afternoon, she was almost asleep in the saddle. A few minutes later she stretched out on her bedroll and was asleep for real.

Travis had chosen this particular place to camp because of the small pool at the edge of the stream, just beyond a thick screen of brush. He and Matt decided to take a swim to cool off.

"Dad, is Daniella sick or something?"

They were nearing the pond when Matt spoke, and Travis eyed his son sharply. "Not that I know of, son. Why do you ask?"

"She sure sleeps a lot, doesn't she?"

"Not really." He thought of Daniella's sleepless nights, the dark circles beneath her eyes, and wondered how much to reveal to his young son. Some inner sense warned him it would be useless to lie; Matt probably knew a great deal about her already. Travis measured his words carefully when he spoke.

"Daniella was taken captive by the Apaches, just like you were. You know that. She has bad dreams about it at night, so she sleeps during the day so the nightmares won't bother her."

Matt's eyes grew large. The blood drained from his face.

"What is it, Matt?" Travis asked anxiously.

"I-I didn't know she was captured. I only knew Cochise adopted her. I don't want her to die, Dad!" he cried. "I like her. She's fun and nice. You like her too, I can tell. I don't

132

want her to die! Don't let her die, Dad!" Matt threw himself at Travis's chest and buried his face against his father's shoulder.

"Hush, son . . . hush. She's not going to die," Travis murmured in an attempt to soothe the boy. "Why would you think a thing like that?"

Matt trembled in his father's arms. "The o-others d-did," he whispered.

Travis felt his blood turn cold. "What others?"

"The other w-women . . . white ladies." Matt looked up at his father with thousand-year-old eyes. "I saw, Dad," the boy cried. "I saw what they did to the white ladies. They did that to Daniella, too, didn't they? All the other ladies died. Don't let her die, Dad," he pleaded.

Dear God, Travis thought. He swallowed with difficulty and hugged Matt to him. To know for certain that his son had been exposed to such brutality, and at such a tender age, was almost more than he could bear. Daniella had been right—Apaches don't shield the children. What could he say to Matt to make the horror of what he'd seen go away?

What would Daniella have him say? After all, it was her they were talking about. There was no point in denying anything, since Matt was sharp enough to have already figured out as much as he had. Travis took a deep breath to steady himself.

"Listen to me." He pushed his son gently away and held him at arm's length. "Daniella is not going to die. What happened to her happened months ago, and she survived. She's the Woman of Magic. Nothing is going to happen to her."

Matt thought about it. Huera said Woman of Magic was big medicine. And Daniella *had* survived, then was adopted by Cochise. Surely the *shaman* had mixed up one of his mysterious potions to protect her.

Most important of all, Matt's father said nothing was going to happen to her. His father never lied.

He nodded decisively. "Okay, Dad." With the lightning-swift change of mood peculiar to the young, Matt grinned.

133

Nodding toward the pond, he challenged, "Last one in's a rotten egg!"

Travis sighed, relieved that his son's worries were so easily put to rest. They raced to get their clothes off, but Matt had a definite advantage. He only needed to pull off his moccasins and untie the string holding up his breech cloth.

They jumped into the cool water and swam, and played, and scrubbed, and played some more. Travis took great delight in having his son by his side again, and swore to himself he would never let any more harm come to this boy who was so precious to him. And he would find some way to repay Daniella for this miracle of happiness.

It had been dark for quite a while before Travis reluctantly allowed Matt to wake Daniella. He and Matt had managed to snare a couple of jackrabbits near the pond at sundown, and Travis had taken his time skinning and cleaning them. He wanted to let Daniella get as much sleep as possible. He would have just let her sleep all night, but he'd promised to wake her. If he didn't, he feared she'd blame him if she had another nightmare.

Snaring those rabbits was a stroke of luck. Travis had been reluctant to fire his rifle to bring down game for their supper for two reasons. The first was in case Golthlay had grown impatient and decided to follow them. Firing off a gun would have been like inviting him to dinner. The smell of roasting meat and the glow of their fire would also alert anyone around to their presence. He was anxious to get the meal over with so he could douse the fire, just in case.

His second reason for not wanting to fire his gun was that it would wake Daniella.

Matt's method of waking her was to tickle her ear with a blade of grass. She woke up laughing, with Matt's devilish grin beaming at her from above.

The aroma of roasting rabbit drifted to her on the light breeze, and Daniella suddenly realized she was starving. She saw Travis turning the meat over the fire and laughed again.

134

"I should have let Matt at you sooner," Travis said softly. "That's the first time I've ever heard you laugh."

The look in his eyes aroused that fluttery feeling in her stomach again, as it had on previous occasions. She turned away, confused. "Well, it isn't every day a girl gets awakened from a sound sleep by a young man tickling her ear." She smiled at Matt.

"Get up, Daniella. Dad's almost got supper ready. We caught a couple of rabbits." He beamed proudly.

"Rabbits, huh? I can't wait. They smell delicious."

It was their first hot meal since leaving the *rancheria*, and they did it justice.

For the past three days, conversation had been almost nil. Tahza's mood had been grim in his determination to get them out of the mountains as swiftly as possible. Now that it was just the three of them, tensions seemed to ease. Matt was the perfect buffer between Daniella and Travis.

But once he started talking, it was hard to get him to stop. He asked his father a million questions. He wanted to know everything that had been happening at home. How many new foals and calves were there? Had Grandad missed him? Had that mean old rooster ended up in the stewpot yet? Had Travis heard how Grandfather White in New Orleans was? Did they have any new neighbors, who maybe had kids his age?

When Matt found out Daniella was their new neighbor, he was ecstatic, even if she didn't have any children.

Travis allowed the fire to die out. "No point in taking chances. It's warm enough since we left the mountains, and there's a full moon tonight."

But Matt wasn't interested in the moon. "How come you don't have any kids? I thought all grownups had kids."

"Matt, it's none of your business," Travis said. "You're not supposed to ask questions like that."

"Don't scold him, Travis. He just wants somebody his own age to be with. Actually, Matt, the reason is, I'm not really a grownup at all," she teased. "I'm just a kid, like you."

135

"Ah," Matt scoffed. "I bet you're pullin' my leg. How old are you?"

"Matt, you're doing it again," Travis warned. "A gentleman never asks a lady how old she is."

"Oh. I'm sorry."

"It's all right, Matt," Daniella offered. "I don't mind. I'm nineteen."

"Nineteen! I told ya you were pullin' my leg. Nineteen's *old!*"

Travis threw his hands in the air. "I give up. See what happens when you indulge him like that?"

Daniella laughed at him. "Don't worry about it. He's right, anyway. Nineteen is old."

"Yeah, ancient." Travis's lips curled up at the corners. At least she wasn't as young as he'd thought, but she was still much too young for him. *What does it matter how old she is? She doesn't want anything to do with me anyway.*

"I've decided you need a shorter name," Matt announced to Daniella.

"You don't like my name?"

"Oh, it's okay. But my name's Matthew, and everybody calls me Matt. So instead of Daniella, we oughta call you Dani. How's that?" Matt waited anxiously for her approval. After a moment, the bright moonlight revealed a slow smile curving her lips.

"It's a lot better than what my family calls me," she said with a laugh.

"And what does your family call you?" Travis wanted to know.

"Oh, no. I'm not about to put that weapon in your hands," she objected. "I hate the nickname they gave me, and you'd probably use it just to make me angry. Just forget it."

Travis and Matt badgered her to tell them, teasing and making outrageously funny threats against her, but she refused to reveal the information. They put forth several guesses of their own, and she laughed until she had a stitch in her side at the ridiculous names they threw at her.

136

As the laughter died down, Travis sent Matt to his bedroll and the camp quieted. In a few minutes, Matt scrambled back up and ran over and whispered something in his father's ear.

"No, a fella never gets too old for that, Matt," Travis answered.

Daniella cocked a brow at the two of them, but they only smiled at her. A few minutes later, Matt spoke again from his bedroll.

"Dani?" His voice was almost a whisper.

"Hmmm?"

"Would you . . . um . . ." Matt looked to his father for reassurance, and Travis nodded his encouragement. "Would you kiss me good night?"

"Why, Matthew Colton, I thought you'd never ask. I'd be honored," she said as she closed the distance between them. She knelt down beside him and he reached his arms up to her. They hugged each other, and she smoothed the tousled golden curls back from his face and placed a tender kiss on each cheek. For once, she wasn't thinking of how much he resembled his father. She saw only a child, thought of the man he would soon become, and felt a terrible emptiness deep inside herself.

"Good night, Dani."

"Good night, Matt. Sweet dreams."

When she turned toward her own bedroll, Travis caught the glimmer of unshed tears in her eyes. He had been about to ask if she would kiss him good night too, but sensed she was not in the mood for jokes. Only he wouldn't have been joking; he wanted her to kiss him. But he knew she didn't feel the same.

"Daniella?" he asked with concern.

Daniella turned her back to him and shook her head, fighting the tears that threatened to fall. When she felt more composed, she sat down and poured herself another cup of coffee. She could hear Matt's even breathing and hoped his sleep would always come so easily.

"You're very good with children," Travis said softly.

137

Her throat constricted. "Thank you."

"You should have several of your own."

Daniella took a deep breath and let it out slowly to still the ache inside. "I love children," she answered. "I always said I'd have a dozen." The ache in her chest grew stronger.

"A dozen? Then you better start pretty soon, hadn't you? I mean, you're not getting any younger, grandma," he teased.

"That was a cruel thing to say." Her aching and bitterness swelled up to turn her voice to ice.

"Cruel? Hey . . . I was only joking. You can't be that sensitive about your age. You're only nineteen, for Pete's sake."

"What has my age got to do with anything?" Her lower lip quivered and her eyes misted over. "It's cruel for you to tease me about something I want very much and will never have."

"Never have? I don't understand."

"Don't understand? Are you so thick-headed that you can't understand I would prefer to have a husband before I have children, Mister Colton? And even if I could stand the thought of letting a man touch me, how many men — decent men — do you know who would marry a woman after half the Chiricahua men of the entire Apache nation have taken turns with her?"

Travis leaped across the dying fire and jerked her to her feet. "That's the first stupid thing I've heard you say." His breathing was heavy. She shrank away from the glare in his eyes.

"Stupid, is it? The Apaches might call me Woman of Magic, but do you know what white men think of me?" She, too, was breathing heavily. All her anger, her pain, her frustration came boiling out. Her voice sizzled and hissed with her ire.

"They think I'm an Apache whore! I see it in their eyes." She took an angry swipe at her damp eyes. "Do you know why I wanted you to come on this trip with me? I could have just gone and got Matt and brought him home to you

138

without having to convince you of anything. It would have been a lot easier on both of us. I knew the Apaches wouldn't harm me. But I wanted you along in case we ran into any white men. Isn't that crazy? The Apaches ruin me, nearly kill me, but they honor and respect me. It's the white men who scorn me. It's crazy! It's backward and all upside down! I think *I'm* crazy!" She struggled frantically to free herself from his iron grasp.

"Be still!" Travis ordered. "I'm going to tell you some things, lady. Things you should have figured out for yourself by now, but you've been too busy feeling sorry for yourself."

"Sorry for myself!" she shrieked. How dare he say such a thing to her!

"Yes. Sorry for yourself. Maybe you have more reason than most people, but I say you place too much importance on what happened to you. You're letting it control you. You need to let go of it, Daniella, put it behind you, in the past, where it belongs."

"So you're the expert now, are you?" she yelled back at him. "I suppose you're going to tell me just how to do it, too!"

"You bet I am. You can start by getting rid of that chip on your shoulder."

"Of all the—"

"And then maybe you should stop reminding yourself and everyone you meet about what happened."

"I don't have to remind anyone of anything. All anybody has to do is take one look at this!" She grabbed a handful of white hair in her fist. "That's reminder enough!"

Travis went on, ignoring her outburst. "You might also try working on getting over this fear you have of being touched. Even with a husband, something like that can make it a little difficult to have children. You did say you wanted children."

"When's the last time somebody told you to drop dead?"

"There you go again," he said, releasing her shoulders.

139

"You've got that chip on your shoulder. Why can't you just admit I'm right?"

"Because you're not right!" she cried. "I don't *let* it control me, anymore than I *let* myself get captured in the first place. I can't help what comes into my mind when I close my eyes at night. I can't help this streak in my hair or the scars on my body. I can't help it if a man's touch reminds me of what happened and scares me half out of my wits!" She was crying now, and didn't try to stop. "I don't want to be afraid. It just happens, and I can't stop it!"

Her tears tore him apart. He reached out a hand toward her. When she backed away from him in fright, he swore under his breath. "After all that's happened in the past week, you're still afraid of me, aren't you? You went to sleep one night holding my hand. Another night, you slept in my arms. I guess both of those times there was something you feared more than you feared me. I don't want to be the lesser of two fears, Daniella. You know I won't hurt you. Why can't you let yourself trust me? You need me right now at least as much as you did those other times."

Daniella trembled and stared at his outstretched hand. How could she tell him that she did trust him, but that the very idea terrified her? She was afraid of the things he made her feel. She was afraid to feel the warmth and safety of his arms, because she knew it was only temporary. When this trip was over, they would go their separate ways. What good would it do her to lean on his strength again tonight, when a lifetime of loneliness stretched out before her? What good, except to remind her of what she would miss.

But oh, God, she wanted to reach out to him, feel his hand in hers, feel his arms around her. He was right—she knew he wouldn't hurt her, not physically. It was her heart she worried about now. How was it possible to need someone so much, so soon? She barely knew him. People don't fall in love that fast. But she was afraid, so very afraid that was exactly what was happening to her. And she couldn't let it happen. Couldn't let it!

"No," she sobbed. She turned away from him and buried her face in her hands. "Just leave me alone."

He came closer. So close she could feel the heat from his body. His breath stirred her hair, and his warm hands gently cupped her shoulders. "Oh, Daniella, I'm sorry. I'm so sorry. I said I'd never hurt you, but I have, haven't I? I only wanted to make you see you don't have to fight all the time. You don't have to be afraid, or alone."

The long fingers on her shoulders flexed, sending warmth and weakness clear to her knees.

"You don't have to do any of those things with me," Travis added. "I won't push you any more, but if you want to lean on me awhile, I'm here. Just please don't cry anymore. I can't stand to see you cry."

She would have been all right, she told herself, if he just hadn't apologized. If he hadn't gone all tender and caring on her. If he hadn't sounded so sincere. If his voice hadn't gone rough and husky.

Her resolve crumbled, leaving her raw and exposed to the night. With a cry of defeat, she turned and fell into his arms. "Damn you, Travis Colton," she sobbed against his chest. "Damn you to hell for making me need you." She pounded ineffectually against him and cried bitterly, great racking sobs that clogged her nose and throat and soaked his shirt.

Travis crushed her to his chest and held on to her desperately. *Damn you, too,* he thought with resignation, *for making me want you so much.* The scary part was, his wanting was much more than just physical. He'd never felt this way about a woman before. His past affairs, even his marriage, had been strictly for convenience. His convenience. There had been no great emotional attachments. He'd never felt this need to hold and soothe and protect a woman, as he did now.

But the physical desire was there too, stronger than ever. The way her firm, generous breasts pressed against him without the barrier of her poncho drove him crazy. Maybe it was just as well Matt was only a few feet away. The sob-

141

bing, trembling woman in his arms was in no shape to serve his baser needs. He'd given her enough to think about for one night.

Travis picked her up and returned to her blanket. He leaned back against her saddle and settled her against his chest.

Daniella was enveloped in a haze of warmth and security, the likes of which she'd never known before. If these few moments were all she would ever have of him, then so be it. She would take them and savor them for as long as she could. Let tomorrow take care of itself.

Her tears gradually ceased, and she relaxed against him. She tried to stay awake, recording every touch, every moment, in her memory. But the warmth of his large hands stroking her back released the last of her tension. His deep voice whispered words of comfort as he buried his face in her hair.

Travis felt the grip on his shirt relax, and soon her breathing was deep and even. As once before, they reversed their roles, and it was Travis who stayed awake all night. God, but she felt good lying against him this way. He treasured every moment of the night. The feel of her slender body pressed against his chest, the clean, spicy fragrance of her hair, the way she clung to him even in her sleep.

No restless murmurings gave any hint that her nightmares had returned, and she slept the night away in his embrace.

It was almost dawn when Travis heard Matt stir. The boy came and stood beside him. Their eyes locked, speaking volumes to each other. Without words, Matt acknowledged that the scene he'd overheard last night was not to be spoken of to anyone. Nor was the fact that Daniella slept all night in his father's arms. Travis motioned toward the trees with his eyes, and Matt silently agreed to stay away from camp until he was called.

Daniella came awake slowly, reluctantly. When she opened her eyes, a wide expanse of brown cotton greeted her. Directly in front of her nose was a deep vee of bare skin covered with tight golden curls, and beneath her ear, a strong, steady pounding. She jerked her head up and stared at Travis in surprise. Memories of last night swamped her, and a fierce heat flooded her face.

"Good morning," Travis said. His soft voice poured over her like warm honey.

"G—Good morning." She lowered her eyes in confusion. "Would you . . . let me up, please?"

"Not until you promise you're not going to get all embarrassed about last night." His arms held her firmly as he waited for her answer.

"I—I'm sorry. I managed to make a pretty big fool of myself, didn't I?"

"No, you didn't. Last night was my fault, and you know it. You have nothing to be embarrassed about."

Chapter Fourteen

It was two more long, hard days before they reached the stream dividing El Valle de Esperanza from Travis's Triple C Ranch. Daniella had withdrawn into herself again, thinking over all Travis had said that night. She realized with reluctance that he was right. She did dwell on what had happened to her, and she had allowed it to control her too much. But she hadn't done those things on purpose, or even willingly, and she didn't have the faintest idea what to do about it.

The best she could do would be to get away from Travis and the unwanted attraction she felt. She needed to get home, throw herself into work, and think long and hard about herself and her future.

She needed to get away from him, but it was the last thing she wanted. To postpone the inevitable good-byes, Daniella asked Matt to get down and walk with her for a moment when they reached the stream.

Travis felt left out, watching the two of them walk away. What could she have to say to the son that she didn't want the father to hear?

When they were far enough away that Travis couldn't overhear, Daniella nodded toward the boundary before them.

"Do you recognize this stream, Matt?"

"Sure. It's the east side of our ranch. Why?"

"It's also the dividing line between your ranch and mine. See those hills there? Just on the other side is my ranch. It's not big like yours, but it's mine. There's another stream that

144

runs down the middle of the valley, and my house is on the other side of that stream."

"Why are you telling me this, Dani?"

"Well, in case you ever want to visit, I want you to know how to find me. You know your father loves you very much. There isn't anything in the world he wouldn't do for you. But sometimes a fella needs a friend. I know fellas don't usually have girls for friends, but I'd like to be your friend, if you ever need one. Okay?"

Matt scrunched up his face in thought. "You mean, like if there's things I don't want to talk to Dad about, I could come talk to you?"

"That's right. But you must promise to tell someone where you're going anytime you come see me. All right?"

"I promise. But can I bring Dad, sometimes?"

Her breath caught for a moment. "You can bring anyone you want," she managed.

"Gee, thanks, Dani!"

On their way back to Travis, Matt stopped and motioned for her to lean down. When she did, he surprised her with a kiss. Her heart felt like it was turning over. How had she grown so fond of him so quickly?

"I sure do like you a lot, Dani."

"And I sure do like you a lot, too, Matt."

"Dani? Thanks for bringing my Dad to find me."

"You're most welcome, love."

Travis stood next to his buckskin, waiting for them. When they approached, he said, "It's my turn now, son. Wait for me across the creek, will you? I won't be long."

Daniella watched the deep frown on Travis's face as he followed his son with troubled eyes. "Don't worry," she said softly. "He's not growing away from you, he's just growing up."

Travis turned and studied her closely. "So, now you read minds, do you?"

"Sometimes," she said with a small shrug.

Travis took a deep breath and let his hat dangle from his fingers. "I owe you, Daniella Blackwood. How do I repay you?"

"You don't owe me anything," Daniella protested, uneasy

with his sudden seriousness.

"Oh, but I do. I owe you my life, and my son, and I owe you an apology for ever doubting you in the first place. If there's ever anything you need—anything at all—just tell me. I can't think of a thing in the world I wouldn't do for you."

He took a step toward her. She backed away nervously. Another step, and she was up against the side of her horse. Travis's hands came up, one on each side of her head, and rested on her saddle. Still he came closer. "I'd like to see you again," he said solemnly. "May I?"

His deep voice sent goose bumps down her spine. "I—I've invited Matt. Y-You're welcome, too."

The tiny gold flecks in his deep brown eyes held her mesmerized, and as he leaned closer, the breath caught in her throat. No part of their bodies touched, until his lips met hers.

He brushed his lips across hers, lightly, slowly, breathlessly. Back and forth, so faint it might not have been happening at all but for the bolt of lightning that shot through them both.

Daniella was lost. She'd never been kissed before. She had no idea something so brief and light could arouse such feelings. She was hot and cold at the same time. Her heart pounded rapidly in her breast.

Suddenly Travis stepped away and dropped his hands to his sides, his dark eyes searching her face, as if committing her features to memory. "Think of me sometimes, and know that I'll be thinking of you."

Daniella looked at him in stunned amazement. As if she'd ever be able to think of anything else after this! Before she knew what was happening, Travis threw her up into her saddle and slapped his hat sharply against her horse's rump, sending her speeding toward home.

"Good-bye, Woman of Magic," Matt called from the stream.

"Good-bye, Little Bear Colton," she returned over her shoulder. "Take care of your father," she whispered to herself.

Daniella had been home for a couple of weeks, but still couldn't put Travis out of her thoughts. She threw herself into work trying to get him off her mind. She, Tucker, and Simon

146

patched the barn roof and mended the corral fence. These tasks and others kept her hands busy, but failed to occupy her mind to any great extent. She had too much time to think, and when she thought, she thought of Travis.

She'd never seen a father display such open affection for his child before. Until her last trip home, she had known her father loved her, but she now realized how restrained, or reserved, the atmosphere in her home had been. Her grandparents demonstrated their affection for her openly, but she thought that was just because they were grandparents. She had no idea parents would act that way. It made her feel as though she'd missed out on something important.

And then there was that kiss. A brief touching of lips, so faint, so light, it might not have even happened. At times Daniella was able to convince herself she'd only imagined it.

Then she'd feel the sun on her face and remember the warmth of tiny gold flecks dancing in the depths of soft brown eyes . . . eyes in which she could lose herself.

The warm southerly breeze recalled his breath, clean and fresh, fanning her face as he came nearer. She could run a finger across her lips and feel again the brief touch of his mouth on hers.

She tried to sleep at night, as she'd done those few times on the trail, but the nightmares were there, waiting for her in the dark. Now she dreamed in the afternoons, too. These dreams were much more pleasant, but just as disturbing. She dreamed of Travis, his lips, his hands, his strong arms holding her.

Daniella knew her dreams would lead to nothing—she wasn't for him—so her afternoon sleep became a thing of dread until she barely slept at all. The mirror showed dark circles beneath her eyes, and when combined with that hideous white streak in her hair, she looked as terrible as she felt.

Even her eating habits suffered. When she sat down to a meal, sometimes the food just stuck in her throat and she couldn't eat at all. At other times, she caught Tucker and Simon staring at her in amazement while she shoveled food into her mouth like a starving ranch hand.

"Keep that up, girlie, and we're gonna have to widen the

doors around this place." Tucker chuckled at his own wit.

Daniella bristled at his humor. Her face and arms were thinner than ever, and she looked downright skinny. No one could call her fat by any stretch of the imagination, unless he happened to realize that the reason she no longer tucked in her shirttail was because she couldn't fasten her breeches anymore. That was something else she tried not to think about.

It had been several days since Tucker's teasing comment, and nothing else had been said on the subject. But as Daniella knelt in the garden, pulling weeds from between tender seedlings, she began to wonder just what was wrong with her. She couldn't go on much longer without decent sleep. And her eating habits were about to do her in completely. Even now she felt sick, and she hadn't eaten more than a bite or two in two days.

Beans simmered right now in the house, and as she caught their aroma on the midday breeze her stomach heaved in protest. She choked and gagged, but nothing much came from her empty stomach. When the feeling passed, she stumbled weakly to the stream and bathed her face in the cool, refreshing water.

"How long was ya plannin' on waitin' before ya told me about the baby?"

The unexpected sound of Tucker's voice startled her nearly as much as the words he spoke. She felt the blood rise to her face, then drain completely away. "I don't know what you're talking about." Her knees trembled. She had to sit on the ground to keep from falling down.

"Don't ya now?"

She finally had to admit the truth to herself. The streak in her hair wasn't the only thing the Apaches gave her that night.

Her time hadn't come since before her capture. She'd heard enough gossip from the girls at school to recognize the signs of pregnancy. And, too, she remembered how her mother had been while carrying the child that had eventually caused her death when Daniella was seven. The child had been born dead, but her mother hadn't lived long enough to know it.

Oddly, Daniella didn't fear her own death in childbirth. But, as if she'd just that moment become pregnant, her

148

breasts and abdomen suddenly felt heavy, weighted down by the unborn child. A bastard. A half-breed Apache bastard.

Oh God, why? Why?

She pressed her hands against her stomach and rubbed hard in a downward motion, as if to rid herself of the unwanted burden. How could she live with such shame? Hadn't her life been ruined enough without this?

"No, no," she moaned. It suddenly all became too much for her. "Oh, Tucker, what am I going to do?" she wailed. Tears seeped from beneath her tightly closed lids.

Tucker laid a gnarled, veiny hand on her shoulder. "Take it easy, girlie. Ain't nothin' you can do about it 'cept make up yer mind to live through it."

"Oh God, Tucker, I can't stand it. The way people look at me and talk about me now is bad enough. I can't let anyone know about this. I can't!"

She sobbed against the old man's shoulder for some time before he helped her to her feet and led her to the house. She spent the rest of the day in her room. She wanted to die. She never wanted to face another living person. She wanted to kill the ones responsible for the thing that grew inside her, the thing she hated.

Lying on the bed was a mistake. She fell asleep. Six leering, copper faces loomed over her. She woke with a strangled scream. It was dark. Outside her small window, the moon rode high. She must have slept a long time before the nightmare woke her, yet she felt far from refreshed. She felt like dying.

What could she do? Was there someplace on earth she could go and hide until this living nightmare was over? And what would she do with the child? She couldn't stand the thought of looking at a living, dark-skinned reminder of that night. She couldn't!

The darkness closed in on her. It seemed to steal the air from the room. To dispel the feeling, she lit a candle.

How would she keep this from her father?

She'd stay in this house and not step foot outside until the child was born, that's what she'd do.

But then what? What would she do with her bastard child?

149

She'd take it to the nearest mission and give it to the sisters to raise. Perhaps they wouldn't hate it the way she did.

But who would help her during the birthing? Her earlier confidence deserted her. The thought of childbirth suddenly terrified her. Her own mother had died in childbirth. Would she do the same? It would be too ironic for her to have lived through her night of captivity to die nine months later from the end result.

A chill swept over her that had nothing to do with the cool night air. Her hands shook and her stomach turned over. She started pacing the floor. *Oh God, why? Why?*

If her father and Sylvia found out about her childbearing state, Sylvia would have Daniella packed up and shipped east so fast it would take a week for the dust to settle.

Daniella halted in the middle of the room. East. Her grandparents! They would help her.

No. She couldn't bring this shame down on them.

But there are ways around that, a voice in the back of her mind whispered. She could claim to have married shortly after arriving home. Her new husband was then killed by raiding Apaches. Since her father hadn't approved of the man, the young widow with a child on the way hadn't been able to bear remaining at home. She'd go to her grandparents for shelter.

That was good. It might work. Unless her grandparents wrote to her father.

But how would she explain giving away her child when it was born? How would she explain a dark-skinned child at all?

An hour later she gave up her pacing, sat on the bed, and stared at the candle flame on her bedside table. No answers came to settle the questions.

The tiny flame before her flickered. Transfixed by the dancing light, she watched, unblinking, as the flame separated itself from the candle and grew until it filled the room with light.

Dark spots transformed themselves into faces. Two dark, young faces belonging to two Apache boys. Each boy was bound hand and foot, and gagged as well. An additional rope looped each thin neck. Now and then the nooses were jerked taut by an unseen hand.

Daniella blinked, and the vision disappeared. The small flame once again stood atop the stubby candle where it belonged.

She shook herself and hugged her arms to her chest. It was the two boys Cochise had asked Travis to look for. She knew it as surely as she knew her own name.

It was such a relief to have something other than her own problems to think about that she concentrated on what she'd just seen.

The two boys had been captured. But by whom? Whites or Mexicans? It could have been anyone. Everyone hated Apaches. And where were they? There'd been nothing else in her vision except a dark shadow in the background. She tried to recall it, but all she could see was a tall shape. With arms? A man?

No! A Saguaro!

Daniella groaned. A Saguaro was no help at all. The tall, stately cactus grew everywhere.

The only idea she could come up with was to ride into Tucson tomorrow. Maybe she or Tucker would hear something. Surely whoever had them would brag about it.

That decision made, she went on to the next one. What would she wear to town? Her usual breeches and poncho, or a dress? Her breeches were so disreputable, it would have to be a dress. But that meant riding in the wagon with Tucker, because she hadn't brought a sidesaddle from her father's ranch.

She supposed she'd live through bouncing on the hard seat for one day. Who knew? Maybe she'd get lucky and fall off. And miscarriages happened all the time.

Hell. Maybe she'd jump.

Chapter Fifteen

Tucson wasn't really an ugly town, as frontier towns went, but there certainly wasn't anything attractive about it either. It wasn't the ramshackle buildings or the smelly garbage in the streets that bothered Daniella. Neither was it the dry, arid desert it perched on, with its giant Saguaro cacti reaching up toward the sky as if beseeching the gods for water. It was the people of Tucson who made her wish she were anyplace else.

Two Mexican women of indeterminate age, both in dire need of a bath and a thorough shampoo, lounged outside the swinging half-doors of a cantina. One of them had one side of her skirt hitched up to her waist, baring a chubby, dimpled and bruised thigh. They were the only females in sight.

The rest of the town's inhabitants appeared to be men. Dirty, evil-looking men. Every one of them had at least two weapons visible, mostly a pistol and a knife. Cartridge belts crisscrossed more than a few chests. There was no law in Tucson, except the law of "every man for himself." Daniella shuddered at the thought of what life must be like in a town where a man couldn't, or maybe wouldn't, walk down the main street in broad daylight without being armed to the teeth.

She clutched the drawstring bag in her lap. The shape and weight of the Navy Colt inside comforted her.

Both the surface and residents of the Tucson streets were rougher than anything the open country surrounding it had to offer. Daniella clung to the edge of the hard wooden seat as she and Tucker made their way through Tucson down dusty, rutted streets toward the market area, where a west-bound wagon train was replenishing its supplies before continuing on toward California.

Their plan was for Daniella to do some shopping while Tucker checked out the saloons and cantinas. One of them was bound to hear something about the capture of two Apache boys.

As they rode through town, Daniella's eyes darted from one side of the street to the other and back again. Nearly every man they passed stopped whatever he was doing and stared at her. Her nerves screamed in protest.

"You're causing quite a stir among the townfolk, girlie," Tucker commented. "But don't take it personal. The only white women they ever see in Tucson are the ones on wagon trains headed west, and they're all a little weather-beaten by the time they've traveled this far. You're quite a sight for them."

"Is that supposed to make me feel better?"

Tucker stopped the wagon in front of William Grant's Mercantile and helped Daniella to the ground. He left the wagon there and went his way on foot. Daniella turned toward Grant's.

The inside of the store was dim, musty, and crowded. Good. Where there were people, there was gossip.

One by one the men in the store—five Mexicans and two Anglos; there were no women—fell silent as they turned to stare at her. Damn. She should have worn the breeches. From the expressions on the men's faces, it must have been a while since they'd seen a woman. At least one wearing something other than faded calico.

But Daniella didn't own a calico dress. Her clothes were the ones she'd brought from Boston—all the latest styles. The walking dress she wore today was one of her plainer gowns, by Boston standards. It was made of pale green poplin. Two wide rows of black lace trimmed the contrasting emerald green sacque. The loose jacket, while too warm, at least concealed the tightness around her waist, where she hadn't been able to cinch her corset in enough to accommodate the dress properly.

With her hair twisted into a knot on top of her head, the

153

wide-brimmed Pamela straw hat, dyed green, with its black lace demiveil hanging down over her eyes, effectively concealed the white streak in her hair. She'd cursed the hat all the way to town when the wind threatened to tear it from her head in spite of the ties beneath her chin. But with the stares she was getting, she was glad she'd worn it. At least no one could see her face plainly.

She desperately wished the men would go about their business and forget her, but it didn't seem likely. She forced a smile and a polite nod in their direction—they stood in a group at the counter—and headed down one of the narrow aisles toward the other end of the store.

A tall thin man with side whiskers came from behind the counter and introduced himself to her as William Grant, the owner of the store. He waited expectantly until she reluctantly gave him her hand and her name.

"It's an honor to have such a lovely lady grace my humble store," he said in a fine Southern drawl. "May I help you find something?"

She asked him for coffee, flour, and sugar, and dawdled as long as possible while he prepared her order.

After a few moments the other men resumed their conversation.

"What news is there of the war in the East?"

Daniella tensed, her back to the men, and listened.

"Ha! What news?" someone answered. "Since Congress moved the Butterfield Stage Line north and cut us off, there ain't any news. Least not in this God-forsaken hellhole. 'Course Congress didn't have much choice, what with Cochise butcherin' everything that moved."

Daniella's throat went dry. *No stage?* How could she get to Boston with no stage?

"Never had no need for no stage just to get news, myself," another man said. "I ain't like you dummies—I can read."

It must have been a long-standing joke among friends, for the other men simply laughed.

"Liked gettin' my news outa the newspaper 'stead of hangin' 'round the stage depot listening for gossip."

"Yeah, well you can be just as dumb as the rest of us now,

Tooley, cuz there ain't no more newspaper. You was just gettin' your gossip second hand, anyhow. Where do ya think the paper found out all that stuff it printed if it wasn't at the stage depot?"

"I know some news," one of the Mexicans offered.

Daniella had to stop herself from leaning toward him to listen.

"Hellfire, Juanito, the only news you know is which one of them *señoritas* down at Raoul's place has got a heart tattooed on her—"

"Tooley, shut up," his friend whispered fiercely. "There's a lady in here, dammit."

Silence echoed through the store, disturbed only by the shifting of crates and an occasional grunt and groan from the back room where Mr. Grant had gone to fill Daniella's order.

She waited in vain. When the talk finally resumed around the counter, it was of horses and cattle. It was useless. Now that they remembered her presence, they weren't going to say anything important.

A few moments later she paid for her purchases and left. After seeing the items loaded into the wagon bed, she crossed the street. She'd try another store.

It was the same everywhere she went. The men acted like they'd never seen a woman before. It was an eerie feeling. She finally encountered two Mexican women at the Tully-Ochoa store, but they were the only women she'd seen except the two soiled doves outside the cantina. With a twitch of her lips, she wondered which "dove" had the tattoo, and where.

After two hours of being ogled, she met Tucker back at the wagon. He hadn't heard anything either. There'd been plenty of gossip in the cantinas, but no mention of two young Apache boys.

"What do ya wanna do now?" Tucker asked.

Daniella sighed. "I guess we'll go home. Nothing else we can do. If I buy any more supplies we don't need we'll go broke.

Tucker helped her up onto the high wagon seat. She groaned to herself as her bruised posterior met hard wood. She couldn't imagine how sore she'd be if it weren't for her thick layer of petticoats.

A train of freight wagons forced Tucker to turn down a side street. Another turn and he had the wagon headed out of town by way of the post office. Once again men turned to stare at Daniella.

"Haven't they ever seen a woman before, for heaven's sake?"

Tucker snorted. "Not a white woman. Not in this town, anyway. There's some Papago women on the edge of town, married ones. And there's a few high class *señoras* and *señoritas,* plus a few low class ones. But no Anglos. 'Cept for the passengers on wagon trains, like I said."

Daniella answered his snort with one of her own. They didn't have to stare so damned hard, did they? Her eyes flicked to the tall, broad shouldered man coming out of the post office, and her heart fluttered up to her throat. Travis!

His penetrating gaze scanned her slowly from head to toe. When his eyes met hers, he smiled with surprise. She realized he'd never seen her in a dress before.

Although she was separated from Travis by the width of the dusty street, her body leaned toward him. When she realized it, she straightened. Whatever he might have felt for her — gratitude, most likely — it was useless now. Even his gratitude for getting Matt back wouldn't extend to overlooking the bastard child growing in her womb.

If she could think of a good enough explanation, she'd be going to Boston soon, provided she could figure out a way to get there. She'd never see Travis Colton again. The thought made her throat close and her eyes water.

The wagon gave an unexpected jerk. Daniella grabbed for the edge of the seat, missed, and nearly fell from her perch. Tucker called to the team and hauled back sharply on the reins. When Daniella righted herself she straightened her straw hat, then noticed the cause of the near-accident.

She'd been so intent on her study of Travis, she hadn't realized a crowd had gathered, blocking the entire road. She'd been completely oblivious to the deafening roar of dozens of men, some on foot, many on horseback, shouting and whooping all around her. The air was filled with flying debris. At first Daniella thought the garbage lining the street had taken wing, then she realized the crowd was throwing it! Her team had lurched when struck by a barrage of rotten fruit.

"What in blue blazes is going on?" she muttered. Beside her Tucker nodded at the center of the crowd.

"Not sure, but I'd guess he's got somethin' to do with it."

Daniella searched the tight knot of men forging their way down the street. People began backing away to make room for some sort of procession. Her eyes grew wide, first with surprise, then with horror.

Leading his recalcitrant pack mule through the throng was Billy Joe Crane, the squatter she'd thrown off her ranch. "It's hanging time!" he shouted.

A cheer rose up from those closest to him. There was something tied on behind the mule, but the crowd blocked Daniella's view. When Crane led the mule past her wagon, she finally understood what was happening.

Two ropes trailed from the mule's harness, each rope bearing a hangman's noose at the end. Each noose fit snugly around the neck of a young Apache boy. The boys she'd seen last night in her vision! Their hands were tied behind their backs, their ankles were hobbled by short lengths of ropes, and their faces were unreadable. Only their wild, black eyes revealed their overwhelming fear.

Shouts of, "Hang 'em!" and "String up the murdering bastards!" turned Daniella's hands to ice.

My God, they're just children! Can't anyone see that?

But the crowd didn't care.

She had to do something! She couldn't let those boys be murdered by a crowd gone mad. Where was Travis? She couldn't see him now for the surge of people. He was supposed to do something. He'd promised Cochise. Where the hell was he?

Billy Joe's obstinate mule gave out a shrill bray and sat down, right in the middle of the street. Crane swore as he tugged on the reins. Three men got behind the mule and pushed. The mule didn't budge.

While the crowd continued jeering and pelting the captive boys with garbage from the gutters, Crane took a whip from someone and started beating the mule. His swings were wild and careless. When one missed the mule completely and struck one of the Apache boys, Daniella couldn't stand any more.

She turned to Tucker. "I can't let them do this."

The old man stared hard at her for a long moment, then let out a resigned sigh. "I know, girlie."

She pulled the Navy Colt from her reticule and climbed down from the seat. For the first time since she entered town, the men's attention was not focused on her. She had to shove her way into the hot, smelly crowd. She got only a few feet when the men closed in around her, paying her no attention at all. She elbowed, she kicked, she screamed at the top of her lungs.

"Let me pass! Move, damn you!"

Nothing. It was as if she were invisible, with no voice at all. With determination, she raised the revolver over her head and fired in the air.

The echoing shot died in the sudden stillness, and a path magically opened up before her. She marched between the gaping men, head high, shoulders back, until she stood in the center of the mob and faced Billy Joe Crane.

"Still abusing dumb animals, I see."

Crane gaped at her a full minute before recognition lit his pale gray eyes. "You! What the hell do you think you're doing?"

She ignored his outburst and nodded toward the two boys, who swayed with exhaustion. "Now I see you intend to take your brutality out on children."

Crane turned his head aside and spat. "Hell. Somebody take that gun away from her before she hurts herself."

A man with the greasiest hair she'd ever seen took a step toward her. She raised the pistol, pulled back the hammer, and took aim on Crane's sunburned nose.

At the same time, she felt the crowd shift behind her. The hair on the back of her neck stood on end. She hadn't thought this through well at all. It would be no trouble for one of them to grab her from behind while her attention focused on Crane.

Too late to worry now. All she could do was try her best.

Then, from behind, came a deep, smooth voice. A familiar voice. "The first man who touches her dies."

A thrill shot clear through her heart. *Travis!*

She couldn't see him, but she felt him when he stood at her back. Pure adrenaline pumped through her veins. In that instant, she understood why some men loved to fight. "Excitement" was too pale a word for what she felt.

To have a chance, however slim, to win against great odds was something she'd never experienced before. They were outnumbered ten to one. It didn't matter. With Travis at her back she could do anything!

If she lived to be a hundred, she'd never forget this moment. And if she died in the next ten minutes, it would be worth it just to feel the headiness threatening to overwhelm her.

But the angry, buzzing mob knew they were only two against the rest. As if on cue from some hidden stage director, each man stepped forward, closing in on Daniella and Travis. Her hand tightened around the pistol. It nearly slipped in her sweaty palm.

"Don't worry none about your blind side," Tucker called. "I got it covered."

Daniella grinned in spite of the overwhelming odds against her and Travis. She couldn't see Tucker from where she stood, but she could picture him standing there in the wagon, shotgun in hand, a devilish grin parting his wiry beard.

His statement had the same effect on the men around her as Travis's had. They stopped moving.

Crane looked ready to burst. His knuckles wrapped around the butt of the whip whitened. "What the hell do you think you're doing?" he repeated.

"I'm taking these boys," she answered firmly.

"The hell you are! They're mine. I caught 'em, and I'm gonna hang 'em." A murmur started somewhere in the back of the crowd and spread. Crane took heart from the show of support. "In case you ain't heard, me and my partners was ambushed by Apaches a few months back. There was five of us, and I'm the only one left. These heathens is gonna pay, by God."

"Don't be any more of an ass than you already are, Crane," Daniella said. "Are you saying that five grown men were attacked, four of them killed, by these two *children?* I don't believe I'd be telling that story, if I were you. It doesn't say too much for you and your friends."

Crane's face turned the same shade of red as his flannel undershirt. He moved toward her. "Why you—"

"One more step and I'll shoot," she warned.

A second later panic assailed her when she felt Travis leave her back, but she didn't dare take her eyes off Crane.

Crane glanced past her shoulder; his eyes bulged. "Goddammit, Colton, you leave them be. They're mine, I tell ya!"

Daniella chanced a quick glance while Crane's attention strayed. Until that moment she hadn't realized how hard her heart was pounding. It leaped with joy when she saw Travis pulling the nooses from the boys' necks and cutting the ropes that hobbled their feet.

She swung her gaze back to Crane and started backing toward Travis.

"All right, you buzzards, make way." Tucker's voice rang out loud and clear in the scorching afternoon heat. "Clear a path to this here wagon for the folks, or I'll clear it myself."

With Travis at her back once more, and the boys in front of him, Daniella inched her way through the hard-eyed men toward the wagon. Travis scared the daylights out of her when he let out a shrill whistle, then shouted, "Buck!" It was a long moment before she realized he was signalling his horse.

With reins trailing on the ground, Buck trotted through the mob, scattering men right and left, heedless of anyone who stood in his way. A big, pot-bellied man grabbed for the reins, but Buck snorted and reared, striking the man on the shoulder with a sharp hoof. With a swish of his tail, he scared off one man who got too close behind him. Another tried, and Buck lashed out with a hind leg. He missed, but the man got the message.

The buckskin stallion shook his head as if ridding himself of flies was his biggest worry. He slowed to a walk beside Travis, thereby protecting the retreating group on one side.

"Cover me," Travis said tersely. He turned and lifted each

boy into the wagon bed. There'd been no time to free the boys' hands. He pushed the boys down behind the two barrels of flour Daniella had bought earlier.

Travis turned again and stood shoulder to shoulder with her. At least, they would have been shoulder to shoulder if she weren't so short and he weren't so tall. With their backs to the stallion, Travis ordered, "Get up on Buck."

Without taking her eyes off the growling men surrounding them, she answered, "No." She knew what he was trying to do. He wanted to make sure she got safely away while he took his chances in the wagon, which would be much slower. She couldn't let him do it. She'd started this mess, and she'd see it through. She'd never forgive herself if Travis were hurt, or worse, trying to protect her.

She ducked under his drawn revolver and scooted next to the wagon, again without taking her eyes off the other men. "Cover me while I climb in," she whispered.

Her skirt and petticoats tangled around her legs while she used the spokes of the back wheel as a ladder. The boys, still crouching behind the flour barrels, stared at her, wide-eyed. Poor things, they had no idea what was going on.

With a flash of black silk stocking, she was finally able to throw a leg over the side and crawl into the wagon bed. "Now you," she said to Travis as she leveled her revolver on the front row of the crowd again.

As Travis swung into the saddle, the mob surged forward. Daniella fired over their heads. Not even an instant later, Tucker gave a fierce shout and whipped the team into motion. Daniella grabbed the side of the wagon to keep from tumbling out.

The wagon pulled away with a jerk. Travis backed Buck down the road to keep the buzzing, cursing men at bay. A shot rang out, then another. He fired into the ground at the feet of the men in front. It slowed them a moment, but he knew it wouldn't be long before they realized he was only one man. He couldn't believe they'd made it this far without getting killed.

If he and Daniella lived through this, he swore he'd wring her neck for such a stunt.

But by God, she was the bravest woman on earth!

He fired three rapid shots over the crowd as he wheeled Buck around. Crouching low, he let out a short, sharp whistle and gave the stallion his head. Buck took one mighty leap, then broke out into a full gallop. Shots whizzed past Travis's ears.

He was gaining on the wagon. Behind him, the crowd broke up as men scrambled for their horses in order to follow. All Travis could do was stay behind the wagon and fire randomly over his shoulder when the pursuers drew near. It might hold them off for a while.

When he neared the wagon, Tucker glanced over his shoulder and gestured wildly toward the wagon bed. He shouted something, but Travis couldn't hear over the thundering hooves, the creak of axles, and the rattle of chains and wagon.

His eyes swept the wagon bed. Where was Dani? My God, where was she? He drew nearer, and Tucker shouted again: "The girl's been hit!"

Travis felt his heart stop and the blood drain from his face. *No! She can't be hit!*

When he pulled alongside the wagon, he saw her. She lay face down across a sack of coffee beans. Her right arm and the right half of her back were covered in blood.

Travis then did something that, in a saner moment, he would never have dreamed of doing. But he wasn't particularly sane just then. He was mad with fear and anger and grief.

He reacted without thinking. He tied his reins loosely to the saddle horn, pulled his feet from the stirrups, and jumped into the wagon bed.

In an instant he scrambled to Dani's side, muttering a prayer beneath his breath. He grabbed her wrist, but the vibrations from the wagon were so strong he couldn't feel a pulse. Terrified, he rolled her over onto his lap and pressed his fingers into her neck beside her Adam's apple. There! Was that a pulse? He couldn't tell.

He bent his head to her chest. A soft moan from her lips finally told him she was alive. For now.

He pulled the bandanna from around his neck and pressed

it against the gaping hole near her shoulder blade. It was soaked through in seconds. He flipped her skirt up and reached to tear a strip from her petticoat to use as padding for the wound. He couldn't put enough pressure on it in the position she was in.

He pulled her up against his chest and wrapped an arm around her, his palm pressing the pad against the wound. With his free hand, he untied the bow beneath her chin and slipped the straw hat from her head. Her long hair slid from its pins and tumbled across her back and his arm.

Beside him, the two Apache boys gasped at the sight. Travis ignored them. He was too busy praying. *God, don't let her die.*

A shot thudded into the wagon seat inches from his ear. He got off a couple of shots that emptied his pistol. Tucker passed him the shotgun. A blast from that, and the riders fell back.

Travis shouted to Tucker that the Triple C was the closest safety, and Tucker agreed. The ride seemed to take forever as Dani's blood seeped from beneath his fingers and ran down his arm. *Oh God, don't let her die.*

Chapter Sixteen

Travis reloaded his pistol and the shotgun with one hand, and fired whenever a rider got too close. Realizing the danger Dani was in, held up against his chest as he had her, he was forced to lay her down out of the line of fire.

The riders were getting bolder now. One of the boldest was Crane. But with the bouncing and jostling the wagon was taking on the rutted, rocky road, there was no way Travis could hope to hit a target. All he could do was fire at random.

A rider pulled up on each side of the wagon. Travis shot one from the saddle, but Tucker sat between him and the other one. The man tried to force his mount into the team to turn them, but Buck had other ideas. He ran on the other side of the team. When they started to swerve, he nipped the nearest one in the shoulder.

Tucker gathered the reins in one fist and groped beneath the seat. He came up with a whip and struck the rider full across the back, knocking him from his horse.

As the others drew near, Travis worried he'd run out of ammunition. A mile from the ranch house, help came. Five Triple C riders burst over the low rise to the left. Travis waved to let them know he needed help.

Five men against the fifteen or so who followed the wagon shouldn't have been enough help, but it was. They swept down on the pursuers, whooping and firing, making as much noise as fifty men. The mob from town fell back. From the other side of the road three more Triple C riders joined in the fray. The pursuers turned back and became the pursued.

An eternity later, the wagon rattled and jolted to a stop before the Triple C ranch house. Travis shielded Dani's face as best he could from the thick cloud of dust stirred up by hooves and wheels. He was never so glad to see home before.

At his shout, Jason, Matt, Carmen, and Juanita, his housekeeper, came running outside.

"Juanita, turn down my bed and fetch Rosita. Dani's been shot. Matt, get up here and untie these boys. Tell them they're safe."

Matt's eyes bulged at the sight of Dani's blood smeared all over his father. He swallowed and looked Travis in the eye. "Is she gonna die, Dad?

"No! Don't even think it."

Travis cradled Dani in his arms and climbed from the wagon while Matt and Juanita rushed to follow his orders.

Travis placed Dani on his bed and gently smoothed back her hair. God, she was so pale. His stomach knotted and his eyes blurred. When he reached for the buttons on the front of her jacket, Juanita objected.

"*Señor* Travis, it is not proper. I will see to the *señorita*."

Travis kept at the buttons without a pause. "I'm not leaving her, Juanita."

Juanita gave in and helped him. They unbuttoned the jacket, dress, and corset cover, then gently turned Dani over onto her stomach and slid the clothes down her arms. The blood-soaked corset ties snarled, and Juanita ended up having to cut them with scissors.

They slid the chemise straps down Dani's arms and pushed her clothes to her waist. Juanita pressed a cloth to the bleeding wound.

Travis stepped back to give Juanita room to work on the wound. Only then did he notice the three long scars across Dani's back. Something lurched in his chest. He'd seen marks like those before, but never on a woman. They were lash marks.

165

Rosita rushed in carrying bandages and hot water, her lips compressed in a tight line. She had been tending and cooking for the Colton family since they first came to this territory. If anyone could help Dani, it was Rosita.

"*Madre de Dios*," she whispered when she saw the wound and the scars. She examined the wound carefully. The bullet had lodged against the bone, keeping the shot from going all the way through the shoulder and out the other side. "You must hold her still, *Señor* Travis, while I remove the bullet."

Dani moaned and tried to pull away from Rosita's probing, but Travis held her down firmly against the mattress. He could almost feel those scissors reaching down into his own flesh, trying to grasp a small lead ball which had invaded his body. Her pain was his, and he nearly cried out each time she groaned beneath the probing. It seemed to take Rosita forever to find that damn lead. When the bullet was removed and the bandage in place, Travis let out a shaky breath and wiped the sweat from his brow with a trembling hand.

"You go now, *Señor* Travis. I will tend her."

"Take good care of her, Rosita."

"*Sí.* I will take good care."

Travis stepped out into the hall and heard voices coming from the salon. Tucker was telling Jason and Carmen what had happened. Instead of joining them, Travis slipped out into the courtyard and found Matt and the two Apache boys.

"Is Dani gonna be all right, Dad?"

"I think so, son. How about these two?" he asked, nodding to the two boys.

Matt introduced them as Shanta and Natzili-Chee.

"Tell them we'll get them home to their families as soon as we can."

Travis felt like a coward when he left a moment later. The two Apache boys looked terrified, and justifiably so. He should spend some time with them, reassure them they were safe. But he couldn't concentrate on talking just then.

His thoughts were too full of Dani.

Dani. He'd been calling her that in his mind for days. Since arriving home, Matt had talked so much about "Dani did this" or "Dani did that" that Travis had unconsciously started thinking of her by that shortened name. It suited her.

He paced the hall outside his room and prayed Dani would be all right. A moment later Juanita came out carrying a clean shirt for him. He followed her to the kitchen, where he washed the blood, Dani's blood, from his hands. After slipping into the clean shirt, he went back to his room. He couldn't stay away.

The women had dressed Dani in a white gown. The sheet, the same sheet he'd slept beneath last night, was pulled up to her shoulders. As his eyes roamed over her colorless features, he saw her bare neck for the first time. Now he knew why she always wore that bandanna. A thin white scar encircled her neck. He remembered talk of Apaches and rawhide leashes. He took a deep breath and forced his eyes away from the vivid reminder of her capture.

Her hair had been brushed free of tangles and lay spread across the pillow. She was so still and pale, and looked so tiny and vulnerable lying there in his big bed.

He pulled a chair next to her and sat down. "I'll stay with her a while, Rosita."

"Sí, Señor Travis, but watch her carefully for any signs of fever. It will probably come, and when it does, we must try to keep it down as much as possible. If the fever gets too high, the poor child might lose her baby."

His breath caught in his throat. "Baby?" he croaked.

"Sí . . . she is expecting a little one. My guess would be that she is about four months along."

Rosita quietly left the room, and Travis buried his face in his hands. Thinking back on their trip home with Matt, he knew she hadn't known about the baby then, or she would never have said she couldn't have children. How did she feel about it? He tried to put himself in her place, but found he couldn't.

167

He knew so little about her, except that she had survived things that would have killed most people. And she was beautiful. The idea of this girl . . . this woman, giving birth to a half-breed Apache bastard and raising it alone depressed him so much he felt like crying. He had no doubt but that the child was the product of her rape at the hands of the Apaches.

Lord, what was the matter with him? He hadn't felt this badly for another person in years.

As he looked down at her face, he thought she looked so fragile she would crumble into dust if he so much as touched her cheek. A fierce desire to protect her rose up within him, and he found himself wishing the child she carried was his.

Fool! he told himself. *If she didn't want anything to do with men before this, she certainly won't let you near her now.* What was wrong with him, that he should find himself caring so much for a woman who carried another man's child?

But that wasn't her fault. It was against her will.

Damn!

After a couple of hours, Juanita came to sit with Dani. Travis went to the salon and found Tucker alone.

"More brandy?" Travis asked, indicating the nearly empty glass in the old man's hand. Tucker had been a surprise to him. On the trail home with Matt, Travis had tried to get Dani to talk about herself, but she was the most close-lipped woman he'd ever met. He'd assumed she didn't live alone, but he sure hadn't expected her to be hooked up with this crusty old prospector.

"Don't mind if I do," Tucker answered. "How's the girl?"

"Rosita says she'll be fine," he answered, unwilling to repeat the rest of Rosita's words.

"Good, good." Tucker's eyes crinkled at the corners. The middle of his shaggy gray beard wiggled, so Travis assumed the old man was smiling.

Travis refilled Tucker's glass, then poured one for himself. He was amazed to find his hands shaking. Now that he was reasonably certain Dani would be all right, he should have

168

felt relieved, but he didn't. Frustration and anger ate at him until he finally exploded.

"Damn it, what the hell did she think she was doing taking on a mob like that? She's lucky she wasn't killed—that we all weren't killed. What the hell possessed her to pull something so stupid?" He glared at Tucker as if blaming the old man for Dani's actions.

"She's a fighter, the girl is. You been on the trail with her. You oughta know that. She seen somethin' that needed doin', and she done it. That's just the way she is. You don't think I could have stopped her, do ya?"

Travis ground his teeth and let the air slowly out of his lungs. "No, I don't suppose anyone could have stopped her, short of hog-tying her."

"Right," Tucker said. Then he chuckled. "She shore is somethin', ain't she?"

Travis smiled in spite of himself. "Yeah," he said, "she sure is something."

He studied the old man for a moment, then said, "Forgive me, but you and Dani seem like a rather unlikely pair. How did you meet her, if you don't mind my asking?" Maybe Tucker would be able to answer some of the other questions which had plagued him since meeting the "Woman of Magic."

"I guess it does look a might odd, an old coot like me and a sweet young girl like her. First time I saw her was the night them murderin' redskins brung her to their camp. What a godawful night that was, to be sure."

"You were there? In their camp?" This must be the same old man he saw her with that first time.

"Yep. Been there a couple of weeks by then, and before you ask, no, I weren't there exactly by choice. They come up on me one day when I was burying poor ol' Jacob, my mule, God rest his soul. They thought I was crazy for diggin' that great big hole to bury somethin' as good to eat as mule meat, but Jacob, well, he was somethin' special, he was. Well, anyhow, I'd heard tell Injuns don't harm crazy folks, so I just kept actin' crazy. They took me back with

169

them and treated me like a guest, 'cept, o' course, they wouldn't let me leave on accounta they thought I might hurt myself, bein' crazy an' all. That's how I come to be there that night when they brung in the girl and them two men."

"What two men?" Travis tossed off the feeling that he was prying into something that was none of his business. He needed to know more about her. He took another sip of his brandy and tried to appear calm.

"They was from the stagecoach the girl was on. They'd been wounded, but not killed, so them dad blamed heathens brung 'em back for a little entertainment, if ya know what I mean. Christ, I wouldn't do to a snake what they done to them men. And there the girl was, tryin' her damnedest to keep from watchin' what was goin' on, but every time she closed her eyes or turned her head away, somebody'd let fly with one of them nasty little whips across the girl's back, tellin' her to watch the fun. I don't know how she lived through that night, I surely don't."

Travis felt a wave of sickness wash over him as he visualized the scene Tucker described. He wanted to stop this conversation, but he couldn't. "I saw the scars on her back." He paused to swallow heavily, and took a deep breath before going on. "And on her neck. I've heard they use leashes. Is that how she got that one?"

"Yep. They like to lead their captives around the camp and show 'em off," Tucker supplied with disgust.

"What else did they do to her, Tucker?"

The old man's gaze turned hard as he stared at Travis. "What the hell do ya think they did to her? You know what they did without me tellin' ya."

Travis hung his head and stared at the glass in his hand. Yes, he knew what they did to her. He was suddenly glad Tucker's answer had been so brief. He really didn't want to know all the details. He was prying enough as it was. But there was something else he had to know.

"What about her hair? I've heard their explanation. Did you see what happened?"

"Well, now, that there is really a strange thing, it is."

Tucker settled himself more comfortably against the cushions of the sofa and took on the air of some great orator. "When them bucks was finished doin' their worst to her, the squaws came next. They beat her with sticks. But that girl, she never quit fightin'. I never seen nobody, man nor woman, red, black or white, fight as hard as she did. Any time anybody got too close, she spit right in their faces, damned if she didn't. Well, one of the older women took offense at bein' spit on and took a great big stick and hit the girl in the head. Knocked her plum out. If they'd done that at the start, maybe she wouldn't be rememberin' so much of that night."

The old man paused and stared thoughtfully off into space. Travis prodded him from his musings. "Then what happened?"

"Well, then they drug her out from the middle of camp and just left her sprawled out on the ground under this big ol' pine tree. Just left her to die, they did. And that's what usually happened to their white captives . . . they nearly always died. It was a might cold up in them mountains, 'specially at night, and her not havin' a lick o' clothes on. I wanted to at least take her a blanket, but them bastards wouldn't let me.

"Afore long, Cochise and the rest of the hunting party came in. That's when they made me go back to my wickiup.

"Yes sir, that's when things started gittin' strange. This big wind come up and it got all cloudy, blockin' out all the stars and the moon. Thunder and lightnin' was everwhere, gittin' closer all the time, but no rain—not a drop. Just about time for the sun to come up, we was all woke up by this big, loud explosion—the ground shook, the air shook—hell, everthang shook. It was real spooky, I'll tell ya that. I thought it was the end of the world, or at least an earthquake. I heard of them before.

"Anyways, we all went out to the middle of camp to see what the hell had happened, and there the girl was, just where they left her, at the base of that pine tree. 'Cept that pine tree wasn't standin' there no more, no sirree. It was

171

split clean in two, right smack dab down the middle, layin' in halves on the ground. That's when somebody noticed the streak in the girl's hair.

"The old *shaman* came forward and said it was a sign. Said the Great Spirit put that streak in her hair so's everybody would know how brave and tough she was. Yep," he added with an emphatic nod. "That's what he said, all right. So who am I to say any different?"

Tucker's version coincided with what Cochise had said at the council that night. Anyway, like the old man said, who was he to say any differently? Besides, there was another question ticking away in the back of Travis's mind.

"When did all this happen, Tucker? How long ago?"

"Ain't exactly sure, but I'd say it was some time in February. Why?"

"I just wondered, that's all." Travis looked away from the old man's squinty gray eyes that saw too much. "I just . . . oh, never mind."

"Well," Tucker said getting to his feet. "Since you say the girl's gonna be all right, I'd better be moseying on home. Simon'll be worryin' 'bout what happened to us. It'll pert near be dark by the time I get there."

"Simon?"

"Youngster the girl took in to look after the sheep."

"Sheep!" *Lord, I'm starting to sound like a parrot.* "You've got *sheep* up in that valley?"

"Not me." Tucker raised his hands in denial. "They ain't my sheep, they're the girl's."

"Good God. Doesn't she realize this is cattle country? She'd better keep them well out of sight, or she'll have nothing but trouble from the ranchers in the area."

"She knows that, I think."

Travis walked out to the wagon with Tucker, and they decided the two Apache boys should stay at the Triple C, since their Spanish wasn't too good, and Dani and Matt were the only ones who spoke their language.

"By the way," Travis said as Tucker was ready to pull out, "did they let you finish burying Jacob?"

172

"Nope. Them sonsabitches ate him."

Travis laughed for the first time that day. "So long. I'll send word how Dani's doing. Come back anytime."

Tucker set the horses in motion and the wagon pulled out in the late afternoon heat. Travis watched him for a while, then turned to go back inside. Carmen met him at the door.

"Why is he leaving the girl here?" she demanded.

Travis walked past her and headed for his study. "She's been shot, Carmen. She's in no shape to travel, and there's no one but the old man and a boy to tend her. We can take better care of her here." He sat down behind his desk and flipped open a ledger, hoping Carmen would think he was busy and leave him alone. He wasn't in the mood for her today. He hadn't been in the mood for her in months.

"You can't mean to let her stay in this house until she's recovered! ¡Dios! You expect me to share a home with a *puta* like her?"

Travis's head snapped up. His hands tightened on the ledger. "I don't expect you to share anything with anyone, Carmen. *I* intend to share *my* home with a young woman who's in need of help, to whom I happen to owe a great deal, if you'll recall. Miss Blackwood is my guest. And in case you've forgotten, you and your aunt share her status. I expect you to treat each other politely. If one guest is rude to another, the first one's welcome soon wears thin."

The look in her eyes told him she understood his meaning clearly, and she didn't like it. Well that was just too damn bad. Maybe she'd finally pack up and leave.

As Carmen flounced out of the room with an indignant rustle of silk against silk, Travis chastised himself. He should have been more patient with her. He knew she had no place to go if she left the ranch. He was good and stuck with her for the time being. Last week she sent out letters trying to locate relatives in Mexico. Until she received a positive reply, he couldn't find it within himself to demand she leave.

For a man who had no desire for a woman of his own, he sure had an uncommon number of them under his roof.

* * *

On his way to find a bed for the night, Travis stopped at his room to check on Dani. When he sat down beside her, she opened her eyes.

"Welcome back." Travis smiled down at her gently. "Can I get you anything?"

She looked up at him through pain-fogged eyes and lifted her hand toward his face. Travis leaned close and took her hand in his. He pressed her palm to his mouth and kissed her damp skin. When he released her hand she traced the scar on his cheek with a trembling finger, sending his blood coursing through his veins. He closed his eyes and gritted his teeth, fighting the sudden urge to crush her to his chest. When he looked at her again, her hand rested on the quilt once more. She was asleep.

He leaned forward and placed a tender kiss on her brow. When he stood, a movement across the room caught his eye. It was Rosita, there to watch over her charge during the night.

Chapter Seventeen

Travis woke the next morning with stiff muscles from sleeping on the too-short sofa in his study. With Dani in his bed, and Carmen having taken a room of her own a few weeks ago, there wasn't a bed left in the house.

With Dani in his bed.

The thought brought a sharpness to his breath and set his heart to pounding. He tried to squelch the idea that he should be in there with her. In bed with her.

With a curse at his own foolishness, he threw off the blanket and got up. He didn't shave or clean up or eat breakfast. Instead, he went to check on Dani.

"How is she, Rosita?"

"She was awake this morning for a few minutes, but now I fear the fever has started." The middle-aged woman frowned.

Travis saw Dani's flushed cheeks and felt concern. Then he noticed the tired slump to Rosita's shoulders. The poor woman had been in this room tending Dani since yesterday.

"I'm going to go clean up and get something to eat, then I'll relieve you for a while. We can't have both of you coming down sick."

Twenty minutes later Travis was back, pushing a reluctant Rosita out the door, stilling her arguments with a stern set to his jaw. Rosita finally agreed to rest for a short time, saying she would be back soon.

Following Rosita's instructions, delivered with the tone of military command, Travis bathed Dani's face and neck with a cool wet cloth. He didn't quite understand why this girl had filled his thoughts so much since the instant he'd seen her, but right now it wasn't important.

Dani opened her eyes and looked at him, but when she spoke, he realized she didn't recognize him.

"But Grandfather, if there's going to be a war now that South Carolina has seceded from the Union, I must go home before travel becomes difficult, if not impossible."

She mumbled something unintelligible, then tossed her head back and forth. Travis fought to keep the cool cloth in place on her brow.

"Papa, why did Mama have to die?" she asked in a little-girl voice.

Travis ached, knowing no way to ease the suffering in her mind or body. She tossed her head again, then took on a lecturing tone as she continued speaking in her delirium.

"Oh, no . . . there's nothing to worry about. The Apaches don't usually bother Americans. It's the Mexicans they fight with. Those riders behind us are probably just out on a hunt."

Dani began tossing violently, and it was all Travis could do to keep her on the bed. When she started to moan and whimper, he felt his insides twist in dread. Her fever was rising. He remembered Rosita's fear that Dani could lose the baby she carried.

Travis stuck his head out the door and bellowed for someone to fetch Rosita.

"No . . . no," Dani murmured in her fever.

"It's all right, Dani. You're safe now. Nothing is going to harm you," Travis told the unconscious girl. "You're safe now."

His deep voice must have reached some part of her fevered brain, for she quieted at his words, even though she continued to speak.

"Look, Tucker . . . there . . . in the flames. It's him! I thought he was dead, but he isn't. See where the flames turn a pale gold around his face?" She smiled at what she saw, but her smile slowly faded. "He searches for someone.

176

The boy! His son! The boy with the golden curls, who looks just like his father. The man's pain is so strong I can feel it. Who is he?"

Travis felt the blood drain from his face as she spoke. No matter what she'd said in the past, he just hadn't been able to accept that she really had visions. Maybe he'd been wrong.

When she spoke next, her voice was bitter. "They honor me and treat me with respect — now. But I'm afraid of them! And I hate them for what they've done to me!"

As Travis continued bathing her brow, she began to plead. "But Papa, don't you love me any more? All I did was come home."

Then she started to cry. "I'm not! I'm not! Papa, please!"

Travis knew he had to calm her somehow before her thrashing reopened her wound. "Dani, hush now. Be still. Hush, love . . . it's all right."

Once more his voice soothed her, and she quieted.

Rosita came. She and Travis spent hours cooling Dani when she was hot and smothering her in blankets and quilts when she grew chilled. At one point, Dani's fever was so high Rosita insisted they remove the girl's gown and bathe her entire body with cool water. The young girl's health, and that of her unborn child, were too important to bother with proprieties.

When they stripped the gown from Dani's fevered body, Rosita and Travis both gasped. They stared in horror at two angry red scars, one on the inside of each of Dani's thighs. "Those are burns, *Señor!*"

Travis's vision blurred. He had to look away before his emotions got the better of him.

My God, my God, Dani, what did those bastards do to you?

Pity and sympathy mixed with the other feelings he held for her but couldn't, or wouldn't, identify.

The wounds were healed, but how many more scars were there, unseen scars? Visions of her lying beneath one Apache after another tortured his mind. Rage and a terrible sense of helplessness filled him. He felt a huge lump in his

177

throat and was consumed again with a desire to protect this woman from any further pain.

For three days her fever raged. Juanita came to relieve Rosita, but Travis refused to leave the room. He caught brief snatches of sleep in his chair beside the bed during Dani's quieter moments, but her slightest movement or murmur jerked him awake time after time.

Rosita returned, then Juanita, then Rosita again, until Travis neither knew nor cared who helped him care for Dani. They spooned warm broth and herbal brews into her mouth periodically, and bathed her often to cool her heated flesh. Beyond that, there wasn't much else they could do, except pray. They did that, too.

As dawn stretched its red fingers across the sky, beads of sweat appeared on Dani's face. Rosita and Travis breathed a joint sigh of relief that the fever had finally broken.

A short time later, Travis locked himself in his study and sought the sofa for some much-needed sleep. He woke late that afternoon and his first thought was of Dani. How was she? Before he even realized it, he was standing outside his bedroom door. He knocked softly, then entered. She was awake. He smiled down at her, noticing how much better she looked after several hours of restful sleep, and sighed in relief.

"You had us pretty worried for a while. How are you feeling?"

"Much better, thank you." Daniella looked down nervously and plucked at the colorful quilt which covered her. "The boys? Are they all right?"

"They're fine," Travis assured her. He sat in the chair next to the bed. "They're with Matt. Tucker went home right after we brought you in, after we were sure you were going to be all right. He said he didn't want Simon to worry."

Daniella closed her eyes in relief. When she'd awakened a few minutes ago, she couldn't remember anything past climbing into the wagon and heading out of town. She was grateful everyone was safe. "No one else was hurt?"

"No. Why'd you do it, Dani?"

Her eyes flew open and searched his face. "Do what?"

"Take on that crowd in town. Damn it, you could have been killed. You almost were." His deep brown eyes bored into her with anger and something else she couldn't identify.

"I couldn't just let Crane hang those boys. I had to do something." She moved then, and her shoulder reminded her she shouldn't have.

"Be still. That wound's going to take some time to heal. We'll talk about this later. You just get some rest."

Before the pain in her shoulder subsided, Travis was gone. She slept the rest of the afternoon. Aside from Rosita and Juanita, who saw to her comfort and brought her a bowl of broth, she was left alone until after breakfast the next morning, when Carmen swept into the room with a swirl of silk and a fragrant cloud of rose-scented perfume.

After taking the chair Travis had occupied only yesterday, the woman spent an eternity arranging her skirts before turning a look of pity on Daniella. "You poor child," she said, clucking her tongue. "We've all been so worried about you. It's good to see you looking better."

"Thank you," Daniella said, wondering where all this concern came from.

Carmen gave her a smile dripping with condescension. "I know we didn't get off to a very good start that first time we met, but that's all behind us now."

Daniella kept her face carefully blank, and thought, *Don't count on it.*

"We're all so grateful to you for finding Matt. Ever since Travis brought him home, well, you wouldn't believe the change in this household. We're a family again."

We? Who was she trying to kid? If Carmen and Travis were a *we,* someone forgot to tell Travis. If he was in love with Carmen, would he have held Daniella in the night the way he had? Would he have kissed her the day they parted?

Maybe, she thought with a sudden wave of weariness. If he'd held her and kissed her out of gratitude. Her heart gave a rapid flutter. Gratitude. Of course.

"Travis and Matt both admire your strength, your courage, and I must say I agree with them. I'm sure I would never have the nerve to do half the things you've done. And with a child on the way, too."

Daniella felt the blood leave her face.

"Oh, don't worry, my dear," Carmen said patting Daniella's hand. "It's not that there's gossip, it's just that I couldn't help but overhear. It really makes me feel quite the coward. In your place, unmarried, faced with raising a half-breed bastard on my own, I'd never be able to show myself again, much less go to town the way you did. I fear I'd flee the territory the first chance I got. *¡Dios!* I'd never have your courage."

The intentional barbs cut deep into Daniella's soul. And it was intentional, she knew. The words were too smooth, too polished. She wondered how long Carmen had rehearsed them.

"But you needn't worry about Travis," Carmen went on. "He's so grateful to have his son back, he can overlook practically anything. Even your present circumstances. In fact, if you did want to go away for a while, I'm sure he'd help you. I've heard him say he would do whatever he could to repay the debt he owes you. And he feels so sorry for you."

Daniella knew Carmen was being deliberately cruel, but there was a ring of truth to her words. Travis himself had offered to repay her for finding Matt. *Anything you need,* he'd said.

That's why he was being so nice, having Rosita and Juanita take such good care of her. He thought he owed her.

A sick feeling churned in her stomach. She wished Carmen would go away and let her sleep. As soon as she could sit up without the room spinning, she'd get out of here. She'd go home. She didn't want his pity or his gratitude.

Travis saw Juanita leave Dani's room early the next morning, and he stopped in to say hello. He was pleased to find some color back in her cheeks.

"Good morning," he greeted warmly.

180

"Good morning." Daniella lowered her eyes in shyness. She struggled to sit up, and he was there instantly to help her with the pillows. She inhaled the clean fresh scent of him. When his arm brushed her shoulder, her pulse quickened.

Then her stomach heaved to her throat and she felt the blood leave her head. *Oh Lord, not now.* She was going to be sick. She knew it. There was nothing she could do to stop the bile rising from her stomach.

"Go—please!" she whispered desperately.

Travis looked at her in confusion.

Just then Daniella pushed him away forcibly and rolled to the opposite side of the bed. The pain in her shoulder seemed to pull the bile up to her throat. She reached beneath the bed for the pot Juanita had just left for her and barely got the lid off before she retched.

Humiliation, hot and devastating, washed over her and made her even sicker when she felt the warm, calloused palm cup her forehead. Strong fingers brushed her hair back from her face and kept it from trailing into the pot. When she calmed, Travis helped her lean back against the pillows and gave her a sip of water, then moistened a cloth from the bedside ewer and tenderly wiped her face.

"Feeling better?" he asked softly.

Daniella felt tears of pain and embarrassment seep from beneath her tightly shut eyelids. God, how would she ever face him again? Her only hope for retaining any self-respect at all around him was that he didn't know the cause of her sudden sickness.

"Hey." He reached out a finger and lifted her chin until she was forced to look at him. "Don't be embarrassed. It happens to most women in your condition, I'm told."

So much for hope. She moaned and turned her head away, the pain in her shoulder nothing compared to the pain of her humiliation. How could he be so kind when he must be thoroughly disgusted that what just happened was due to the half-breed bastard she carried? He knew about the baby, that much was certain. She squeezed her eyes shut even tighter and felt herself blush. She wouldn't look at him. She couldn't. Not ever again.

The bed jiggled as he pushed away from it, then she heard him sigh. "I've got some work to do, so I'll leave you to rest. And I expect you to do just that—rest—all day."

Daniella refused to look at him or say anything, and he finally left the room. Why was he being so nice? Then she remembered his words from the day they brought Matt home, and Carmen's words yesterday. It was gratitude. He felt he owed her something.

But God, she didn't want his gratitude or his sympathy. She wanted his lips to touch hers again. Then she remembered the way his eyes had taken her breath away last night, and she grew frightened.

He was a strong, virile man. He would never be content with just kisses, she knew. But anything more than that terrified her beyond reason. She would surely be more of a whore in his eyes than she already was if he knew how badly she wanted him to kiss her again.

Chapter Eighteen

Travis was like a mother hen with one chick, trying to make certain Daniella got the proper care and rest. He ordered her to stay in bed, much to Rosita's and Juanita's amusement and Daniella's confusion. He finally relented when Rosita warned him Daniella's shoulder would grow stiff if she wasn't allowed to exercise it.

After that one morning when she had thrown up in front of him, Travis didn't visit her at such an early hour again. When he did visit, Matt was usually with him. And sometimes, the Apache boys, Shanta and Natzili-Chee. Neither Travis nor Daniella ever spoke of her morning sickness or her childbearing state.

Daniella mentioned going home once, but Matt and Travis both protested that she couldn't possibly leave until after La Fiesta de San Juan, which was still three days away. They decided she certainly wouldn't be well enough to travel until then. They would invite Tucker and Simon, and those two could see that she got home safely.

Daniella was familiar with the practice of celebrating St. John's Day on June twenty-fourth in the homes where a Juan, Juana or Juanita lived. When she was a child, one of her father's ranch hands had been a middle-aged man named Juan. She could still remember going with all the other children on the ranch for the traditional four-in-the-morning swim, and then an entire day of singing, dancing, and eating.

The memories of her happy childhood, especially when her mother was still alive, haunted her now. She saw much love and laughter in this house, and wondered what the future held for her own child. If she ended up having to raise it, she feared she'd never be able to show it love or laughter. She thought about it a great deal throughout the day, and later that night when she was alone in her room, but could find no answers to the questions tossing in her head.

Realizing she had no gift for Juanita, Daniella persuaded Travis to send a message to Tucker as to what he and Simon should bring with them when they came for the fiesta. When the messenger returned, he brought all the things she had asked for. She was surprised at Tucker's efficiency in filling her request so quickly, and pleased that she wouldn't have to worry and wait until the last minute to prepare her gift.

She had chosen a delicate lace shawl she had purchased in Boston as a gift for Sylvia, but had never given to her. It would be perfect for Juanita. Also included in the bundle were some of her own clothes for the evening of dining and dancing.

Daniella threw herself wholeheartedly into the preparations for the event, offering her help wherever she could. Everyone on the ranch kept an eye on her to make sure she didn't overdo, and she found it increasingly frustrating to be told to go sit down and rest, but she could not find it in herself to complain.

These people were so kind to her that she knew she'd miss them all terribly when she left. Everyone who lived and worked on the Triple C loved and respected Travis and Jason and doted on Matt. They quickly extended their affections to Daniella, if for no other reason than she had helped the family.

The only damper on the days was Carmen. She, too, expressed concern for Daniella's well-being, but only with words. Her eyes told a different story, as did her behavior toward everyone but Travis. Around him, she was as congenial as the next person. But when he wasn't around, she dropped the act. She spoke sharply to the servants, ignored Matt entirely, and treated Shanta and Natzili-Chee with open scorn. The servants, for the most part, stayed as far away from her as they could get.

Many of the Colton employees were related to each other in some way. Three young ranch hands, Carlos, Jorge, and Benito, were Rosita's sons. Luis, their father, also worked with them. Davita, Carlos's wife, and Consuela, Benito's wife, helped their mother-in-law in the kitchen. Then there was Juanita, the housekeeper. She was Rosita's older widowed sister. Even the old gardener, Emilio, was family, being Luis's father. They were all happy and easy in each other's company, and Daniella felt good amid such a loving, laughing group of people.

The only time Daniella saw Travis now was when the family gathered at mealtimes, and even then she felt uneasy in his presence. The way he looked at her when he thought she didn't notice disturbed her. Sometimes his look was merely thoughtful, as if he pondered some minor puzzle. At other times she would catch such a look of tenderness from him that it caused her throat to constrict.

But it was the look he wore now that scared her. He was looking at her as if he could see straight through her clothes. She'd seen that look before on men, the most recent being Golthlay. She knew what that look meant, and it was hard for her to admit that Travis wasn't all that different from other men.

"Oh, Señorita Dani, you look beautiful," breathed nineteen-year-old Davita. The girl had just finished arranging Daniella's hair in a mass of curls on top of her head and stepped back to view the overall picture.

Daniella studied herself in the long mirror. It did feel good to wear one of her own gowns for a change. The waist had needed letting out, but the full gathers hid her protruding stomach. The neckline was scooped just low enough to reveal the swell of her breasts without being too suggestive.

She tied a strip of lace around her throat to cover the scar that remained there. The deep green of the gown contrasted sharply with the pale blue of her eyes, making them appear darker than usual. Ivory lace trimmed the neck and sleeves and brought out the golden tan of her skin. Miss Whitfield would cringe at the sight of that tan.

The look pleased her, but she was nervous about appearing before Travis dressed like this. With the exception of the high necked, long sleeved dress she'd worn to town, the only clothes he'd ever seen her in were her breeches and the full, colorful skirts and loose white blouses loaned to her this past week by Rosita's daughters-in-law. What would he think? Would he think she was seeking his approval, or trying to entice him?

Was she?

Of course not!

The entire day had been one of fun and gaiety, with piñatas for the children and presents for Juanita. The food seemed neverending, and the wine flowed freely. No one worked on this holiday, except for necessary chores, therefore Travis had been nearby constantly. Daniella noticed that if he was not at her side, then he was watching her from only a short distance away. He was always somewhere near with a ready smile. She felt young and carefree again under his pleasant attention. She forced the dark looks Carmen cast her way to the back of her mind. She wouldn't let Carmen ruin this day.

To everyone's relief, a small thundershower descended on the ranch in the middle of the afternoon. Not that the rain was needed so much at this time of year, but according to legend, if it didn't rain on the day of La Fiesta de San Juan, the rest of the year would be dry. Daniella used the rain as an excuse to retire to her room for a nap, in order to be refreshed for the evening of dancing ahead.

"You've done wonders with my hair, Davita. Thank you. You'd better go now and see to yourself before the music starts."

Daniella liked Davita. She was a pretty, lively girl, and

the two of them were the same age. Daniella didn't let herself dwell on the idea that she felt years older than this vivacious dark-eyed girl who helped her dress for the party.

After Davita left, Daniella made her way nervously down the hall toward the courtyard. Travis's father greeted her.

"My dear, you look lovely. You honor our home with your beauty." Jason bent down and placed a fatherly kiss on her brow, bringing a light blush to her cheeks.

"Thank you, Jason. And may I say you cut quite a dashing figure yourself," she answered with a smile. His black suit made his silver hair glow in the light of the torches around the courtyard. His smile was open and friendly, as usual, and his hand on hers was warm and reassuring.

A moment later she felt the hair on the back of her neck stand out and knew she was being watched. Realizing there was no danger here, she forced herself to relax. Turning slowly, she found Travis's hot gaze on her as he approached. Her heart fluttered rapidly when he smiled at her. He, too, was dressed in black, and its effect on her was devastating.

Travis took her hand from his father and brought it to his lips. Her breath caught in her throat. His eyes finally left her face to travel the length of her body and back up, resting briefly on her trembling breasts before returning to gaze into her eyes.

"Isn't she lovely?" Jason said, breaking the silence.

"Beautiful," Travis breathed.

And suddenly Daniella felt beautiful. She smiled radiantly. "Thank you," she murmured.

"Goodness gracious, Simon, would you look at that. Is that our girl?" Tucker's voice broke the spell that held Daniella and Travis motionless.

"Tucker!" She was astonished at the old man's changed appearance. His hair and beard were clean and neatly trimmed. He must have borrowed the pants and shirt he wore, for she knew he possessed nothing more than the baggy garments she had first seen him in. She kissed his cheek, and this time it was Tucker who blushed, drawing a round of laughter.

187

"They must be takin' good care of ya, girlie, 'cause you sure look fine."

"Thank you, Tucker. They're taking excellent care of me. In fact, you may have trouble with me when we get home. I've become positively lazy," she laughed.

At her mention of home, the smile on Travis's face disappeared.

"Simon, I've missed you." Daniella threw her arms around the young giant and planted a kiss on his chin. Even standing on her toes, his chin was as high as she could reach.

Travis was startled and none too pleased to see Dani wrap her arms so familiarly around this good-looking young man whom he hadn't met. He fought hard to keep the scowl off his face. Tucker had mentioned Simon, of course, but he'd called him a boy and indicated he was much younger.

A peculiar sensation ran through Travis, one he'd never felt before and refused to examine closely, when Dani pressed her lips to Simon's chin. It surged and strengthened as he read the obvious affection in her hug, her smile, her eyes.

The only others he'd seen Dani so free with were Tucker, Cochise, Dee-O-Det, and Matt. Matt was a child, and her friend. The others she regarded as . . . family.

He relaxed. Family. She considered Simon family. That's why she was so free and easy with the young giant.

And why, he asked himself, was Daniella Blackwood's family reduced to this boy, a crusty old prospector, an ancient Apache *shaman*, and a fierce Apache war chief?

Where was her real family? John Blackwood had been her uncle. That made Howard Blackwood her uncle, too. Or did it?

Snatches of her fevered ramblings floated through his mind.

But Papa, don't you love me anymore? All I did was come home.

Travis frowned, trying to remember what she'd said that first night on the trail about Howard Blackwood. Something about trading her absence from his home for the deed to El

Valle.

Could Howard Blackwood be her father? It didn't make sense. After what she'd been through with the Apaches, her own father wouldn't have wanted "her absence from his home." He would have wanted to shelter her, protect her, give her all the love and support she needed to get over what had happened.

No. Howard couldn't be her father. But who was?

Travis forced the puzzle to a back corner of his mind. This was a night for celebration. He intended to see that Dani enjoyed herself.

". . . another one of her strays she picked up," Tucker was saying.

Dani and Simon both looked affronted by whatever the old man was talking about.

"Now don't be alookin' at me like that, you two. That's what you and me both are, Simon. A couple of old strays she felt sorry for and took in."

"Sorry for! Why, I never—"

Tucker's rasping laughter cut her off. He gave a big wink, and Simon broke out in a grin. Dani sputtered to a halt. A moment later she laughed with him.

Travis listened with interest and amusement as Tucker went on to tell how Simon had come to join him and "the girlie." No doubt the old man embellished the tale somewhat, judging by the looks Dani and Simon gave each other.

"Sheep!" Dani jumped at the boom of Jason's voice. "This is cattle country. You can't have sheep in cattle country."

Travis smiled. He'd forgotten to warn his father about the sheep.

Dani gave Tucker an exasperating look. The old man just smirked at her, his expression saying, *Get yourself outa this one, girlie.*

Simon frowned, and Dani patted his massive shoulder in reassurance before turning back to Jason.

"The Triple C may be cattle country, Jason, but El Valle de Esperanza has sheep." She looked up at him in defiance.

189

"Well, Dad," Travis drawled. "What can you say to that?"

Jason took a deep breath and the scowl on his face eased into a smile. "Just keep your damned—I mean, keep your sheep away from our cattle, young lady."

"I intend to," she answered with a grin. "Simon would never let one of his beloved sheep stray so far, would you, Simon?"

The big giant just smiled down at her and shook his head. As she turned back toward Jason, Simon tugged gently on her sleeve. She looked up at him in question, then shrugged her shoulders.

"Simon wants to know why you don't like sheep, Jason," Dani said.

Jason and Travis both looked at her curiously.

"The boy don't talk," Tucker explained.

Simon tugged on Dani's sleeve again. "He knows you talk to me, Simon. He just means you don't talk with your mouth and tell everything you know, like he does."

Travis looked on in wonder as Dani held a one-sided conversation with her silent friend.

"Don't you never talk with your mouth, boy?" Tucker asked in frustration.

Simon grinned at the three men who looked at him expectantly, and settled his gaze on Tucker. "Never."

Dani and Tucker stared at Simon in total amazement.

Matt ran up and tugged on the big giant's hand. "Come on, Simon, let's get outa here before they pester you to death. A guy'd think they never heard anybody talk before." Matt hauled a grinning Simon off toward the food-laden table where they each began filling their plates.

"What's the matter with you two?" Travis wanted to know. Tucker and Dani were still staring at Simon's retreating back.

"Did I really hear that . . . with my ears?" she asked.

"You musta, 'cause I surely did," Tucker answered.

"What are you two so excited about?" Jason asked.

"Oh, nothin' much," Tucker said. "It's just that that's the first word we've ever heard the youngster speak."

190

Just then the traveling band of musicians hired for the occasion began to play, and Carmen made what Travis knew from past experience was a perfectly timed grand entrance. If the woman's purpose was to impress him with her beauty—and she was definitely beautiful—her efforts were wasted. Travis gave her a polite nod, then swept Dani away to the area set aside for dancing. As they swirled to the music, he noticed how perfectly her small hand fit in his.

The evening progressed rapidly, and Travis kept a close eye on Dani, who spent most of the time dancing. Everyone danced with everyone else, and laughter filled the warm night air.

Carmen was in her element, preening and demanding Travis's attention constantly. It was late when he was finally able to disengage himself from her clinging arms and pass her along to Jason. When his father led her out in a dance, Travis turned and saw Dani sitting alone on a bench, watching the dancing.

"Having a good time?" he asked.

"Oh, yes. It's a wonderful night."

Her smile lit her face with an inner glow, and Travis was unable to stop himself from reaching for her hand. He wanted her. It stunned him how badly. Wanted her here, now, always. "Walk with me?" he asked softly.

When she stood, he placed her hand on his arm and led her around the vine-covered trellis and out of the courtyard. The air was fresh and clean, and as the music faded with the increasing distance, frogs and crickets sent up their own nighttime chorus beneath the cottonwood trees, only to hush when the humans intruded into their domain.

They stopped beneath the branches of a huge old cottonwood at the edge of the creek. "I hear from Matt you plan on leaving tomorrow," Travis said softly.

"It's time." Daniella, too, spoke quietly, afraid to disturb the peacefulness in the air. Inside, she was anything but quiet. Her heart pounded so hard she was afraid he would hear. Would he kiss her? *Please, Travis, kiss me.*

"Is there any way I can convince you to stay longer, until

you're fully recovered?"

"I am recovered, Travis." She looked up into his face, and his eyes seemed like black pools. Moonlight flickered through the leaves of the tree, sprinkling his golden hair with silver patches. She held her breath as he leaned forward, and his lips finally touched hers. The sensations aroused by his nearness and the warmth of his mouth were exquisite.

"Dani," he whispered roughly against her lips. His arms came around her and urged her closer, his kiss deepening as his breathing became ragged.

Travis pulled her unresisting body fully against his own and felt the roundness of her stomach, but her breasts pressing against his chest overwhelmed all other thoughts, and he moaned deep in his throat. He'd wanted this for so long.

When her mouth went slack beneath his, he wasted no time in invading that soft warm cavern with his tongue, taking her breath away. Slowly, shyly, her tongue met his. His heartbeat increased. His arms held her even tighter.

Suddenly Daniella panicked. She was suffocating! His two arms became a dozen in her mind, tearing at her, pulling her down. She knew it wasn't happening, but was powerless to stop the terror engulfing her. Dark leering faces swam before her closed eyes. She struggled to free herself from imagined horrors.

Travis felt her body stiffen against his, felt her pushing him away. Not understanding what was happening, he held her even tighter, pressing her against the tingling warmth in his groin.

Daniella felt that part of a man she had learned to fear rise up and harden against her. Sheer terror gripped her. She tore her mouth free. "No! No!" she cried hysterically, struggling to free herself completely.

The terror in her voice penetrated the fog of lust enshrouding Travis's brain and cooled him as effectively as a bucket of cold water. He loosened his grip and she tore herself away and tried to run, but tripped on the hem of her dress and fell to the ground.

"Dani!" he cried. When he knelt beside her and reached for her, she tried to scramble away. "No, Dani, I won't hurt you." He managed to wrap his arms around her shuddering form and held her still. "Ssh . . . it's all right, Dani . . . I'm sorry. I didn't mean to frighten you." He tried to comfort her with words the same way he had when she was delirious with fever a few days ago.

Daniella took in great gulps of air and finally realized where she was and who she was with. She went limp in his arms.

"Are you all right now?" he asked tenderly, smoothing a stray curl from her face.

She nodded, unable to speak, and pulled herself free of his warm, comforting, yet threatening embrace. She rose on shaky limbs and walked away a few paces, rubbing her hands on her arms to ward off the sudden chill.

"I'm sorry, Dani. I didn't mean to frighten you."

"I know that. It wasn't your fault." She was still shaken. Her voice quivered with emotion.

"Look at me," he insisted.

Travis tilted her head up. Her eyes, silver in the moonlight, were full of pain and despair. "I'm sorry. It was my fault. I should have remembered . . ." He took a deep breath and silently cursed himself for a fool. "Come on. It's late and you're tired. I'll see you to your room."

Daniella voiced no objections as he led her back to the house. They walked side by side, each with similar troubled thoughts. Avoiding the courtyard, Travis took her back to her room. He whispered a tender good night and placed a fleeting kiss on her brow before leaving her at the door.

Was she destined to humiliate herself in front of him every time they were together? First her disreputable clothes, then her nightmares on the trail, the time she'd broken down and cried all over him, the trouble in town, morning sickness from her detestable condition, and now this. Lord, what must he think?

As tired as she was, she refused to sleep that night. After acting like a maniac over a simple kiss, she had no intention of waking the entire household in the middle of the night with screams. She'd been lucky so far. No nightmares had plagued her during her recovery. She didn't intend for them to start now.

She changed into her borrowed nightgown and paced the length of the room and back for hours. As dawn lightened the sky, she dressed in more borrowed clothes—an embroidered skirt and white blouse, and waited until time to go to breakfast.

When voices carried down the hall and she was sure the household was awake, she opened the door and stepped out into the darkened hall, only to stop short at the sight that greeted her.

Two doors down, Carmen stood in front of her open bedroom wearing a pale, thin nightgown, her arms wrapped around Travis's broad shoulders, her lips pressed tight against his mouth. Travis's hands gripped Carmen's bare shoulders.

"Mi querido," Carmen whispered harshly against his lips.

Holding her breath lest she make a sound, Daniella moved silently back into her room and closed the door. She leaned back against it and let out her breath. A trembling seized her from head to toe. To see him in the arms of another woman was more painful than anything she could imagine.

But she wasn't really surprised by what she'd seen. Carmen was a beautiful, desirable woman who undoubtedly knew how to please a man. Daniella would bet her last pound of sugar that Carmen didn't panic in his arms and try to run away. No, she invited him with her hot, black eyes and soft, red lips. She wasn't afraid of men.

And she didn't have a hideous streak of white in her hair, either. Nor was she looked upon with pity and scorn for carrying a half-breed bastard in her womb.

Of course Travis would prefer Carmen. What man wouldn't?

Swamped by despair, Daniella moved to the bed and sat down. Her original idea of going east to have the child now took on a note of desperate importance. She'd go immediately. As soon as she figured out how to get to the nearest stage.

She waited a few minutes, then, with every ounce of courage she possessed, she opened the door a crack and checked the hall. Relief flooded her. The hall was empty. As quietly as possible, she avoided the front of the house and slipped out the back way. She met Tucker and Simon as they came out of the barn, where they'd slept.

In as few words as possible, she told them she was heading home immediately. Tucker studied her sharply for a moment, then gave a jerky nod of his gray head and started hitching the team to the wagon.

"What about the boys?" he asked.

Damn. She'd forgotten about them. She couldn't very well leave them with Travis. Taking them home complicated her plans for going back east. Yet what choice did she have? Rescuing them had been her idea, so they were her responsibility. "They're coming with us."

Travis took his place at the head of the table and reached for the cup of coffee next to his plate. It was the closest thing at hand to wash the taste of Carmen's kiss from his lips.

He wanted to swear; he wanted to hit something. A man his age should be flattered when a beautiful woman accosted him—that was the only way he could describe what Carmen had done a few minutes ago in the hall—she'd accosted him.

But damn, he wasn't flattered. He was disgusted. And angry. To have the bittersweet memory of Dani's eager, inexperienced response last night—eager at least until her mind had played tricks on her—overshadowed by Carmen's unwelcome attentions made him madder than hell.

His desire for Dani was growing into a gnawing hunger. He felt a smile starting. He'd just have to wipe out Carmen's kiss with another one from Dani.

After breakfast he'd get her alone in his study on some

195

pretext or another. Only this time he'd go slowly and not scare the wits out of her. He nodded to himself. It was an excellent idea. Right after breakfast.

So where was she? Dani should have been here by now. She was an early riser, he knew. Matt, too, was late. Were the two of them together? As if thinking of his son conjured him up, Matt walked in just then and took his place at the table. With eyes lowered, the boy started filling his plate.

"Good morning, son."

Matt heaved a sigh and picked at his food. "Morning."

"Why the long face?"

Matt kept his gaze on his plate and sighed again. "I just wish Dani didn't have to go, that's all. And I wish she didn't have to take Shanta and Chee with her."

"We haven't decided what to do about Shanta and Chee yet. There's no need to worry about it so soon."

Matt's head snapped up. His wide brown eyes settled on Travis. "Well *somebody* decided, cuz she took 'em home with her."

"What are you talking about?" It was a stupid question, because Travis already knew the answer. Dani was gone. That's why she wasn't at breakfast. She was upset about last night, so she left. Without a word. *Damn it*.

"I'm talking about Dani. Her and Tucker and Simon and Shanta and Chee left."

Travis let out the breath he'd been holding. His gaze caught Jason's frown, and for a brief instant, a look of smug satisfaction in Carmen's eyes. "When?" he asked Matt.

"A few minutes ago."

"Did you see her? Did she say anything?"

Matt shrugged. "She just said she was all well now and it was time to go home. I wish she'd stayed."

Me too, son. What he wanted to do was ride after her and bring her back. She had no business going home now, with a child on the way and only Tucker and Simon to help her.

It was all he could do to keep from jumping up, riding after her, and bringing her back. But knowing Dani, *bring*

196

isn't what he'd have to do to get her back here. He'd have to drag her. And after last night, she'd probably shoot him before she let him get near her.

No, he couldn't go after her. Not now. He'd give her a day or two, then he'd pay a visit.

Damn, but it wasn't like her to sneak out without a word. She might be upset about last night, might even be a little afraid of him because of what happened, but she was no coward. So what had sent her running?

Chapter Nineteen

Carmen knew she couldn't just prance her horse down the middle of Tucson asking everyone she met if he knew Billy Joe Crane. Word would surely get back to Travis if she did something so bold and foolish. And Travis must never know.

So she skirted the edge of town and came up behind a row of four crumbling adobe huts where a group of children played. For a silver dollar, the oldest boy agreed to find out if Crane was in town and if so, to bring him to Carmen.

Dios, it was hot. She tugged at the high neck of her blue velvet riding habit. It was most certainly too hot for velvet, but one must dress properly for each occasion. If she was right, this meeting with the *gringo* named Crane, the one who had reason to hate the Blackwood bitch nearly as much as Carmen did, would be one of the most important occasions in her life. Daniella must leave the territory. If the girl was reluctant, Carmen was counting on Crane to persuade her.

The scant shadow behind the adobes, where Carmen sought what relief there was from the unrelenting desert sun, grew several inches longer before she saw the boy returning. She pursed her lips at the sight of the man with him.

She'd known, of course, that Crane was a *gringo,* but not that he was quite so unkempt, so big, or so dirty. As he came closer, she added, *or so stupid looking.*

198

"Boy, if you're aleadin' me down the garden path, I'll bust your backside," the redheaded giant threatened.

"No, *señor*, see? *Aquí, aquí.*"

Crane paused a moment. His eyes raked her from head to toe. Curious eyes, narrowed in thought. Or just against the glare of the sun? *No*, Carmen thought. *He's not stupid at all.* An unexpected shiver of excitement slithered down her spine.

When he and the boy stood before her, she tossed the boy his promised dollar. *"Gracias, muchacho.* Run along."

The boy let out a whoop of delight and caught the shiny coin in the air. He spun on his bare heel and ran off toward his friends.

Carmen and Crane stood staring at each other. "You are the one called Billy Joe Crane?"

He snorted. "Who wants to know?"

She stood beside her horse and trailed a gloved hand along the animal's neck. "I am Carmen Martinez. I understand you have a . . . shall we say, a quarrel, with a certain young lady who does not like trespassers on her property, and who has a fondness for young Apache boys."

Crane angled his head and looked at her with one eye. "Could be."

"I, too, have a quarrel with the girl. Is there a place we can go, a place that is private, where we can talk?"

A slow grin disturbed one side of his bushy red beard. "Private? Sure."

He took the reins and led her horse behind the last adobe, there tying it to a low clump of brush. Carmen was both surprised and amused when he extended his arm in a semblance of gentlemanly conduct and escorted her across the cracked, sunbaked ground. They went up an alley, cut between two squat, crumbling houses, and up a rickety set of stairs to a dark, musty room.

The only window was covered by a moth-eaten blanket. A small table, held upright by three legs and a rusted rifle barrel, bearing a mismatched pitcher and bowl with matching cracks, stood next to an ancient, stained feather tick spread out on the floor. The rest of the room, barely enough space for the two of them to stand, was empty.

"Now," Crane said, "what's on your mind, *señorita?*"

"I will be blunt with you, Señor Crane. I want to get rid of the girl. I think, perhaps, you want the same thing."

The man scratched at his beard with a beefy, work-hardened hand and moved to lean against the wall. With the toe of his boot, he kicked the door closed. The only light left was a few thin beams coming through the moth holes of the blanket over the window, and a narrow crack around the door.

"What'd ya have in mind?"

"Well." Carmen licked her lips and strolled the cramped confines of the room, sending her velvet-clad hips swaying. "I'm not really sure. All I care about is that she leave the territory."

"Why? Why do you want her gone?"

"She is an obstacle. I want her removed. She is too close to the Triple C and its owner."

"You mean Colton."

"Yes. I mean Colton. Travis belongs to me, and I intend to marry him. But the girl and her problems have distracted his attention."

Crane did nothing but look at her. She forced herself to relax her hands to keep from fidgeting under his steady regard.

"So why'd ya come to me with your story?"

She tossed her head and gave him a slight smile. "I understand you're a prospector, that you occupied El Valle de Esperanza for some time. Did you find anything worthwhile there? Perhaps you would like a longer look?"

His eyes narrowed to slits. "Meaning?"

So. She had his interest. There was something in the little valley he wanted. "I propose we strike a bargain, you and I. If you get rid of the girl, run her off her land and out of the territory, I will marry Travis Colton and ensure that you have no trouble from the Triple C when you take over El Valle."

200

"What makes you think I want El Valle?"

Carmen let her eyes roam over the massive size of him suggestively. She didn't need to feign interest when her gaze settled on the telltale bulge in the front of his pants. That tingling excitement that struck her when she first saw the spread of his shoulders rose to a fever pitch. He was huge and strong, and had a look about him suggesting meanness, even a hint of cruelty. Her smile widened.

"Come now, *señor*. A man like you would not distance himself from the excitement and . . . pleasures . . . to be found in town, not without a reason. A very good reason. I think perhaps you found something in that valley that interested you. I care not what it is. Whatever you find is yours. All I want is for you to get rid of the girl. Are you interested?"

She let her gaze drift slowly down his body again, deliberately lingering on the very real evidence of his interest. She felt her breasts swell in response.

"I could be, if you'd be willin' to, ah, sweeten the pot a mite."

Reluctantly, she pulled her gaze back up to his face. Her tongue came out slowly and stroked her upper lip. When his eyes widened and his breath grew ragged, she dropped her gaze again and gasped. He had to be near bursting! She felt her knees go weak as moisture pooled in heated desire between her legs.

Being deliberately provocative, she slowly pulled the gloves from her hands and let them drop to the rough plank floor. "What," she said, her voice suddenly husky, "did you have in mind?"

With a low growl, Crane sprang forward. "This." One huge paw grabbed her breast and squeezed. Carmen made no pretense about not wanting him. This was no time to be coy. She'd been too long without a man.

Daniella sat sideways on the bed, feet stretched out in front of her, and leaned back against the cool adobe wall.

201

She stared out the window across the room, determining the window's location by its different shade of black from the wall surrounding it. A cricket chirruped somewhere just outside.

She rolled her head against the wall and wished she were that cricket. Then she wouldn't have to worry about what to do.

She'd been home from the Triple C for two days and hadn't made a move to leave. How could she go back east to have the child and expect Tucker and Simon to stay here and do all the work? They'd spent most of the day tracking a coyote who'd killed a sheep the night before, so the hay they'd cut earlier was still stacked next to the barn. She wanted to get it up into the hayloft before the next rain. There was so much to do.

Then there were Shanta and Chee. She'd have to take them to Cochise before she left. And if she didn't take them soon, her condition would be obvious to her observant adoptive father. She had no desire to discuss it with him.

And when she left for Boston, what would Travis think? Not that she'd find out, because she had no intention of telling him her plans, or even seeing him again, for that matter.

Daniella sat in the darkness for hours as her thoughts rolled round and round. Eventually the square that was her window took on an orange tint. She stared unblinking, and it grew brighter. The others would be up and about any moment.

She sniffed and caught a whiff of smoke. Someone must already be up and starting a fire for breakfast. Probably Tucker. She'd been so deep in thought she hadn't heard him.

What an odd color the sunrise had this morning.

Daniella straightened away from the wall and sat upright. Another trace of smoke reached her nostrils. *That's not wood smoke.*

She made it to the window in a single leap. The orange glow wasn't coming from over the mountains in the east,

202

but from somewhere on the other side of the house!

Fire!

She raced out of her room, banging on Tucker's door as she flew past. "Fire! Fire, Tucker!" She didn't wait for a reply, but ran out the front door and into the night, heedless of her nightgown and bare feet.

The haystack was burning! And it was entirely too close to the barn for comfort.

Flames crackled and leaped up one side of the stack, great gray and black clouds of smoke rising and hovering. At least the horses were out in the pasture. Thank God there was no wind to spread the fire.

Daniella had no idea how to put out a burning haystack, but instinct sent her racing to the well. By the time she lowered the bucket and raised it again, she knew it would take too long to do any good. But she didn't know what else to do!

When she returned to the fire, Simon, who'd been sleeping in the barn, was there with a shovel. As fast as he could, he shoveled as much dirt as possible onto the burning side of the haystack. Around behind, where the fire hadn't reached, Tucker wielded a pitch fork for all he was worth, tossing the unburned hay as far away as his skinny arms could manage. Shanta and Chee, who'd been sleeping in the barn with Simon, were helping Tucker, carrying hay in their hands.

Daniella started to toss the water from her bucket onto the flames, but Simon waved her away and pointed at the barn. He meant for her to wet down the dry timber to help keep the fire from spreading.

By her third trip from the well, the flames were out. All that was left was a small pile of smoldering hay. Simon had ended up leaving off with the dirt and resorted to beating the flames with the shovel.

Tucker and the boys had managed to save about a third of the stack.

Soot, ashes, and exhaustion covered all five of them. Daniella was vaguely surprised to notice dozens of tiny black-ringed holes in her nightgown. Caused by sparks, no doubt, although she was too tired to care.

She made one more trip to the well, but this water was for drinking. The five of them drained the bucket in a hurry. No one had yet spoken a word since Daniella had shouted "Fire!" at Tucker's door.

Tucker finally broke the silence. "I'll swan, girlie. A body never gets bored around you, that's for certain. Did ya smell the kerosene?"

Daniella jerked her head up. "What kerosene?"

"The kerosene I smelled when I first came outside. The kerosene what started this fire."

Daniella hadn't thought to wonder how the fire had started. She hadn't had time. She glanced at Simon, and he nodded that he, too, had smelled kerosene. But none of them had heard or seen anything.

A deep shiver ran through her. Kerosene meant arson. There was no way any of them had spilled the stuff anywhere near the haystack. Someone had deliberately set the fire. But who? Why?

"Soon's it's light, me an' Simon an' the boys'll have us a look around. See if we can spot anything. Sun'll be up soon, girlie. Why don't you go get some sleep?"

After being up all night, then fighting the fire, Daniella was too tired to argue. She nodded her head then stumbled to the house. She didn't even wash the soot from her face and hands or change her gown. Instead, she fell onto the bed in a stupor and went to sleep.

The first thing Travis noticed when he rode through the narrow entrance to El Valle a few hours later was a heavy layer of gray smoke hanging thirty feet off the ground from one end of the valley to the other. He knew instantly there'd been a fire. Worried, he kicked Buck into a gallop and raced toward the small cluster of buildings at the other end.

When he reined Buck in at the house, Tucker hailed him from in front of the barn.

"What happened?" Travis demanded as he dismounted and tied the stallion to the porch post.

Tucker snorted. "Fire."

"No kidding," Travis said, rolling his eyes. He caught sight then of the smoldering remains of the haystack. "You people should be more careful. You could have burned the whole place down."

"The kinda care we need ta take ta keep from havin' fires like this one is ta post guards around the place."

Dread knotted in Travis's stomach. "You mean it was set?"

"Yep."

"How? Who did it? Was anybody hurt?"

Tucker lifted his hands and counted off on his fingers as he spoke. "Kerosene, got no idea, and no, nobody was hurt. The girl's in the house. Might still be sleepin'."

Travis closed his mouth with a snap. He'd looked for Daniella, hadn't seen her, and was just about to ask where she was. Was he so obvious that the old man could see right through him?

He didn't care. Right now all he wanted to do was see Dani, see for himself she was all right. He started toward the house, then stopped.

"Any tracks?" he asked Tucker.

Tucker aimed a stream of tobacco juice at a lizard and missed. "Yeah," he said. "Too many, and all ours."

Travis walked into the house and looked around. There were dishes stacked in the wash tub, and coffee sat warming on the stove, but no Dani. He stepped quietly to the closed door at the other end of the room and stopped. If she was asleep, he didn't want to wake her. He tapped lightly. No answer.

He should leave. He should go outside and wait until she woke up. He wanted to talk to her about the way she'd sneaked off from his ranch the other day. It wasn't like her to take the coward's way out, and it wasn't like her to be rude by not telling anyone but Matt good-bye.

He'd gritted his teeth for two days before riding over here

205

to see her. Before his conscience spoke up, he turned the knob and eased the door open a crack. As his eyes searched and found her sprawled face down across the bed, he chastised himself. Since when had he stooped to spying on a sleeping woman? It made him uneasy. He started to close the door and step away, but then his brain registered what his eyes were seeing.

Good God.

Her bare feet, hanging off the bottom corner of the bed, were covered with dirt and soot and what looked like dried blood. An angry red burn marred the inside of her left ankle.

The white cotton nightgown that would hang to the floor when she stood was bunched up around her knees, leaving her soot-streaked calves bare. The whole garment was pockmarked with burn holes, and the ruffle at the right wrist was singed half away. Her long black and white hair spread out in tangles across her back and shoulders.

Travis took it all in in seconds, then shoved the door open. Damn, couldn't she stay out of trouble at all? He made no effort to be quiet when he stomped back to the kitchen, then returned a moment later with a bowl of water and a rag.

Daniella heard the clomping of boots on the wood floor. She groaned and mumbled, "Go away," but it may not have come out right, because the boots didn't leave. She eased back into sleep and dreamed of splashing water and something cool, wet, and soft on her feet. It felt wonderful. She sighed and rubbed her cheek against the pillow.

Then something warm and hard—fingers?—touched the bottom of her foot, and it tickled. She giggled in her sleep, but the sound of her own voice woke her. With a yawn, she stretched and arched and wiggled her toes. The warm thing was still there.

Cool wetness touched the raw burn on her ankle. It stung. Daniella jerked her leg and pushed herself up on both elbows.

"Be still."

206

The deep, familiar voice froze her muscles for a moment. Then she kicked the hand from her foot and scrambled across the bed until she sat, panting, with her back to the wall and her nightgown tugged down tight over her bent knees.

"What are you doing here?" she demanded, her eyes wide, her chest heaving, and her wits scattered.

Travis knelt at the corner of her bed, one knee on the floor, the other foot flat, knee raised. He propped one hand on his hip and leaned an elbow on his upraised knee. A wet, dirty rag dangled negligently from his hand. He raised his eyebrows in feigned innocence and said, "Washing your feet."

Daniella frowned, lifted the hem of her gown just enough to see her toes, then frowned some more. She raised her gaze back to his face. "Why?"

Travis snorted. There was no other way to describe it. It was a snort. "Somebody has to look after you. You couldn't stay out of trouble if you tried, could you?"

"What are you talking about?"

His face hardened and his mouth tightened. "You had no business running around in the middle of the night trying to put out a burning haystack. Look what you've done to yourself!" he said sweeping a hand in the air. "You could have been seriously injured, or worse."

"I'm supposed to ignore a fire that close to my barn? This whole place could have gone up in flames if we hadn't got that fire out when we did."

"And you damn sure had no business doing it barefooted, and in your nightgown."

Daniella ground her teeth in righteous indignation. "What I do, how I do it, and what I wear while I'm doing it are none of your business. Get out of my room."

"If I do, will you get dressed and come out so we can talk?"

"What time is it?"

"I don't know. Around ten, maybe."

"Then no, I won't get dressed. Now go away. I've had maybe three or four hours of sleep. I'm tired."

"If you'd learn to sleep at night, like a normal person—"

"My sleeping habits are none of your business."

"Dani—"

Daniella closed her eyes in frustration. "Get out."

"Not until you tell me why you left the way you did the other day."

She opened her eyes. "I left because it was time to come home."

"You sneaked off like a thief in the night. Why?"

She felt her face heat up. "I did not sneak."

"Neither did you bother to tell anyone but Matt you were leaving."

She looked away, unable to meet his direct stare. In her mind she saw him again as she had that morning, his lips glued to Carmen's, Carmen's arms wrapped around him, his hands on Carmen's shoulders.

Travis dropped the rag he still held into the bowl of water by his knee. "Was it . . . because of what happened? Because I kissed you?"

Her face grew hotter.

"Dani, you must know I want you. But surely you also know I wouldn't hurt you or scare you for anything. You know that, don't you?"

She glanced at him, saw the earnestness in his face, and glanced away. "I told you. It was time to come home. It had nothing to do with . . . the other."

"Prove it," he said softly.

Her gaze jerked back to him. Her heart whacked against her ribs. "What—" She swallowed and tried again. "What do you mean?" Did he mean to kiss her again? Here? In her bedroom? Her mouth went dry.

"Come home with me."

It was the last thing she'd expected to hear. "What for?"

Travis heaved a sigh and flexed his shoulders. "Because in your condition you've got no business trying to work this place."

She'd been expecting—no, to be truthful, she'd been hoping for—a kiss. Instead, he brought up a subject she'd just as soon never discuss. Her eyes narrowed as she glared at him. "How indelicate of you to say so, Mr. Colton."

Travis matched her glare. "Well damn it, somebody's gotta look after you, 'cause you damn well don't look after yourself."

"I can look after myself just fine."

"Sure you can. That's how you got yourself hooked up with me in the first place, looking after yourself. You try to do me a favor, and you end up in a knife fight with an Apache. You try to sleep and you wake up screaming. You go to town and get yourself shot. You come home and get yourself burned. That's how you take care of yourself. And what are you going to do up here with no one around but Tucker and Simon when the baby comes? You going to take care of yourself then, too?"

Daniella gasped. Unmarried men and women simply did not discuss things like having babies. It just wasn't done. "I think this conversation has gone far enough. You can leave now. Thank you for your concern, but I assure you, you needn't worry about me. I'm not your responsibility."

"Changing the subject won't make it go away, Dani."

"I should be so lucky," she muttered to herself.

"At least think about coming back to the ranch. You'll have your own room, and I won't bother you. You won't have to lift a finger, and Rosita and Juanita can take care of you when the baby comes. You shouldn't be up here working this place in your condition."

"So I'm supposed to just leave? Leave Tucker and Simon with all the work?" As she spoke the words, she realized their truth. If she went to Boston, she'd be abandoning Tucker and Simon, shirking her responsibility to them and El Valle. She buried her face in her hands and groaned. She couldn't leave. Not for Boston, not for the Triple C.

"Think about it," he said softly. "Meanwhile, at least let me send one of my men up here to help you keep watch."

209

"Keep watch for what?" she asked, raising her head but not looking at him.

"For whoever set that fire last night. Do you have any idea who might have done it?"

She gave a little half-laugh. "Anyone from town? I'm sure I made more than a few enemies that day."

"Especially Crane. Isn't he the one you said was squatting here when you first came?"

She nodded. Travis was right. Crane now had a double grudge against her. It could have been him who set last night's fire.

"I'll send Benito as soon as I get home."

"No," she said quickly. "There's no need. We'll keep our own watch. Besides, Consuela and the children need him. I don't."

"Dani—"

"Travis, please. I appreciate your concern, but it isn't necessary. I thank you for everything you've done for me. You think you owe me something, but you don't. Any debt there may have been was canceled when you stood with me in town the other day. Just go home, Travis. I'm tired."

She watched first anger, then frustration flash across his face before his expression went carefully blank. He stood slowly and towered over her.

"All right. I'll go," he said softly. "But I'll be back."

And before she could guess his intentions, he leaned down and kissed her, hard, right on the lips.

Chapter Twenty

A week later, from his hideout in the hills, Billy Joe Crane watched the lights in the small valley below flicker out one by one. He would have wished for a darker night, but he was tired of waiting. That fire he'd set last week in the haystack hadn't done the trick. It was time to give the girl reason to move on.

He glanced up at the sky again. The heavy cloud cover was lit from behind by a full moon, leaving the sky a whitish gray instead of black. What the hell—at least he'd be able to see what he was doing.

The big dummy, the one who didn't talk, had moved the sheep and that damn dog to the other side of the stream. That should keep the dog from smelling him, at least long enough for what he had in mind.

Crane's eyes focused on the pale outline of the house. He knew the girl would be sitting out front, like she'd done every night for the past week. When did the little bitch sleep? He sure hoped tonight put the fear of God into her. Or the fear of Crane. He grinned at the thought.

Yep. It was time she left. He wanted that house. And the valley. And the gold he knew was there.

Prospecting was a damn uncomfortable way to live, and dangerous, too. He and his four partners learned that lesson last summer. Camped out in the open, as usual, the damned Apaches took them by surprise, sneaking up on them just before sundown while Two-Fingers Dan was turning that scrawny jackrabbit over the fire.

It had happened so fast they hadn't even been able to get to their guns. When Crane came to the next morning his shoulder was pinned to the ground by a six-foot lance. Two-Fingers Dan and the others were dead. The horses were gone.

Goddamn, he hated Apaches.

Ever since then, he hadn't been overly fond of camping out, either. But how's a fella supposed to find gold while sleepin' in a house?

The adobe in El Valle was the answer to all his problems. He could live inside its snug walls at night and dig up the gold during the day.

And gold there was—high grade ore. He reached into his pants pocket and pulled out the small, fist-shaped nugget he'd found in the dead man's pocket last summer. It was smooth and warm, and its little friends, wherever they were hiding, would set him up for life. All he had to do was find them. That might take some doing. It was a cinch they weren't laying up on the porch where the dead man had been. But he'd find them, all right.

Yes sir. Billy Joe Crane was gonna be somebody in this territory. Somebody important. Just as soon as he got rid of the girl and her friends so he could get to all that shiny yellow gold.

He started down the hillside one careful step at a time. He was gonna be real quiet. He wasn't gonna kick any rocks or breathe loud or nothin'. He wasn't even gonna let the kerosene slosh in the can he carried.

He thought of the girl down there and ground his teeth. That interferin', breeches-wearin', Apache-lovin' bitch. After tonight she'd leave this valley, and it would be his. He'd set himself up like a king. Maybe even invite that Mex slut—what was her name?—Martinez. Carmen Martinez. Maybe he'd let her visit now and then whenever she needed a good bangin'. He grinned and rubbed his crotch. She was a hot one, all right. She'd be back for more of what he had. Just thinking about it made him hard.

An hour later he was still hard when he crept from the

last line of hills to the back of the barn. He'd kept the barn between him and the house so he wouldn't be spotted. Now he moved to the corner and peeked around the side.

He watched, holding his breath, as the shadowy form of the girl stood in front of the house. She stretched her arms over her head and yawned. The action drew the white shirt tight across her breasts. Crane rubbed his crotch again and thought he'd like to give her a try.

But he'd rather have her house and the valley.

She picked up her rifle and strolled off toward the creek on the other side of the house. He relaxed. Damn, she was makin' this easy.

Crane started to pour the kerosene along the back wall of the barn, then stopped. He remembered seeing the big dummy and those two little Apache nits go into the barn every night. They were in there now. Them gut-eaters owed him four lives, by God.

Near the front corner of the barn he found a six-foot tree limb that hadn't been cut into firewood lengths yet. Hefting it in his arms, he carried it—quietly—to the big single door in the front. He butted one end against the ground and the other against the door. No one would get out that way, and even the girl wouldn't be able to move that brace. He repeated the procedure at the rear door.

Daniella breathed in the warm night air as she picked her way across the narrow creek in the darkness to check on the sheep. At least her sleepless nights could now be put to use standing guard.

She remembered last week's fire with a shudder. Even now she could smell the burning fumes of kerosene. Would the smell never leave her?

The sheep moved restlessly at her approach, but Simon's dog whined a greeting and butted his nose up against her hand. He'd been up in the hills guarding his flock the night of the fire, otherwise they might have had some warning.

Warning. If she'd had warning the day after the fire—

warning that Travis would kiss her — she might have avoided him. Avoided those firm, demanding lips. Thrilling lips.

Her hand was halfway to her lips, intent on rubbing them. She stopped and made herself stroke the dog instead. No matter how many times she tried, she would never be able to wipe away the feel of that disturbing kiss. Disturbing, because it hadn't scared her. And *that* scared her.

The dog stiffened beneath her hand and raised his nose in the air. He growled low in his throat, then barked and took off toward the creek. With her mind still reliving Travis's kiss, Daniella turned to see what excited the dog.

Light flickered through the trees. *Light?*

Not light! *Fire!*

Daniella pointed her rifle in the air and fired three rounds as she ran. The light grew brighter with every leap she took. When she broke through the trees and dashed forward, the barn was engulfed in flames.

Tucker, wearing nothing but his long flannels and boots, met her in front of the house. They each spotted the brace on the barn door at the same time.

"No!" she screamed. "Simon! Chee! Shanta!"

The log itself wasn't burning yet, and neither was the door. But Daniella and Tucker together couldn't budge it.

"The axe! Where's the axe?" Danielia screamed.

Tucker found it stuck in a log just around the corner. As he reached for it, a shot rang out and whizzed past his shoulder. He sprang back around the burning corner of the barn. Daniella realized she'd dropped her rifle in front of the house. She made a mad dash across the clearing. Another shot barely missed her feet. She reached her gun and threw herself against the front of the house.

Where? Who? Why? she wondered frantically.

"Came from over yonder," Tucker shouted, pointing a gnarly finger toward the northeast.

Daniella's mouth went dry and her heart clapped like racing hooves on hard ground. They were pinned down good. Any move they made could be seen for miles because of the fire, while whoever was shooting remained hidden in darkness. And the boys were trapped in the burning barn. She could hear them coughing and choking and pounding on the door.

By God, she wasn't about to let them burn alive in there! "Get ready to grab the axe, Tucker! I'll cover you."

Tucker gave a sharp nod and pushed up the sleeves of his faded red undershirt. "Let's do it, girlie!"

Daniella darted from the end of the house and fired in the direction Tucker had pointed while he grabbed the axe. Thank God and Mr. Spencer for her repeating rifle. She followed Tucker back around to the front of the barn where they were out of the line of fire.

While flames licked hungrily up the dry, weathered walls and crawled across the roof, Tucker hacked away at the brace holding the boys trapped inside the inferno. By the time the brace gave way, the hinged side of the door was in flames. The latch was so hot he had to use the axe to release it.

From inside, the boys threw themselves at the door and it crashed open. Tears of relief washed clean streaks down Daniella's soot-covered cheeks.

An instant later, as Daniella and Tucker helped the choking, gasping boys away from the barn, the roof caved in with a tremendous crash and roar. A wall of flame shot high into the sky and danced there for long seconds before collapsing down upon itself.

When Travis rode in the next afternoon Daniella swore under her breath. At least this time he'd waited until she'd gotten some sleep.

He reined the buckskin to a halt and leaned down on the saddle horn while staring at the charred remains of the barn. Little tendrils of smoke still rose from a few smoldering piles of rubble. A muscle in his jaw ticked as his eyes narrowed. "Son of a bitch," he said through clenched teeth.

When his gaze shifted and settled on Daniella, she braced herself for further outburst. She didn't have long to wait.

He swung down from the saddle, dropped his reins to the

ground, and started toward her. She turned her back on him, not willing to cope with his obvious anger. What did he have to be angry about? It was *her* barn, damn it.

An instant later Travis grabbed her arm and jerked her around to face him. When his voice came, it was rough and hard, and it shook with barely checked fury. "Damn you, Dani. If you'd listened to me and let me put a guard at the mouth of the valley this wouldn't have happened. We might have even caught the bastard."

She yanked her arm free of his grasp, vaguely aware that his anger and his harsh grip hadn't frightened her. It was something to think about, perhaps when she had more time. But right now he needed to be set back on his heels.

"For your information, Mr. Know-It-All Colton, your guard at the entrance would have been useless. Whoever set fire to the barn came and went from the hills," she said, nodding toward the northeast.

Travis's brown eyes narrowed even more. "How do you know?"

"Because that's where the shots came from."

Daniella closed her eyes and thought, *Damn you, Tucker, keep your big mouth shut.*

"Shots?" The coldness of Travis's voice sent chills of dread racing down her arms.

She ignored the feeling and glared at him. "Yes, shots."

"That cuts it. You're not staying here. You've got five minutes to get your things together."

She shook her head. "I'm not going anywhere with you."

"You're coming home with me if I have to drag you kicking and screaming all the way."

"Over my dead body," she hissed. "If you think for one minute I'll stay in your house and watch you drape yourself all over that—" She clamped her mouth shut. Her eyes popped open wide. *What have I said?*

The brown slits of Travis's eyes slowly opened to reveal dancing gold highlights. He threw his head back and roared with laughter. When he could speak again, he said, "Is *that* why you left the ranch?"

Mortified, the heat in her face nearly suffocating her, she pretended ignorance. "I don't know what you're talking about."

His grin was disgusting. "You're jealous."

"I most certainly am not," she said, recovering her composure. "You have to like somebody to be jealous. And right now I don't like you, Colton, not one little bit. You and your know-it-all attitude aren't welcome here, so just go home where you belong. We don't need you or your help."

"I think you do," he said softly, his grin fading away.

"Well you're wrong."

Travis stared at her a minute, then glanced away. "All right, I'll leave. But I'm sending some men back to stand watch over this place."

"They won't be welcome."

"And they'll stay until we catch whoever's setting these fires, or until you come to your senses and come home with me. It's not safe here, Dani. I only want to keep you safe."

A few minutes later she watched him ride out. A dozen different emotions swamped her, the most prevalent of which was disappointment. He hadn't kissed her.

Next came confusion, although there was nothing new in that. She'd been confused since the day she met Travis Colton.

Even with Tucker, Simon, and the boys around her, she felt an overwhelming sense of loneliness press against her. The child in her womb chose that moment to make its presence known. It was the first time she'd felt it move. The reminder of its existence—as if she needed a reminder—was enough to make her want to crawl into a hole and hide.

Pure stubbornness kept her on her feet.

That afternoon Daniella watched as Benito and Carlos rode through El Valle and took up positions in the hills north and south of the house. So. Travis had done it. She had no doubt their younger brother, Jorge, was at the main entrance to the valley.

She felt trapped—trapped by Travis and his men, and by

whoever was trying to burn her out of her home. It had to be Crane, she was sure of it. She'd run him out of the valley and stolen Shanta and Chee out from under his nose. From his view, he had reason enough to hate her, and that meant whoever stayed at El Valle with her was in danger. She tried again to think of a way out, a way to protect everyone on the ranch and save what was left of her reputation.

Since the stage line no longer came through Tucson, she didn't see how she could get to Boston. She didn't know the territory she'd have to cross to the north to find the stage, and she didn't know the Apache tribes that roamed there. As much as she wanted to be relieved of the burden of her child, she wasn't willing to die trying.

Travis's offer of help till the baby came was unacceptable. Aside from the fact that she'd have to watch Travis and Carmen together and suffer their sympathy and pity, no one on the Triple C would take the child and raise it. The child would be much better off with someone other than herself. She'd never be able to give it the love every child deserves.

That left only one place where she had any hope of giving the child to someone else to raise, and it would also serve another purpose.

At supper that evening, she told Tucker and Simon she was taking Chee and Shanta home.

"When?" Tucker asked.

"We'll leave as soon as it's full dark. The boys will have to ride Butch and Ben. That'll leave you two with just the mules."

"We ain't goin' nowheres anyhow. How long you gonna be gone?"

The look in Tucker's eyes told her he had a good idea what she was planning, so there was no use in denying it. "If they'll have me, I'll be staying several months."

"If they'll have ya," Tucker said with a snort.

"I think you and Simon should take the money from my . . . father . . . and go stay in town until I get back."

"What the devil'd we wanna do that for?"

"Because until we get rid of whoever's trying to get rid of

us, it's too dangerous to stay here. Simon and the boys were nearly killed last night, and you were shot at. I don't know who we're up against, but it's me he's after. I won't have either of you hurt because of me."

She and Tucker argued for several more minutes, with Simon looking more distressed with each word, before Tucker relented.

"All right, dangit," he said. "We'll go to town. You jist be careful on the trail, ya hear?"

Daniella reached over and squeezed his hand, making him blush from the top of his beard to the roots of his thinning hair. "Thank you, Tucker. It'll ease my mind knowing you and Simon are safe. When I come back we'll rebuild the barn and start over."

Tucker lowered his gaze to his plate. "We'll rebuild the barn."

Simon reached across the table and grabbed Daniella's sleeve. He shook his head vigorously, not wanting her to go.

"I'm sorry, Simon. I have to go. It's just until . . ." She couldn't even say the words, and ended by waving her hand in front of her stomach. Simon blushed and ducked his head.

"Then what?" Tucker demanded.

"Then I'll come home."

"Alone?"

Daniella watched Chee and Shanta struggling with the forks she'd insisted they learn to use and ignored the feeling that she would be betraying a helpless child, *her* child, abandoning it. Her voice hardened with determination. "Yes. Alone."

A few hours later, Daniella, Chee, and Shanta slipped out of the valley under the cover of darkness. They took a seldom used game trail that led to the stream separating El Valle from the Triple C, the place where she'd told Travis and Matt good-bye that day. No one would cross the Triple C to get to her valley—they wouldn't dare—so she knew Carlos would be stationed farther east in the hills.

She was right; they went quietly, undetected, and headed

southeast. When they reached Cochise's summer stronghold high in the pine-covered mountains five days later, Daniella was ready to drop from exhaustion.

After so many silent days on the trail, the sudden wave of sound that crashed over them when they burst into the clearing was a shock. An old yellow dog greeted them first. It darted from beneath a bush and nipped at Blaze's heels. The mare kicked out and the dog gave a yelp, tucked its tail between its legs, and lit for cover.

Five nearly naked toddlers sat playing in the dirt beside the second wickiup. As Daniella and her two companions rode near, first one child then another raised his head and stared, until they all gaped at the riders. One youngster jumped up and ran around the wickiup toward the front shouting, "*Shimá! Shimá! Shuh!*" Mother! Mother! Look!

The woman came out. Her eyes widened upon spotting Woman of Magic. When she saw who rode with her, she shouted. Others came at her cry. As Daniella, Chee, and Shanta rode through camp a joyous procession formed behind them. Women left their chores, and men and children left their games to welcome home two they'd thought were lost to them forever.

By the time they reached the center of camp, the riders were forced to stop by the crowd of people around them.

Cochise came forward and greeted the newcomers, then gave his usual frown at Daniella's breeches and shook his head. But when he put his hands on her waist to lift her from the saddle, the welcoming warmth in his eyes turned to confusion, then stunned amazement.

"*¡Tu es encinta!*"

Daniella felt her face heat up unbearably as the eyes of the crowd all turned to her as one. She felt the stares drill into her abdomen and wanted to crawl off like some wounded animal and hide. Just beyond Cochise, Loco caught her gaze and grinned. A chill ran down her spine.

Cochise lifted her to the ground and the attention was drawn from her—thank God—when Shanta and Chee started telling how they'd been captured by the big white

220

man with hair the color of flames, then saved by Woman of Magic and her friends.

An impromptu celebration broke out. Songs were sung around the campfires of the Chúk'ánéné of how Woman of Magic, with the help of the Yellow Hair and the Crazy Old One, saved the two boys from the enemy. It was past dark before Daniella was able to slip into the empty wickiup Travis had slept in when they had come for Matt.

Loco followed her and stood outside her door. She knew he was there, but refused to acknowledge him. He would not enter without permission—that sort of thing was not done among Apaches—so she ignored his calls. After a few minutes Cochise came and sent him away, then asked for admittance.

Daniella closed her eyes and took a deep breath. She'd seen him staring at her protruding stomach all afternoon and evening. Him and everyone else. Knowing it would do no good to put him off, she called for him to enter.

As was his way, it took Cochise nearly a half hour of small talk to get to the point. "You are with child. Have you taken a husband?"

When he mentioned her condition, Daniella lowered her eyes and studied the turned-up tab at the toe of his moccasin. His second sentence, however, brought her gaze up to his with a jerk. "A what?"

Before he could answer, Dee-O-Det called for admittance. Grateful for the interruption, she ignored Cochise's scowl and invited the *shaman* within.

When the old man was seated, Cochise said, "She is with child. I have just asked her if she has taken a husband yet."

Dee-O-Det grinned. "Of course she is with child."

Daniella frowned. Cochise clenched his fists. "You knew she was with child?"

"Naturally," the old man said as if he'd just been asked if he knew his own name. "It is what a *shaman* is for, to know these things. I also know she has not taken a husband. When would she have time to even think over such a serious matter, when she's been so busy rescuing everyone else's

221

children? Now that she has returned to us, we can settle the matter. Take her to Nali-Kay-deya's wickiup and stay there with her until I come for you. Do not permit yourselves any visitors."

Daniella tensed. What was he cooking up? Whatever it was, she didn't think she wanted any part of it. "I don't need a husband."

"Of course you do," Cochise said emphatically. "I have heard that among your people an unmarried woman who has a child is looked upon with scorn. It is the same with our people. We will do as Dee-O-Det says. Come."

Dee-O-Det placed a gnarled hand on her shoulder and smiled at her. "Do not worry, child. I have seen your future, and it is a good one. You will be happy with what comes to pass."

Giving her no chance to protest or question, Cochise took Daniella gently but firmly by the arm and led her to Nali-Kay-deya's wickiup, as Dee-O-Det instructed. Kay, as Daniella called her, was one of Cochise's two wives, and mother to Naiche, Cochise's youngest son.

Cochise refused to speak to Daniella about Dee-O-Det's plans. Instead, he rolled himself in his blanket and went to sleep next to his wife. Across from Daniella, she saw that Naiche, too, was asleep.

But even as exhausted as she was by the grueling trip to the stronghold, Daniella could not sleep. Fear of her nightmares was so strong that she never fell asleep in the dark any more, even when she tried. Because the mountain night was cold, she spent the dark hours until dawn feeding small sticks to the fire. As the sun came up, she was finally able to close her eyes.

Dee-O-Det left his chief and Woman of Magic and returned to his own fire within the ring of sacred stones surrounding his wickiup. There he studied the flames and listened to the wind as it whispered through the tops of the pine trees, waiting for the answer to his question. As the *diyini*, or "holy one," the spiritual (and sometimes the physical) well-being of the band depended on him. Woman of Magic's future would directly affect that of the band. Of this Dee-O-Det was certain.

In less than an hour, he knew. Yellow Hair, the white man called Colton, would come for the girl. Dee-O-Det knew what Yúúsń had planned, but the girl was stubborn and afraid, and others among the band had their own ideas of what her future should hold. For things to turn out right, Dee-O-Det knew his timing must be perfect.

Just before dawn, the *shaman* sent his young apprentice to watch the trail. The old man waited inside his wickiup, not wishing to talk with anyone for the time. It was nearly noon before his apprentice came secretly, as instructed, with the news that the Yellow Hair had just passed *t'iis nasitaa*, the leaning cottonwood. Dee-O-Det smiled and gave the young man further instructions.

Dozens of voices outside the wickiup woke Daniella when the sun shone directly down the smoke hole above her. Cochise sat in his place of honor across from the doorway on his bed of furs. His eyes were fixed on the halter he was braiding from strips of rawhide. Nali-Kay-deya and Naiche were gone.

Daniella had scarcely sat up when Dee-O-Det's voice rang strong and clear from outside, calling for Cochise and Woman of Magic to come out. Daniella opened her mouth to speak, but Cochise motioned her to silence and led her through the doorway.

She blinked at the bright midday light and shaded her eyes with one hand. What were all these people doing here? What was going on? When the crowd to her left parted, she saw Loco approaching, leading five mustangs. He kept his eyes from hers as he walked to her side and tethered the horses in front of the wickiup. He then walked about ten feet away and turned back toward her, standing there, feet spread, arms folded across his sturdy, bronze chest, a grin

223

playing about the corners of his wide mouth. Daniella had the sudden urge to seek the relative shelter of the wickiup.

At a shout from her right, she turned and saw the people open up another corridor, this time for Golthlay, who also led five horses. Daniella's heart knocked against her ribs. He must have stayed behind when Mon-ache rode out. If she'd known Golthlay was here, she might have waited to bring the boys home.

When he'd tied his horses on the other side of the door-way, Daniella glanced nervously at Cochise, who stood expressionless beside her, then at Dee-O-Det. The *shaman* winked at her!

She was still puzzling over that when two men she didn't know came forward, one from Loco, one from Golthlay. Stunned beyond speech, Daniella listened through the sudden buzzing in her ears as each man, acting as an official go-between, offered Cochise the five horses as a bride gift and asked for Woman of Magic in marriage for the man who sent him.

The buzzing in her ears lessened as Cochise turned to her. "Well, daughter? Which man will you choose as husband?"

"You can't be serious!"

"I am serious," Cochise snapped. "You cannot raise the child alone. Who will provide for you? You must have a husband. You will not leave here until you are married."

Daniella was stunned. He was serious! He actually expected her to marry one of those . . . those . . .

For one brief moment she was nearly overwhelmed by fear. In the next instant she shoved it aside and straightened her shoulders. All Cochise was asking—no, telling—her to do was marry. Well, she wouldn't do it. It was out of the question.

Chapter Twenty-one

"She did *what?*" Travis bellowed.

"Like I said—"

"No." Travis raised a hand to stop Tucker from repeating himself. "I heard you. Damn her! What the hell was she thinking, setting off alone like that with those boys? What the hell were *you* thinking to let her?"

"I suppose you could have stopped her?"

The laughter in Tucker's voice set Travis to grinding his teeth in frustration. "When did she leave?"

"Last night, just before midnight."

"Damn her. Why didn't you go with her? Now she'll have to ride back alone."

"Did I say she was comin' back?"

Travis felt his skin turn cold. "What do you mean?" he said with a growl. "Don't play games with me, Tucker. This is Dani we're talking about. Of course she's coming back." He wished he was as sure as he sounded.

"You're right," Tucker agreed with a nod. "She'll be back. As soon as the kid is born and she finds a family to raise it."

"What?"

Tucker opened his mouth, but Travis cut him off with an enraged snarl. In utter frustration and nearly choking on his own anger, Travis spun and rammed his fist against the wooden post supporting the thatched roof of the porch. Grass and dirt filtered down on his head and shoulders.

When he turned back around, massaging his bruised knuckles, Tucker had gone into the house. The old man

225

came out a moment later carrying a canvass bag and a bed-roll.

"What's that for?"

"For you," Tucker said calmly.

Travis frowned. "What for?"

Tucker spoke as if explaining something to a dimwitted child. "So when you ride after the girl, you'll have food and blankets."

For the first time in what felt like weeks, Travis threw back his head and laughed.

Tucker agreed to send Jorge back to the Triple C with word that Travis was going after Daniella.

"By the way," the old man said, "she thinks me and Simon are stayin' in town till she gets back. I wouldn't wanna be the one to tell her otherwise, if I was you."

Travis grinned and nodded. In less than five minutes after Tucker brought out the sack and bedroll, Travis was on his way.

She was less than a day ahead of him, and he intended to catch up with her by tomorrow or the next day. He found her trail easily—she'd made no attempt to cover it—and smiled to himself. He'd have that stubborn little baggage within reach soon. After all, she was five months pregnant. How fast could she travel, anyway?

Pretty damn fast, he thought grimly, days later when he knew he'd been spotted by Cochise's trail guards. He'd be at the stronghold in a couple of hours, and he'd never even caught sight of her. He knew he hadn't passed her or missed her, because he'd followed her tracks all the way.

Damn her. What was she trying to do, kill herself? He was half dead from exhaustion, and he wasn't a frail, pregnant woman having to worry about the safety of two young boys.

When he reached the edge of the *rancheria*, a young Apache greeted him, saying in halting Spanish that he was sent by Dee-O-Det, and Yellow Hair was to follow him. Another boy ran up to take Travis's horse, so he dismounted, remembering to unstrap his gunbelt and hang it over his saddle horn, and followed the *shaman's* messenger.

He would have thought the arrival of a white man would have caused a bit more notice, even if he had been here before. Yet the part of camp they walked through seemed deserted. Up ahead he heard voices, and then he saw a crowd had gathered.

Travis recognized Cochise's deep voice at once, but didn't catch the words, only the serious tone. Dee-O-Det's young helper led Travis around the edge of the crowd and up beside a wickiup. Travis didn't know what was going on, but Dani and Cochise and two strings of mustangs seemed to be the center of attention. Two men, one of whom was Golthlay, stood before them, and Dee-O-Det stood behind the two men.

The old *shaman's* gaze caught Travis's, and Dee-O-Det grinned at him. Travis would have stepped forward to make his presence known to Cochise and Dani, who had their backs to him, but Dani's word's in Spanish stopped him cold.

"I am sorry, but I cannot marry one of these men."

Cochise folded his arms over his chest. "Choosing to remain unwed is not one of your options, daughter. Tell me what is wrong with these men."

Travis couldn't believe this was happening. Cochise expected Dani to *marry* one of them! A shiver of rage ran through him. He would have spoken then, but Dee-O-Det had worked his way through the crowd to Travis's side. The old man grabbed his arm and shook his head. "Wait," he hissed.

"They are both fine, strong warriors, in need of a wife," Cochise was saying. "Mexicans killed Golthlay's wife many winters ago. Loco, too is without a wife. She took his son and daughter and left him after, well, for reasons which you know. To either man, you would be an only wife, at least for a while. They are good men, and would treat you with honor and provide well for you."

"Honor. Ha." Dani scoffed. "I can't believe you would even listen to Loco's offer, after what he did to me. We all know that's why his wife left him. He only wants me so people will stop laughing at him."

The two prospective grooms had moved closer. Loco bristled under her insult and glowered his anger at her. Golthlay chuckled.

"What are you laughing at?" Daniella demanded of Golthlay. "We both know why you offered for me. You don't want a wife. You want revenge because I beat you at your own game."

Dani faced Cochise once more. "I will not choose to tie myself to one of these men. If you choose for me and force me to marry one of them, then his death or mine will be on your head, for I swear to you, before the wedding night is over I will slit his throat, if he doesn't kill me first."

Cochise glowered at her. "I tell you, you must take a husband! If these two who have offered for you are not to your liking, then name another. I well send for him and see you married. Your child must have a father. And do not tell me your white father will help you, because I will not have it. Any man who would turn away his own daughter for something that was not her fault shall have nothing to do with my grandchild."

Daniella tried to stifle her anger, for she knew harsh words would get her nowhere. "*Shitaa,* you saved my life, and my mind. I love and honor you for that. Please believe I mean no offense when I say I could never live with the Chúk'ánéné every day for the rest of my life. I like my bed up off the ground, and a solid roof and walls around me that don't leak when it rains. I'm too soft and spoiled to be happy living any other way."

"Then choose one of your own kind. I do not care, so long as you marry a good provider who is strong, and who will take your child as his own."

"There is no need to find a father for the child." Loco stepped forward until he was a mere three feet away.

228

Daniella's first urge was to step back, but she forced herself to be still.

"Part of the child is mine, and I will take the whole."

Daniella knew he referred to the Apaches' belief that a child was made one part at a time. To make a whole child, a couple must mate many times. Even their word for bastard, *yúútatske'*, meant "many fathered." They believed that each man who'd raped her had sired part of her child.

Her stomach contracted, threatening to send its bile up her throat. She swallowed heavily as her mouth filled with saliva. She turned to Cochise and muttered, *"Shishxéná!* If he says another word, I shall kill him!"

With a flick of his wrist, Cochise sent Loco back to the edge of the circle. To Daniella, the chief said again, "Then choose one of your own kind."

"Shitaa, that's just not possible," Daniella claimed. "My people will never accept this child, just as they don't accept me. My child will be a half-breed bastard, and to white men, I'm just an Apache whore—a *puta!* No man wants a whore for his wife."

Someone grabbed her from behind, and a harsh voice sounded in her ear—in English. "Stop it! Don't say things like that about yourself!"

"Travis!" Daniella felt her knees turn to water. If Travis hadn't been holding her arm so tightly she would have fallen. A strange sense of relief flooded her at the sight of him.

But that was ridiculous, she told herself. His presence would only complicate her predicament. "What are you doing here?"

"Did you think I wouldn't come? Did you think I'd just let you ride off like that and not come after you? What the hell is going on here, anyway?"

She gave a short, bitter bark of laughter. "It seems everyone's decided the whore needs a husband."

"That's enough!" His fingers dug painfully into her arm. The look in his eyes was enough to kill.

Daniella tossed her head in defiance. "Well, it's true!" she cried.

"It's not." His grip on her arm tightened. You're nobody's whore. I won't have you even thinking it."

"Español, por favor," Dee-O-Det drawled. This was what he'd been waiting for. He restrained a grin, barely, when Travis addressed Cochise in Spanish.

"They each offered you five horses?"

"Sí."

"I'll make it ten horses, plus ten head of cattle."

"Travis, no!" Daniella shrieked.

"I accept. *Nzhú*. It is good."

"It is not good. *I* don't accept."

"Yes you do," Travis said calmly. "I'm your only logical choice."

"Travis, be serious!" Daniella switched to English. "Just stay out of this. I can outwait him. In a few days he'll give up and leave me alone."

"No he won't. You know that. Besides, I happen to agree with him. I think you need a husband."

"Well I don't!" It was time to end this farce. She switched to Spanish. "I did not come here to find a husband for myself or a father for my child. I came to find a couple willing to raise this child as their own, because I don't intend to raise it at all."

Stunned silence greeted her statement. She knew what she proposed was unheard of among the Chidikáágu'. Children were so valuable to them that if a couple could not have any, they stole one from an enemy and raised it as their own. It was the only way the tribe could survive. And here she was, trying to give her child away. No wonder Cochise and Dee-O-Det were looking at her as if she'd grown another head.

Dee-O-Det uttered a strangled cry, then shouted, "No! It cannot be allowed!"

Daniella had known the old man might disapprove, might even be shocked and angered, but she hadn't counted on his outright interference. She'd come this far; she wasn't about to give up now.

"You would have this child raised by a woman who will hate the sight of it?" she cried. "For I swear, every time I look at it, I will be reminded it was conceived in violence and hatred, and I will soon grow to hate the child, through no fault of its own."

"But you are wrong, my child," Dee-O-Det cried. "This child you carry is not from any violence or hatred."

"What are you talking about?" she demanded. "There is not a person here who does not know what happened to me that night. And if you think I've been with any—"

"No! That is not what I meant. Hear me, Woman of Magic, and listen to my words. The burden in your womb was not placed there by angry, drunken warriors. When they finished with you and dragged you to the base of the sacred pine, no seed had taken root. It was the bolt of lightning from the Thunder People at the right hand of Yúúsń that set seed to fertile ground. The same bolt that placed the streak of white in your hair to mark you as Woman of Magic. You do not carry one child from being violated. You carry two, both from the hand of Yúúsń, and both children, a girl and a boy, will wear the mark of Yúúsń's favor, just as you do."

The people standing around were as speechless as Daniella. Loco clenched his fists and scowled, while Travis held his tongue.

"It's impossible!" Daniella cried. "Things like that just don't happen, and you know it."

"Ah," the old man said. "But it *has* happened. All was set in motion a hundred winters ago when Yúúsń planted the sacred pine in our winter stronghold, where no other pine trees can grow. It is Yúúsń's will, and no mortal can change what will come to pass, not even Woman of Magic."

Daniella could see how sincerely Dee-O-Det believed his own words. She glanced at Cochise and saw that he, too, believed. Perhaps this was her way out. "If what you say is true, and my child—children—are so special, then I am right to come and leave them with you. Surely the Chúk'ánéné do not want the children of Yúúsń to be raised by a white woman. I will stay among the Chúk'ánéné until the birth, and leave the children with you."

The *shaman* started shaking his head before she'd even finished. "It cannot be. All will be lost if Woman of Magic does not raise her own children. It is your magic that will make them special. The boy and girl will grow to be an important link between your people and ours in years to come."

Great! Now I'm supposed to give in and agree to raise half-breed twins because of the old man's superstition. If it really is twins.

"Yúúsń does not make mistakes. Surely Woman of Magic is not so cold and unfeeling as to cast aside her own flesh and blood, the way the rancher she called 'father' cast her aside. Surely she is not such a monster."

Daniella flinched as though she'd been slapped. She battled the tears that formed in her eyes and fought the memories that flooded her mind. Memories of her father's total rejection of her.

Oh, God! Am I like him? Willing to throw away my own children because of some sort of stupid, misplaced pride? Because I fear what others might say about me?

No! She was not like Howard Blackwood! She wouldn't be!

At that precise moment she felt a feather light stroke on her abdomen. She gasped. It was from the inside! The child—or children—in her womb moved gently beneath her breast, and she knew, as if from a voice inside her heart, that she couldn't abandon her own flesh and blood. Dear Lord, she couldn't.

Travis looked over her head at Dee-O-Det for some kind of sign. He had it an instant later when the old man smiled and nodded at him.

"Dani?" Travis said softly. He turned her by the shoulder and placed his hand beneath her chin, forcing her to look at

232

him. Her pale blue eyes swam with tears she tried to blink away. "Marry me, Dani," he said in English.

She stared at him blankly for a moment, then stepped away with a gasp. "Just because I may have changed my mind about giving up my child doesn't mean I'll marry you. I can't marry you, Travis."

"Why not? I'm willing." He looked deeply into eyes the color of the morning sky. Oh yes—he was definitely willing.

"I can't be your wife, Travis. I can't be any man's wife," she cried.

"If you're talking about what happened the night of the fiesta, forget it. We'll work it out."

"What do you mean, work it out? How can we work out something like that? Getting married isn't going to magically make my fears go away, or my nightmares."

"We just take things one step at a time, Dani. I've got a hold of your arm right now, and you haven't even batted an eye. When we first met, you'd have panicked and probably shot me if I'd grabbed you like this. It just takes time, that's all." He eased his grip and massaged her arm with his fingers. "I'll give you all the time you need, I promise. I won't push you to do anything you're not ready for. I want you. Sometimes I want you so much I ache. But I'd never try to force you, you know that. I might try to persuade you," he said with a crooked grin. "But I'll never force you. Let's just get married and let everything else work itself out."

Daniella searched his face intently, trying to reason out why he was doing this. Then she remembered his words. *There's not a thing in the world I wouldn't do for you.*

"Travis, look," she said. "I know you think you owe me something for helping you get Matt back. But whatever you may have owed me you more than paid back when I got shot. I can't let you do this out of gratitude. It wouldn't be fair. It's all too one-sided."

"Why is it one-sided?"

"Because I get everything! I get a husband, a . . . a protector, a beautiful home full of loving people, and a name

233

and a father for my child. You get nothing."

"Nothing? Oh, no. I'll tell you what I get. I get a beautiful woman to grace my home, a friend to talk with, a wife and the child she carries, a mother for my son, a lover some day, and maybe even more children. What man could ask for more?"

Daniella couldn't believe he was actually saying these things. It would be so easy to give in, to say yes, to marry him. She found herself wanting it so much it hurt. But she had to make him realize it would never work. She shook her head.

"I'll tell you what you really get," she said. "You get a wife who's looked on as a whore by nearly every white man in the territory. A wife who either paces the floor all night or wakes the whole house with her screams. A wife who's afraid to let you touch her. In a few months, you get a half-breed Apache bastard—maybe two—who'll grow up calling you Daddy."

"Like I said before, I'm willing. Anyway, you really don't have much choice, do you?"

Daniella swallowed hard. It was tempting. So tempting. It would be so easy to stop fighting him, stop fighting herself, and just give in. So tempting. To go home with him to the Triple C, to all those friendly people. . . .

She swallowed again. "I think you've forgotten something."

"What's that?"

"Carmen."

"What about her?"

"That's my question."

A smile played about the corners of his mouth. "Jealous?"

"Don't be ridiculous," she snapped. "I can see certain advantages to the situation, from your point of view. A wife who can't . . . you know, and a mistress who not only can, but will. What I can't see is why you'd want to bother with me at all. Why not just marry Carmen?"

Travis's smile grew until he laughed outright. He ran a

234

knuckle across her cheek, sending hot shivers down her spine. Then he sobered. "Whatever there once was between Carmen and me ended months ago, Dani. Before Matt and I left for New Orleans last fall."

"I think someone forgot to tell Carmen that."

Travis shrugged. "It's not that I haven't told her—more than once—it's just that she doesn't listen."

Daniella dropped her gaze from his deep brown eyes. So far he hadn't said anything to reassure her where Carmen was concerned.

"Look at me, Dani." He waited until she did. "I know you saw me with her the morning after the fiesta, but—"

"It doesn't matter, Travis," she lied, shaking her head.

"It does matter, if it makes you think I care about her. For the record, I wasn't the one doing the kissing, she was. She draped herself all over me, clung to me, and no—before you ask—I didn't like it."

Curious, Daniella asked, "You don't like women who cling to you?"

He grinned slightly. "Not when my mind is on someone a little more independent."

"Never mind." What had made her ask that, anyway? She shook her head and looked away. "It doesn't matter who was kissing who. Even if I were your wife in name only, I wouldn't want to share my husband with another woman. That's not exactly fair, and I know it. But that's the way I'd feel."

With a cupped hand, Travis turned her head back around and smiled. "I'm glad you'd feel that way. You might have to share me with my son, my father, and the ranch, but believe me, not with Carmen or any other woman. The only reason she's even still around is because she doesn't have anyplace else to go. She sent out letters a few weeks ago to try to locate relatives. As soon as she hears from them she'll be gone. Until then, I can't see myself just kicking her out."

Daniella studied his earnest expression. Did she dare trust him in this? Was it true he didn't care for Carmen, that she'd be leaving soon?

"Travis, I—"

"¡*Basta!*" Cochise cried. "Enough! *Habla español.* Do you accept his offer?"

"I—" She looked from Cochise to Travis. What should she do? Was it wrong to want something so much? Would Travis be able to rid himself of Carmen and rid Daniella of her fears? Did she want him to? Or would he end up hating her? "I—"

"She does," Travis said firmly.

"*Bueno.*" Cochise nodded.

Dee-O-Det let out the breath he'd been holding and allowed a smile to spread across his wrinkled old face. "*Taeh! Gutál nt'aa,*" he shouted. "There is to be a ceremony. Tonight at the central campfire Woman of Magic will be joined to Yellow Hair Colton. *Nzhú.* It is good."

Chapter Twenty-two

Daniella lowered herself to a fallen tree trunk, then heaved a sigh. Normally she enjoyed the quiet, fragrant peacefulness of the forest. Today she didn't even notice it. Instead of breathing deeply of the pine-scented air or listening to the breeze that sounded like a roar in the needled tops of the pines, she stared blankly at a shiny-backed beetle making its way across the mountains and valleys of decaying leaves and needles near her foot.

She needed this time alone in the forest to come to terms with what she was about to do.

Coward, she thought. *Tell him. Tell them all you can't marry him.* But she knew she wouldn't. She'd keep her mouth shut and go through with it, then pray for a miracle. It would take at least a miracle to keep Travis from growing to hate her, and to keep her from running off screaming into the night when he grew tired of being patient.

But Travis had been right that day at El Valle when he said she'd need help when her time came. It would be doubly true if Dee-O-Det was right and she did carry twins.

That was the practical reason for marrying him. She had other reasons, less practical, more emotional. Reasons she was afraid to examine.

So for now she would go along with everyone else's wishes. She would marry Travis and live at the Triple C. After the birth, when she was more able to cope, well, by then he'd probably be only too glad to see the last of her. She could go home to Tucker and Simon.

Lord, she was tired. She shouldn't have ridden so hard to get the boys home. The poor babe in her womb was probably regretting being placed in a woman who had no care for its comfort.

Daniella straightened abruptly. It was the first time she'd thought of the child with anything other than scorn.

My child.

She still wasn't overjoyed at the prospect. She didn't share Dee-O-Det's belief. She knew exactly how she'd gotten this way, and it wasn't from any damn bolt of lightning. But maybe if she concentrated on Dee-O-Det's story, she could at least keep herself from hating her own flesh and blood.

God, help me, please.

Behind her a twig snapped. She slumped. Someone was coming. Probably Travis. She wasn't going to be given enough time to sort things out in her mind.

She braced her hands against the log, but before she could rise, a hand came around her head and clamped itself over her mouth. In the brief glance she got, she knew instantly it was not Travis's hand. It was much too dark, and it was scarred. She closed her eyes and shivered as she pictured that scar. It was in the shape of a bite mark. A human bite mark. Hers.

In an instant she was thrust back in time, back to *that* night. Dark hands throwing her to the ground. Dark hands tearing at her clothes. A dark hand covering her mouth. She could still taste the blood as she remembered sinking her teeth into that hand with all the strength her jaws could command.

That memory triggered a fear so strong it threatened to rob her of her sanity. When she began to struggle, a deep voice hissed Spanish words in her ear.

"Be still, and I will not harm you. Struggle, and you will die, very slowly."

She nodded her head slightly that she understood, and the hand came away from her mouth. Her attacker stepped

238

over the log she was seated on and turned. A violent trembling seized her when Loco faced her. He was one of them, from that night last winter. She could never forget that big lumpy nose and those small beady eyes. His thin lips twisted in a grimace of hatred. Quicker than a snake, his hand flashed out and struck her across the face.

She clutched the log desperately with one hand to keep from falling over backwards. The other hand flew to her throbbing cheek. When she steadied herself, she felt her lip carefully and her fingers came away with a smear of blood. Loco stood glaring at her with black eyes full of hatred.

Her fear fell away as an avalanche of anger rolled over her. She pushed herself up and faced him boldly, fully realizing he could kill her at any moment. That thought, too, made her angry . . . That she was at the mercy of this bastard only fueled the fire in her blood.

"Why has no one cut off your nose?" Loco demanded. "That is what our people do to whores!"

"You dare to call me names, you bastard? Why have you followed me? What do you want?"

"I want what you stole from me."

"I've stolen nothing from you. Now get out of my way." Daniella made as if to brush him aside and walk away. Loco grabbed her by the hair. A knife magically appeared in his free hand. She stumbled and fell, and he yanked her up by her hair. In addition to the pain in her scalp, the sudden movement caused a wrenching pain deep in her abdomen. She screamed.

Loco ignored her. "After that night we took you, my wife left me. You know that." He gave her hair another painful tug. "She took my son and daughter and all her belongings and left me because of you. She made me the laughing stock of this band. It is all your fault."

He tugged her closer, so close his breath nearly gagged her. "I thought you could replace her," he said, practically growling in her face. "I offered for you, and what did you

239

do? You threw my offer back in my face! You laughed at me! You chose a white man over me! Again I am laughed at—because of you!" There was a feral gleam in his eyes. His lips drew back in a grimace.

Was it her imagination, or were his teeth really pointed like a wolf's?

He thrust his scarred hand before her eyes. "You left your mark on me. Now I will leave mine on you. You will pay for what you have done to me."

In the face of his threat, Daniella's anger fled and her fear rose rapidly. The knife, held in his scarred hand, flashed before her eyes. Her knees buckled. He held her off the ground by her hair.

Just when she expected to feel the cold steel cut into her nose, she was jerked sideways, and his hand released her hair. She fell to the ground in a haze of pain and fear. She tried to scramble away, but was halted by the log. She lay on her side, her back against the log, and gaped in astonishment as Travis and Loco circled each other warily.

She blinked, and over the roaring in her ears she heard voices and shouts through the trees. Cochise and Dee-O-Det stood to one side of the small clearing, with Golthlay behind them. It looked like everyone who'd been witness to the marriage offers was coming to circle the clearing.

Her attention swung back to the two before her just as Loco lunged and swung his knife in an arc, barely missing Travis's ribs as Travis jumped back.

"This is not your concern, white man," the Apache warned, his breathing already heavy. Both men stood crouched, arms outstretched. It was then Daniella realized Travis was unarmed. His hands were empty! "The bitch is mine to deal with. If you interfere, you will die."

"She is mine! You're the one who will die for touching her." As he spoke, Travis reached a hand toward Hal-Say. The man who had adopted Matt passed him a knife.

Daniella bit back a cry of alarm. She couldn't distract

240

Travis now, but she was terrified. She'd heard stories of Loco's fighting skills. He was invincible in battle. Her eyes pleaded with Cochise. He shook his head and motioned for her to keep quiet. Daniella swallowed nervously and tasted fear. Not for herself, but for Travis. *Dear God! Somebody stop this!*

Travis didn't take his eyes from his opponent when he asked, "Are you all right, Dani?"

"Travis, don't do this! He'll kill you!" she cried.

Loco lunged for Travis again and missed. Travis's knife flashed out. A streak of blood appeared on Loco's arm. Travis smiled grimly. "Does that mean you care, Dani?" he asked without looking at her.

Fear clogged her throat and prevented her from answering when Loco leaped into the air toward Travis. She struggled to sit up as the two men rolled on the ground, each fighting to gain the upper hand. More blood appeared, this time on both men, as knives flashed and each man grunted with the effort of his struggle.

When he regained his feet, Travis knew he was up against a skilled opponent. He had no energy to waste on useless emotions—regret over not imprisoning Dani in his home when he'd had her there, fear for her safety during the last few days, and murderous rage at this son of a bitch who'd threatened her.

He'd seen Dani walk off alone and decided to give her some time to herself. Her whole world was spinning out of control. He didn't blame her for being bitter and upset, even frightened.

He'd worked his way toward the edge of camp, intending to wait for her. Cochise and the old *shaman* stuck to him like a tick on a hound, saying he wasn't allowed to be alone with her until after the ceremony.

Then he'd heard her scream. When he'd rushed through the woods and found her with a knife in her face he'd nearly died on the spot with fear. An instant later he was swept with the most violent rage he'd ever known.

Travis knew Loco was one of the men who had raped Dani. That knowledge shone deep within the black eyes that glared their hatred at him as the two men again circled each other. A moment later Loco taunted him with it.

"She had no right to choose you, white man. Even if you've already had her in your blankets, I had her first."

Travis knew what the bastard was doing. He was trying to rile him into making a stupid move, into rushing him. But even knowing that, it took all his willpower to let the words slide away and concentrate on the business at hand.

The Apache didn't let up. "Did you hear me, white man? I had her before you. I had her before any man. I remember the feeling of tearing into her virgin flesh. That is something you'll never have from her, because it is mine! I took her maidenhood! Me! Loco!"

"And you will die for it." Travis feinted right, then dodged left and opened up another slit in the Apache's hide, this one across the ribs. Loco's blade flashed and drew a long red line down Travis's forearm, then he lashed out with a foot and caught Travis behind the knee. Travis hit the ground with a solid *thud*, his breath gone, then rolled quickly, causing Loco to miss him entirely and land face down on the ground.

Before Loco could move, Travis rolled again and landed on the man's back, with a knee placed firmly against Loco's kidney. Loco heaved, trying to unseat the white man from his back. Travis grabbed a handful of long, black hair and yanked, raising Loco's head from the ground. Then he slammed the man's face into the dirt. The satisfying *crunch* told him the Apache's nose was broken.

Loco managed to brace himself with one knee and dislodge Travis, but before he could strike, Travis rose onto his knees and swung his fist, landing it directly in what used to be Loco's nose. The Apache fell back, striking his head on the base of a tree. He was out cold.

Travis dropped to all fours and hung his head low between his shoulders, trying to catch his breath. When he thought he could stand, he struggled to his feet and staggered toward Dani, who still crouched on the ground against the log. He dropped to his knees again before her.

Tears streamed down Daniella's face; she didn't care. Her wide eyes roamed over every inch of him, searching out his wounds. With each one she located, a sob shook her. Blood oozed from dozens of tiny nicks and scratches, and at least a half-dozen larger cuts. Because of her. He was bleeding because of her.

She had watched him fight for his life, for her life and her honor. While she'd watched, a realization came over her. Her hatred and fear of Loco and the others who had attacked her suddenly paled before her feelings for Travis. What would she do if anything ever happened to him? How could she go on? To live without his tender touch, his gentle, warm eyes, his soft lips, his strength, his sense of humor, seemed too horrible and barren to even contemplate. Each time Loco's knife found its mark, she felt as if it had struck her. When Travis bled, she grew weaker.

She loved him!

It didn't matter that he didn't return her feelings. It was enough that he not be killed. And if he still wanted to marry her and take her home, she vowed she'd find some way to make up for all the trouble and pain she'd caused him.

She looked up at him and wept harder at his injuries. A movement behind him caught the corner of her eye. She went rigid with shock. Loco was up and moving, lunging for Travis's back!

Travis saw her eyes lock on something over his shoulder. Her look of alarm was all the warning he needed, but even then, he was almost too late. He thrust her aside and came to his feet, turning and raising his knife as he rose. His other hand swung out, knocking Loco's knife sideways. The

243

blade grazed his shoulder, but missed his neck, where it was aimed.

Loco roared with rage and flung himself at Travis. The shock of impact knocked Travis to the ground, Loco going down on top of him.

Daniella screamed in horror, watching Loco land on top of Travis. But the duel was over. In his desperate effort to rid himself of his foe, the Apache had thrust himself directly onto Travis's knife.

Travis rolled Loco's body over. Daniella stared, aghast at the sight of the knife protruding from the dead man's chest. Tears of relief poured down her cheeks, and she longed to reach for Travis, to be enveloped in his arms and rest her head on his chest. The look on his face held her still.

He stared at Loco's body with contempt, but when he turned his eyes on her, his expression did not change. Daniella struggled to her feet as Travis got up, but he did not lend a hand to help her. A sob clogged her throat. She took a step back, putting more distance between them, her eyes wide with pain and dismay at his obvious contempt for her.

All the rumors around the territory about her, the names people called her, her pregnancy, the streak in her hair, he'd accepted all that with a calm that had amazed her. Now she understood. None of those things had really sunk in for him. Until now. Now he'd been face to face with a man he knew had raped her. She read the knowledge in his eyes. Now it was all real to him.

When he met her gaze over the dead body of her attacker, Travis saw the look of horror and dread fill her eyes. He had heard her scream, had seen the Apache threatening her with a knife, and now she acted horrified that the man was dead. *Damn.* Would he ever understand her? What had she expected? That he would tap the man on the shoulder and politely ask him to leave her alone? Goddamn! She was his! That bastard had treated her like she was a common whore!

When Travis bent to retrieve the knife Hal-Say had lent

him, Daniella closed her eyes briefly and took a deep breath to help control her tears. Now that she finally realized how much he meant to her, it was too late. He wouldn't marry her now. He would leave her here with Cochise. Or maybe, if she asked him, he would take her home. But she would never be able to bring herself to ask him for anything. He'd done enough for her—more than any other man would have. She had no right to expect more.

Daniella turned to go, but as she took her first step, Travis grabbed her none too gently by the shoulder and turned her around.

"Oh no you don't," he said, his breath still coming in harsh gasps. With the bloody knife still gripped tightly in his other hand, he led Daniella to where Cochise and Dee-O-Det stood, keeping himself between her and the sprawling corpse that was, even now, being carried away by three men.

"We'll be married *now*," he said, his tone daring anyone to disagree.

Cochise and Dee-O-Det looked at one another for a moment, then nodded.

"Give her to the women so they may prepare her. The ceremony will take place in two hours."

"No." The fingers grasping her shoulder tightened. "I'm not letting her out of my sight for even a minute. You see what happens. She can't stay out of trouble long enough to bat an eye. We'll be married *now*."

Again Cochise and Dee-O-Det looked at each other, and again they nodded.

"Follow me," Dee-O-Det said.

The old *shaman* didn't waste any time. He led them back through the forest to the center of camp, where he had them wait, Daniella in her breeches and Travis covered with blood. While Dee-O-Det walked away, saying he'd be right back, Cochise's two wives forcibly dragged Daniella from Travis's side and into Nali-Kay-deya's wickiup.

"You cannot be wed dressed as you are," Kay scolded. "You will shame Cochise."

"As well as yourself and your husband," Tesal-Bestinay added.

Ignoring her protests, the two women stripped her in seconds. When Kay unrolled the clothing she intended Daniella to wear, Daniella gasped. The soft yellow buckskin skirt and poncho-style blouse were covered with exquisite beadwork and hundreds of metal bugle beads that gave off a soft tinkling sound with every movement. Long fringe decorated every edge of the garments.

The matching moccasins, or *kébans,* bore strips of beadwork and reached nearly to her knees. When Daniella was dressed, the distinctive tabs on the toes poked out from beneath the fringe of the skirt. The two women draped her neck in yards and yards of tiny black beads, half of which hugged her throat, the other half hanging down to rest against her breasts.

The softness of the clothing against her bare skin sent heated yearnings to her very core, shaming her, scaring her with their intensity. When she stepped out of the wickiup, Travis's eyes lit with appreciation.

Was that a drumbeat pounding in her ears, or the sound of her own heart?

By the time her trembling legs carried her to Travis's side, Dee-O-Det was back. He nodded his approval at her clothing. He positioned himself on the opposite side of his sacred ceremonial log from them, then began a chant, keeping time with the sacred spirit rattles, he pulled from a leather pouch at his waist. Suddenly he quieted, pulled out a silver ceremonial knife, and held it high.

All sound seemed to stop. The dogs stopped barking; the people stopped talking; the wind in the trees quieted; the birds fell silent, waiting; even the usual gurgling of the nearby stream sounded subdued to Daniella's dazed mind.

From out of nowhere Dee-O-Det produced a long wand

tipped with pine needles. He moved it in an arc above the couple's heads, and *tádídíń,* the sacred pollen of the tule, fell down on them. Travis sneezed. Dee-O-Det was startled out of his somber mood long enough to grin.

Sobering quickly, Dee-O-Det knelt before Daniella and Travis and motioned for their hands. He swiftly made a small cut on Daniella's right wrist and Travis's left, then wrapped their bleeding wrists together with sacred binding.

"You have two bodies," the *shaman* said. "But now only one blood. You are one." He pulled the binding from their wrists with a flourish. *"Nzhú!"*

It was done. They were married.

With the *shaman's* shrill cry of victory, an explosion of sound hit Daniella's ears. Dogs yapped, children shrieked, adults cheered. Birds resumed their calls, crickets their chirps. Cochise's deep voice rumbled in his chest as he congratulated Travis. The wind in the pines resumed its gentle roar. The stream gurgled. Things seemed back to normal.

But they weren't. She was married. Dear God, what had she done?

Before she could gather her scattered wits, she found herself stooping to enter the empty wickiup where Cochise and Dee-O-Det had found her that first night back in camp.

First night? It was last night. How could her entire life have changed so drastically in one short day?

She stared around blankly and slowly realized the wickiup was no longer empty. Cochise's wives had been busy. To one side was a bed of grass. Daniella recognized the blanket from her bedroll spread over it. The one folded at the foot of the bed must be Travis's.

A small pile of firewood rested opposite the bed. Next to it was a pitch-covered water basket, a gourd cup, her saddle and Travis's, her clothes, their weapons, saddlebags, bridles, and horse blankets.

And behind her, just inside the doorway, stood Travis Colton. *Her husband.*

247

As if her thoughts brought him to life, he stepped around her and crossed toward the bed. "I realize it's not the usual thing for a bridegroom to fall asleep right after the wedding," he said with a crooked little smile as he sat on her blanket. "But then the wedding itself was a bit unusual, wasn't it?"

While he talked his fingers worked the buttons of his shirt free and Daniella once again became aware of the blood. *His* blood, spilled for her. At the same time she realized he was taking his shirt off, she also realized much of the blood had dried and the cloth was stuck to a dozen different cuts.

"No!" she cried.

But she was too late. Just as she cried out, he yanked the shirt from his body and started a fresh flow of blood.

Travis winced, feeling his skin tear with the tug of his shirt. When Dani cried out, he stiffened. Did she think he was undressing for the wedding night? That he was getting ready to attack her? "No what?" he bit out. Damn, he'd promised, hadn't he? She didn't trust him. But then, with the hardness in his loins growing by the minute, he wasn't sure he trusted himself.

"You idiot," she said. "You just reopened half your wounds, pulling your shirt off like that."

He wanted to cry with relief. Her eyes had lost that dull glaze that had come over them during the fight. They were filled with life now, and, he thought, biting back a grin, irritation. Her face was animated. Her whole body, in fact, as she posed there with feet spread and hands on hips. Every movement made her dress jingle. He wanted to jump up and grab her and kiss her, or better yet, drag her down to the blanket. But that would send her running for sure. Bad idea.

"How else am I supposed to get this rag off?" he asked, forcing the laughter from his voice.

Daniella rolled her eyes and shook her head. *Men,* she thought. "I could have soaked it off in a few minutes and

248

you wouldn't have started bleeding again. Give me that." She grabbed the shirt from his hands. The only part that wasn't bloody was the back, but it was covered with dirt. The tail was clean, so she tore it off.

That would have to do to bandage the worst cut, the one on his forearm. She still needed something to clean him with and found a dirt-free spot along the upper back and shoulders. She tore it off and discarded the rest of the shirt. After wetting the rag in the water basket, she knelt next to him on the blanket.

"If you're tired, lie down. This is going to take a while." She was a little surprised when he complied without a word. He lay there, stretched out before her, bare and bloody from the waist up. Remembering the last time she'd touched his bare chest, tending another wound that was directly her fault, as were these new ones, she was grateful this time when he closed his eyes.

She wiped gently at the smear of blood on his cheek. It must have come from his hands because his face wasn't cut, thank God. One scar on that ruggedly handsome cheek was enough.

After wiping the smear away, she bathed the rest of his face and neck. His eyelids twitched once, but didn't open. His lips flexed when she ran the damp rag over them. She remembered the feel of those lips on hers. Soft, yet firm. Gentle and teasing at first, then full and forceful. Demanding. Her hand shook.

It was a relief to leave his face and tackle the cuts and scrapes on his arms and chest. The bleeding had stopped everywhere but on his forearm. She saved that gash for last and cleaned the rest of him as gently as she could, being careful not to soil her borrowed clothing.

Every place her fingers met his warm skin, the muscles beneath her touch quivered. It was unnerving, making a man's muscles quiver. His face looked relaxed, his eyes remained closed, so she tried to ignore the sensation. But something deep inside her responded to each of his muscle spasms with spasms of her own.

When she finally cleaned off his forearm, the gash didn't look as bad as she'd feared. At least, it didn't appear to need stitching. She took the salve from her saddlebag and smeared it on every cut and scratch, with special attention to his forearm.

She folded the severed tail of his shirt into a pad and placed it over the wound, but she didn't have any rags left to tie it in place. She laid his arm down gently, not wanting to disturb the slow, even rhythm of his breathing, and reached across him for the bandanna laying on top of her breeches and shirt. Just as she reached it, Travis sucked in his breath.

Daniella straightened abruptly. His eyes were open and staring at her chest.

He grinned slightly. "The beads are cold."

She wasn't sure why, but when she removed the necklace, her hands trembled. Without thinking, she also took off the short strands of beads encircling her throat.

"It's almost gone," he said.

Daniella's heart gave a thud and she dropped the bandanna at the unexpected sound of his deep voice. Her gaze flew to his face again to find his gaze had risen slightly. She swallowed and took a short breath. "What?"

Travis raised his injured arm and ran a single fingertip across the front of her neck, sending hot and cold shivers down her spine. "Your scar. It's almost gone."

She lowered her gaze from his face and removed his hand from her neck. She hadn't meant to let him see the scar. He had reminders enough of who and what she was without that. But she'd forgotten about the damned thing.

With her lips pressed tight, she repositioned the folded pad along his cut and wrapped her bandanna around it to keep it pressed tightly in place. "There."

As she turned away, she noticed one small nick she'd

missed just above his belt. When she picked up the wet rag she'd been using her hand trembled again. *One more touch,* she told herself. If she could make it through one more touch, she'd be finished. Then she could leave his side and maybe breathe again.

The wet cloth and the side of her little finger touched him and brought a sharp gasp from him which sucked in his stomach and made the muscles jump beneath her hand. Both his hands twitched. Her startled gaze flew to his face. His eyes were closed again, but his jaw was tense.

"Did I hurt you?"

He cleared his throat, but his voice still rasped when he said, "No."

"I'm almost finished."

So am I, Travis thought. Lord, if she touched him again it was going to be all too apparent just how close to being *finished* he was.

She touched him again, this time with salve on her finger. He forced himself to relax and recall the first time he'd witnessed Dani having a nightmare. That picture alone was enough to cool the fire in his blood. This time.

Lord, what had he got himself into? How was he going to be near her day after day and keep his hands off? Impossible as the task seemed, he knew he had to somehow keep his promise not to rush her. It was the only way he'd ever gain her trust.

"I want to thank you for what you did for me today. I was in a tight spot, and you got me out of it."

Travis smiled, his eyes still closed. "Don't mention it."

"I have to mention it," she went on. "I want you to know how much I appreciate it. The balance has tipped the other way, and now I owe you. I'm not sure how I'll ever repay the favor."

Travis opened one eye, then the other. She had something on her mind, and he had a feeling he wasn't going to like whatever it was.

"I don't want you to feel like you're bound to me in any way," she said. "No one outside this camp knows what's happened. Maybe it's best if we keep it that way. I promise I won't cause you any trouble or make any claims on you."

Frowning, Travis raised up on one elbow. "What are you talking about?"

"I'm talking about forgetting this ever happened."

"You mean the ceremony? You mean when we leave here, you go your way and I'll go mine? Is that what you mean?"

She nodded, not meeting his eyes. "Yes."

"Not on your life, woman." She looked at him then, startled. "As far as I'm concerned, you and I are man and wife."

"Don't be ridiculous, Travis. You don't have to—"

"Maybe I don't have to, but you do. You think Cochise won't hear about it if you stay at El Valle while I live at the Triple C?" He snorted and lay back down. "He'd hear about it within a week and you know it. Besides, he'll be coming to pick out his horses and cattle this fall. Then you'll be right back where you were. No, Dani. We're married, you and I, and I intend to see we stay that way."

"But why, Travis? I don't understand why you did it in the first place, much less why you'd want to stay married to me."

He'd been anticipating that question. No lie would do, but neither could he bring himself to tell her the complete truth. She wasn't ready for that yet. It would be a long time before she would be at ease enough to accept his feelings for her. So he settled for other, lesser truths. Mainly because he wasn't quite sure what the real truth was.

"Partly because you needed me to marry you. Because Cochise expected it. I think Dee-O-Det knew all along what was going to happen. But mostly I did it because I wanted to."

Bemusement filled her mind as Daniella studied this man, her husband. Did he want a mistress for his home and

252

a mother for Matt so badly he would marry someone like her? That didn't make any sense.

"Go ahead and say what's on your mind," Travis said.

"What's on my mind," she answered slowly, "is how much I fear you're going to regret this."

"I won't regret it, Dani. Especially if you try a little, and meet me halfway. Now stop worrying, and trust me."

That's easy for you to say, husband.

Travis sat up and pulled off his boots, then held out his hand to her. "Come on. Get some sleep. You look as tired as I feel."

Daniella looked everywhere but at the hand he extended. Did he actually expect her to lie down next to him and *sleep?*

"Just sleep, Dani."

Her cheeks burned. Had he read her mind?

Still avoiding his gaze as well as his hand, she glanced at the crack around the buckskin door flap and heaved a sigh of relief. "No thanks," she said. "It's almost dark."

Travis dropped his hand. "What's that supposed to mean?"

"You know I don't sleep at night."

"Still? You slept all night on the trail a few times, as I remember."

"That was different."

"Yeah, I know. You slept with me."

"You can't compare then with now."

"No, I guess not," he answered. "Now we're married. Husbands and wives do that, you know—sleep together."

Husbands and wives did more than that. Daniella felt her nerves stretch taut. "This afternoon you promised—"

"I know what I promised," he interrupted. "And I intend to keep that promise. Until you tell me you're ready for more, bedtime is strictly for sleeping."

"Do you mean that?" she asked hesitantly, still unable to meet his gaze.

"Yes, I mean it. Dani, you can't go on catching snatches

253

of sleep every now and then. It's not good for you, it's not good for the babies. You need a full night's sleep, every night. I can't promise you won't ever have bad dreams again, but if you do, I'll be here, right beside you, with whatever help I can give. You've got to try, Dani."

On that, she knew he was right. If she didn't start getting a regular night's sleep soon, she'd go crazy. If she didn't collapse first.

Travis held out his hand again. "Trust me," he said softly. *Trust me.*

The words echoed in her head. She shouldn't have to work at trusting him. He had never given her any reason to doubt or fear him. She *didn't* fear him. She should be able to lie down with him, offer him what any bride would offer her husband on their wedding night.

She understood that while what happened between a man and wife was similar to what the warriors did to her, a caring husband would not hurt her, and would not press her too often to fulfill his needs. Travis would never resort to violence or cause her pain.

She should do it. She should tell him she was ready to be a real wife. He deserved that much from her.

When she tried to picture the act in her mind, she was surprised and grateful to realize she saw none of the terrible violence from before. Simply a man fulfilling his needs with his wife.

Then from nowhere a sudden heat rushed over her, tingling across her breasts and down her belly to settle between her thighs. What was happening to her? A craving emptiness spread from the heat. Dear Lord, the shame of it!

She turned abruptly away from Travis before he could see the wantonness in her eyes and grow disgusted with her.

"Dani," he said, clasping her arm.

Fire spread from his fingers to her flesh.

"Sleep, Dani. Let's start out the way we mean to go on. With you sleeping beside me at night."

Daniella took a deep breath. Already those shameful feelings were fading. Thank God.

Sleep, he said. Yes, she needed sleep. But God, if she woke up screaming just one more time, she was afraid she'd just keep screaming and screaming and screaming.

As tired as she was, she knew she'd probably fall asleep sometime during the night. At least Travis had already seen her at her worst.

Slowly, reluctantly, she started to take his hand. Bugle beads tinkled in the silence. "I can't lie down in this," she thought aloud.

Travis turned his back while she removed the borrowed clothes and donned her own dirty breeches and a clean shirt from her saddlebags.

When she approached the blanket where Travis lay, he once again held out his hand to her. Hesitantly, she took it and allowed him to pull her down next to him on the blanket. When she tugged to free her hand, he simply threaded his fingers through hers rather than let go.

She lay there next to him, her blanket beneath them, his at their feet. It would get cold during the night. She should have started a fire.

That was her last coherent thought. She never knew it when sleep and Travis Colton wrapped their arms around her.

Travis was dreaming. He knew it, yet didn't want to wake. The hot, throbbing dream had teased him many times since he'd met Dani. He relished it, for only in his dreams did she come so willingly into his arms. She felt so real, warm and vibrant against him, her lips soft and pliant. In his dream, she had no fear. She came to him eagerly, stunning him with her passionate response, making him so hard he hurt.

Real. She was so real. Nothing had ever felt so perfect as

255

her arms around his neck, the shape of her breast in his hand. He teased a nipple with his thumb. She gasped loudly in his ear.

Loudly?

Good God.

Travis tore his mouth from hers, appalled to find himself suddenly awake, looming over Dani. The dim moonlight drifting through the smoke hole was barely enough to see, but see he did.

No dream. Not this time. She was here, in his arms, her breathing as labored as his. She looked as stunned as he felt.

"Dani, I . . ." What could he say? She hadn't pushed him away yet. Was that a good sign? He swallowed. "Even in sleep, our bodies know what should happen between us."

Daniella stared up at his shadowed face . . . *our bodies know* . . . But her mind didn't. Her mind knew a dozen different fears, not the least of which was her body's reaction to Travis's touch. The tingling heat had started before she woke. How was she to stop it?

He loomed over her, the moonlight on the back of his head creating a silver halo effect. He was waiting for something from her. But what? What was she to do, to say, while his hand still cupped her breast. It felt good. Too good.

Then she realized something else. Of all the things she feared—saying or doing the wrong thing, feeling things she was sure good girls don't feel, being married to him, not being married to him, the mating act itself—she felt no fear of *him*. He hung over her in the dark, had total possession of her body; she lay helpless beneath him. Yet in her heart, and yes, her mind, she knew Travis would not hurt her.

So why was she hesitating? This was her chance to prove, to him and herself, that she could be his wife. *Our bodies know.*

With her heart thundering in her ears, she looked steadily at him and whispered, "Yes."

256

She felt him stiffen at her answer. "Yes?"

She whispered again, "Yes."

He didn't move, didn't seem to breathe. "Are you sure?"

Sure? Daniella couldn't remember the last time she'd been sure about anything. Even though she knew he would never deliberately cause her pain, she couldn't help the question that rushed from her lips. "Will it hurt?"

"No. God, no, Dani. I'd never hurt you."

She closed her eyes and prayed. "Then yes, I'm sure."

"You're not afraid?"

When she looked up at him, she couldn't help the nervous little smile on her lips. "Only a little, but not of you."

Still, Travis hesitated. "Please," she said. "I want to do this." *For you. I want to do it for you.* And for herself? No. For herself, she could live a lifetime without this physical joining. The heat, the yearning, the terrible restlessness generated by his nearness confused and frightened her. She didn't need it. Didn't want it.

But she knew no man would keep a wife who wouldn't mate with him. It was what wives were for. And if she knew nothing else, she knew she wanted to remain Travis Colton's wife. "Please."

Travis's heart raced. He hadn't meant to make her beg, but he hoped she was sure. The way he felt just then, he didn't know if he could pull away from her.

Her fingers moved through the hair at his nape, sending hot shivers racing down his spine. He was lost. He pressed himself against her thigh.

Her eyes widened. She stopped breathing.

"Easy," he whispered. God, he was ready to explode. *Slow down, slow down.* He brushed his lips across hers. "Easy. It's all right." At least, he hoped it would be all right. He hoped he could control himself enough to keep from ripping her clothes off. He hoped he could go slowly enough to bring her pleasure. He hoped he wouldn't do anything to scare her, to bring back her nightmare.

So many hopes. All dependent on his fast-disappearing control over his desires. He reached for the top button of her shirt and found his hand trembling. He couldn't remember ever wanting a woman so much that he trembled with it. *Careful. Easy.*

But when he kissed her, it wasn't careful or easy. It was raw and deep and filled with months of yearning, of wanting and not being able to touch.

Lord, how was he going to keep from scaring her? He was scaring himself.

He tried to ease the kiss, but deepened it, instead. When he finished the buttons on her shirt, he pushed the fabric aside and raised his head. Her skin gleamed pale and creamy in the darkness. The dark centers of her breasts pointed at him, taunting him, daring him.

"Beautiful," he whispered. "So beautiful." He bent his head and touched his tongue to one sweet nipple.

Daniella gasped and arched from the ground. Fire and lightning shot from his tongue through her breast, and gathered between her legs. She lost herself to Travis and his magic.

Her breast filled and swelled. Her nipple tightened, begged. For what, she didn't know.

Then Travis took the aching peak into his mouth and suckled, and she knew. *This* was what she wanted.

Vaguely, she felt him unfasten and tug off her pants, but her senses were totally centered on what his mouth was doing to her breast. At her other breast, she felt his hard, calloused hand. Then the hand drifted lower, over the mound of her belly.

The mere reminder of her child-bearing state should have cooled the heat in her veins. That it didn't, scared her. How was she to control this terrible pressure building inside her?

Then his hand moved lower, lower. No! He couldn't touch her *there*. If he did, he would feel the embarrassing, shameful wetness she couldn't control. Desperately she clenched her thighs together. But when his knee nudged between hers, she couldn't help but accommodate him.

Lower, lower, went his hand, until he touched the very center of the frightening fire consuming her. His hard yet gentle fingers touched, explored, probed. Of their own accord, her hips began to rotate.

His mouth left her nipple. She moaned in protest. The cool night air prickled her moist flesh. Travis kissed his way across her chest to lavish equal attention on her other breast. His breath was hot against her sensitive skin.

"You taste so sweet," he whispered.

He made as if to leave her breast altogether.

"No," she gasped. She threaded her fingers through his soft hair and held his head in place.

She was torn between the fire caused by his mouth at her breast and that from his hand between her legs. The pressure inside her built to a nearly unbearable level. How much more could she stand?

Then he moved and lay between her legs. He took his hand away. She whimpered. His mouth left her breast. She moaned, suddenly too weak to hold him there.

"It's all right," he whispered.

All right? How could it be all right? She was dying.

When his mouth took hers again, a tremendous heat pressed between her legs. Daniella stiffened. This was it. He was going to do it. If she closed her eyes now, would she see Travis, or her nightmarish tormentors?

She kept her eyes wide open.

And then he was pressing into her, slowly, purposely, steadily. God, it was . . . it was like nothing she'd ever imagined. He filled her completely. There was no pain. Only heat, and so much more pressure, more pleasure, she knew she would soon explode.

Helplessly, she closed her eyes. A wide, dark chasm waited for her. She could feel herself slipping toward it, being pushed, led, by each thrust of Travis's hot, hard flesh.

The chasm awaiting terrified her. When would Travis finish? Would he stop before she exploded from these frightening feelings? Before she slipped off the edge of reality and into that terrifying darkness?

It was too much. The heat. The pressure. The restless, empty yearning. And yes, the heart-pounding excitement. The profound, tingling pleasure.

This wasn't right, wasn't normal. She shouldn't be feeling these things. Suddenly from out of that dark chasm loomed her father's accusing eyes. Eyes that screamed, *whore!*

"No!" More terrified than she'd been on the night of her attack, she opened her eyes and pushed against Travis's shoulders with all her strength.

Chapter Twenty-three

Travis, his eyes closed to better savor the exquisite feel of Dani's silken depths, felt the change in her almost at once. At first he thought she was with him, frantically seeking that same pinnacle of pleasure toward which he now raced. But when he opened his eyes and saw her face, stark and drawn with sheer terror, he cursed himself.

She pushed against his chest and lunged beneath him. That one thrust of her hips sent him over the edge to a violent climax.

Daniella knew she was crying, but couldn't help it. She'd been so close to that deep, black chasm, so close to shooting off over the edge. Too close.

When Travis stiffened and shuddered above her, within her, she knew it was over, but still she could not stop the tears. She turned her head away so that as he braced himself above her — how odd, his arms were trembling — he wouldn't see her tears.

When his harsh breathing slowed, he withdrew from her trembling flesh and rolled to his side. Even as she sagged with relief that he was finished with her, she nearly cried out in protest at the raw, throbbing emptiness he left in his wake.

Travis lay beside her, feeling as if her silent tears were being ripped from his soul. "I'm sorry, Dani."

She didn't respond.

God, how could he have done this to her? He'd given his word not to rush her. He was a fool. A greedy fool.

And a tired one, too. He'd ridden like the devil to reach the stronghold, then fought Loco. He'd left his life's blood in the soil, his life force deep inside Dani.

His last thought before falling into exhausted sleep came from out of nowhere. *You're not only a fool, but not much of a man, either. A real man satisfies his woman.*

Her tears should have been tears of pleasure. He knew they were not.

Daniella woke to the steady beat of a drum. It was barely light enough to see inside the wickiup. Something heavy pressed down on her shoulder, and the drumbeat quickened.

An instant later she realized it was no drumbeat, but a heartbeat thundering in her ear. Travis's heartbeat. The weight on her shoulder was the arm he had draped around her. And she found herself wrapped around his long, hard body like bark on a tree. One arm encircled his broad, hairy chest, her head lay nestled in the hollow of his shoulder, and—

She gasped and jerked her knee away from where it rested intimately over his private parts. His *hard* private parts.

She would have rolled away, but the arm around her back and over her shoulder held her firmly in place. The scratchy blanket covered them both.

"Let me go."

"Dani—"

"Please. Just let me go."

He didn't. "Look at me."

She couldn't.

"Dani." He cupped her cheek and turned her head to face him.

Involuntarily, her gaze travelled up his throat, over his beard-roughened jaw, to his eyes.

"Dani, I . . ." His Adam's apple bobbed on a swallow. His gaze fell from hers. "God, I'm sorry. I promised you time,

262

then rushed you into something you weren't ready for. I know after last night you have no reason to believe me, but I swear it won't happen again. Not until you convince me you're ready."

Daniella flushed. He blamed himself, when she was the one who had urged him on. She shook her head. "It wasn't your fault."

He met her gaze again. "I—"

"Let's just forget it, all right?" Forget it? What a stupid thing to say. She knew hell would have icicles before she forgot it.

She pushed away and sat up. That's when she finally remembered—she and Travis were both naked. With a gasp, she jerked the blanket up to her chin.

Her action left Travis totally, vividly exposed to her horrified gaze. She spun away from him, her cheeks on fire. "I'm sorry."

Travis watched her long hair slide down, hiding her pale skin and the three parallel scars across her back. With any other woman, he might have laughed at such a reaction to his naked arousal. But this wasn't any other woman. It was Dani. He swore under his breath.

Trust me, he'd said. Then he had proceeded to use her to satisfy his own needs. And had terrified her in the process. He had obviously brought back all her fears and nightmares. God, how could he have been so depraved?

He swore again and tugged on his pants. To her back, he asked, "Would you rather rest a day or two, or are you up to starting home today?"

Home. Daniella clutched the blanket tighter. Yes, she was ready to leave this place. Maybe once they reached open country she could forget those searing, shameful things she had felt when he touched her in the darkness. "I'm ready to go whenever you are."

"You're not too tired?"

"Why should I be tired?" she asked, turning away from him.

263

"By all rights, you should probably be dead. If I hadn't followed your tracks all the way here, I'd almost swear you flew from El Valle. I started out a half a day behind you and nearly rode Buck into the ground. I never got near you."

She shrugged. "I was in a hurry."

"Fine. We'll leave as soon as you're ready."

An instant later, she heard the hide flap over the doorway rustle. He was gone.

Now what happens? she wondered while she hurriedly dressed. Her attempt at being a real wife had failed miserably. He was surely disappointed. He'd said he was sorry. He blamed himself.

Yet she knew it wasn't his fault. She had asked for last night. Begged for it. It was her own frightening response that had ruined things. She had no idea what to do about it, other than keep out of his reach until she was certain those strange feelings wouldn't recur.

After braiding her hair, she tugged on her moccasins, gave her saddlebags a final check, and stepped out into the sunlight.

They were saddled up and on the trail within an hour. Travis led the way, with Daniella's two geldings, Butch and Ben, in tow; Daniella brought up the rear. She was glad to simply follow for a change. All that sleep last night—she wasn't used to that much sleep at one time—had left her groggy.

She'd been so tense and worried for so long, she hadn't permitted herself to feel tired. She'd simply ignored the exhaustion, the aches and pains of being in the saddle all day. But now that her body had nearly a full night's rest, it seemed determined to make up for lost time. It was letting her know it would no longer be ignored. She kept dozing off in the saddle.

She couldn't remember the last time she was so tired. Staying in the saddle soon became a real chore, until she wasn't sure how much longer she could do it. And if her sheer fatigue wasn't enough, the burden in her womb was also making itself felt. Daniella was being kicked and poked and prodded from the inside. After about an hour it stopped. Then her troubles really began.

She was ready to swear Dee-O-Det was wrong. There had to be more than two babes in there, and they were all sitting on each other in a pile, directly on top of her bladder. She was forced to stop frequently to relieve herself.

Travis made no comment about her frequent stops, for which she was grateful. She was slowing them down, she knew, but she couldn't help it. He waited on the trail for her each time, never leaving her behind, never complaining.

Each time she got on and off her horse was harder than the last. It took a real effort to pull herself into the saddle. Her arms trembled with weakness and her legs were nearly numb, not to mention the unaccustomed soreness from last night's—no. She wouldn't think of last night.

By the time they stopped for the night she was far beyond uncomfortable, past fatigue. She was incapable of thought or movement. When Travis lifted her to the ground, her legs wouldn't hold her, and she started to collapse. He caught her to him and lifted her effortlessly in his arms. He cursed under his breath, then out loud.

"Goddamn. Why didn't you tell me you were about to collapse? Are you trying to kill yourself, along with these babies?"

Daniella forced her eyes open and peered up at his furious face, but was too exhausted to even speak. She tried, but all that came out was a low moan. Travis muttered another curse, then laid her down on the ground so he could set up camp.

As he looked down at the dark circles beneath Dani's eyes, he sharply berated himself for a fool. He should never have urged her to leave so soon. He should have stayed to let her rest longer, or left her there.

Her exhaustion shook him more than he cared to admit. He'd never seen Dani other than strong and alert, except on rare occasions. It was obvious she'd been pushing herself to the limit, and everything was catching up to her. Using her the way he had last night hadn't helped. If he wasn't careful, this trip would kill her.

He spread out their bedrolls side by side, then placed her gently on the blanket and covered her. The sun was going down and the air was cooling. They were still in the mountains; it would be cold tonight. He built a fire.

He wasn't worried about attracting attention this close to Cochise's *rancheria*. No one but Apaches would be anywhere near, so they were safe for tonight.

With a frown, he watched the tiny flames come to life. What a strange thought. He and his family and everyone he knew had been fighting Apaches on and off for years. But now, if the Chiricahua were near, he knew he was safe.

Because of Dani.

When the fire was going strong, he heated up a chunk of the venison one of Cochise's wives had given them this morning, then woke Dani. Well, he didn't actually *wake* her. He sat her up and forced her to eat.

Daniella wasn't even aware of her surroundings. She chewed when Travis told her to chew, swallowed when Travis told her to swallow. At least, she thought it was Travis.

Her mind hazily questioned how it was possible for a person to eat and sleep at the same time, but she wasted no great amount of energy trying to figure it out.

When her head kept drooping until her chin rested on her chest, Travis laid her back down and stared at her thoughtfully. The front of her shirt moved. He reached out a hand and gently stroked her rounded stomach. Beneath his touch, the babes quieted.

What was he to do? He wanted to take her home, but if she was this exhausted after only one day, she'd never survive the four or five days their slow pace would require to get them home. But they could be back with Cochise by this time tomorrow night. Could he do that? Take her back there and leave her until he could return for her?

The very thought of going home without her was too

bleak to even consider. If he wasn't able to come back for her any time soon, she might very well be past the ability to travel at all until after the babies were born. *Damn.* He wanted her children born in his house. In his bed.

The notion startled him. He'd been aware for some time that he had strong feelings for Dani. They were mixed up feelings, and he hadn't yet sorted them all out. There was gratitude, of course, for getting Matt back, but there were other feelings. He wanted to protect her, to make sure no one or nothing ever hurt her again. After last night, he realized *he* was one of the things he must protect her from. How was he to do that, without letting her go?

He wanted to share things with her, ordinary, everyday things. There'd been dozens of times since they'd brought Matt home when Travis would go about his daily chores and think, *If Dani saw this she'd smile,* or he'd sit down to dinner and wonder, *Does Dani like peaches?*

Then there were the times he lay in his bed at night, alone, and remembered the feel of her body next to his, the sweet, innocent taste of her lips, and knew without a doubt that he wanted her.

He wanted her beside him, day and night.

But what did his wants matter in the face of Dani's health?

Travis bitterly regretted kissing her the night of the fiesta. If he hadn't tried to rush her, she wouldn't have run off the way she did. He'd have been able to convince her to stay with him. She would have been safe at the Triple C instead of up at El Valle fighting fires and getting shot at. And she wouldn't have come to the mountains and nearly been killed by Loco.

If he hadn't been so foolish, so stubborn, so damned stupid that night of the fiesta, none of this would have happened at all, and Dani would be at home, in his bed, and by now he would at least be lying next to her, touching her.

Obviously he hadn't learned his lesson. Last night was proof of that. He had rushed her, pushed her. Used her.

Terrified her. And if he were honest with himself, he would admit what bothered him perhaps most—he hadn't satisfied her.

He wasn't sure he was ready for that much honesty.

Still, he wanted to hold her. How long would it be before she let him get that close again? If he took her back to Cochise, he might never get the chance to regain her trust.

Right now she was so exhausted, she wouldn't know if he touched her or not. He could lay beside her, hold her . . .

No. It wasn't right to take such unfair advantage.

Yet even as he told himself that, he knew what he was going to do. He lay down next to her and slipped his arm beneath her shoulders, turning her slightly until she rested against him.

She felt fragile, so fragile and precious. She felt as though the smallest movement might shatter her into a million pieces.

He ran his hand down her back and fingered her thick black and white braid. Pulling on it gently, he tilted her face up and placed a soft kiss on her lips. She sighed in her sleep and buried her face against his neck.

Travis lay awake for hours, savoring the feel of her in his arms. Whether he took her back to Cochise tomorrow or not, it could be months, or longer, before he had this pleasure again.

The sun was just coming up when Travis gently shook her awake. Daniella was groggy and disoriented, but the hot coffee he furnished helped clear her head. She mentally braced herself for another grueling day. A shudder of apprehension shook her at the sight of Travis's grim expression. He must be furious that she was slowing them down so much.

When they were ready to mount up, Travis stood and stared at her for a long moment, his expression forbidding. He closed his eyes briefly and seemed to come to some sort of decision, then lifted her carefully, almost gently, to her saddle.

Daniella made an effort to appear alert and energetic, but she failed miserably when she discovered she couldn't even keep her eyes open. The bright morning sun shot tiny daggers of fire directly into her brain. She had to close her eyes against the blinding glare.

But if the sun was in her eyes, that meant they were heading east! Home was west! Suddenly she had no trouble at all keeping her eyes open. She pulled up on the reins, bringing Blaze to an abrupt halt. "Why are we headed east?" she demanded.

Travis stopped his horse a half-length ahead of hers and kept his eyes trained on the trail. "I'm taking you back." His voice was emotionless. No, not emotionless. It was hard, cold—and it sent a shiver of apprehension down Daniella's spine.

"Back to Cochise?"

"Yes." He still didn't look at her.

In that moment Daniella's world came crashing down around her. He'd changed his mind. He didn't want her after all. Her emotions seesawed between hopeless despair and righteous anger. The anger won out. "No!" she cried.

This time he looked at her, in surprise. "What do you mean, no?"

"I mean simply that. No." She thrust out her chin. "I won't go."

"Look, Dani. I've thought it over—"

"You've thought it over? You've thought of nothing but yourself. You're always trying to tell me what to do. You told me to come home with you, but I didn't, so you came after me. Then you told me to marry you. Now you've changed your mind and decided you don't want me after all. Fine! After what happened when we—" Her cheeks stung something awful. "I don't blame you for not wanting me around."

She squared her shoulders and sat up straighter, deter-

269

mined not to cry. "But *I* decide where I'll go. Not you. I do have other options besides just you and Cochise. I can go to my own ranch. I won't go back to Cochise."

"You didn't let me finish," Travis said, a gentleness creeping into his voice. "I haven't changed my mind. I've never changed my mind about wanting you. But you'll never make it, Dani. You collapsed after just one day. You'll never last another four or five days on the trail. I *have* to take you back, for your sake. You've pushed yourself too hard for too long. You're not up to a trip like this."

Daniella looked deep into his eyes and was warmed by the genuine concern she saw there. He could just be using this as an excuse, but she didn't really believe that. She didn't want to believe it.

"If I jumped to conclusions and misunderstood, then I'm sorry, Travis. But I won't go back to Cochise. Yes, I was tired last night." She ignored his snort of exasperation at her obvious understatement. "And I'll probably be just as tired when we stop tonight. But I'd rather spend the next few days being tired and end up at home, yours or mine, than be left with Cochise. That is what you were planning, wasn't it? To leave me there?"

Travis sighed and looked away. "Only until you were rested and I could come back for you."

"And how long would that be? A week? A month? Or would you change your mind again and just leave me there?"

"No!" he objected. "You're my wife now."

Her heart thudded. He still wanted her? Even after—

"You belong in my home," he said firmly, interrupting her thoughts. "But if you try to make it all the way back now, you'll either lose the babies or kill yourself, and I won't let you do that."

"I won't go back to Cochise, and you can't make me."

She might as well have thrown a glove in his face as a formal challenge, for that was the effect of her declaration. Travis worried his horse around until he was beside her. Be-

270

fore she could prevent it, he pulled her from her saddle and planted her in front of him on his own mount. "I can."

Daniella wiggled and kicked her feet to get loose, but the buckskin was unaccustomed to such activity and reared in protest, nearly unseating both riders. Butch and Ben joined in the fray and jostled each other and tugged on the lead line, further upsetting Buck. Daniella threw her arms fearfully around Travis and hung on tightly.

Travis held her to him with one hand and tugged the reins with the other, trying to control the horse. He wanted to concentrate on the fact that Dani had just voluntarily put her arms around him, albeit in fear, but was instead forced to pay close attention to the struggle with his mount.

"Do that again," he said harshly, "and you might break both our necks."

"I'm sorry," she said, properly chastised. Then something flickered across her eyes. She tossed her head and glared at him. "Do you plan to carry me all the way there?" she asked peevishly.

Travis forced himself not to grin at such a welcome thought. It would satisfy his own craving to hold her, and if he behaved himself, might help her get used to his touch. He gave a decisive nod. "That's exactly what I intend to do."

"Please don't take me back there, Travis," Dani pleaded.

Travis thought he detected a note of fear in her voice. He studied her closely. "Are you worried that something like what happened with Loco will happen again? Are you afraid to go back?"

"And if I am?" Daniella looked down at her hands and twisted her fingers in agitation. The truth was, she was more afraid that Travis would not come back for her, but she couldn't tell him that. After the way she had behaved on their wedding night, he wouldn't understand. She should try to explain—just as soon as she figured it out for herself.

"If you're afraid," Travis said, "I'd tell you not to worry. Cochise won't let you out of his sight. Nothing like that could ever happen again. No one there would dare try to

271

hurt you."

Daniella realized they were moving, and they were still headed east. She couldn't let him take her back. "I feel it's only fair to warn you," she stated with a calm she didn't feel, "that as soon as you start for home, I'll follow. Don't worry, though," she added. "I won't force my company on you. I'll go to El Valle and we can do as I suggested, and pretend none of this ever happened. But I won't stay with Cochise."

Travis halted his horse again, this time in defeat. She was just stubborn enough to pull such a stunt. "Dani, be reasonable," he tried one last time. "The trip all the way home would be too hard on you right now. I know you don't believe me, but I really am only thinking of you."

"You be reasonable," she stated stubbornly. "The trip won't be any easier on me as I get larger. Unless, of course, you were planning on leaving me there until after I shed this burden, in which case I must remind you that then there will be two squalling babies to worry about. If that's what you're planning, then I can only assume you don't intend to come for me at all. I can't really say I blame you, though," she said quietly. "I did warn you this would happen, that you'd regret our marriage. But in any case, I'd rather be in my own home, with Tucker and Simon, than in the mountains with Cochise. Please, Travis."

Travis closed his eyes in frustration. She had voiced his own fear that their separation might be a long one if he took her back to Cochise. But she thought he was using her health as an excuse to be rid of her. She had no idea how wrong she was.

"All right," he sighed. "I'll take you home, but only under one condition."

"What's that?"

"That when you get tired, you tell me."

Daniella's shoulders slumped with relief, and she nodded in agreement. Travis turned her face up to his and looked at her sharply. "Promise?"

His face was so close she could feel his breath against her

272

cheek. His eyes were dark, captivating. "I promise," she whispered.

He studied her a moment longer, then wheeled his horse around and headed west. Blaze trailed along behind the other horses.

Daniella had won this battle, but she wasn't sure just what that meant. He was taking her home, but to whose home? His, or hers? That was one question she couldn't bring herself to ask. She'd be finding out soon enough. But she also wondered why he was still holding her.

"Aren't you going to stop and let me get on my own horse?"

"Are you uncomfortable?"

"A little," she admitted. A saddle horn was not the softest of seats.

Travis levered himself up and over the cantle, settling on the saddle skirt, leaving Daniella the seat of the saddle. He had one arm in front of her, pressed intimately across her breasts, and one arm supporting her back as he held the reins in both hands. He released one hand and pressed her head down on his shoulder. "Better?" he asked.

"Yes. But you surely don't intend to carry me all the way home. This can't be comfortable for you at all, and Buck will get tired with all this extra weight."

Travis chuckled. "My saddlebags weigh more than you do. Buck's fine. I'm fine. You just relax." Why hadn't he thought of this sooner? Now he could hold her in his arms for days.

"I'll relax, under one condition."

"What's that?" he asked with caution. What had she come up with now?

"That you promise to tell me when your arms get tired."

The soft, tender look in her eyes nearly took his breath away. A slight smile tugged at the corners of his mouth. "I promise."

She returned his smile, then snuggled—snuggled!—against his shoulder and went instantly to sleep. Travis vowed he'd hold her until his arms fell off before he would willingly let her go.

She slept several hours, and he savored every minute of holding her. But when she woke, she insisted on returning to her own horse. Reluctantly, he let her go.

Daniella breathed a sigh of relief. Waking in his arms had seemed natural, right. Then those hot, scary feelings had swept over her. She was learning from experience that the only way to stop them was to get away from Travis.

For the rest of the trip, she insisted on riding Blaze. She had to keep out of his reach or risk his discovery of her feelings. If he knew how he frightened her, there was no telling what he might do.

When they reached the last creek and Travis headed for El Valle rather than the Triple C, Daniella nearly choked on the tears she tried to hide. Had he seen her new fear of his touch, or were there other reasons—her reputation, her childbearing state, their disastrous wedding night—reasons that made him decide he didn't want her at the Triple C?

Daniella stared dully at Butch's rump—or was it Ben's?—and was scarcely aware when they reached her house. In the back of her mind she'd been hearing a hammering since they entered the valley, but it had stopped a moment ago.

Tucker's shout brought her eyes into focus, but she didn't believe what she saw: the raw skeleton of a new barn! "What the—"

She slid from Blaze's back and ran to meet Tucker and Simon. She hugged each one and laughed when they blushed. "What's going on around here? I thought you two were going to stay in town. Where did you manage to get all this lumber?"

"Whoa, girlie." Tucker caught her head in the crook of his elbow and laughed again. "One question at a time."

"Hold on there, Tucker," Travis called as he dismounted and came toward them. He grinned and said, "That's my wife you're manhandling."

Daniella's startled gaze flew to Travis. Why'd he have to

274

go and say that if he'd brought her here to leave her?

"Wife, you say! Well, I'll be damned. I don't believe it." Tucker hooted and threw his hat in the air while Simon grinned. "Not that I didn't think you was smart enough to know a good thing when you saw it," Tucker added to Travis. "But I sure never thought she was smart enough to go along with ya."

Daniella jabbed an elbow in Tucker's ribs. Travis laughed and said with a wink, "She didn't have much choice in the matter."

Then to Daniella he said, "Gather up what you need to see you through tonight and I'll send someone after the rest of your things tomorrow."

Stunned, Daniella stood and stared at him. He wasn't leaving her here! He actually meant to take her home as his wife. Despite—

In a daze, she walked to the house and opened the door to her room. But instead of gathering clothes, she sat on the edge of her bed and stared at the wall, trying to sort out her emotions.

On the trail she'd talked herself into believing she and Travis could never work out their problems—*her* problems. Yet her hope had never completely died. Then when he'd led her into the valley and she'd thought he meant to leave her here, she'd felt a kind of relief. Sure it was tinged with disappointment, but the relief was there as well.

Now she knew he meant to go through with it. To take her home and introduce her as his wife. How was she to face all those people at the Triple C? It was one thing to be treated warmly when she was a guest. Now that her role had changed, Jason and the others, with the possible exception of Matt, would be horrified that Travis had actually gone and married a woman like her. A woman who'd been with Apaches and now carried the proof before her for all to see. A woman who, in a few short months, would present her husband with a couple of half-breed Apache bastards. A woman who experienced the most shameful, frightening

275

feelings when her husband touched her.

Damn it, she wouldn't put herself through that hell, and she wouldn't let Travis put her through it either. What right did he have to send her emotions seesawing back and forth while she tried to guess what he really intended to do with her? Why should she leave any of this up to him? It was her life and her children they were dealing with.

She wouldn't do it. She wouldn't be his wife and hold herself up to the scorn she knew his family and friends would show her. She wouldn't subject herself to the terror she'd known when they mated. It would be bad enough to live through the next years on her own. It would be even worse to drag Travis down with her.

Travis stood in the doorway with his hat in his hand. "You're not packing. Are you feeling all right?" It was a sure sign of how troubled she was that she didn't even hear him enter the house.

"I can't do it, Travis."

He sauntered into the room and stood looming over her. "Do what?"

She took a deep breath and stared at his knees. "I can't go home with you and pretend to be the happy, blushing bride. It won't work."

"It *will* work, and you *will* go home with me. And I don't expect you to pretend anything. I just want you to be yourself. Now, unless you want me to pack for you, I suggest you hurry."

She started to argue, then stopped. Despite everything—even despite their wedding night—she still wanted to be his wife, share his life. She wanted what he was offering too badly to keep trying to talk him out of it. She walked to the battered wardrobe and selected two dresses and a nightgown.

"I've talked to Tucker and Simon," Travis said while she packed. "They'd like to stay on here unless you want to sell the place. I told them it was up to you and them."

Daniella nodded and stuffed her few belongings in her

carpetbag. She didn't want to sell the place. It would help to know she had some place to go if Travis changed his mind about her. But she couldn't expect Tucker and Simon to stay on for nothing, and she had no way to pay them.

Then an idea came to her. With a smile of determination, she found the leather pouch containing the deed to El Valle and added their names to hers, making the three of them equal partners.

When she showed the deed to Tucker and Simon, they refused to accept her offer. When they finally realized she was adamant, that she was dead set on having partners, they insisted that she own a full half, and they'd split the other half between them.

After finally giving in to their demands, Daniella let Travis help her mount, and the two of them rode out. She tried to clear her mind of what would happen when they reached the Triple C. The unpleasant possibilities were endless.

The next time she allowed herself to relax was hours later, in private.

The rocking chair made a slight creak every time it rocked forward, kept in motion by Daniella's toes pushing against the floor. The chair hadn't been in Travis's room before. Neither had the vanity, mirror and stool on the far wall, the extra wardrobe beside her, nor the dressing screen behind her. They had all been added since Travis had brought her home this evening and announced they were married.

Though she had tried not to think, she'd worried and fretted all the way from El Valle about how Travis would break the news of their marriage. When they'd ridden up to the house Matt had come running outside. Travis had dismounted and grinned. "Come say hello to your stepmother, Matt. Dani and I got married."

What a stir that had caused. A slight smile curved her lips when she remembered Matt's reaction. He'd gone wild

277

with joy. "No kidding?" the boy had shrieked.

Travis had laughed back at him. "No kidding."

"Hey, Grandad!" Jason was just coming out to see what all the fuss was about when Matt yelled. "I've got a new mom!"

Travis repeated the announcement for Jason. If she didn't know better, she would have sworn there was a touch of pride in Travis's voice at the time.

Jason had surprised her. She'd worried all the way from El Valle about his reaction to his son marrying a woman like her. He knew all about her and her unwanted pregnancy, yet when she'd dismounted, he'd given her a big hug and a kiss on the cheek and said, "Welcome home, daughter."

Then Travis had performed that ridiculous stunt of swinging her up in his arms and carrying her over the threshold. By then Rosita and the rest of the servants, as well as Carmen and her aunt, had come out front to see what all the commotion was about. Travis stopped right in the middle of the doorway, turned around so everyone could see, and planted a big, wet, noisy kiss on her lips. She remembered the heat of the blush that had stained her cheeks at the time. His boisterous laughter filled the air at her astonished look.

As his lips had neared hers, she'd seen Carmen's face go pale, then red with fury. Travis hadn't so much as looked at the woman. The thought occurred to Daniella that perhaps he was using her to rid himself of Carmen, or to make Carmen jealous.

The first was all right with Daniella. She wasn't sure what to think about Travis's explanation about his relationship with Carmen, but if Daniella was really going to be his wife, she'd just as soon Carmen wasn't around.

Would Travis use her like that?

Daniella frowned. Wasn't she, after all, using him? She'd used him to get out of a tight situation with Cochise, and was using him still to give a name to her children, so wasn't

278

he entitled to use her in return?

But what if her second guess was closer to the truth—that he was using Daniella to make Carmen jealous?

That was ridiculous. He surely wouldn't go to the trouble of marrying one woman just to make another jealous—unless he was planning on getting rid of his new wife somehow. If that were true, however, he wouldn't have introduced her as his wife in the first place. Their marriage probably wasn't legal anyway.

Then he'd plastered her with that kiss and blocked Carmen from her sight.

Daniella closed her eyes and remembered that kiss again. It had been expected by everyone, she realized. But Travis had made sure he delivered it in such a fashion that there was no way her fears could have been brought to the surface. It was the wettest, noisiest, sloppiest kiss possible. Almost like being licked in the face by a dog. A big dog.

She wished she'd changed clothes at El Valle, instead of meeting her new family in her trail-worn britches. At least she'd been able to change into a dress before dinner tonight. It was high-necked and long-sleeved, and concealed not only the evidence of her pregnancy, but also the scar on her neck.

Now she sat here, rocking, waiting, in Travis's bedroom—*their* bedroom. Waiting for him—her husband. Would he keep his word and not try to force her?

Maybe, she thought. Maybe for a little while. He hadn't tried anything, not even a kiss, since that one disastrous night in the mountains.

Maybe that was his way of getting her to come home with him. Maybe he'd change his mind now that they were home.

But no, that didn't make any sense. Whatever else he might be, Travis Colton was an honorable man.

As if thinking his name conjured him up, he entered the bedroom and closed the door behind him. "You're still up," he said with mild surprise. "You must be exhausted by now.

I thought you'd be asleep."

"No, I'm fine, really."

Travis unbuttoned the cuffs of his shirt and pulled his shirttail from his trousers.

Daniella's eyes flitted away from the disconcerting sight of him undressing. She cleared her throat. "Has everyone gone to bed?"

"Everyone but you and me." Travis held out his hand. "Come on. Let's go to bed."

Daniella tried to control the shudder of something other than fear that ran down her spine. If she'd been thinking straight, she'd have been in bed by now, pretending to be asleep. Now she'd have to get up, undress, and purposefully crawl into bed beside him. Damn! Why hadn't she gone to bed?

"Nothing's changed, Dani. The bed is for sleeping. Trust me," he said softly.

Lord help her, she did trust him. And that was the scariest thing of all.

Slowly, reluctantly, she took his hand and allowed him to help her out of the rocker. She went behind the dressing screen and found that someone, probably Juanita, had already laid out her nightgown. While she got ready for bed she heard Travis moving around the room. His boots hit the floor, one at a time, sounding unnaturally loud in the otherwise quiet room. She jumped at each sharp thud.

When she came from behind the screen, Travis was already in bed. The covers stopped at his waist, and his bare chest glared at her, threatening to destroy what little nerve she had left. Before she could change her mind, she slipped into bed, hovering as close to her own side as possible.

But Travis had other ideas. He turned down the wick on the lamp, plunging the room into darkness. When his hand reached across her waist, she squeaked with fright.

"It's all right. I just want you to come over here and sleep next to me. We wouldn't want you to fall out of bed in the middle of the night." He pulled her next to him until her

280

head rested on his shoulder. She lay stiff and unyielding beside him, knowing he must be able to hear her heart pounding in her chest.

"By the way," he said, his tone light and easy. "Tonight I made some arrangements for us I hope you'll approve of."

"Oh?" That was the best she could manage through her tight throat.

"Yeah. There's a wagon train due in Tucson any day now. Benito's going to ride out, try to find it, and see if they've got a preacher with them. Many wagon trains on the way to California do."

She frowned in the darkness. "A preacher? What for?"

"Well, don't get me wrong—as far as I'm concerned, you and I are as married as any two people can be. But some day down the road we may need to have some sort of proof, for the twins' sake. I'd like to have something in writing. You don't mind, do you?"

"You mean . . . you want a preacher to . . . marry us?"

"If it's all right with you."

"You'd do that? Go to all that trouble, just to protect my babies?"

"Now they're my babies, too, Dani." He rubbed his left wrist against her right one, where they each bore a small scar from Dee-O-Det's sacred knife. "I know I didn't plant the seed, but if my blood now flows in you, then it flows in them, too. That makes them mine."

Daniella felt tears sting her eyes. She couldn't talk past the lump in her throat. He cared! He really seemed to care! What could she possibly have done to deserve such a man as Travis Colton?

Travis and Daniella were married for the second time a week later by a dour little reverend named Smithson who'd stopped in Tucson on his way to California. When Carmen heard the news—that their marriage was now legal—she flew into a rage. She packed her bags and her aunt, and

281

headed for Tucson.

Once there, she headed straight for Crane.

"You fool! You idiot! Can't you do anything right? You were supposed to get rid of Daniella Blackwood!"

Crane took a half a step back then stopped. "Now hold on there, *señorita*. I done just like you wanted. She ain't been in that valley in purt near four weeks. I figure it's just a matter of time before them two pals of hers leave, too. I run her off, just like I promised."

" 'I run her off,' " she mimicked. "*Sí*, you ran her off, *amigo*. But you ran her straight into Travis Colton's arms! He went and married the little *puta!*"

"Married her?" Crane looked stunned.

"I can't guarantee you access to that valley as long as she's alive. Now you're going to have to kill her."

Crane frowned and looked doubtful. "What do you mean, kill her? I ain't no murderer."

"I mean—" she drew a gloved forefinger across her throat in a sharp, cutting motion. "—kill her!" She glanced down at her hands and started tugging off the tight gloves. "That way Travis will own the valley. He'll be the bereaved widower. Yes," she said with a slight smile. "This might work out even better than we'd planned. He'll be so upset over the little bitch's death, he'll need consoling."

She watched him lick his lips. His gaze followed her fingers as she began unbuttoning first her jacket, then her blouse. "And when he marries me I'll insist he get rid of that valley, which will be such a *painful* reminder of his sweet young wife. He'll sell it to you."

With narrowed eyes, Crane studied first Carmen, then the floor between his rough boots. "And supposin' he don't sell to me. Hell, I ain't got no money anyhow."

Carmen waved away his objection and watched his gaze devour her firm breasts beneath her thin chemise. "A mere detail. I'll lend you the money, and you and I will be partners." She tossed her gloves, jacket, and blouse to the dusty floor. "You can pay me back out of the gold you find."

282

"Supposin' he sells to that old man, the one the girl lived with?"

"You'll just have to kill the old man, too. And while you're at it," she said, slipping the straps of her chemise down her shoulders, "you might as well get rid of that young one, the big dummy. They'd just be in our way." The chemise slipped down and caught on her hardened nipples. She took a deep breath and felt them swell and point at and beg for the man who stood three feet away, obviously as ready as she was. "For a man like you, they should be easy enough to take care of."

"Sure." Crane's eyes glazed over. "Ambush. But that won't work with the girl. If she's livin' at the Triple C, I ain't gonna be able to get near her."

"Of course you can." Carmen smiled and bared one nipple. "She likes the outdoors. She doesn't stay in the house all the time. All you have to do is find a hiding place, watch, and wait. Sooner or later you'll catch her alone, away from the house. It would be best, of course, if you kill her quickly and leave the body. That way there will be no question as to her fate, and Travis will accept her death and marry me that much sooner. And I don't need to tell you, *amigo* — you have to kill the girl soon."

No, she don't need to tell me, Crane thought. *Gawdamighty! The slut really expects me to do murder!* A shiver ran down his spine.

Hell, I ain't no murderer, he thought. *Especially not of a girl, an old man, or a dummy.*

He conveniently forgot about locking Simon and the Apaches in the burning barn. Hell — Apaches didn't count anyway. He wanted the valley, all right, and the gold he knew was there. But he'd damn sure never done murder before and didn't intend to start now just because some bitch in heat had an itch she wanted scratched. And he intended to scratch it like it had never been scratched before.

But where did that leave him?

It left him with no access to the gold, that's were it left

283

him. And he wasn't willing to give up that gold, dammit.

In a moment he grinned. He'd get rid of the girl all right, but he'd do it his own way. Hell, he didn't need Carmen to get at the gold, all he needed was to get the people out of the valley. He didn't want to own the damned place, just mine it.

And what he had in mind for the new Mrs. Colton would serve his purposes just fine. He'd get even with her for the things she'd done to him. Make her pay. He'd take her up in the hills for a while and tie her up, enjoy her sweet little body. Then when he got tired of her, he'd take her down below the border. Might have to go over as far as Chihuahua, but maybe not. There were plenty of whorehouses in Mexico that'd pay top dollar for a looker like her. And he'd make sure she knew how to please a man in every way there was. He could get more for her that way.

It wasn't like she was a virgin or nothin'. He'd heard the stories about her and the Apaches. He'd keep that to himself, though. Even the Mexican whorehouses wouldn't want Apache leavings.

But Billy Joe Crane wasn't so particular. No sirree, he wasn't.

"The sooner you kill her," Carmen went on, "the sooner I can marry Travis, and the sooner you can get what you . . . want."

With a growl, Crane grabbed her and slammed her back against the wall. "I can get what I want right now. And what I want is them damned skirts of yours outa my way."

"*¡Sí! ¡Sí!*" She tugged frantically at her skirts. "*Yes.*"

Chapter Twenty-four

With Carmen now in Tucson, everyone—most especially Daniella—breathed easier.

As one week extended into two, Daniella realized with some amazement that not only had her morning sickness not returned in some time, but she was sleeping every night, with Travis, still without nightmares. Her overall health improved so much she almost didn't recognize herself in the mirror. Gone were the bruised-looking eyes with their dark circles. They went the same way as her pale, sunken cheeks and the lines of fatigue around her mouth.

Instead of the gaunt features she had almost become accustomed to, she now saw rosy cheeks and sparkling eyes in the mirror. Sometimes she even caught a glimpse of the old Daniella, the one who knew who she was and what she wanted, the one who liked herself and her life.

But it was, after all, only an illusion. She didn't know or feel any of those things, and she never would unless she stopped behaving like a fool and tried to establish some sort of communication with Travis.

With that in mind, she decided it was time to stop avoiding his company. He had been true to his word and had made no move toward any type of intimate relationship. They slept together in the same bed each night and he'd done no more than put his arm around her and give her a peck on the cheek. She may not be able to please him the way he wanted, but surely there were other things she could do to create a little harmony between them and alleviate some of the tension whenever they were together.

It was this determination that sent her down the hall this morning toward his study, where she knew he was working. She intercepted Consuela as the girl carried a fresh pot of coffee to her employer. Daniella relieved her of the tray and took it in to Travis herself. It was as good a way to start as any.

Travis was so engrossed in his account books that he didn't even look up when she placed the tray on the corner of his desk. He mumbled to himself over a column of figures as she walked behind him and peered over his shoulder. He muttered a curse and threw down his pencil in disgust. Leaning back in his chair, he began to massage the tight muscles of his neck.

"Here," Daniella said softly, startling him. "Let me."

He turned his head and looked at her in surprise. She forced his head back around and brushed his hands aside. Her nimble fingers began their work and she could feel the tenseness leaving his neck and shoulders. "You've been bending over these books too long. Why don't you go get some air and let me finish for you?"

Travis looked around at her again in mild surprise. "Do you understand this sort of thing?" he asked, indicating the mess on his desk.

Daniella grinned. "Probably at least as well as you do." This was finally something she could feel confident with. "I used to do all of my grandfather's book work for him."

Travis shouldn't have been surprised. There probably wasn't anything she couldn't do, except love him. But it was too soon for that, he cautioned himself. Other women he'd known had said they loved him, and all they knew how to do was look pretty and demand all his attention. Dani was different. There were other things he wanted from her besides her body, and this was a start. She had come to him and offered her help. It was a good start.

"If you're sure you don't mind, I'll be glad to let you do it."

"I don't mind at all. I would enjoy doing something useful around here for a change."

Travis stood and gave her his chair. "I thought you'd been keeping fairly busy lately."

"Oh, I have," she answered, seating herself in the massive chair and tilting her head up to look at him. "But everything I do is for myself. I'd like to do something for you."

Travis leaned over her with one hand on the arm of the chair and the other on the chair back. He gazed into her eyes and felt his heart slam against his rib cage. *I don't want you to do it just for me,* he thought. He wanted her to do it for *them,* for herself.

Her nearness was intoxicating. The only time they even got close to each other was in bed, and then he spent so much energy trying to douse the fires ignited by her warm, soft body pressed against his side that he wasn't even able to enjoy holding her in his arms. "There is something you can do for me." His voice was low, their faces only a hand's width apart.

"What is it?" Daniella felt captured by his eyes and could not look away. That fluttering feeling was back in her stomach, and she knew it wasn't the babes she was feeling. Nor was it fear. Her legs and arms felt weak, and her pulse pounded in odd places in her body. She waited breathlessly for his reply.

"Kiss me," he whispered. But he made no move toward her.

"I . . . I don't think that's such a good idea," she whispered back, still unable to tear her eyes from his.

"I think it's a very good idea."

In spite of her protest, she waited breathlessly for him to lower his lips to hers. When he didn't, she understood—it was her move. The decision was hers. Only it wasn't hers at all. It was as though she had no will other than his. Her hand reached out on its own and pulled his head down until their lips met. The only kisses she'd ever received had been from Travis, therefore her experience was lacking. She

287

merely pressed her lips softly to his, then released him.

But Travis was by no means disappointed. He was ecstatic. She did it! She actually kissed him, just because he asked her to. His knuckles whitened as he gripped the chair with all his strength to keep from grabbing her and pulling her completely into his arms. Slowly. He must go slowly. But holding back just then was probably the hardest thing he'd ever had to do.

He lowered his mouth slightly and returned the feathery kiss with one of his own. "Thank you," he whispered roughly. He eased himself away and forced himself out of the room. Once outside, he sat down abruptly to still the trembling in his limbs.

Daniella shook herself from her daze and realized Travis had gone. She collapsed back into the chair and covered her flaming cheeks with icy hands. *My God!* How scary; how frightening; how thrilling! Such a small thing, that kiss she'd just given him. But she felt like she'd just climbed the world's highest mountain and now stood triumphantly at its peak.

It was some time before she came back down to earth and was able to concentrate on the account books. A little while later Travis returned to escort her to the noon meal, looking for all the world as if nothing earth-shattering had taken place that morning. Following his example, Daniella did her best to appear calm and casual.

It wasn't easy. Every time she saw him, she remembered the thrilling rush of sensation when their lips had touched.

If she could have that feeling, and the sense of safety she felt when he held her, without those darker, violent passions he could so easily stir, those passions that so terrified her, life would be nearly perfect. And for the next several days, it was.

Then a friend of Travis's, Lucien Renard, came, and the two men plus Jason stayed up nearly till dawn arguing politics. Daniella didn't like spending the night alone. She barely slept at all without Travis beside her.

Yet she understood the importance of Renard's visit. There was a move on by many of the area residents to send a representative to the Confederate Congress to have a separate territory established—the Arizona Territory.

Anti-United States feelings had been running high for months because the requests to make a new territory had been all but ignored by the U. S. Congress. President Buchanan had been in favor of the idea, but he was considered pro-Southern. The northern states absolutely did not want, and would not allow, another territory sympathetic to the Southern cause to enter the Union. Now Lincoln had his hands too full to even consider it. Consequently, any time the resolution came up for a vote, which wasn't often, it was defeated.

That left self-proclaimed Arizona as part of the Territory of New Mexico. The nearest seat of civil government or law and order was hundreds of miles to the east, and the citizens of Arizona, as they called themselves, were constantly plagued by Mexican *banditos* and American outlaws, fugitives from justice and the civilized world, not to mention the Apaches.

Now the army had left them with no protection from *banditos* and Apaches—the troops had burned their forts and headed east to meet the rebels in Texas. The cry echoing across the territory was, "The Union deserted us!"

Since the U. S. government had moved the Butterfield Stage route in March and *The Weekly Arizonian* had ceased publication, the people in the area felt isolated. No stage, no army, no telegraph, no newspaper, no railroad, no judge, no sheriff. Something had to be done!

Renard and a few others were going from ranch to ranch inviting everyone to the upcoming meeting, where they planned to elect a representative to send to the Confederate Congress in Richmond.

Daniella woke from a light sleep around dawn when Travis finally came to bed. She supposed he would take it wrong if she thanked him for staying up all night and giving

289

her the pleasure of waking up in his arms. He usually got up before she woke.

She slept awhile longer, but woke to something tickling her nose. She smiled. It was the crisp, curly hair on Travis's chest.

She sat up carefully so as not to wake him. That's when she realized he'd kicked the covers off and lay next to her, naked and exposed. She gasped at the sight of him. It was only the second time she'd seen her own husband completely naked. The first had been that morning in the wickiup, when she'd been too mortified by her own behavior of the previous night to notice anything other than his nakedness. But now she noticed. He was magnificent.

A quick glance at his face showed him still asleep, so she allowed her gaze to roam. His chest was broad, his stomach flat and ridged with muscles. Just below his waist, where she'd never really looked, his skin was whiter. His hips were lean and firm. Cradled in the bushy nest between his thighs—

Heat stung her cheeks. She gulped and jerked her eyes away to scan down his long, muscular legs dusted with dark gold hair to his feet. Then slowly, while her heart thudded painfully in her chest, her gaze traveled back up to that part of a man she'd learned to hate and fear.

She held her breath and forced herself to look. The breath eased out gently after a moment. His manhood lay limp and peaceful, so harmless looking. After a moment she relaxed. There was nothing threatening about what she saw. It was a part of the man she most wanted to be close to. She wasn't afraid of Travis, so how could she be afraid of his body?

She wasn't, really. She only feared the things his body did to hers. Yet even as she watched, the thing seemed to grow. Daniella's eyes widened. Was it her imagination? Her fear taking over? No! It *was* growing! Her mouth went dry. She tried to swallow. Her throat wouldn't work.

It was time to leave. She had to get away before she did

something stupid. The fear and the nightmarish memory of that huge black chasm that had tried to suck her in swarmed in her brain and made her angry. She wasn't afraid of Travis. She wasn't!

Besides, he was asleep. She intended to leave him that way. With an involuntary jerk, she started to scramble across the bed. A hard, calloused hand grasped her arm. She let out a startled squeak and whirled on her knees. She met deep brown eyes, wide awake and studying her closely. She tried again to swallow.

"Do you find my body so repulsive?" he asked softly.

Unable to speak past the dryness in her throat, she shook her head from side to side.

"Then come here."

Travis pulled gently but firmly on her arm, sliding her across the sheet until her knees touched his bare hip. What was he doing? Did he mean to use that thing on her now? To go back on his word? Against her will, her gaze dropped. At the sheer size of his hardness her heart stopped beating altogether.

If she didn't get away—and soon—her own body would start to shame her. Already she felt a hot throbbing, low and deep. Any minute her breasts would swell, her nipples would flush and harden. And he would know.

Her voice came out in a panicked rush of air. "No. Let me go."

Somewhere in the back of her mind she knew she was making a mistake. She should talk with him calmly and rationally, explain how she felt. But she couldn't think straight when he was in such an obvious state of arousal. She couldn't simply sit next to him on the bed, knowing that at any moment she might . . . might what? Throw herself at him? Or scream?

"Let me go."

Something inside Travis snapped. Weeks of lying next to her in bed, touching her, but not able to *touch* her, of watching her fear slowly slip away, watching her grow more comfortable with him day by day, and now, here she was, terrified at the sight of him!

"Goddamn." He sat up and held her by both arms, facing her practically nose to nose. "What's the matter with you? You act like I'm going to attack you. I'm not the one who raped you, and I'm damn sick and tired of being treated like a leper because of something someone else did. I've never hurt you, and I never would." As he yelled at her he knew it was the wrong thing to do, but he couldn't help himself. His frustrations got the better of him, and his anger rose even higher.

"What you're staring at is called a hard-on, in case you didn't know. It's what happens to a man when he wakes up in bed and finds a beautiful woman—his *wife*—with her eyes all over his naked body."

Dani whimpered and tried to pull away, her chest heaving, her eyes wide with terror. With a low growl of frustration, Travis released her and climbed out of bed.

"I can't believe you're so naive you don't understand this can happen to a man whether he wants it to or not. Grow up, Dani. My face isn't the one in your nightmares. I'm not the villain in your dreams, so stop acting like you think I'm going to rape you any minute. Right now you couldn't pay me to touch you. I prefer a *woman* in my bed, not a frightened, irrational child."

He clenched his fists to keep from reaching to shake some sense into her. "I know I scared you the one time we were intimate. But you urged me on. I thought you were feeling the same things I felt, the things a man wants his woman to feel. I was wrong. I'm sorry. I said it wouldn't happen again, and it won't. Not until you're writhing beneath me, begging for it."

He jerked on his pants, grabbed shirt, socks, and boots, and stomped from the room, swearing with every step. The door slammed behind him.

Daniella flinched. It sounded so final, that slamming

door. With a choking cry, she threw herself down on the bed and buried her face in his pillow.

Dear God, what had she done? Had she driven him away for good? There'd been such anger, such frustration in his eyes. But it was that other emotion she'd seen, so poignant, so real, that she'd see in her mind for the rest of her days — his pain.

She had hurt him. A wife shouldn't hurt her husband, shouldn't refuse him in bed. A real wife would submit.

But the things he made her feel, the rushing heat, the breathlessness — the fierce yearning for something she didn't understand — made her want to do so much more than submit. And that's what shamed her, *terrified* her. If she behaved the way her body wanted to, Travis would be repulsed. He had told her he didn't like clinging women. What she wanted went far beyond clinging.

The words Travis had spoken just before he had stormed out of their room did not sink in until late that night, when Daniella lay in bed — alone.

I thought you were feeling the same things I felt . . .

Daniella sat up, her eyes wide. Could he have meant . . . did he *want* her to feel those things she felt?

. . . the things a man wants his woman to feel.

Was that what she had experienced?

The memory of racing toward that huge black nothingness in her mind still had the power to make her heart race, her mouth go dry. To terrify her.

Yet Travis would never hurt her. Why would he want her to fly off into that fearful chasm? Or had he no idea what she'd seen in her mind?

It would take courage — perhaps more than she possessed — to talk to him about this, but she knew the discussion was long overdue.

She kicked back the covers and was almost out of bed before she remembered the reason she was alone in the first place. Travis was out on the range somewhere with his men. She strongly suspected he was staying away on purpose

293

because he was still angry with her, and still hurt. She vowed to do her best to correct the situation the minute he came home tomorrow.

But when tomorrow came, Travis didn't. Daniella lay awake for a second lonely night. All the next day she waited and paced.

He didn't come.

In the wee hours of her third morning alone, she grew too restless to stay in bed. She lit the lamp and got up. The room suddenly seemed too big, too empty.

She put on her robe, picked up the lamp, and crept quietly down the hall. With no real destination in mind, she roamed through the dining room and salon, finding nothing there to hold her interest. She stepped into Travis's study and halted. He was there, slumped over his desk, his head resting on his folded arms. He'd returned, and hadn't even told her. The room reeked with stale cigar smoke and whiskey fumes. At his elbow stood a nearly empty bottle with only an inch or two of amber liquid remaining. He had obviously been home awhile.

Daniella thought he was asleep until the hand holding an empty glass began to move. She approached cautiously. "Travis?" she whispered.

At the sound of her voice his head jerked up. When the light from the lamp stabbed his bloodshot eyes, he squinted and grimaced. She was appalled by his dirty, unshaven appearance and the dark circles beneath his eyes. She reached out a suddenly trembling hand toward his face, but he jerked away from her touch.

"No!" he cried hoarsely.

"Travis, come to bed."

"Huh? What for?" he grunted in disgust.

"You need some sleep," she replied with amazing calmness, ignoring the real meaning of his question. "And when you're rested, I think we need to talk."

"We don't need to talk," he growled. "You need to get the hell away from me and leave me alone. Just go. Get out."

Dani felt the blood leave her face. *Get out.* It seemed to bounce off the walls and echo in her ears. His eyes pierced her like daggers, saying he wanted no part of her. With a strangled cry, she fled the room and the hatred churning in his face.

Back in the bedroom, she set the lamp down and paced the floor in agitation. As she paced, her sense of rejection gave way to a sense of injustice and anger. How dare he do this? She tried to talk to him, to work things out, to share with him the way he'd asked her to, but would he listen? Would he try to see her side of things? Understand her feelings? No. He didn't want to.

I won't let him treat me this way. I won't stay where I'm obviously not wanted. I won't stay here and be the object of your scorn, Mr. Colton. Get the hell away, you say? Well that's exactly what I'll do, you stubborn, self-centered ass.

From the bottom of the wardrobe she pulled out her small carpetbag and started cramming clothes into it. The only place she had to go was home to Tucker and Simon. Home. Funny how El Valle didn't really seem like home any longer. She'd grown to love the Triple C.

Daniella shoved the thought and its accompanying sense of loss aside. A new thought intruded. El Valle was so close. It was the first place Travis would look. Would he come after her?

Get out!

She blinked at the stinging sensation in her eyes. No, he wouldn't come after her.

She crossed to the dresser and picked up her brush and comb. Just as she placed them in her bag the door crashed open. She jumped and squeaked. The carpetbag fell to the floor, spilling its contents.

From the doorway Travis glared at her. His gaze took in the spilled clothes on the floor then raised to her face. With his eyes locked on hers, he kicked the door shut.

"What in hell do you think you're doing?"

Daniella took a step back from the heated, drunken glare

in his eyes. "I'm doing what you asked," she said breathlessly. "I'm getting out."

Travis took a step forward and swayed. "Women," he said with a snort. He closed his eyes, took a deep breath, then looked at her. Before she realized it, he was standing only inches away. The backs of her knees were already against the bed. She was trapped.

The babes in her womb, perhaps objecting to a lack of oxygen since she'd been holding her breath, chose that moment to kick—hard. Daniella gasped and placed a hand on her stomach.

Travis frowned. "What is it?"

She tried to smile, but couldn't. "Nothing. Just a kick."

He raised a hand and stroked her stomach with one gentle finger. After letting out a deep sigh he said, "I only meant for you to leave the room, not—not leave *me*."

Daniella's heart skipped a beat. "You did?"

He blinked like an owl. "I drank too much."

"You did."

"We need to talk."

"We do."

"I need to sleep."

"Yes."

He stumbled around her, fell onto the bed, and pulled her down beside him. For a moment she thought he was already asleep, then he whispered, "You won't leave?"

She sighed and laid her head on his shoulder, feeling the rightness of being next to him. "I won't leave."

With his eyes still closed, he said, "Promise?"

She heard the vulnerability in his voice and smiled through gathering tears. "I promise."

He answered with a soft snore.

An hour later she slipped out of bed without disturbing him. She was wide awake and he was out cold. She doubted if a stampede would wake him. Still, she was quiet when she dressed and left the room.

The day stretched and so did her nerves. He'd wake up

soon. What was she going to say to him? He thought she was afraid of *him*. How was she going to explain, to make him understand the nature of her fear?

Oh, why didn't he just wake up and get this discussion over with so she'd know where they stood with each other?

By late afternoon she was ready to scream. She was in the kitchen when word came that Travis was asking for a bath. He was up, then. She'd have to face him soon.

With nervous fingers, she added wood to the fire beneath the big black kettle hanging in the hearth. The dry cedar caught and flared, sending out a pleasant aroma.

Daniella stared at the flames, mesmerized. They raced along the wood like wild mustangs across open grasslands. She could even picture riders clinging to the backs of the fiery steeds. Dark-skinned, barechested riders with flowing black hair.

In the next instant the picture turned sharp and clear. The riders were Apaches, herding cattle and horses away from a ranch. One warrior dismounted and entered the small adobe house, emerging a moment later with a terrified white woman in tow.

Daniella's heart pounded forcefully in her chest. The Apache flung the woman to the ground, flipped up her skirt, and threw himself down on top of her. Daniella stuffed her knuckles into her mouth to stifle a scream.

She tried to tear her gaze away from the vision in the flames but couldn't. It was as though there was something she should see, should know.

Yet the woman, whose face Daniella would never forget, was unfamiliar to her, as was the house. Why then, was this violent scene being forced upon her? Why was she made an unwilling eyewitness?

Then she saw what she was meant to see. It wasn't the woman she was supposed to recognize, it was the Apache. At the sight of that embittered face, those thin, cruel lips and black, beady eyes, Daniella moaned and spun away from the flames. The vision disappeared.

But never would she forget the sight of Golthlay forcing himself on that poor woman. Golthlay, who, if not for Travis, might have become Daniella's husband.

In spite of the intense heat of the room, a cold shiver ran down her spine. When Rosita and Juanita entered the kitchen a moment later, Daniella kept her back toward them. She had to get out of the house, at least for a few minutes, no matter how hot it was outside. "I think I'll take a walk," she announced to no one in particular.

With decisive steps bordering on flight, she left the house by way of the courtyard and headed for the line of cottonwoods along the creek.

The creek was dry now, but she didn't care. The cottonwoods offered shade and privacy. It wasn't until she was there that she remembered. This was where Travis brought her the night of the fiesta. The night he'd held her and kissed her so passionately. The night she'd panicked and fought him.

With a cry of denial, she stepped toward the creek and stared blankly down the steep, five-foot incline to the dry, rocky bed. That night of the fiesta was weeks and weeks ago. So many things had happened since then. She was his wife now. She thought she'd changed so much. Yet the vision of Golthlay brought back all her old fears.

Chewing on her lower lip, she stared into the dry, rocky creek bed. Maybe that vision was *supposed* to remind her of her old fears. Maybe it was meant to show her that what happened to her at Travis's touch was *not* to be feared. Maybe—

Somewhere close a twig snapped. She stiffened. Her heart pounded. This was it, then. She'd have to turn and face him. Ask him, beg him if necessary, to give her another chance.

But she couldn't turn around. Her legs refused to move. In a ragged voice she said softly, "I'm sorry."

"So am I, little darlin' " came the rough, gravelly reply.

Her heart stopped. That wasn't Travis's voice! Before she

could turn around or even take a breath, a large, beefy hand clamped over her mouth and jerked her back against something . . . a man's chest!

A scream built in her throat.

Chapter Twenty-five

Travis woke with a groan. His eyes were glued shut. His mouth tasted like a moldy cow patty. And somebody was driving a railroad spike through his brain. A dozen somebodies.

Lord, what had he done to himself? And why?

An instant later he remembered.

Dani.

He forced his eyes open and hissed at the stabbing daggers of light. After several slow, painful blinks, the room was almost in focus. But even as he coerced his creaking muscles to turn his head to look for Dani, he knew he was alone. He felt her absence every bit as strongly as he'd ever felt her presence.

Judging by the angle of light, it was late afternoon. He'd slept the entire day!

When he finally sat up he didn't know which to grab first, his pounding head or his churning stomach. He groaned again. Somehow groaning seemed to ease the misery.

He had to find Dani. He had to convince her to give him another chance. And he swore to himself he'd never blow up at her again the way he did the other day. God, what a fool he'd been to lose his temper like that. She couldn't help the way she felt. It was just going to take more time, that was all. He prayed fervently she'd give them both that time.

But he couldn't face her looking like a derelict. He'd slept in his clothes, hadn't shaved in four days, and he smelled like the inside of a keg of cheap belly-wash. That last thought brought indignation. The brew he'd drowned himself in last night was definitely not cheap.

It took him less than an hour to shave, bathe, and dress. By the time he left the bedroom he felt almost human again. And hungry. The queasiness had left him. But food would have to wait. Dani was more important than his stomach.

Yet he couldn't find her anywhere. He checked room by room, but she wasn't in the house. In the kitchen he finally learned she'd gone outside. He knew where to look then. He left through the courtyard and headed for the creek.

"Goddammit!" Billy Joe Crane struggled to hold on to the woman in his arms. She was slipperier than a snake. She squirmed every which way and used her small feet like lethal weapons. His shins would be bruised for months.

But he didn't dare let go of her now that he had her. He couldn't believe she could still fight like this with him squeezing her breast as hard as he could. Maybe if he let go there and wrapped his arm around her waist he could—

Good God Amighty!

She was . . . she was gonna have a baby! He'd never even spoken to a woman who was gonna have a baby before, much less *touched* one! Lordamercy! If he caused harm to a woman in a family way, he'd never be able to sleep nights for the rest of his life.

Why hadn't that Mex slut told him about this? There was no way in hell he'd go through with his plans now. No sirree, not Billy Joe Crane. *Not on your life.* That bloodthirsty *señorita* would just have to wait, or get somebody else to do her dirty work. It damn sure wasn't gonna be Billy Joe Crane, by God.

The woman in his arms whimpered, reminding him he still held her. His arm pressed tight against the bulge of her stomach. He let go so quick they both stumbled. He had to get away, and fast. A man could hang for what he'd just done. Not to mention what he'd planned to do.

When Colton's new wife righted herself, her back still to him, Crane gave her a slight shove that sent her staggering forward, then he hightailed it for the bend in the dry creek bed where he'd left his horse.

Daniella stumbled forward, carried by momentum to the crumbling edge of the bank. With her heart in her throat, she hung there a second, waving her arms frantically to catch her balance. The loose rocks beneath her feet shifted, then gave way. All she could do was flail her arms and shriek as the rocky creek bottom rushed up to meet her.

Travis was about a dozen yards from the line of cotton-woods when he heard a high-pitched shriek from directly ahead. The hair on the back of his neck stood up. He sprang forward at a run. "Dani!"

He broke into the trees and slowed, his eyes darting all around, searching, searching frantically. "Dani!"

No answer.

He whirled, ran a few feet right, then left. *Stop! Think!* Dani was in trouble. She needed him. Now was no time to panic, regardless of the fear that threatened to suffocate him. He turned in a circle again. Where was she?

"Dani!"

No answer.

He came out of the trees at the edge of the creek. Three steps to the bank and he saw her. "Dani!"

Terror clutched his heart and threatened to render him senseless at the sight of her still form lying at an odd angle on the rocks below.

If he scrambled down the bank where he stood, he'd shower her with rocks. He had to move several feet left. That's when he heard another sound that sent his hackles rising.

Hoofbeats.

Someone had been there! Someone had been there and

302

left Dani lying limp and lifeless on the rocks. And Travis couldn't give chase because he couldn't leave Dani. Was she dead?

God, please, no. "Dani!"

No answer.

He leaped from the bank and disregarded the sharp, tearing pain when he wrenched his knee upon landing. He reached Dani in an instant and knelt beside her. Her breath was shallow, but it was there, thank God. With trembling hands he felt for broken bones and gratefully found none. But the knot on the side of her head worried him.

"Dani?" He shook her gently and got no response. "Dani, can you hear me?"

He had to get her to the house. Rosita would know what to do. Rosita always knew. He forced his arms beneath her and lifted her to his chest. With terror clutching his throat and his heart slamming against his ribs, he carried her out of the creek bed, through the cottonwoods and brush, across the barren, sunbaked ground to the house.

He went in through the courtyard and bellowed for Rosita. At their bedroom, he shouldered the door open and placed Dani carefully on the bed. Hurried footsteps sounded in the hall, then Rosita and Juanita burst into the room.

"*¡Dios!* What has happened?" Juanita cried.

"She's been hurt," Travis answered needlessly without taking his eyes from Dani's face. "I don't know how bad or by whom. There's a knot on her head."

Dani rolled her head on the pillow and moaned. A second later her eyelids fluttered open. While she blinked and tried to focus, Travis brushed a loose strand of hair from her face. At his touch her eyes widened with fright and she gasped.

"It's all right, Dani," he said softly. "You're okay now."

Her fear-glazed eyes darted around the room. Travis eased away from her. Was it him she reacted to, or the memory of her attacker? Either way, now wasn't the time to find out. He stood and moved aside so Rosita and Juanita could care for her.

"Señor Travis," Rosita said over her shoulder, *"por favor,* bring some warm water from the kitchen. We will see to *la Señora."*

Travis backed out of the room mutely, reluctant to take his eyes off Dani. On his way to the kitchen he ran into Jason and told him all he knew of what had happened. "Get the men out and see if they can pick up any tracks. I want that bastard found, whoever he is."

"Consider it done," Jason said.

A few moments later Travis carried a bucket of warm water to the bedroom. Juanita took it, then ushered him out with words of reassurance as she firmly closed the door in his face.

Travis clenched his fists at his sides and stood waiting in the hall, staring at his bedroom door. The women would take care of her, and she wouldn't draw away from their touch, like she would from his. But oh, God! How he wanted to touch her, to hold her, to protect her.

He paced the hall and cursed, waiting for word of Dani. Protect her. Hell! She'd been attacked practically on his very doorstep. Some fine protector he was!

Finally, after what seemed like hours, the bedroom door opened and Rosita came out into the hall.

"How is she?"

Rosita placed a plump, workworn hand on his arm. "She will be fine. She has many bruises from her fall, and the lump on her head, that is all."

"That's all!"

"She is lucky. It could have been worse."

Travis paled. Rosita was right. Dani could have been killed or raped or shot, or any number of other unthinkable things. "Can I see her?"

Rosita patted his arm the way she did for Matt when telling him the pudding was all gone. "Let her rest for a while. Juanita will sit with her. You are so upset yourself, you will only upset your wife more."

Reluctantly, he left.

Three generations of Colton men sat down to a late supper that night. Earlier Travis had explained to Matt as best he could what had happened. He cautioned his son to stick close to the house for safety's sake.

The news about Dani upset Matt. Travis knew the boy worshipped her. He'd had to assure him over and over that Dani would be okay, and hoped all the while he wasn't lying.

Jason's news hadn't lightened the oppressive atmosphere any. He had found where the rider sent his horse up the creek bank into the hills, but they'd lost the trail in the rocks.

After supper Travis went to check on Dani. Juanita, wearing a concerned frown, met him halfway down the hall. Alarm shot through him at her expression. "What is it?" he demanded. "What's wrong?"

"La Señora, she is having *la pesadilla*—a bad dream, and keeps calling your name. I have tried to wake her, but she does not hear me."

Travis was down the hall and through the bedroom door by the time Juanita's words were out. When he neared the bed, Dani was tossing her head back and forth on the pillow, sobbing pathetically, calling out his name. Cautiously, he sat down next to her on the bed, indecision washing over him. He wanted nothing more than to respond to her cry, to hold her and comfort her, but if she recoiled from him in fear, he didn't think he could stand it.

"Dani," he called tentatively.

"Travis! Travis!" she cried in her sleep.

"I'm here, Dani." He caught a flailing arm and held her cold hand in both of his warm ones. "It's me, Dani. It's Travis. I'm here."

Dani continued tossing her head and moaning, occasionally crying out his name, while Travis talked to her in a soothing voice, trying to calm her. Her cries grew stronger

305

and stronger, until, with one final anguished cry of his name, she woke herself. Her eyes flew open. Travis winced at the mixture of pain and pleading he saw there.

"I'm here, Dani. It's all right now. You were having a bad dream."

She stared at him, tears coursing down her face, her hair a streaming mass of tangles across the pillows. Her chest rose and fell rapidly. She clenched her swollen eyes shut and covered her face with her free hand, holding onto Travis with the other. When she spoke, her voice was choked with misery and tears.

"I needed you. Oh, God. I called, and called, and you couldn't hear me. You wouldn't come."

"It was just a dream, Dani," he said, trying to reassure her. "I'm here. It's all right now."

Travis watched helplessly as she sobbed out her misery. Tears streamed from the corners of her eyes, made paths across her temples, and ran down into her hair. He ached with the need to reach out and wipe them away, but held himself in check. If he frightened her now, he didn't think she would be able to take it. She'd had a bad scare this afternoon and was much too fragile to cope with another one from him.

"Dani?" he questioned tentatively. "Dani, love, please stop crying. You're making yourself sick. Please stop."

Dani tightened her grip on his hand and sobbed all the harder. "I c-can't st-stop," she wailed.

He leaned toward her and blinked the moisture away from his own eyes. "Tell me what to do, Dani. I can't stand to see you suffer this way. I'd do anything to make your pain go away."

Daniella looked at him through her flood of tears. She cried even harder and gripped his hand tighter. Why couldn't he put his arms around her, make her feel safe, warm?

Tell me what to do . . .

Could she?

"Tell me how to help you, Dani. I . . . I want to hold you, and comfort you, but I don't want to frighten you. Tell me what you need," he pleaded with her.

"You-you want t-to hold me?" Her words were interspersed with sobs and sniffles, her eyes wide, her breathing heavy. Her heart refused to beat until she had his answer.

"More than anything in the world," he said, his voice quivering with emotion.

Daniella studied him closely through tear-filled eyes. What she saw sent her heart pounding at a rapid pace. There was no anger from their previous quarrel in his face; no contempt or even pity. Instead, she saw a tenderness that took her breath away, and a longing so great she felt certain it nearly matched her own. She cried out his name and reached for him, and he came to her, wrapped his strong, warm arms around her. As he stretched out beside her on the bed she buried her face against his neck.

Neither of them heard the soft click as Juanita gently closed the bedroom door on her way out.

Travis turned toward Dani and covered her legs with one of his. He reigned kisses on her hair, cradled her head in one hand, and held her as tightly as he dared. She cried so hard he felt her shuddering sobs to the depths of his soul, but he didn't tell her not to cry this time. He understood these tears, for they matched the ones in his own eyes. Tears of overwhelming relief. Relief that, at least for this moment, they could touch and hold each other, each giving and taking comfort. It seemed like years since he'd held her.

"Oh, Travis," she cried between sobs. "Hold me. Hold me tight." She clung to him with a strength that astounded him. He held her so tightly he was afraid he might hurt her, but she pressed even closer.

"I'm holding you, love, and I won't ever let go." He rocked her in his arms and stroked her hair, her back, her arms.

"How can you even stand to touch me after the way I've acted?" she wailed.

"*Not* touching you is what I can't stand," he said fiercely. "I've been going out of my mind for days wanting to hold you and touch you." Her sobs were quieting now, and he continued stroking her. "But I was afraid I'd scare you again, turn you away from me. And then, today at the creek, when I saw you lying there on the rocks, I thought I'd die. What happened? Can you tell me?"

"Oh, Travis, I was so scared! There was a man!"

A shudder ripped through her. Travis held her closer and murmured, "I know, love, but he's gone now. Did you see who it was? What did he want? What happened?"

Daniella took a deep breath and concentrated on Travis's warmth surrounding her, on his hands stroking her, his lips in her hair. It helped. She wasn't afraid anymore. Nothing bad could happen to her when he held her like this. In a steady voice, she told him everything that happened at the creek.

"What about his voice? Did he say anything?"

She tried to remember every detail, but things were fuzzy in her mind. "He said something," she murmured, rubbing her forehead. "I don't remember what, though."

"Think. Did you recognize his voice?"

She shook her head and frowned. "No, but . . ."

"But?"

"But I feel like I should have."

"What do you mean?"

She squeezed her eyes shut a moment, then looked up at Travis. "I don't know. I remember thinking when he spoke that I should know his voice, but . . . I was so scared."

She wrapped her arms around his neck again and held him tight. Travis felt every muscle in her body tense. He tried to ease away, but she wouldn't loosen her grip.

"It's okay." He rocked her back and forth and whispered in her ear. "You're safe now. I've got you, and I won't let anything happen. I promise."

She quieted while he spoke, and eased the choking hold she had on him. He only meant to kiss the tears from her

308

cheek, but as his lips neared, she turned her head and her lips met his. The shock was instantaneous. Travis felt his blood catch fire and center in his loins. He pulled his head back, feeling lower than a snake for wanting her so badly when she was so distraught.

An apology formed on his lips, but died in his throat when he felt her hand at the back of his head, urging him down. Her lips parted, trembling. When he looked into her eyes his breathing grew ragged. There was no fear in those pale blue depths. She met his gaze with a steadiness that fanned the flames of his desire.

Her hand pulled him toward her, and her head raised to meet him half way. Their lips met, gently at first, tentatively. Travis's tongue traced the path of her lower lip and Daniella felt tingling waves of heat and pleasure wash over her. She felt the smooth, yet rough texture of his tongue as it slipped into her mouth, and she moaned deep in her throat as her muscles quivered and her bones melted.

The kiss became desperate, demanding, on both sides, and they clung together in mutual need. She met his passion with her own inner fire, surprising them both with the depth of her response. When he withdrew his tongue from her mouth, she followed him, shyly at first, then boldly as she felt his trembling response. This time it was Travis who moaned against her lips while his hands continued caressing her back and hips.

Travis pulled away, breathless, stunned by both the emotions and physical responses generated by the kiss, and by the violent upheaval going on in her womb. The twins were strongly objecting to being squashed between two larger bodies. He stroked gently, the way he used to when the babes kicked.

But his eyes were locked on her face, anxiously waiting. Slowly, slowly, she opened her eyes and looked at him. He stared in amazement at the look of total wonder in her eyes.

"Is this what you wanted me to feel?"

He searched her eyes and found the answer. "Yes. This is

what I want you to feel."

Suddenly Daniella understood. The passion and yearning, the desire, the craving for his touch—those were the things a man wants his woman to feel. And she felt them all. For him. She was his woman.

Her new knowledge burned bright in her mind and heart, chasing away her feelings of shame at sensations she hadn't understood, her fear of that deep chasm looming close. It wasn't a black emptiness to be feared. It was a dark, cozy sanctuary where Travis would take her. A special place they could go together.

All that remained was for him to show her the way.

With one trembling finger, she reached up and traced the outline of his lips. "Oh, Travis," she breathed. "How could I have ever been so foolish as to be afraid of you? Can you ever forgive me?"

The breath caught in his throat. "You're not afraid now?"

"No," she whispered, staring directly into his eyes.

Their lips met hungrily. Daniella clung to Travis as a drowning person clings to a lifeline and felt certain the room must be spinning. Her blood soared through her veins in answer to the pounding of his heart against hers. She had never allowed herself to feel passion before and reveled in the waves of heated pleasure that washed over her. His tongue searched out the inner recesses of her mouth, demanding a response she could not possibly fail to give.

He eased his lips away and left a trail of fire down her neck as he kissed his way over her thin cotton gown toward the breast he cupped in his strong, calloused hand. Tears gathered behind Daniella's closed lids. When his hot, wet mouth closed over the throbbing peak, raw emotion burst in her veins. He teased with teeth and tongue until her nipple stood hard and erect beneath the wet spot on her gown. He sucked gently, tugging on invisible cords that reached to the very center of her being, where she felt an emptiness despite the babes in her womb. An emptiness that swelled and throbbed with need, a need only Travis could fill.

His hand stroked her belly, and his lips followed. His fingers reached beneath her and kneaded her soft buttocks. She moaned with pleasure at the sensations he created, but flinched and gasped sharply when his fingers hit a tender spot.

Travis felt her stiffen. He raised his head and swiftly withdrew his hands. "What is it? Did I hurt you?"

"It's nothing." She still felt the pleasure he had created in her body, the brief pain already forgotten. "It's only a bruise." She ran her fingers through his thick, wavy hair, wanting him to resume what he'd been doing.

A picture of Dani lying limp and lifeless on the rocky ground flashed in his mind and abruptly cooled his passion. "Where?" he insisted. She had landed hard on those rocks. He pushed her gently to her side and drew the back of her gown up her legs.

She tried to stop him, but he brushed her hands away. He frowned at the large area of discolored skin. "Just a bruise? You're black and blue all over," he cried. He ran his fingers over the bruised flesh, barely touching it, and she flinched again. "I'm so sorry, my love."

His eyes sought hers for forgiveness for hurting her, and she smiled at him tenderly. "It's not as bad as it looks," she said.

Travis scanned the room and spotted a familiar-looking small brown jar next to some larger bottles on the bedside table. He reached for it and sniffed its contents. It was one of Rosita's secret concoctions for cuts, burns, and bruises.

Daniella watched as he dipped his fingers into the fragrant herbal mixture and gently applied the cool cream to her bruised flesh. She stared, mesmerized by his hands. Hands powerful enough to grasp a knife and kill a man, yet so infinitely tender when he touched her. Hands that could set her heart pounding and her blood singing with a mere touch. Hands that would, one day soon, cradle her children safely in their strength. Cradle them, God willing, with love.

311

Travis concentrated on his task, aching for her injuries. When he finished he smoothed the gown back down over her hips and rolled her carefully onto her back, then reached to undo the tiny buttons that started at her neck and ended at her toes.

She halted his hands. "No. Please don't," she whispered.

He searched her eyes and tried to identify the emotion that flickered briefly there. His heart sank when he recognized it. "You are still afraid of me, aren't you?"

Chapter Twenty-six

"No!" She cried out fiercely and gripped his hands. "I'm not afraid of you. Not . . . not like you mean. It isn't that."

"Then what is it?" Travis lowered his head and kissed her hands, never taking his eyes from her face. "I only want to look for more bruises."

"I know. It's just that . . ."

He watched closely as blood rushed to her face. Tears again filled her eyes and she blinked rapidly. "What is it? Tell me," he insisted gently.

"Oh, Travis," she wailed. "I'm so f-fat and ugly!" She threw an arm over her face. "I don't want you to see me like this," she cried.

"Oh, Dani, Dani." He raised up and lay down next to her, forcing her arm away from her face. She tried to turn away, but he slipped a hand behind her head to hold her, and kissed the tears from her cheeks. "You're not fat and you could never be ugly," he whispered. His other hand began to gently stroke her stomach again. "You're just six months pregnant, that's all. You're supposed to look like this. Don't hide from me. Share this with me, please."

The whole time he spoke, he placed soft, tender kisses across her face. Now his lips settled on hers, and Daniella forgot her embarrassment, her shyness, in the tenderness of his kiss. Before the hunger could build, Travis freed her lips. He reached for her buttons again as their eyes remained locked on each other. She lost herself in the golden flecks of his dark brown eyes and couldn't think of a single

313

reason why her own husband should not undress her.

Travis finished unbuttoning the gown, then slipped it from her shoulders and arms, leaving her totally exposed to his gaze. He reached to cup her milk-swollen breasts, longing to feel their weight in his palms, then froze with his hand still in the air. Her left breast bore a ring of five bruises, each in the distinct shape of a man's fingertip. His heart burned with rage. "I thought you said he didn't hurt you."

He watched her surprise as she discovered the bruises. "I guess I was too scared to notice."

With a trembling finger, Travis traced a fine blue vein that ran between two bruises. He wanted to kill the one responsible for marring her delicate flesh, but for now he must settle for soothing her pain. He leaned down and kissed each mark, then reached for the brown jar again, reminding himself he was supposed to be taking care of her injuries, not fondling her.

He proceeded to inspect every inch of her flesh. Each time he came across a bruise, he kissed it first, then soothed it with the cream. He rolled her to her side again and found one last bruise on her left shoulder. He treated it the same as he had the others.

After setting the jar aside, he gently massaged her lower back. She moaned softly and arched in pleasure. Travis kept massaging until he felt the tight muscles on each side of her spine relax.

When she tried to draw the sheet up over herself he tugged it from her fingers. "Is it this you don't want me to see?" He ran his fingers lightly across the hard mound of her belly. "Or this?" He slid his fingers down her thigh and settled on the scars on the inside of each leg.

With a sharp intake of breath, she turned her head away. Her cheeks turned pale. Her lips trembled.

"Look at me." At his gentle insistence, she complied. "I've seen them before, you know." At the startled look in her eyes, he continued. "When you were shot I helped Rosita bathe you. I've seen all your scars, so there's no reason to be shy with me."

"But Travis," she gasped, blushing from her navel to the roots of her hair. "We weren't even married then! We barely knew each other."

A slow grin spread across his face. "I know." He wriggled his eyebrows suggestively.

"And you still married me?" she asked in wonder.

"Of course I married you. What do a few scars have to do with anything?"

"You wouldn't say that if you knew how I got them," she said tightly, her gaze darting away from his. With a sharp tug, she jerked her nightgown over herself to hide her nakedness.

Travis moved up beside her again and turned her face toward his, but she refused to look at him. "How did you get them?" he asked softly.

She swallowed hard and stared at a point below his chin. In a shaky voice she said, "Believe me, you don't want to know."

Travis smoothed a knuckle across her cheek. "I do, Dani. I *need* to know. I need to know everything about you." When she didn't answer, he went on. "It was the Apaches, wasn't it?"

She squeezed her eyes shut and inhaled sharply.

"You've never said much about that night," Travis said quietly, his knuckle still stroking back and forth across her silky cheek. "You keep it all locked up inside, and it sits there between us and festers. Let it out. Talk to me. Let me share the pain, and maybe then it won't hurt so much."

She shuddered violently. With a sob, she rolled toward him and buried her face against his shoulder. Her words came out in a tortured whisper. "You don't know what you're asking."

Travis cupped the back of her head in his large palm, careful not to touch the tender lump she'd received this afternoon. "I'm asking you to let me carry part of your bur-

315

den. Nothing you can say will change the way I feel about you. Just talk to me, Dani."

She lay there so long, her face pressed against him, her breath coming in short, rapid little gasps, Travis feared she wasn't going to say anything. Then another hard shudder ripped through her, and her voice came, low and anguished.

"It was a stick. From the fire. I wouldn't . . . I . . . oh, God!" she cried.

Travis held her close and soothed her with his hands and voice. After awhile she calmed. Then, in a voice devoid of all emotion, she told him everything, from the attack on the stagecoach until she came to the next morning with the streak of white in her hair.

When she told of how she'd locked her ankles together, and of a warrior pulling a burning stick from the fire, thrusting it between her thighs to make her spread them, Travis felt bile rise in his throat. It stayed there, choking him, as she told of one man after another, seven in all, taking her brutally, there on the ground, beside what remained of the two men who'd been captured with her.

Travis fought to control the sickness in his gut and the rage in his heart. It was all he could do to just hold her and let her talk.

When she was quiet for a while, he stroked her hair and rolled his face against the pillow to wipe the dampness from his lashes. Then she started talking again, in that same lifeless voice, telling him about her recovery, her adoption by Cochise, her visions of Travis and Matt, her friendship with Dee-O-Det, her trip home, when Travis and his men had tried to ambush her and her escort, and finally, she told him about her father, stepmother, and the little brother they tried to keep from her.

Her own father! How could the man be so damned cruel? Travis wanted to rush out across the mountains and kill Howard Blackwood, strangle him slowly with his bare hands. But he didn't. He'd been right—she needed to talk,

316

to finally get everything out in the open. He'd known what she'd gone through had been horrible, but until now he'd had no idea just how big a miracle it was that she was even alive, let alone sane.

She kept talking, telling him everything right up until the day she'd come to the Triple C that first time.

Travis held her for a long time after she finished speaking. When he felt her start to relax, he turned her face up to his and kissed her forehead, her nose, and gently as he could, her lips.

"It's over, Dani. All the bad things are over now. The scars may always be there, but like I said, what do a few scars matter? You may even get a few more, you know." He ran his hand over her stomach again. "From the babies."

"Rosita says I won't," she said shyly. At his questioning look, she pointed to one of the bottles on the bedside table.

Travis reached for it, pulled the cork, and poured thick, fragrant lotion into his palm. He spread it liberally over her abdomen, smoothing it into her skin. "I can't believe something so delicate can possibly stretch so much." When her stomach was smooth and dry to the touch again, his lips followed the paths his hands had made. Then he poured more lotion and massaged it gently into each breast, wringing a moan of pleasure from her.

Daniella's eyelids grew heavy, and she couldn't hold them open. That empty, tingling sensation deep inside was back, and this time she welcomed it. She arched, pressing her breasts more firmly into Travis's hands. When his lips touched hers, she opened her mouth, hungry for the taste of him. He pressed himself along her side, and she felt the proof of his desire hard and throbbing against her hip. The thought of shying away, of being afraid, never entered her mind. She moved instinctively against him in a gesture as old as time, somehow knowing the greatest pleasure in the world awaited her.

He pressed himself against her hip, then groaned and pulled away. He flung himself onto his back and covered his

317

face in the crook of his arm while his breath rasped in his throat. His other hand covered his groin.

"Travis?" she asked anxiously. She rolled to her side and rested a hand lightly on his chest, feeling his heart pound against his ribs. "Travis, what is it?"

His arm came down from his face and he gripped her fingers in a crushing hold. "God, Dani, I'm sorry. I never meant to lose control like that." He brought her hand to his cheek and held it there. "It's just that I want you so much."

Daniella gazed at him steadily. "Then why did you stop?" Was that her voice? How could she sound so calm, when her heart was sending pulsebeats to places in her body that had never pulsed before?

"I don't want to stop." He smoothed a strand of hair from her face. "But you took quite a fall today out there at the creek. You're bruised and sore, and these babies are due in a few weeks." He held a palm firmly against her stomach. "If we don't stop I might hurt you or the babies. As much as I want you, I just can't take that chance."

She studied his expression closely, trying to determine the truth of his words. Were those his real reasons for pulling away from her? Panic raced through her veins, dousing the fires of passion. "Or is it the things I told you?"

She didn't realize she'd spoken her fear aloud until she saw Travis's fierce frown. He turned until they lay face to face and gripped her shoulders tightly. "No!" he cried. "Dani, no. It has nothing to do with that."

He saw the panic in her eyes and knew he hadn't convinced her. She didn't believe him. All her old insecurities were back full force. "I swear it, Dani. Nothing you've told me tonight could make me not want you." He gazed into her eyes steadily, willing her to believe him.

"I hate what they did to you, the Apaches, your family. I'd like to kill every single person who ever hurt you," he said fiercely. He ran a hand around her hip and gripped the inside of her scarred thigh. "And the first bastard I'd like to kill is the one who did this."

Her bright blue eyes swam in pools of tears. She swallowed once, then whispered, "You already have."

For one brief instant, Travis stared at her in disbelief. Then he understood. Loco. All the pieces fell into place. Her reaction on the way home when Matt mentioned Loco. Loco's own boastful words about how he'd been the first to—

Travis pulled Dani to him roughly and buried his face in her long, soft hair. His voice, when it came, was choked and harsh. "I wish I could bring him back from the dead, just so I could kill him again, slower this time. It was too damn clean the first time, too easy. He deserves—they all deserve the slowest, most hideous torture possible for what they did to you."

He pulled away from her and forced her to meet his gaze. "But Dani, nothing, not them, not what they did to you, *nothing* can make me not want you. I swear it."

Her eyes darkened with pain and doubt. "Do you want me? Do you really?"

Bruised and heavy with child she might be, but Travis was starting to understand that her emotional bruises were far more important than the physical ones.

The eyes looking up at him were deep pools of need. Not physical need, but emotional. She needed his lovemaking to prove her father wrong. To assure her that what she'd endured in the past did not keep him from wanting her. That even in her childbearing state she was a desirable woman.

One glimpse of that stark, devastating need, and he was humbled. And lost.

He wondered if he had the strength to control his near violent desire for her enough to be as gentle as she needed him to be. If he hurt her in any way he'd never forgive himself. And he understood now that denying her what she needed at this moment would be the cruelest hurt of all.

Slowly, deliberately, he took her hand and placed it against the front of his pants, letting her feel the pulsing hardness that lay beneath the fabric. "Feel how much I want

319

you," he whispered roughly.

Her eyes, still locked on his, widened. Travis swallowed heavily when her pink tongue darted out to swipe her upper lip.

"Then please don't stop."

As she spoke the words, her hand squeezed him, wringing a groan from deep in his throat. Travis closed his eyes briefly, then looked at her again. "Do you know what you're saying?" He held his breath, waiting for her to change her mind.

Instead, her hand squeezed again, and she said softly, "Make love to me, Travis."

Slowly, cautiously, praying he was doing the right thing, he brushed his lips against hers. Once. Twice. His voice came on a whispered breath. "If I do anything that hurts, anything you don't like, anything that scares you, you tell me, all right?" She sighed and nodded, and he lost himself in the warmth of her kiss.

As the kiss deepened, Daniella forgot. She forgot the Apaches, her father and stepmother, her attacker this afternoon. She forgot about pain and humiliation. She forgot about insecurities. She forgot her fear of the things he made her feel. She forgot her own name. She forgot to breathe.

There was only Travis, with his warm lips and questing hands. She stopped thinking, and simply felt. Like a woman. For the first time in her life.

He left her lips and trailed a searing string of kisses down her neck, over her collar bone, across the nightgown she'd pulled up to shield herself with earlier. When his hot mouth settled on the tip of her breast, she arched toward him with a gasp. He was pulling those strings again, the ones that ran from his lips, through her breast, clear down to the heavy throbbing between her legs.

She cried out in protest when he pulled away, but he only kissed a path to her other breast. She put a hand on his cheek to stop him. "Wait," she whispered.

Travis froze. His eyes flew to hers, questioning, wary.

320

She smiled and tugged the nightgown out of the way. His gaze flew to the newly exposed flesh and he sucked in his breath. Tears stung the back of her throat when she realized the big, calloused hand reaching for her bare breast was trembling. Somehow, she hadn't expected him to be as affected as she was.

With her own hands none too steady, she guided his mouth to her breast. This time there was no tentative brushing of lips, but an all out, passionate assault. He tongued and teethed and suckled until her breath rasped in her throat.

She'd never felt this way before, never dreamed there were such feelings. Without her fear, everything was intensified a hundredfold. When his hand slid over the mound of her stomach and cupped her between her legs, she thought she'd die with the sheer pleasure of it. Surely nothing could be better than this.

In the next instant his flexing fingers proved her wrong. Passionately, excitingly wrong.

As if guided by instinct, she caressed his hardness in rhythm with every movement of his fingers.

"Oh, God," he said against her hardened nipple. His tongue lapped once, twice. "You taste so good." The hand between her legs shifted. When his finger slid into her, she gasped. "And you feel so good, so hot, so ready."

With a moan, he ground himself into her hand.

Suddenly Daniella wanted to feel his bare skin against hers. Needed it. Frantic, she tugged at his shirt, pulling it from his pants, and ran her free hand beneath it up his bare back.

Then he was pulling away from her. She whimpered in protest until she saw him jerking at the buttons on his shirt. With eager hands she reached to help him. When he tugged it from his arms and tossed it to the floor, her fingers, hungry for the feel of him, threaded themselves through the golden curls on his chest.

Travis threw back his head and closed his eyes. Her

touch! How he'd craved it! Her small, inexperienced hands did things to him no other woman had ever done. Right then he was sure he'd never even known another woman. There was only Dani. And she was his.

He opened his eyes and watched her face as she stroked his chest, his shoulders, his stomach. When she raised her gaze slowly, deliberately it seemed, to his, the look in her eyes took his breath away. This wasn't the look of the half-scared, totally defiant girl who'd come to his house and claimed to know where his son was. It wasn't the look of a woman who'd looked death and defilement in the face and lived to tell about it. Nor was it the look of the woman he'd terrified with his actions a few days ago.

This was a look as old as time, one women had been giving to men since Eve first bit into the apple. It was the look of hot, sultry passion. The come-hither look of a woman who wanted her man, and wanted him now. It was a look that could bring a man to his knees and crumble empires.

If he'd had an empire, he would have let it crumble in that moment, just to see that look in her eyes for him. For him alone.

Sweat beaded across his brow and the tightness in his loins became unbearable. With a groan, he took her lips fiercely, demanding the response her eyes promised. And she gave it.

The true test came a moment later when, with heaving chest, he tore his lips and hands free and shed the rest of his clothes. He tensed, feeling her eyes on him as though they were hands. He was hard and boldly ready for her. Would she draw back, shrink from him in fear and revulsion? He held his breath.

She stared at him so long, not moving, not speaking, he closed his eyes in dread. He'd done it. He'd scared her with his eagerness, his loss of control. He should have gone slower. He should have doused the light so she couldn't see him. He should have—

Warm, soft fingers touched his aching hardness. He

322

gasped. He groaned. "Oh, yes," he whispered hoarsely. "Touch me, Dani, touch me."

At his desperate plea, something warm and wonderful burst in Daniella's heart, sending bubbles of ecstasy shooting to her fingers and toes. He wanted her! He wanted and needed her as much as she did him.

With a woman's confidence, she stroked him and smiled at his jerking reaction. Then his hand closed over hers and wrapped her fingers around him. He guided her hand up and down, up and down, then, with a ragged breath, he drew her hand away.

Before she could ask what was wrong, he rolled her over until her back was to him. He wrapped his body around hers from behind until they were like two spoons nestled together. What was he doing? "Travis?"

"It's all right, love. Trust me." He tucked a pillow beneath her upper knee, then swept the hair from the back of her neck and placed hot, fevered kisses along her nape. "This way I won't crush you." His hand roamed over her stomach and down between her legs again, working its magic until she was once again breathless. She felt herself grow hot and heavy.

When his fingers slipped from her she wanted to cry out in protest. But in the next instant, she felt the hot, hard length of him slip inside her.

She moaned in pure pleasure.

He stopped. "Am I hurting you?"

His voice was rough with passion, and so was hers when she answered, "No! Don't stop."

Travis steeled himself for control and eased forward, pushing himself into her hot, sweet depths. Depths so tight, so virginally tight, even though she wasn't a virgin. His control slipped. He gasped and grasped for it, but it was gone. He buried himself within her, and buried his face in her hair.

He was the first. No matter who had gone before him, he knew he was the first to make her eyes flutter closed, to make her moan deep in her throat that way, to put that secret, woman's smile on her lips.

His body screamed for release. With trembling fingers, he found the tiny bud of pleasure between her velvet folds and massaged it in time to his slow, rhythmic thrusts.

Somewhere in the back of her mind, Daniella wondered if a person could die from so much ecstasy. She moaned and moved her hips against him. The tempo of his lovemaking increased. She met him move for move.

Suddenly she felt herself climbing, higher and higher, faster and faster, until she flew off the edge of the world. Directly into that deep, dark chasm. But it was no longer fearful, no longer dark. Bright rainbows of light exploded all around her. Her body convulsed again and again. She cried out for Travis. And he was there.

He stiffened and gave one last, deep thrust, and answered her cry, joining her in his own release.

Minutes, maybe hours later, when their breathing had slowed, Travis slipped from her body, moved over and rolled her to her back. His hand shook as he smoothed long tangled tresses from her face. "Are you all right?" he whispered.

Slowly, with great effort, Daniella opened her eyes and met his anxious gaze. With a hand on the back of his neck, she pulled him close for a soft, sweet kiss. "I've never been this all right in my life."

When he smiled, she smiled back.

She watched his every move as he pulled the sheet up over their bodies and turned down the wick on the lantern till the light went out. With a sigh, she felt his arm slip around her. She curled up against his side, placed her head on his sweat-dampened shoulder, and fell asleep.

Daniella dreamed she was floating on a cloud, drifting lazily along on a gentle breeze. She woke slowly. Her ear was pressed against her husband's chest and she heard the strong beat of his heart. *Her husband.* He truly was now. She smiled and ran her hand through the crisp golden curls on his chest.

She felt a kiss on top of her head and raised up on an elbow to look at him. "Good morning." Her voice was husky with sleep. She lost herself in the brown and gold depths of his tender gaze.

"Good morning." With his hand behind her head, Travis pulled her down until their lips met in a gentle searching kiss. He threaded his fingers through her hair and moaned against the softness of her mouth.

A hesitant knock sounded on the bedroom door. She jerked away.

Travis froze, trying to read the expression in her eyes. She wasn't as desperate to be held this morning as she'd been last night. Was she having regrets? He saw the blush creep up her neck and cover her face. What was she thinking?

"Dani?" With a finger to her chin, he forced her to look at him.

A slow smile spread across his face, and Daniella felt her blush deepen. She knew he must be reading in her eyes what she felt in her body. That surging warmth was flooding her again, the same as it had last night when he kissed her, held her, made love to her. She wanted him to touch her, and she wanted to touch him, all over.

She felt his laughter start deep in his chest, and by the time the booming sound of it filled the room, he was hugging her tightly and she was laughing with him. She wanted to tell him all the things she was feeling right then. The euphoric sense of freedom that swept through her was exhilarating. For the first time she understood what it was to be free of fear. She'd never felt so safe and cared for in her life as she did at this moment.

But even more important to her than that was the knowledge that she could simply reach out and touch her husband any time she wanted, and he would be there. He could touch her, and she would revel in it. She wanted to tell him all of this, but the words stuck in her throat, and all she could do was laugh with him, and hold on to him and to this moment, and pray he understood that the tears on her face were not tears of sorrow.

He gently kissed her tears away and pressed her head to his shoulder before calling an answer to the knock at the door. Juanita entered the room carrying a tray with their morning coffee, and at the sight of the two of them curled up together in bed, a wide grin split her face. She placed the tray on the bedside table and quickly scurried from the room, shutting the door as she left.

Travis sat up to drink his coffee, and Daniella decided to get dressed. Still too shy to walk around naked, despite last night, she slipped her arms through the sleeves of her nightgown before tossing the sheet back and climbing from the bed.

At the sharp rattle of cup and saucer, followed immediately by a low, vile curse, Daniella gripped the gaping front of her gown closed and whirled toward Travis. His face was nearly as white as the sheet, and he stared down at the bed. She frowned. "Travis, what's wrong?"

Her gaze automatically followed his. Her knees trembled at the sight of the dark red spots on the sheet where she'd lain. It was blood. Her blood!

"Get back in bed, Dani," Travis said, his voice rough with emotion. "I'll get Rosita."

Travis's hand shook as he helped her back into bed. Dear God, what had he done? He'd given in to the fierce desire that had been burning within him for so long. He'd taken advantage of her vulnerability last night, knowing all the while he shouldn't. And now she was bleeding. Because of him.

He brushed a tender kiss on her brow, then yanked on his pants and ran — *ran* — for Rosita.

He spent the next half hour as he'd spent much of the previous evening, pacing the hall outside his closed bedroom door. He aged ten years waiting for that damn door to open.

When it did, he stiffened with dread, remorse over his actions last night in that very room eating him alive. "How is she?" he demanded. "Should I send for a doctor?"

Rosita raised one disdainful brow at the unintentional insult, then shook her head and rolled her eyes. "It was only a few spots of blood. With rest and care, and no more bed play," the woman announced boldly, "*la Señora* will be fine."

"Are you sure?"

Rosita smiled and patted him on the cheek as if he were Matt. "*Sí*, I am sure. You go to her now."

Travis was still too worried to be relieved as Rosita left and he sat down on the edge of the bed.

"I'm all right," Dani told him, reaching for his hand.

He clutched her hand tightly while searching her eyes. There was a look of such tenderness in those pale blue depths it nearly took his breath away. "Are you sure? How do you feel?"

"I feel fine. Rosita says this just happens sometimes. I'll be all right. But we can't . . ."

"I know, love, I know. I knew last night we shouldn't. I'm so sorry. If anything happens to you or these babies because I couldn't control myself—"

"Travis, no. It isn't your fault. It could have been caused by the fall I took yesterday. In fact, that's probably the case. Besides," she added with a blush and a slight grin, "the way I remember it, I . . . well, I sort of threw myself at you."

He felt himself smiling at her candidness as well as her enchanting blush. He leaned forward and brushed his lips across hers. "You only gave me what I wanted more than anything in the world," he whispered. "I've never received a more precious gift in my life."

Carmen checked to make sure her bodice was properly buttoned as she stepped out into the blinding afternoon sun

327

and started down the rickety steps leading from Billy Joe Crane's room to the alley below. *Dios,* but the only thing worthwhile at all about that stupid *gringo* was what he had between his legs. Imagine him getting squeamish just because Travis's little wife happened to be expecting.

What earthly difference that made, Carmen couldn't figure out. If he was going to kill the interfering bitch anyway, what did it matter? Even when Carmen had told Crane Daniella was only expecting an Apache bastard—maybe two, if ranch gossip were to be trusted—he'd still refused to go back and finish the job.

He'd said he didn't care if the kid was red, white, or green, he wasn't about to harm a "mother-to-be."

Dios, what a stupid fool! Now he was refusing to even go near the Triple C until the new Mrs. Colton gave birth. Apparently it was all right to kill a new mother, but not an expectant one. Who could understand a *gringo* anyway?

At the bottom of the stairs Carmen's skirt caught on a loose splinter. She gave a sharp tug, then cursed under her breath at the sound of ripping fabric.

Next week Travis would be coming to town. All the farmers, ranchers, and businessmen were coming for some sort of election. How she longed to see Travis!

But no. The time wasn't right. Not yet.

She could, however, arrange to have a little pressure put on him, pressure for him to get rid of his wife. Yes. A few suggestions whispered in the right ears over the next few days, and Travis's own neighbors might convince him of the wisdom of sending Daniella packing.

And if that didn't work, she'd grit her teeth and bide her time until Crane took care of the problem once and for all.

Chapter Twenty-seven

Travis hated leaving Dani for the day or two the meeting in Tucson would take, but she had insisted that he go. One of his biggest worries was that now that she was no longer confined to bed she would overdo and tire herself out. Before he and Jason had ridden out that morning Travis had made Rosita and Juanita swear they'd keep a close eye on her. That helped, but not enough. He wanted to keep his own eyes on her.

Yet she was right; this meeting was important. Now that the U. S. Army had pulled out and left the Territory defenseless, left it with no remaining doubts as to the contempt the Union held for Arizona, it was imperative that they get a representative to the Confederate Congress as soon as possible. Today in Tucson the citizens would elect the delegate. Travis and Jason wanted to make sure the man they sent was the right man for the job.

"Would you look at that," Jason said as they neared Tucson.

Travis narrowed his eyes and peered down the dusty road. The town was bulging with people. Wagons lined the streets and tents spilled from the edge of town out into the desert. "Surely they didn't all come for the meeting," he said more or less to himself.

As they slowly made their way through the tightly packed streets toward the livery, shouts and snatches of conversation explained the situation. Many had come for the meeting, but most were refugees from Tubac, down near the border.

Apache attacks had become so frequent and vicious, everyone from Tubac and the surrounding ranches and farms had fled north for the dubious safety of Tucson. They were tired, scared, and angry over the loss of their homes.

Travis smiled grimly to himself. The vote should go quickly. These people wanted action, and they wanted it now.

By the time the meeting came to a close that night, Travis was pleased. By an overwhelming majority, the citizens elected Tucson resident Granville Oury as the Arizona delegate to the Confederate Congress.

"Have you seen Renard anywhere in this throng?"

Jason frowned and shook his head. "Not a sign of him."

Travis shouted across the crowded room, asking if Renard was present. Josh Hamlin elbowed his way toward Travis and called out, "Hell no, he ain't here. You didn't hear what happened?"

Something in Hamlin's eyes sent prickles of foreboding down Travis's spine. "What happened?"

Hamlin's gaze flicked toward Jake Alverez and Burton Schmidt, who joined him facing Travis. "He weren't home two days after tellin' all of us about this here meeting when he was hit by Apaches. They took all his stock, burned down his house, and some heathen buck . . . well, let's just say Sarah Renard won't never be the same after what he done."

Travis lost track of the voices around him as he pictured pretty little dark-haired Sarah Renard, Lucien's wife. Hamlin didn't have to explain the details. It was clear from his tone and the look on his face that Sarah had been raped.

The buck called himself Geronimo.

Golthlay? That sorry bastard!

"So what happened?" Jason demanded. "Where are the Renards?"

"They lit out," Hamlin answered. "He said he was takin' her back to her brother's in Santa Fe."

"Damned shame, if you ask me," Alverez commented.

"Yeah," Schmidt said. "A man ain't safe nowhere these days, least of all in his own home. But then, guess you don't have to worry about your place being attacked by Apaches, now, do ya, Colton? Is that what the rest of us gotta do to keep our homes safe? Take up with Apache leavings?"

Travis felt the blood roar in his ears. Without so much as a blink of an eye, he swung his fist into Schmidt's face and broke the man's nose. Schmidt reeled and took three men down with him when he fell.

"What the hell!" someone shouted. A cry went up in the throng.

"Fight!"

Daniella let Matt stay up later than usual with the excuse that he needed to study his lessons. The truth was, however, that she wanted to postpone going to bed without Travis for as long as possible.

Since the night they'd made love she'd felt so close to him, even when they were apart during the day. She knew that when night came they would lay down on the big bed in their room and hold each other.

She hadn't rid herself of all her fears, but he'd helped her over that biggest one—her fear of intimacy. The biggest thing left for her to face was the birth of her twins. No matter what Travis said, she feared his reaction when they were actually born. When presented with a constant physical reminder of her past, how would he react? How would *she* react?

Seated on the edge of the bed, Daniella stared at the glow of the lantern and tried to banish that particular worry from her mind. A moment later, images formed before her eyes. She tried to blink them away—she didn't want any more visions—but her lids refused to lower.

The scene before her sharpened to show a crowded,

331

smoke-filled room. Men shouted, although she couldn't hear them. In the center a brawl was taking place. Two blond men stood back to back and fought off a half dozen others. Fists flew and boots kicked. Arms and legs tangled as some of the combatants crashed to the floor. It was impossible to tell exactly what was happening until it was all over, and the two blond men stood back to back again, glaring a blatant challenge to anyone else who cared to take them up on it.

Just as the scene started to fade, Daniella gasped. It was Travis and Jason! When the vision disappeared, she buried her face in her hands. Travis and Jason had been in a fight. What had caused it? Had the political meeting gotten out of hand?

That didn't make sense. Travis and Jason held opposing views on the matters being discussed, yet they'd fought together, not against each other.

With a sinking feeling of dread and guilt, she somehow knew the fight had something to do with her.

When the men got home the next day, Travis frowned when he located Dani on her knees in the courtyard watering flowers.

"Is this how you rest and take care of yourself?"

She dropped the watering gourd into the bucket next to her with a splash and whirled on her knees to face him. "You're home!"

The smile on her face and obvious delight in her eyes stirred a warmth and yearning deep inside him. With a crooked smile of his own, he helped her stand, then sighed with satisfaction when they embraced.

Their lips met in hungry reassurance that they were together, that her fear of him really was gone. Even though they'd made love, Travis had half expected her to withdraw from him again during the past days. He thanked God that it hadn't happened.

She pulled back slightly and he felt the touch of her eyes on his face.

"Are you all right?" she asked breathlessly.

"Now that I'm home with you, I couldn't be better," he answered with a smile.

"No," she said shaking her head. "I mean the fight. Were you injured?"

Travis stared down into her face, confused. "What are you talking about?"

She took another step back and pursed her lips. "I'm talking about the fight you and Jason were in, about this bruise on your cheek," she said, running a gentle finger over the spot in question. "What happened, Travis?"

Puzzled, he asked, "How did you know Dad and I were in a fight?"

She closed her eyes briefly, but not before he saw the flash of pain and uncertainty there. "Dani?"

"I . . . I saw it."

"You couldn't have. You were here the whole time. Weren't you?"

She nodded and swallowed. "I was here, but . . . I saw it."

Travis felt a coldness prickle along the back of his neck as understanding dawned. She'd had another vision. As far as he knew, it was the first time in months this had happened to her. He knew her visions frightened and confused her. He had hoped for her sake she wouldn't have any more. He pulled her gently back into his arms. "Are you all right?"

She looked up at him earnestly. "I asked first."

Travis forced a smile to his lips. "I'm fine. It was nothing."

"But what started it? What was the fight about?"

"You didn't see that, too?" he asked carefully.

"All I could see was the fight, and that you and Jason won. I couldn't hear any voices, so I don't know what started it."

The smile returned to Travis's lips, this time without force. Not for his life would he tell her what that damned fight had been about. The lie came easily to his lips. "You know how some men get when politics is the topic of conversation. Things just got a little out of hand, that's all. It was nothing important, I assure you. There was no real harm done."

When Dani changed the subject and asked about the Renards, he tensed again. This, too, was something he didn't want to tell her. It was unlikely that anyone would ever inform her of the cause of the fight, but she was bound to hear the truth about the Renards eventually. He couldn't lie about it, but he didn't necessarily have to tell her the whole truth, either.

His abridged version only mentioned that Renard's ranch was attacked by Apaches, and that the Renards had gone back to Santa Fe. He didn't mention what had happened to Sarah.

But yet Dani knew. He saw the knowledge in her eyes.

With a shake of her head, Dani changed the subject again, and Travis was relieved to hear her ask about the election.

"We're sending Granville Oury as Arizona's first delegate to the Confederate Congress."

"Now what happens?"

"Now we wait and see how he's received when he gets there."

"Oury. I've heard that name before. Do you think he'll be able to do us any good?"

"If anyone can do us some good, he can, I suppose. He's been here for several years and knows our problems as well as anyone else. He's smart and he's honest, and he seems to understand the inner workings of government. He's probably the best man for the job."

Travis stopped and stared at Dani. It suddenly dawned on him that he'd never had a serious discussion of this sort with a woman before. He'd never been around a female who even cared about such things, much less understood them. The more he was around Dani, the more he learned about her, the better he liked her. He'd never *liked* a woman

334

before, except his mother and the women who worked on the Triple C.

The thought of his employees reminded him that the political meeting wasn't the only thing that happened in Tucson yesterday. "Damn," he muttered.

"What?" Dani asked.

"We started talking about that meeting and I forgot the real reason I came looking for you just now. There's someone in my study I want you to meet."

"Now? But . . ." She looked down at herself and brushed at her skirt, trying to knock the dirt from the flower bed off.

"You're just fine the way you are. They won't mind."

"Who is it?"

"Just come with me and you'll see."

With a shrug of her shoulders, she took the arm he offered, and they walked back into the coolness of the house. When they entered the study, he smiled at her surprise when she saw the old Mexican woman and the young girl waiting for them.

Dani's first reaction was pure reflex: her hand went up and touched the white streak where it began at her temple. The two strangers responded automatically by following her hand with their eyes, but their facial expressions did not change. They each wore a tentative, hopeful smile.

"Dani," Travis began. "This is Señora Rivera and her granddaughter, Lucinda. They're both looking for work. I thought perhaps Tucker and Simon could use someone to look after them. What do you think?"

"Oh, Travis," she cried. "I think it's a marvelous idea. I've been so worried about them, up there all alone with no one to take care of them and see they eat properly."

"I thought you might feel that way." Travis smiled down at her. "Lucinda says she's had some experience with babies, and has agreed to come back here in a couple of months to help you, if you wish. In the meantime, she'll go with her grandmother. If you like, we can take them up to El Valle

335

this afternoon. That is, if you feel up to it, and if Rosita says it's all right."

Dani gazed up at him with gratitude shining in her eyes. He forced his breathing to remain normal, but he thought if she didn't stop looking at him like that he might startle everyone present with his actions.

"I feel fine," she declared. "I'd like to see Tucker and Simon, and there are still a few things I'd like to bring from there. Can we take the wagon?"

"I thought we would. We can start right after we eat whatever it is I smelled when I passed the kitchen earlier."

"You're right," Dani answered. "We must feed them first. We wouldn't want them to have to eat Tucker's cooking their first day there, or they might leave." She smiled warmly at the two new employees, and they smiled back shyly in return.

After dinner, Travis, Daniella, Lucinda, and Señora Rivera climbed into the wagon for the trip. The two-hour ride went quickly for Daniella. When they arrived at El Valle, Tucker reached up and lifted her to the ground. With a laughing hoot, he said, "You've put on a few inches, girlie."

"A gentleman is not supposed to notice," Daniella scolded.

"Gentleman! Huh."

"We brought you a surprise," she informed him. "Señora Rivera and her granddaughter, Lucinda, are here to cook and clean for you, and to generally keep you and Simon out of trouble."

"Well, ain't that a wonder. They surely are welcome, ain't they, Simon?"

The silent giant grinned and nodded. As far as Daniella knew, Simon hadn't said another word since the night of the fiesta. "We're both a little tired of my cookin' already," Tucker added with a laugh.

Daniella showed Señora Rivera and Lucinda around the house and grounds, then she had her remaining belongings, including her spinning wheel, loom, and a good supply of wool, loaded into the back of the wagon.

"You look good, girl," Tucker told her when the two of them were alone. "They treatin' you all right down there?"

"Oh, yes." Her eyes locked on Travis as he approached. She felt her heart swell. "Everyone is very good to me."

Travis reached her side. "It's getting late," he said. "Ready to go?"

Daniella smiled. "Yes." She was ready to go wherever he led.

He helped her to the wagon seat, and after cheerful goodbyes, he headed the wagon home. The trip was filled with easy, quiet talk and long, comfortable stretches of companionable silence. When Travis pulled to a halt before the ranch house, he helped Daniella down. She leaned heavily against him.

"You're tired," he said. "We were gone too long. Why don't you go rest for a while?"

"Thank you for what you did today," she said. "It was very thoughtful and kind of you to think of Tucker and Simon. I know they're grateful, and so am I." She stretched up and placed a soft kiss on his cheek, then left him standing by the wagon with a wide grin on his face.

Chapter Twenty-eight

"Juanita, would you please inform Dani we have guests, and ask her to join us?"

"*Sí, señor,*" Juanita replied.

Travis turned back to the two men in his study and poured them each another drink. Both men were about his age. One he'd known since childhood, the other was a stranger.

Calvin Watson and Travis had played together as boys and had been best friends, then each drifted off to pursue his own dreams. Travis came West and became a rancher. Cal attended law school in Philadelphia, and then he, too, came West. He settled in Santa Fe and opened a law office.

Cal was half a head shorter than Travis, and of a much lighter build, almost too thin, in fact. His curly brown hair and sparkling hazel eyes gave him a carefree, boyish appearance.

"My wife doesn't know anything about these papers I asked you to prepare, Cal, so I'd appreciate it if you didn't mention the subject in her presence."

"She's not in favor of the idea?" Cal asked in alarm. "You realize the papers aren't valid unless she signs them willingly." He rubbed the back of his neck as if it ached.

"I understand that," Travis replied, ignoring the questions in Cal's eyes. "It's just that the subject hasn't come up yet. I'm hoping she'll want this as much as I do, but if she doesn't, well, it's her decision."

Travis tried to shrug off the idea that Dani wouldn't be

338

pleased about this surprise he'd been planning for months. She surely would see it was the best thing for all concerned.

He turned his attention to his other guest, not quite sure what to think of this man who called himself Tom Jeffords. Jeffords claimed to be a former captain in the U. S. Army, now operating a mail contract to and from Tucson and points east. Cal and Jeffords had met in Tucson and found out by accident that they were both headed for the same place—the Triple C.

Cal's excuse to Travis for coming to visit was that the mail was too unreliable, with Cochise shooting up everything that moved now that the army was gone. He dismissed the danger of traveling by stagecoach along the Gila River, then south by horseback to Tucson, as so much nonsense. Travis figured at least part of the reason Cal was here was to get a look at the new Mrs. Colton. Ever since Julia, Cal hadn't trusted Travis's judgment when it came to women.

Besides, Travis had flatly stated for years that he'd never remarry. For Cal to get a letter from him stating he was marrying a woman who was already pregnant, with twins, and by another man yet, was more than the lawyer could stand.

Jeffords was also here because of the mail problem. His riders were being shot out of their saddles so often these days he claimed it was nearly impossible to find anyone willing to take on the job. The reason was Cochise. Jeffords had it in his head that if someone just sat down and talked with Cochise, explaining that the mail and the riders who carried it were no threat to him, the problem could be resolved.

To this end, he came to the Triple C looking for Woman of Magic. He'd been told she could lead him to Cochise.

"What do you know about Woman of Magic, Jeffords?" Travis asked cautiously.

"Not a whole helluva lot, really. Some Apaches who scouted for the army just said she's a white woman, and that

339

the Apaches, the Chiricahua in particular, consider her big medicine. They say she's got a streak of white in her hair, put there by their Great Spirit. That's all I really know."

"Had any of those scouts ever seen her?" Travis was curious and concerned about the rumors about Dani.

"Naw. They did say, though, that no Apache, be he Chiricahua, Mescalero, or whatever, would dare harm her. Apparently all their medicine men have warned them she's not to be touched. Knowing one or two medicine men myself, I figure if she's that important, she must be at least ninety, and if she's got all her teeth missing and a wart on the end of her nose, I won't be a bit surprised."

Travis had just taken a sip of whiskey when Jeffords made that last comment. He choked on the mouthful of liquid and nearly spewed it all over his guests, but finally managed to swallow it.

"You all right, Travis?" Cal gave his friend a sharp slap on the back to help clear his throat.

"Fine. Fine," Travis gasped. A *wart!*

When he could breathe again, he sighed with relief. It was good to hear that Dani's protection extended to the other Apache tribes.

But a *wart?*

Guests? Guests! Daniella rushed to the bedroom to change clothes.

Well, perhaps "rushed" was too strong a word. She huffed and puffed, and moved as fast as she could, and it *felt* like rushing.

She stripped off her peasant garb and washed herself as best she could from the ever-present pitcher of cool water. She caught sight of herself in the mirror and groaned. She was out of breath, her cheeks were flushed, and her hair streamed down her back in windblown snarls.

She slipped into one of the dresses she'd made recently, which buttoned up the front so she didn't need help getting into it. It was a simple, long-sleeved, scoop-necked, pale yellow muslin, and had a high waist to accommodate her girth. She liked the way the color complimented her skin. She put on a pair of tan kid slippers, left over from her days in Boston, then frantically yanked a brush through her hair and tied the curls at her nape with a yellow ribbon. Another yellow ribbon encircled her throat, hiding the scar.

Whoever these guests were, Daniella was pleased Travis had asked her to join him. This was the first time they'd had guests since she'd been here. She only wished she'd had time to make herself more presentable.

When Daniella, still breathless from having hurried, stepped into the study, all three men rose to their feet immediately. Travis held out his hand to her with a warm smile, while the other two men stared with identical stunned expressions.

"Gentlemen, my wife, Daniella," Travis announced proudly.

Daniella's eyes sparkled with pleasure when she read the admiration and total approval on her husband's face.

Travis stepped forward and met her in the middle of the room, then placed an arm about her waist. She leaned into him slightly, and when she raised her face to his, he placed a brief, tender kiss on her lips. For a long moment, they lost themselves in each other's eyes.

Cal snapped out of his trance and thought, *My Lord, she's breathtaking!* His eyes went from the white streak in her coal black hair, over her glowing face, sparkling eyes, pert, turned-up nose, soft pink lips curled up in an intimate smile, down her dainty chin and the slim white column of her delicate throat, across her ample breasts, to her huge, swollen abdomen. His mind raced. . . . *pregnant when I met her . . . Woman of Magic . . . white streak . . . big medicine . . . pregnant when I met her . . .*

Whatever Travis Colton had gotten himself into this time, he certainly seemed to be enjoying it. Cal burned with curiosity and vowed to find out all he could about this new Mrs.

341

Colton. Was she as grasping and deceitful as Julia had been? She didn't look the type, but then, Julia had been beautiful, too.

Travis tore his gaze away from Dani and caught Cal's expression. He could almost hear the questions whirling in the lawyer's head. Cal never could stand a mystery.

"Dani, I'd like you to meet my oldest and closest friend, Cal Watson, from Santa Fe. Cal, this is Daniella."

That was twice since she'd entered the room that Travis had called her Daniella. It was the first time he'd called her that since before they were married. His arm came around her back and he gripped her shoulder firmly. It struck Daniella that both gestures, the use of her full name and the grip on her shoulder, were blatant attempts to demonstrate his possession of her. She stole a quick glance at him and bit back a smile. He was jealous!

She extended her hand to Cal, and with a flourish, Cal bowed and placed a kiss just above her knuckles in the best of old world tradition.

Daniella laughed gaily at his extravagant style. "Welcome to the Triple C, Mr. Watson. I'm delighted to meet a friend of Travis's."

"Please, call me Cal. It's a pleasure to meet you, Mrs. Colton."

"Thank you. But if I'm to call you Cal, then you must call me Daniella." She felt Travis relax when she used her full name. She smiled to herself.

Travis turned her toward the other man in the room and introduced them to each other.

"You've got a mean streak in you, Colton, letting me run off at the mouth that way, knowing what a fool I was making of myself." Tom Jeffords shook Daniella's hand in a firm, no-nonsense grip.

Puzzled, she looked to Travis for an explanation.

"Mr. Jeffords came here looking for Woman of Magic. He was under the impression that you were, uh, well, much older."

She knew by the smiles on their faces that there was more to it than that, but she let it go. "What can I do for you, Mr. Jeffords?" She sat down on the chair Travis had vacated. Travis stood behind her with his hands resting possessively on her shoulders.

Cal and Jeffords resumed their seats, Cal leaning forward intently to catch every word.

"Then you really are Woman of Magic?" Jeffords asked.

"To some people, I am." Surely if the man were here to scorn her, as others had, Travis wouldn't have introduced him. She tried to relax.

"Mrs. Colton," Jeffords began. "I have a problem, and I've been told you might be able to help me with it. You see, I've contracted to carry the mail to Tucson over a couple of hundred miles of pretty rugged territory. For months now, my riders have been harassed by Cochise. Many of them have been killed. Now the way I see it, a man as powerful as Cochise must also be pretty smart. My men don't carry any military dispatches, just civilian mail. What I'm hoping to do is explain this, in person, to Cochise, and try to convince him to let the mail carriers through. That's where I need your help."

As Jeffords spoke, Daniella watched him carefully. He was a large, solid man, with a trim red beard and long auburn hair hanging down past his collar. But it was his eyes she searched. They were brown and keen, and they studied her carefully, even as she studied him. Her first, overall impression was that Jeffords was an honest, sincere man.

"You want me to talk to Cochise about this? Is that why you're here?"

"Well, no, ma'am. Truth is, I wanna talk with him myself, face to face. I just don't know how to find him. All I want from you is some directions. I'm told you know where his stronghold is."

"I see," she said slowly. "And if I give you these directions, how do I know you won't lead the army there to wipe him out?"

343

"You don't," he answered bluntly. "But I'm not a complete fool, Mrs. Colton. I'd guess that it'd be near impossible to get within a day's ride of Cochise without him knowin' about it. He'd definitely have the advantage, and he'd be able to wipe us out, probably without us ever even seeing him. I guess I'm asking you to trust me. I plan to go alone. I believe that's my only chance of gettin' to meet him."

Daniella thought hard. Should she trust this man, this stranger? If she did, and it was a trick, well, he was right — Cochise could definitely protect himself. And if it wasn't a trick, if this man was sincere, it might be just what Cochise needed to see that Travis wasn't the only white man he could trust. Cochise would certainly admire a man brave enough to enter the stronghold alone. *If* Jeffords made it in alive.

"You put me in a difficult position, Mr. Jeffords. I think I trust you. But if I tell you how to find Cochise, and you should betray him, or harm him, I'd never forgive myself."

"You're that close to him, then?" Jeffords asked intently.

"He saved my life. That's something I'll never be able to repay him for. I would never willingly betray him."

Her candid answer obviously surprised him, but he seemed to recover quickly. "I understand your position, ma'am. All I can say is that I assure you, I'm going on my own, not as anyone's messenger or representative, and all I want to do is talk with him. If you decide not to help me, I'll just have to try some other way of locatin' him."

Daniella didn't know what to do. Her instincts told her this could be a good thing, both for Jeffords and Cochise. But the very fact that she was so willing to trust this stranger made her shy away from him. She needed time.

"I'd like to think about your request for a little while," she said hesitantly. "If you'll stay and join us for dinner, I'll have an answer for you then."

Tom Jeffords split his red beard with a smile. "Ah, Mrs. Colton. Even if you decide you don't want to help me, I

344

could never pass up an invitation to a homecooked meal."

Daniella extended her invitation to Cal, too, who readily accepted. After a few minutes of polite chit chat, Travis and Danielia left their guests and went to their bedroom.

"Well, what do you think?" Travis asked.

Daniella paced the floor nervously. "I think if Jeffords is really what he says he is, Cochise needs to meet a man like him. He needs to know you aren't the only honorable white man in the world."

"And if it's a trick?"

"If I was sure it was a trick, I'd give him directions to Mon-ache. He'd kill him on sight. What do you think? Do you trust him?"

"It doesn't matter what I think, Dani. He's not asking me for information about my adopted father."

She understood then—it was to be her decision. Then she started laughing.

"What's so funny?"

"I just realized that I can't tell him what he wants to know, even if I wanted to. I wouldn't know how to describe which canyon leads into the *rancheria*. The best I could do would be to tell him to ride east until Cochise finds him."

Travis smiled. "That's not a bad idea, you know. We could tell him how to get within range of Cochise's scouts, and let them take him in from there. If you trust him, that is."

"It's perfect!" she cried. She stood on tiptoes and kissed him on the cheek.

His arms slid around her and pulled her close. Their lips met in a gentle, searching kiss. It was several moments before they pulled apart.

As they left the room together, Daniella stopped Travis with a touch on his arm. "I think I want to talk to Jeffords some more before we tell him anything. Do you mind?"

"Of course not, love." He bent down and kissed her on the nose. "I promise not to tell him anything unless you say it's okay."

They rejoined their guests and took them to the main salon to wait for Jason and Matt. They didn't have long to wait.

"Uncle Cal!" came the shriek from the doorway. Matt was a blur of motion as he streaked through the room, nearly upending a small table in his haste. He threw himself at Cal's slender chest. Everyone looked on indulgently as the two hugged each other. After a minute, Cal lowered Matt to the floor and stood back at arm's length.

"Let me look at you, boy. I hear you had quite a little adventure after you left Santa Fe on the stage. But Matt, the next time you get a burr under your saddle, try something a little more tame, like busting broncs or wrestling a bear. Getting captured by Apaches is not what I would consider a fun thing. But you don't look any worse for the experience. In fact, I'd say you've grown several inches since last winter."

"Have I really? Dani says I'm gonna to be as big as Dad, someday," Matt said proudly. "But the Apaches weren't too bad, once they decided to keep me. But I wanted to come home, and they wouldn't let me. Then Dani brought Dad, and Cochise let me come home with them."

Cal and Jeffords both eyed Daniella carefully, questions plainly visible in their eyes. She blushed. This wasn't something she wanted to talk about with strangers. Jason came to her rescue.

"Calvin Watson, you old bookworm. What's the matter? Did Santa Fe finally get too tame for you, or did you figure we needed a bit of your version of law and order out here in Apacheria?"

"Jason!" Cal greeted. "It's good to see you! Actually, I had some important papers for Travis and didn't want to chance the mail, no offense intended, Jeffords. So I used that as an excuse to come and meet your new daughter-in-law."

The two men shook hands exuberantly, then Travis introduced Tom Jeffords to Jason and Matt.

"What brings you to the Triple C, Jeffords," Jason wanted to know. They were all seated around the dinner table now.

"I came to see if Mrs. Colton could help me locate Cochise," Jeffords answered truthfully.

Matt looked up sharply. "What do you want with Cochise?" he wondered aloud.

"I want to ask him if he'll consider letting the mail go through to Tucson unmolested. You think he will?" the man asked the boy.

"You just gonna ride up to him and ask him, just like that?" Matt was plainly skeptical.

"That's my plan, if I can find him."

Matt turned his troubled gaze on first his father, then Daniella. *"Shimá,* what if he's an *'iitkúi?"* Matt asked.

Daniella felt a lump in her throat. He'd called her Mother! He'd never done that before. But the question he asked was one she'd been asking herself for the past hour.

Jeffords laid his fork down on his plate and looked at both of them. "I assure you I'm not a troublemaker."

Matt flushed guiltily at being caught calling the man names. Daniella was shocked that Jeffords had understood. "You know their language?" she asked in amazement.

"I learned it from the same scouts who told me about you. How else am I going to be able to talk to Cochise if I can't speak his language? It seemed like it would be worth the trouble."

This was not a common thing, for a white man to learn an Indian language, Daniella knew. Indians were usually considered stupid and illiterate because they didn't speak English. Jeffords had definitely gone to a lot of trouble.

"You have to understand, Mr. Jeffords, that I can't guarantee your safety. You could very easily be killed without ever seeing Cochise."

"And I might fall off my horse and break my neck just over the next hill, too. Life's full of chances. I'll take mine."

Daniella made her decision. "Tell him what he wants to know, Travis."

347

* * *

Tom Jeffords left for Cochise's stronghold the next morning at first light. It would be weeks before anyone at the Triple C learned if he even made it alive past Cochise's trail guards, let alone if he got to talk with the great chief himself.

Cal Watson was fascinated by everything he learned about Daniella Blackwood Colton. He stayed several days, until he finally had the entire story out of Travis. By the time he headed back to his law practice in Santa Fe, he was convinced that Travis and his new wife were very much in love with one another. He admitted to himself that his concerns had been groundless. Travis was happy, and Daniella was a worthy object of his affections.

With the autumn rains came cool, almost cold nights. Daniella's spinning wheel was moved to the main salon where the family now gathered each evening. She spent hours spinning wool into fine yarns and threads while Travis and Jason told her what all was happening around the ranch, and Matt studied the lessons she gave him.

With the heat from the fire on her face, Dani draped her shawl on the back of her chair. She was unaware that every time she bent to check or change the spool beneath her spinning wheel, the front of her loose blouse fell open to an alarming degree, causing Travis considerable discomfort.

Jason chuckled. Travis flushed in embarrassment at being caught ogling his own wife.

"Come on, Matt. I think it's past our bedtime," Jason suggested with a laugh.

When Daniella and Travis were alone, she looked at him uneasily. He'd been glaring at her all evening. She tried to think of what she could have done to cause his ill temper.

"Travis?"

"Um?" He stared into the fire and nursed his third glass of whiskey.

348

"What's wrong?"

He scowled at her from beneath lowered brows. "Nothing's wrong," he growled.

She stared at him in disbelief until he turned his gaze back to the fire and downed the rest of his drink. She bent to replace her full spool with an empty one.

"Damn." He squeezed his eyes shut for a moment, then rose from his chair and turned his back to her.

"Travis, what is it?" she asked desperately. "Why are you so angry?" They'd been getting along so well lately. He'd been so tender with her, so thoughtful of her every need. This mood of his tonight was one she hadn't seen in a while, and it worried her.

He spun around and threw his glass into the fireplace. "I'm not angry."

Daniella raised her chin a notch. "Then why are you scowling and shouting at me? You certainly act angry, and your anger seems to be directed at me. Just tell me what I've done."

"I am not angry," he said between clenched teeth. She moved to lean down again to untangle her thread and Travis groaned. "Stop! For God's sake, Dani, you're driving me crazy when you bend over like that."

She followed his gaze and the blood rushed to her face at the sight of her breasts completely exposed. She sat up abruptly and clutched the front of her blouse around her neck. "I'm sorry," she said in embarrassment. "I didn't realize—"

"No, love, I'm sorry." Travis came to her and placed a hand on her shoulder. "I didn't mean to shout at you." He gave a harsh laugh. "Restraint is something I've never been very good at." He looked down at her in apology. "Let's go to bed. I need to at least hold you in my arms."

She couldn't resist the plea in his eyes. She stood and went into his open embrace with a sigh, and Travis picked her up and carried her to their bedroom. Once they were in bed, Daniella in her nightgown, Travis naked, as always, he reached for the bottle of lotion. He'd been applying the lotion for her every night since he'd first done it that night weeks ago, the night they made love.

Daniella was still sensitive about having him see her in her present condition. In her opinion, his seeing her belly stick out like some old fat sow about to farrow should be enough to cool his lusts, but she'd found out in the past few weeks that it did no such thing. She knew he wanted her and understood his frustration.

"Travis." She reached out to halt his progress on her buttons. "You don't have to do this tonight . . . if you'd rather not."

He leaned down and kissed the hand that covered his, then looked at her steadily. "Most of the pleasures in my life lately stem from you, and touching you is one of them. I want to do this. I *need* to do it." His eyes held hers for a long moment, asking permission.

She sighed and released his hand. In truth, she wanted this as much as he did. She loved the feel of his tough, calloused hands against her skin. His fingers were so gentle as they stroked her, and she was coming to crave the fires he ignited within her with his touch.

By the time he finished with the buttons on her gown, the babes in her womb were trying to adjust to her new reclining position, and were tossing and kicking violently. Travis grinned and began to smooth on the cool lotion.

"They certainly are violent tonight," he teased. "I've never seen an Apache war dance, but it sure feels like that's what's going on in there."

Travis both felt and heard Dani's quick intake of breath. His gaze flew to her face and he saw her eyes darken with despair. "Don't look at me like that," he said. "No one hates how you got these babies more than I do, except you. But the fact that they're half Apache is not something we're going to be able to ignore, not ever."

She tried to turn her face away, but he reached out and held her chin. "With all my heart, I wish the seed they

350

sprang from was mine, but it isn't and there's nothing you or I can do about that now. But these are going to be my children, Dani. They'll carry my name, and be raised with Matt as his brother and sister, and I'll love them and protect them till my dying day.

"Even if we tried to keep it from them, they're going to know before too many years that I'm not their sire. Cochise will be back to see them. I have a feeling he's going to take his role as grandfather quite seriously. If you want to fight him on that, then I'll do my best to keep him away. But I'm not sure that would be wise, or even fair. The Apaches are a very proud people. These two little ones have the right to know about that side of their heritage, Dani. I don't want them to be confused, or torn, or have their loyalties divided, but . . . they're going to need to know. Am I making any sense?"

She blinked back the tears that pooled in her eyes. "I guess so, but . . . I just don't see how you can simply accept them so easily."

Travis read the pain and confusion, and even the doubt in her eyes. "That's easy, love," he said with a soft smile. "They brought me you."

Chapter Twenty-nine

Daniella's pace slowed considerably during the last weeks of her pregnancy, but she went about her days with a light heart. When her burden lowered, she found it difficult to get around, but Travis was nearly always at hand to help her. The entire household noticed the difference between husband and wife and smiled when they saw the tender looks that passed between the two.

Indeed, it would have been impossible for anyone to fail to notice the difference. Daniella fairly glowed under Travis's care, and Travis was more relaxed than anyone ever remembered.

The only dark spot for Daniella was Travis's occasional joke about being kicked awake in the middle of the night by the twins. "How can you sleep through that?" he would ask with a mock groan. She knew his jokes were meant to tease away her concern, so she hid her worries as best she could.

"I think I'm getting used to this," Travis announced one morning during the latter part of November.

"Used to what?" Daniella had been awake for some time. An ache in her lower back had disturbed her just before dawn.

"I slept through all the night time wrestling matches," he replied with a grin.

She should have told him then that the babes hadn't kicked in hours. She should have told him they were too busy preparing for their imminent birth. But she didn't.

Travis had had no trouble controlling his lust lately. As he

352

saw Dani's discomfort grow daily, he was far more concerned with her welfare than his own needs. Her time was near, and he worried about the ordeal she'd be forced to endure.

"Did you sleep all right?" he asked, concerned.

"Mostly," she answered truthfully. "I just can't seem to get comfortable any more."

Travis rubbed a soothing hand over her taut stomach. "It won't be long now. They're getting lower and lower." He continued stroking the tight mound until he felt the muscles relax somewhat. "Are you worried about the birth?"

"No," Daniella answered softly. It was true. She really wasn't worried. "Juanita and Rosita assure me I'll be fine." She laughed at his doubtful expression. "I think that means they won't allow me to be anything other than fine. I'm not worried, so you shouldn't be either."

Later that morning, Daniella met Juanita in the hall. "There is a man here to see you," the woman said.

"Me, not Travis?"

"Sí."

Daniella smiled. "Is it Tucker?" she asked eagerly, her spirits lifting at the thought.

"No, *señora*, this is a man I do not know."

Daniella's smile died. A feeling of unease raced down her spine, followed swiftly by another wrenching spasm in her lower back, the same kind she'd been having all morning. She gasped with the intensity of the pain.

Juanita reached for her arm. "Is it *los niños?*"

Daniella relaxed as the pain passed. "No, it's just my back."

The housekeeper gave her a knowing look. "Just your back," she said with a nod. "Stay on your feet as long as you can. I will be nearby when you need me."

Daniella waved away the woman's words. "I told you, it's just my back. I'll be fine."

As she walked toward the salon to greet her visitor, she wondered again who it could be. With her luck, it was

353

probably that despicable Billy Joe Crane. A shudder ran through her at the thought.

When she entered the room a moment later, she almost wished her visitor was Crane. He would have been more welcome.

"Hello, Ella," her father said.

A deep coldness seeped into her bones. As if it were happening all over again, she could feel the blade of his betrayal twist in her heart. Forcing all emotion from her voice, she asked, "What are you doing here?"

She watched as he ran his gaze from her head to her toes. "I came to—" On the way back up, his gaze stopped at her stomach, and for a moment Daniella feared his eyes would pop right out of his head. "Good God! You're—you're—" His face turned dark red and he clenched his fists at his sides.

"Damn!" He tore his gaze from her abdomen and raked her from head to toe again. With a sneer, he said, "I came looking for you, thinking maybe I was wrong, the way I treated you when you came home last spring." He paused and gave a sharp bark of bitter laughter. "Only I wasn't wrong, was I? It sure as hell didn't take you long to find yourself a man, did it? What's the matter? Apaches leave you with an itch you couldn't wait to scratch?"

Daniella felt the blood leave her face and wished desperately for something to lean on. From behind her came a low snarl. A second later a dark blur shot past her. Travis!

He reached her father in two long strides, and before Daniella could wonder what he was about, Travis grabbed the shorter man by the collar and lifted him off the floor. His fist swung and connected with a loud whack to Howard's jaw. Travis released him and Howard staggered backward, his eyes wide with shock, his hand clutching his aching jaw.

"Colton! What the devil's got into you?"

"Shut up, you miserable bastard." Travis swung again, this time knocking Howard to the floor. "If you ever, *ever*

354

talk to my wife like that again, I'll kill you with my bare hands! I'm more than tempted to make her an orphan here and now."

Travis practically breathed fire while Howard, a look of total shock on his face, struggled to sit up. "Your *wife?*" he croaked. His face seemed to crumple. "Daughter, I—"

Daughter! Daniella thought with scorn. How dare he call her that!

"I'm . . . sorry," Howard managed.

With her face held expressionless, she said, "So am I," then left the room.

A moment later she stepped into the bedroom and closed the door, grateful to be alone with the conflicting feelings roiling inside her. *Pain*. The renewed pain of her father's callousness. *Love*. Love for Travis for defending her nonexistent honor so gallantly. *Hope*. A tiny flame of hope brought on by her father's reason for coming here in the first place.

And disgust. Disgust with herself for allowing that hope to exist at all.

She hadn't made it halfway across the room when the door opened and Travis came in. He immediately took her in his arms and held her. "Are you all right?" he whispered against her hair.

Daniella sighed. "I suppose so."

Travis ran his fingers through her hair and stroked her back. "Don't worry, love, I'll straighten him out."

She felt herself sigh again. "Don't bother. He made up his mind about me a long time ago. He won't change it now."

A few minutes later Travis left her alone in the room, and she paced the floor, trying not to think about her father. Trying not to think about why he'd come.

It wasn't hard to keep her mind off him, she found. The ache in her back was getting stronger, more persistent, more frequent. And it was developing a set of fingers that reached around her stomach.

Soon Juanita came to check on her, and while the housekeeper was there, Daniella's water broke. After she and the floor were both cleaned up, she paced again, waiting for the pain to worsen, as she knew it must. But it didn't. The ache in her back settled to a dull, constant nuisance, but didn't get any worse.

Daniella skipped dinner, but joined the family for supper. It was a mistake. She'd hoped her father would have been gone. Instead, he sat at the table with a sorrowful look on his face and watched her every move with anxious eyes.

She couldn't eat. The very thought of food was revolting to her. Instead, she sipped her coffee and pushed the food around on her plate.

Matt and Jason chatted about their day, and Jason finally drew Travis into the conversation. Daniella wasn't following the talk. It merely buzzed in her ears as the dull ache in her back turned into a definite pain. Every few minutes it grew sharper. She ground her teeth against it, letting out a soft sigh every time it eased.

Getting up from the table at the end of the meal was a relief. She silently led the way into the salon and the others followed. Concentrating on not groaning aloud, she didn't watch where she was going and stumbled into a small side table. With a jerk, she reached out and barely saved the lamp from crashing to the floor.

The sudden movement brought back the sharp pain she'd been fighting. She gasped and clutched her stomach.

Breathe! she told herself.

Travis started forward, but was nearly bowled over by Howard, who reached his daughter first. "Ella! Are you all right?"

"Oh God!" She laughed hysterically, releasing the tension she'd been holding in so tightly all day. "What I would have given to have heard those words from you months ago." Her laughter died as swiftly as it had come, and so did the pain. She looked at her father calmly. "But it's all right now, Papa. I've met too many people since then who feel the same way you do for me to let it bother me anymore. If you can't accept what's happened to me, can't accept these babies I'm about to give birth to, then it's your problem, not mine." The pain came again, and Daniella gritted her teeth for a long moment until it passed.

Breathe!

Travis had never been more proud of anyone in his entire life than he was of Dani at that minute. He just prayed that she believed what she just told her father.

A knowing look passed between Dani and Juanita, and the housekeeper rushed out of the room. Travis was puzzled by the exchange and went to his wife's side, slipping an arm around her. He was appalled when he felt the rigidity of her body. With a finger on her chin, he turned her face toward his. "Dani?"

"Could you help me to our room, Travis?" she asked between gasping breaths. "When I said I was about to give birth, I'm afraid I meant any minute."

Travis stared at her in stunned amazement. "My God!" His expression slowly turned to one of horror as he understood. She was in labor! "Why didn't you say something?"

Travis picked her up in his arms, carefully, as if she were the most fragile piece of china and might shatter at any sudden movement, and carried her out of the salon. When he reached their bedroom, he started to lay her on the bed.

"No—please. Not yet," she said between gasps. She squeezed his shoulder in a grip of steel as the pain washed over her again.

Rosita and Juanita began undressing her. They slipped a fresh nightgown over her head while Travis stood by, helpless and bewildered. He caught a brief flash of bare extended belly, and wondered how such a fragile creature as Dani could possibly endure the ordeal ahead.

When the two Mexican women helped Dani onto the bed, she lay back against the pillow and sighed. Travis saw the braided rawhide strip tied from post to post across the headboard. When Dani reached for it, he broke out in a cold sweat.

357

"More pillows. I need—" Her voice broke off in a gasp of pain, but Juanita was there, lifting her head and placing more pillows behind her. Finally Dani was propped up in a half reclining position, which allowed her some ease from her discomfort. Her knees were drawn up, along with her gown. Travis felt completely out of place, but his feet refused to carry him to the door.

"I see the head now. When the next pain comes, Señora, push hard," Rosita instructed calmly.

Travis swallowed heavily. How could they all be so calm? Dani was covered with a sheen of perspiration and her hair clung damply to her pain-contorted face. Twisting her hands in the barbaric rawhide strap, she pulled with her hands and pushed with her body. The thin strap broke, and she cried out at her sudden loss of support.

Travis wasn't given time to think as Juanita shoved him onto the bed. In seconds he was behind Dani, his legs drawn up against the outside of hers. She leaned back against his chest and reached blindly for his arms. He held them out to her, finally understanding the role he was to play. She gripped and squeezed until he thought his bones would snap.

"One more push now, and the shoulders will be out."

Travis felt Dani tense as the next pain came. Her scream echoed in the room. He felt the blood drain from his face. A moment later there was another cry, this one from a new voice never heard before.

"It's a boy!" came the cries from the sisters.

Dani gasped for breath and laughed at the same time. She loosened her hold on Travis, and he smoothed the hair back from her face with a trembling hand and kissed the top of her head. He was breathing and sweating just as hard as she was.

The bloody, squalling infant waved tiny fists in the air, angry at being so rudely thrust from his warm nest. Travis stared in awe, feeling suddenly proud and humbled at the same time.

"Let me see him," Dani begged.

"Just let me clean him up a bit—there you go, little man. Here's your mama, sweet boy," Rosita crooned.

"Oh," Dani sighed as she held her son for the first time. "He's beautiful! Isn't he beautiful, Travis?" She looked up over her shoulder. Her face still showed signs of pain, but her eyes shone with an inner light that nearly took his breath away.

"Beautiful," he murmured. But he was looking at the mother, not the child.

Rosita took the boy and placed him in Lucinda's waiting arms. Fifteen minutes later, Dani's daughter was born. When the baby girl was presented to her, Dani gasped in dismay.

"Oh, no," she moaned. The baby had the same thick, black hair as her brother, but there, at her right temple, was a short, narrow tuft of white. Dani closed her eyes and swallowed heavily.

Travis witnessed her dismay and knew its cause. "Hush, Dani. She's beautiful. She looks like you—she's perfect."

Dani sniffed back her tears as Rosita took the baby from her arms. Under orders from Juanita, Travis left the bed and stood aside. The babies and Dani were cleaned up and the bed linens changed, then the twins were taken to the nursery and given over to Lucinda for the night. When all the activity was over, Travis found himself alone with Dani.

"My God, Dani," he said, sitting carefully at her side. "You were magnificent."

Dani sighed with satisfaction. "You were pretty wonderful yourself. Thank you for staying with me, for helping."

"Any time, love." Travis bent down and kissed her tenderly, and she closed her eyes in exhaustion and slept. He left the room to find a stiff drink and a bed for the night.

He spent a long uncomfortable night on the sofa in his study. It was way too short for his long frame, and too narrow as well. He would have gone back to his own bed, but he was afraid of disturbing Dani. She was so exhausted and worn out, as well she should be. He marveled again at the miracle of life he'd been allowed to witness, to take part in. He felt a closeness with Dani and the twins that had been missing from his life.

In the past few weeks, since she had let go of her fears, he'd seen her blossom like the petals of a rose kissed by the summer sun. She'd become carefree and happy, quick to laugh and a sheer pleasure to be near. He prayed the scene with her father this morning had done nothing to change the warm, loving woman she'd become.

Loving—now there was a word. Did she love him? Or was she just grateful to him for helping her through a trying time in her life? It had to be more than gratitude he'd seen shining in her eyes these past weeks. It had to be! He needed her love, needed to be able to show his love in return. He'd hidden it from her far too long now.

When dawn finally came, Travis knew he'd never spent a more uncomfortable night in his life.

On the way past the nursery door, Travis heard the babies fussing and Lucinda's gentle murmur as she tended them. Realizing Dani must still be alone, he hurried to his bedroom door and entered quietly, without knocking.

"What in the hell do you think you're doing?" he bellowed.

There was Dani, so stiff and sore she could barely move, trying to make her way across the room. At the unexpected sound of his voice, she jumped and uttered a squeak of surprise.

"Travis! You scared the daylights out of me!"

"What are you doing out of bed?" he demanded.

"I was just getting my brush."

Travis swung her up in his arms and placed her back on the mattress. "You're supposed to be in bed. You want something, you ask for it." He brought her brush to her and watched with pleasure while she brushed the tangles from her long curls.

He peeled his wrinkled shirt off and splashed water from

the pitcher into the bowl on the dresser. The cold water revived him, driving away the fog of the sleepless night.

"Travis!" Dani cried.

"What is it?" He crossed to her side quickly, instant worry consuming him. "What's wrong? Are you in pain?"

"What happened to your arms?" She stared, wide-eyed, at his bare forearms.

"What?" What the hell did his arms have to do with anything? "What's wrong, Dani?" he repeated, reaching to grasp her shoulders as she sat and stared at him.

"What have you done to yourself?" Dismay colored her voice, and she gently ran her fingers over his skin.

Travis followed her fingers with his eyes to the scratches and bruises on his forearms. "Oh, that," he said with relief. Nothing was wrong, after all.

Dani looked at him with concern. "What did this, Travis?"

"Not what, love, but who." A slow grin spread across his face, and he leaned to press a tender kiss on her lips.

Slowly her expression changed as he watched her remember his part in last night's events. Her eyes clouded. "I did this, didn't I?" she asked softly. Her hand spread across his skin and her fingertips matched his bruises. "Oh Travis, I'm sorry. I didn't mean to hurt you."

"Hush, love." He kissed her lightly again. "I wasn't the one hurting last night. You were. How are you feeling this morning?"

"I'm fine. A little stiff and sore, though," she added with a grimace.

"Only a little?" he asked doubtfully. After another kiss, Travis slipped on a clean shirt, then helped Dani pile extra pillows behind her back. He was just drawing a chair up next to the bed when Lucinda and Juanita entered with the twins.

"Señora, this son of yours is most unhappy. He says that if you do not feed him at once, he is likely to starve to death in the next few minutes." Lucinda offered the squalling in-

361

fant to his mother, and Dani reached for him with eager
arms. When she held him close, he immediately quieted
and began rooting around on her breast.

Daniella laughed and blushed slightly as she opened the
front of her gown. The baby latched onto her nipple with
amazing zeal, and she gave an involuntary jerk with his first
sucking action.

She whispered a short prayer of thanks, both for her children, and for the realization that her fears had been
groundless. The twins weren't even a day old, but she loved
them. Fiercely. They were her own flesh and blood. How
could she have thought she wouldn't love them?

Travis watched the child knead her breast with tiny fists,
and a wealth of emotions rose up within him. In all his
thirty years, he had never seen a mother nurse her babe.
Julia hadn't shared the experience when Matt was born. He
thought this was the most poignant event he'd ever witnessed.

It had been many years since he'd held his own infant son
in his arms, and he wanted to hold these babies close to him
now. Before he could make a move toward the baby girl,
however, Juanita thrust the child into his arms.

"Here, Señor Travis, take her. Lucinda and I must
straighten the nursery." When the two women left the room,
a strange sound floated out behind them and Travis's
stunned gaze followed them. Dani asked him what was
wrong.

"Nothing," he said with a laugh. "I've just never heard my
staid, dignified housekeeper giggle before." He looked down
at the precious bundle in his arms and smiled. "She's got
your ears, and your eyes, too, I think. And your mouth."

"And my hair." Dani's unhappiness over that point was
obvious.

"As a man, I happen to find that streak in your hair very
attractive. If you're not careful, you'll give this little girl a
complex."

When the baby boy's mouth finally went slack, Dani

362

and Travis traded bundles, and Dani pressed her daughter to her other breast.

Travis studied Dani closely as he cradled her newborn son in his arms. She had a new look about her that hadn't been there before. A glow, a self-confidence, an inner peace, radiating from her entire being. The only word he could think of to describe the change in her was "magical."

A knock on the door a few minutes later startled Travis and Dani from their separate reveries, but didn't disturb the now-sleeping twins. Travis called a reluctant admittance to whoever was disrupting their privacy.

"I hope we're not intruding, but the suspense was killing us." Jason and Matt had come to see the newest members of the Colton family.

Howard Blackwood sipped on his brandy and stared at the crackling flames in the fireplace. A grimace of self-loathing marred his features. Even as he'd spoken those harsh, bitter words to his daughter all those months ago, he'd known he was wrong. But how could he ever explain to her?

How could she possibly understand how easy it had been for him over the years to forget the past? When he'd sent her away to Boston, he'd honestly thought he was doing what was right for her. She'd needed some of her rough edges smoothed away.

Then, while she'd been gone, it was easy to pretend, with his new, young wife, that he was young again himself. Young and virile and just starting out in life, with no painful memories of the past.

There was no way to justify how he'd listened to Sylvia, let her lead him around by the nose, let her turn him against his only child.

Then Ramón had come along, and the past had been even easier to forget, to ignore.

He closed his eyes in pain. Good Lord, he was a grown

363

man. An old man, even. Weren't *men* supposed to be able to think for themselves? He'd been such a fool, listening to Sylvia's worries about the gossip surrounding Ella's time with the Apaches. Such a stupid, worthless fool.

Just when she'd needed him the most, he'd turned his back on his daughter, his own flesh and blood, and cast her out. She'd never forgive him for that. He'd never forgive himself.

What she'd had to endure, first from the Apaches, then from her own father! But she was married to a good man now. Travis Colton was a son-in-law to be proud of.

He rubbed his jaw with a grimace. *And he's got a powerful right hook.*

With Colton at her side, Howard could hope that Ella would be happy now, but he didn't really see how she'd ever be able to put the past behind her after giving birth to a couple of little half-breed Apache bastards.

He shook his head in wonder. Travis had carried the twins around in his arms like he was the proudest new father in the world. Like he didn't even notice all that wrinkled brown skin and coal black hair. Or the streak of white in the little girl's hair. How could a man accept a thing like that? Why would he even try?

Love, came the unbidden answer. Travis Colton loved Ella. It was in every look, every word the man uttered. A man could overlook a lot of things for love of a special woman. Hadn't he, himself, shunned his own daughter for the woman he loved?

With another sip of brandy, he silently wished Colton good luck. Love could make a damn fool out of a man, if he was stupid and weak enough to let it.

But he would let Colton worry about his own troubles. Howard had enough to deal with. Colton might claim to accept — no, not claim, he really *did* accept — the twins as his own. But how was he going to deal with having half-breed Apache grandchildren?

Grandchildren.

The word seemed to age him by just flitting through his mind. Wasn't it only yesterday that Ella was born? And Ramón wasn't even three yet. How could he have a three-year-old son, and *grandchildren?*

He pictured Ramón in his mind as he'd looked right after he was born. Wrinkled brown skin and coal black hair.

Wrinkled brown skin and coal black hair.

Howard sat up straighter. Good Lord, it was true! With the exception of that little tuft of white at the girl's temple, those twins looked remarkably like his own son had when he was a newborn.

He smiled slightly. He'd been fooling himself for so long, what could it hurt if he let himself believe one more lie? He'd think of the twins as Mexican! His wife was Mexican, his son was Mexican, so why not his grandchildren?

If he could think of them that way, maybe he'd be able to keep from opening his big mouth and hurting Ella again.

"Ahem. May I come in?"

Daniella looked up from handing her new son, whom she had named Pace, to Lucinda, and found her father standing hesitantly in the open doorway. Serena, Pace's sister, had already been taken to the nursery, and Daniella had just begun to wonder if someone would come to help her pass the time of day. She had not expected it to be her father.

She gave a hesitant nod, wondering why he was here. She was in much too good a mood today to hold a grudge any longer against the man who, until a few months ago, had been the light and love of her life. She had Travis to thank for that.

She smiled at her father. "Pull up a chair and sit down. I was just wondering what I was going to do for company this afternoon, since Travis thinks I'm an invalid and won't let me out of bed. I'm glad you came."

Howard looked at his daughter skeptically. "Are you? After what I did to you, I'm surprised you want to see me at all."

"I've learned a lot since then, Papa. It hurt, what you said to me, but I've put it behind me. I have a family of my own now, and things are better than I ever dreamed possible."

"I'm glad to hear that. I've had a lot of time to think since you left, and I've learned a lot since then, too." He threaded his fingers and cleared his throat again nervously. "I just want to say that—well, that I'm sorry for what I did to you. I was wrong, and I didn't mean any of those terrible things I said. I know that doesn't help anything now, but I just wanted you to know."

"Thank you, Papa," she said softly. The word "papa" rolled off her tongue easily, naturally, as if she'd never cursed it, never denied it. "It does help, it does matter. You're still my father. There were too many good times before I went back east for us to let this one thing stand between us, don't you think?" Tears clouded her vision. When she tried to blink them away, they overflowed and ran down her cheeks.

Howard's eyes, too, misted over. He moved to the edge of the bed and Daniella went willingly into his arms. They held each other and cried, ridding themselves of any remaining bitterness and sorrow. Howard looked sheepish and embarrassed as he wiped the tears from his face, and he and his daughter both laughed, further clearing the air between them.

"So," he said firmly. "How are you feeling?"

"I'm feeling fine. Have you . . . seen the babies?"

"Yes, as a matter of fact. Your husband brought them into the salon earlier. I believe he said you were napping at the time. Yesterday he told me he intends to be their father, and he seems to be taking his role to heart."

"Yes, he does, doesn't he? He's very good to me, Papa. I don't know what I would have done without him."

"You're happy here, then?" he asked, searching her face.

"Very much so." She watched as his face began to relax.

"I'm glad for you," he said. "You deserve to be happy. I've

known Jason a number of years. He's a good man, and apparently his son is, too."

"I think so," she said with a smile.

"I'll let you get some rest now. I was warned not to tire you. I'll leave in the morning, but I'll stop in before I go."

When he was gone, Daniella lay back against the pillows, sighed with contentment, and fell asleep smiling.

"Do you have a few minutes to spare me, Colton?"

"Only if you promise to call me Travis," he answered, coming from behind his desk to greet his father-in-law.

"Ah. Does this mean I'm forgiven?" Howard asked with a tentative smile.

"You've never done anything to me that requires my forgiveness. If you're talking about what passed between you and Dani last spring, well, all I can say is, if she hadn't left home, I might not have ever met her. Maybe I should thank you for that, but somehow it just doesn't seem proper." Travis smiled at Blackwood and extended his hand in friendship. Dani told him earlier that she and her father had settled their differences and made peace. If it was good enough for her, he would give Blackwood a chance.

"I told you I came here because I heard in Tucson that Ella was here," Howard stated. "But I think you should know, there's talk in town about Ella, about her being friendly with the Apaches, bad talk. I just thought you should know . . ." Howard's voice trailed off as Travis burst out laughing.

"I'm sorry," Travis said when he could speak again. He had to choke down another burst of laughter before he could continue. "I appreciate the warning. That's not what I'm laughing about."

Howard just stood there staring while Travis struggled to control himself. "Have I said something amusing?"

"No," Travis answered. "Well, yes, I guess maybe you did. What was it you called her?"

"Who? Ella?"

Robust laughter filled the room again as Travis lost control. "I'm sorry, Howard." Travis choked and wiped the tears from his eyes. "I don't mean to offend you. I've just never heard anyone call her that before. When Matt asked if he could call her Dani, she said she liked that a whole lot better than what her family called her. No offense, but I think I have to agree with her." His shoulders shook as he restrained his hilarity, but he couldn't keep the grin from his face. "I've never heard a name suit anyone less than Ella suits her."

A slow grin spread across Howard's face until he was chuckling right along with Travis. "I suppose you're right about that. She always did hate it. If I remember, I started calling her that shortly after her mother passed on. Daniella was always traipsing around after the men, wanting to do everything they did. I think calling her Ella was my attempt to remind the little tomboy in boots and pants that she was really a girl."

Chapter Thirty

"Where did you sleep last night?" Daniella asked. "And the night before?" The question had plagued her while she lay in her lonely bed for two nights since the birth of her twins.

"On a very short, narrow, lonely, uncomfortable sofa in my study."

"Why?"

"You needed your rest. I was afraid I'd disturb you."

"I've had so much rest the past two days I could scream," she said with feeling. "Will you sleep here tonight?"

"Is that an invitation?"

"It's an invitation to sleep in your own bed. I'm afraid that's the best I can offer, for now."

"I know," he said with a smile. "I was only teasing. But let's talk about this 'for now' part." He gave her a slightly lecherous grin, and she smiled back and laughed as his face drew nearer to give her a brief kiss.

Daniella motioned toward the sheaf of papers Travis held in his hand. "Are you bringing your paperwork to bed these days?"

"Not exactly," he replied, his expression turning sober. "It's something I want you to look over. I've already signed it, and my father and yours have witnessed my signature. The only thing left is for you to sign it, if you approve."

"What is it?" What could make him turn so serious all of a sudden?

"Just read it."

Hesitant, she took the papers from him and started reading. Amazement swamped her. Halfway through the first page her vision blurred. She blinked the moisture away and looked up at him. "You want to adopt my babies?" She was stunned. This was totally unexpected.

"Yes." The intensity in his voice left no room for doubt. "Both of our fathers have toasted their grandchildren. Matt can't talk about anything else but his new baby brother and sister. Everyone accepts that I'm their father, except you. You're the only one who doubts me. Please sign it, and don't doubt me any more. For my sake, as well as for the twins. Maybe then you'll stop calling them yours, and start calling them *ours*."

"But—but it must have taken weeks, months even, to have these papers prepared. How did you get them?" She was stalling for time, and they both knew it. Could she let him do this? Saddle himself with two half-breed Apache children for the rest of his life? It seemed like too much to ask of any man.

"I wrote Cal the week we were married and asked him to start drawing up the papers. He brought them when he came last month."

If Daniella was stunned before, it was nothing to what she felt now. Tears overflowed her eyes and ran down her cheeks, barely missing the legal documents in her hand as the wet drops landed on the front of her nightgown. She remembered back to that day Cochise had ordered her to marry. Travis had said then that he was prepared to accept her children as his own. She could have saved herself so much heartache and uncertainty if she'd only taken him at his word. But then, as now, it seemed too simple, too good to be true . . . too much.

"Why, Travis?" she asked breathlessly, hope rising in her despite her efforts to still it. "Why would you do that? How could you have accepted everything so easily?"

"You really don't know, do you?" he asked. Daniella shook her head slowly in reply. Travis spoke again. "At first

370

I was angry that day, but only for a minute, and not for the reason you think. I was angry because Cochise was forcing you to accept me, and I was afraid you'd get stubborn and refuse. But when you finally agreed, I realized Cochise had probably saved me weeks, if not months."

"I—what do you mean?"

"I followed you into the mountains, Dani, to ask you to marry me. If you hadn't been pregnant, Cochise would never have tried to force you. So I'm very grateful for the twins. If it weren't for them and Cochise, I might still be trying to convince you to marry me. I'd do anything for Pace and Serena. I want to protect them in every way possible, with my name, with these adoption papers, and any other way I can."

"But Travis, I . . . I . . . why would you *want* to marry me?"

"Don't you understand, Dani? Don't you know how much I love you? How much I loved you even then?"

Daniella squeezed her eyes shut, sending a fresh wave of tears down her cheeks, then opened them again to stare at Travis in wonder and disbelief. Her doubts melted almost instantly when she saw the look in his eyes. There, in those warm brown depths, was all the love a woman could possibly dream of wanting.

With a choking cry, she flung herself at him and buried her face against his neck, sobbing his name over and over. The adoption papers fluttered to the floor, temporarily forgotten.

"My God, my God, Travis. You don't know how long I've prayed to hear those words from you."

He crushed her to him in a desperate grip and trailed moist, fevered kisses down her cheek. "How long? How long, Dani?"

"Forever," she breathed, her tears having miraculously disappeared with his first kiss.

"Forever?"

Daniella pulled back and cupped his face in her hands,

371

looking him directly in the eye. "Forever. Because that's how long I've loved you," she whispered.

They clung to each other, arms entwined, while Travis covered her mouth with his. Daniella surrendered completely to the heat and hunger of his kiss. A low moan escaped his throat, or was it hers? He leaned forward, pressing her down on the bed. His hand roamed down and cupped a large, full breast, then down farther, to the new emptiness of her abdomen. He drew back slightly.

"I do love you, Dani," he whispered against her lips. "More than words can say. But maybe I should stay on the couch." He raised his head from hers slowly. "Without the twins here to kick at me, I might forget myself entirely."

"No, don't go." Daniella wrapped her arms around his neck and pulled him down until their lips were only a breath apart. "I love you."

"Say it again."

"I love you. I love you. I love you."

And he did stay in their bed that night. He knew she wasn't over the childbirth yet, so he tempered his cravings and reveled in the knowledge of her love.

They settled into a routine, beginning each day with Lucinda bringing the twins for their morning feeding. Travis always stayed for this. It was a special time for him; he loved watching Dani nurse the babies. Aside from bringing them all closer together, it gave him his only chance of the day to view a part of Dani he longed to taste for himself.

One morning when the twins were barely a week old, Dani rushed to the window and leaned out. "Hear it, Travis?"

"Hear what?" he asked, shifting Serena's weight in his arms as he stood.

"A signal horn! Someone's coming!"

Travis heard the Apache signal horn and feared some of the people on the ranch might not realize this was a friendly visit rather than a raid. The Apaches had never raided the Triple C before, but stories of raids farther south and east kept everyone on edge. He handed Serena to Dani and hurried to make certain no one took any pot shots at the approaching visitors.

By the time Daniella made it outside, Matt was already there, blowing an answer on his own signal horn.

Eight dark riders approached the house slowly on rangy mustangs. As they neared, Daniella recognized Cochise and Dee-O-Det in the lead. Behind them rode four warriors whom she recognized, but whose names she couldn't recall. Her eyes widened with surprise when she realized the last two riders were boys—Chee and Shanta.

Nearly all the Triple C employees had gathered out front by the time the Chiricahua dismounted. With a nervous smile, Daniella introduced everyone to Cochise, wondering all the while just what Travis's father and friends thought of the situation.

Cochise introduced his men, then Travis said, "I'm glad you've finally come for your cattle and horses."

Cochise nodded. "*Sí*, we come for the bride gift, and other things."

Daniella tensed. What other things? Then she asked the question aloud.

"I seek—"

A low cough from Dee-O-Det cut him off. One corner of Cochise's mouth twitched. "My business can wait. The Old One claims his business must come first. He has come, as *shaman*, to perform the sacred bestowal ritual on your new children."

While Cochise spoke, Dee-O-Det turned and unstrapped a large bundle from his wood-and-cowhide saddle.

"Bring the babes," the old man said. "This must be done outdoors."

Unsure of just what a "sacred bestowal ritual" was, Daniella nevertheless knew she trusted Dee-O-Det with her life. "Let's go to the courtyard."

Of the eight Apaches, Cochise and the two boys were the only ones who'd ever been inside a white man's building before. The others had to be coaxed inside. They were amazed at and somewhat skeptical of the solid walls, ceilings and floors, and the many different rooms and strange furnishings. All of them visibly relaxed when they entered the courtyard.

Daniella and Travis each carried a child out into the courtyard, and the rest of the family gathered around in curiosity.

Dee-O-Det carefully unwrapped a double-sized cradleboard. Cochise whispered between Daniella and Travis that the *shaman* had spent the last month constructing the *ts'al* and praying over it. The frame was made of oak, as was each footrest at the bottom edge. There was a canopy, for shade, woven from the stems of the red-barked dogwood. The back was divided in two, one side of sotol stalks for the boy, the other of yucca for the girl. Buckskin stretched across the top of the canopy.

"The designs in the top will tell you which side of the *ts'al* is for which child. The half-moons are for the girl, the cross is for the boy. You must always put each child on the proper side," Dee-O-Det explained to Daniella. He then pointed out the protective amulets tied to the canopy. There was a bag of sacred pollen, some turquoise beads, and over each side hung a charred piece of wood from the pine that had been struck by lightning.

Dee-O-Det opened his bag of *tádídín* and put four dots of the dust on Pace's face. For Serena, he drew a powdery line across her cheeks and the bridge of her nose. Muttering a sacred chant, he held up the *ts'al* to the east, then south, then west, then north, stopping when he faced east again. He set the cradleboard down and picked up Pace. After three ritual feints, he placed the boy in the *ts'al*, then did the same with Serena, grunting his approval of the white tuft in her hair. Pace and Serena simply stared at the old man, neither making a sound.

Dee-O-Det's emphatic *"Nzhú!"* marked the end of the ceremony.

A few minutes later, after the twins were back in the nursery with Lucinda, Daniella led the guests to the dining room. There they met with more confusion when introduced to tables, chairs, plates and silverware. They weren't quite sure what to think about all of it, but out of politeness to their host and hostess, they refrained from scoffing openly.

Then the feasting began. Daniella had no idea where Rosita came up with all that food on such short notice, but there was plenty for everyone. Dee-O-Det won the cook over by playfully asking her to leave her husband and run away with him. He said he'd rather die of overeating than of old age.

The afternoon was half gone by the time Cochise and his party were ready to head out. As the others mounted, Cochise paused. "There is a thing I would ask you," he said to Travis. "We have seen that your bluecoats have gone. Many of our people believe it means we have defeated the American soldiers in battle so many times that *Los Goddammies* have run away. Some of us do not think this is so. Can you tell us why they have gone?"

Travis worried over what to say. If he confirmed that the soldiers were gone completely, would the Apaches run wild and try to kill everyone? Or would they relax, seeing the threat against them leave with the soldiers? Either way, he was not prepared to deal with the consequences of having Cochise find out later that he'd lied. Cochise was a man of honor, even if it was a different kind of honor than Americans understood. He deserved the truth.

"The soldiers did not leave because they thought they were beaten." This comment brought mumblings from the men with Cochise, but Travis ignored them. "Far to the east there is a new war they go to fight. The states in the North are fighting the states in the South. All soldiers have been called to those battles. The fighting could move to this territory, and then you'll have two armies here. But if that doesn't happen, then be certain that as soon as the war is over, the soldiers will return."

Cochise stared into Travis's eyes for a long minute, then nodded sharply. "I believe you. Thank you for telling me."

Some of the men with Cochise were obviously displeased with their chief for his decision to trust the white man, but Cochise seemed to accept their displeasure as a matter of fact.

"And now, my friend," Cochise said to Travis, "I have a favor to ask of you."

"If it's within my power, I'll be glad to do you any favor."

"My people need to understand more of the white man's ways, and your language. I have two young boys with me who would like to work for you and learn these things, if you have need of extra workers." Cochise motioned and Chee and Shanta came forward.

"You've been listening to my prayers, Cochise." Travis grinned at the two boys. "Are you two any good at breaking wild mustangs?" he asked them. Both boys nodded yes with caution. Travis turned back to Cochise. "We have a couple of dozen wild mustangs that need a lot of work. I could use the extra help."

"It's settled then. Shanta and Natzili-Chee will work for you, and you will teach them your ways." Travis and Cochise shook hands in the white man's fashion. "We must gather my cattle and horses and go. We have many miles to cover before the moon sets tonight."

Cochise and his men herded the bride gift of ten head of cattle and ten horses off toward the east, leaving two suddenly uncertain boys behind among strangers.

Daniella and Matt took the two boys in hand and tried to make them feel welcome, but it was Rosita they took to. Over the next week the cook tempted and coaxed them with special treats. By the end of two weeks, the boys had settled in amazingly well to ranch life.

Also by then, Travis noticed, Dani had her old figure

376

back, with the exception of her increased bustline. He enjoyed this new trim wife. Her skirts swayed gently when she walked, and he yearned for the day they could share a more intimate relationship.

Each night was torture for him as he lay next to her in their bed. Most of the time he had to turn his back on her just to be able to sleep. But usually he woke during the night with her soft warmth pressed against his bare back, and it was all he could do to keep from attacking her.

The days turned into weeks, and as Christmas drew near, secret smiles and hushed whispers filled the house. An odd combination of pine boughs and piñatas decorated the rooms. Tempting aromas drifted from the kitchen.

On Christmas Eve, Jason and Travis presented their gifts to the staff at the annual Triple C Christmas party, and laughter echoed through the house. Everyone was in high spirits. Everyone except Travis. Daniella noticed he was unusually quiet. Every time she looked his way he was pale one minute, flushed the next.

"Are you feeling all right?" she asked.

He took another healthy swallow of brandy and stared off at some point beyond her shoulder. "I'm fine," came his curt reply. His lips curled up, but it could not be classified as a smile.

Something was definitely wrong. All evening he'd been either staring daggers at her or ignoring her completely. "If you aren't ill, then are you angry about something?"

"No. I'm not angry." His eyes flicked down the length of her, then away.

Daniella put a hand on his arm and felt him shudder. "Travis, what is it? What's wrong," she whispered, not wanting to be overheard.

"What's wrong is that goddamn dress you're almost wearing!"

Daniella fought to stifle a girlish giggle. The dress in question was made of crimson velvet, and was the best dress she owned. It had long, fitted sleeves and a full gathered

377

skirt. The neckline was extremely low, and her waist was cinched in tightly by her corset. As a result, her breasts thrust upward to a nearly scandalous degree. She'd worn it on purpose. She was tired of having him turn his back to her in bed each night, not believing she was recovered from the birth of the twins. The dress was an open invitation she hoped he'd be unable to refuse.

"You don't like it?" she asked innocently.

"Like it?" he croaked. "It's not that—it's—damn, Dani, it looks like you're going to fall out of it any minute!" He reached up and tugged on the neckline, trying to raise it a notch or two, oblivious to the watching eyes and secret grins around the room. His knuckles rested boldly against the creamy softness of her swelling breasts.

Daniella felt branded by the heat of his fingers against her skin. "You think it's a little low, then?" Again she wore that wide-eyed, innocent look. However, the rapid pulse fluttering at the base of her throat would have given lie to her calm voice, if Travis had been capable of raising his gaze that far above the temptation of her breasts.

"Yes! It's a little low!" he hissed, yanking his hand away as if he'd been scorched.

Daniella placed her hand on his chest and looked up at him. "Then maybe I should go take it off," she purred. "But I'll need help with the fastenings." Surely he couldn't mistake the provocative look she gave him.

Travis swallowed, feeling his pulse race out of control. "Are you being a tease, wife?"

"A tease? I always thought a tease was someone who promised something but refused to deliver. I wouldn't dream of teasing you, husband."

The way she said it, her voice low and husky, her eyes full of promise, caused such a tightening in his loins that Travis nearly groaned out loud. Without another word, he grabbed her elbow in a bruising grip and practically dragged her from the room.

Jason watched them go, a knowing smile playing about

the corners of his mouth. Maybe after tonight his son wouldn't take his short temper out on everyone else any more.

"Where's Dad and Dani goin', Grandad?" Matt wanted to know.

"They're both tired, Matt. I don't think we'll be seeing them again tonight. Any more of those cookies left?"

"Do you mean it?" Travis asked once they were behind the closed bedroom door. "Are you sure?"

Daniella inhaled sharply at the intense passion burning like golden flames in the depths of his hot brown eyes. She stood on her toes and pulled his head down. Just as their lips met, she whispered, "Yes."

His arms came around her and crushed her to his broad chest as the kiss continued. His tongue plunged deeply into her mouth. She tasted the brandy he'd been drinking, thinking it strange that just tasting it on his tongue could make her feel so lightheaded. She never knew it when her dress and petticoats landed on the floor with a soft *whoosh*.

His lips left a trail of fire down her throat and across her shoulders. The straps of her chemise fell away just as she felt her corset come loose. Travis held her desperately, as if he feared she might disappear, and arched her backward over his arm. His lips continued their descent to her breasts, and his hands ran the length of her, pushing the chemise to the floor.

Then his large calloused palm cupped her bare breast. The heat of his fingers shot through her like lightning. His teeth took tiny tingling nibbles along the full underside of her breast, then his mouth settled where they both craved it most, on the tight, dark peak. Daniella cried out at the sensations he created. It had been so long!

He circled the nipple with his tongue and then sucked gently, scraping lightly with his teeth. She felt a tugging sensation on some invisible string that ran from her hardened nipple, down inside her to that secret, woman's place, now throbbing with want. Her knees went weak.

She stood in nothing more than her shoes, stockings and garters. His hands were everywhere on her flesh, searing her with their heat. She felt the hardness of his desire throbbing against her abdomen. Stretching up, she pressed against him, trying to satisfy her flaming need.

Travis lifted her in his arms and placed her gently on the bed. He kissed her again, long and thoroughly, until the blood pounded in odd places in her body. She tasted her own milk on his tongue, where it mingled with the brandy, giving it a creamy, smokey flavor. There was a moist swelling between her thighs, and she moaned against his mouth.

"I want you so much," Travis whispered hoarsely. "I've waited so long to have you, touch you, feel you next to me this way again." He raised up and removed first one slipper, then the other, kissing the sensitive arch of each foot in turn through her stockings, turning her bones to jelly. Then came the garters. When he reached for her stockings, he rolled them down one at a time, slowly, following each with his lips. Her body swelled with desire, and her heart with love.

When she lay naked before him, Travis stared in awe at her beauty. As his eyes lowered, her hands spread to cover her thighs.

"No," he whispered. He brushed her hands aside and bent to run his tongue lovingly over the scars she tried to hide.

He raised again and knelt above her, searching her face for any sign of uncertainty, but the only emotion in her eyes was passion, and it was for him. His heart swelled to near bursting when she opened her arms and clung to him with all her strength.

His lips on hers were fierce, demanding, and Daniella answered with a passion that shook them both. She fumbled with the buttons on his shirt, desperate for the feel of his skin on hers. She wanted to touch him, to cover him with kisses as he had her. His fingers brushed her trembling ones away and he stripped off his shirt, then the rest of his clothes, tossing them carelessly to the floor.

When he lay back down, half covering her body with his own, Daniella gasped with pleasure at the warmth and solidness of his chest pressed to her breasts. Then his lips caressed an erect nipple and she dug her fingers into the bulging muscles of his shoulders. His right hand trailed down until his fingers rested intimately in the hair at the juncture of her thighs. Lower they slid, until he cupped that place that throbbed and ached for his touch. His fingers slipped ever so slowly into her hot moist depths, halting her breath in her throat. When he moved his fingers gently, she thrust against his hand and moaned in ecstasy.

Her heart pounded and her breath came in great heaving gasps. She writhed beneath his skilled touch. When his hand slipped away, she whimpered in protest. But then he was parting her thighs with his knee and lowering himself on top of her. Nothing could possibly feel so right, so wonderful, as his weight pressing down on her, shielding her, loving her. She felt his pulsing hardness seeking entry. She reached between their bodies and touched him, tentatively at first, then she boldly wrapped her fingers around him.

When her warm hand enclosed his engorged manhood Travis threw back his head and sucked in his breath. He wanted to laugh and shout out loud in triumph, but he couldn't. He grasped her hips and lifted them slightly.

Daniella guided his entrance home, and he pushed deep within her warm wetness. When he began to move, she caught his rhythm instantly and met him thrust for thrust, wrapping her legs around him instinctively and soaring with him.

Higher and higher they climbed, until they reached the peak of pleasure together. Daniella cried out his name in wonder as a thousand colors burst inside her head, and her entire body became one huge, pulsating organ, throbbing with each ragged breath she took.

Sometime later, when they drifted down from the clouds,

Travis rolled to his side and held her tightly to him. It was only a matter of minutes before Daniella felt him growing hot and hard again against her thigh.

Travis grinned at her look of amazement.

She started to speak, but the words turned into a moan of pleasure as his hands worked their magic on her once more. By the time his lips closed over a still-sensitive nipple, she was mindless with wanting him again.

With heated touches and fevered kisses, they climbed the mountain of ecstasy again, cresting the peak and hovering there, then plummeting to the other side in shared bliss, together.

Chapter Thirty-one

"I'll be back by dark," Travis said in answer to Daniella's question.

"You've been around the house so much lately, I'll miss you if you're gone all day." She nibbled at his chin, eliciting a groan from deep in his throat.

"Ah, wife, you make it hard to leave."

She grinned. "I make it hard, do I?" She rubbed her leg back and forth against his and moved her body suggestively beneath him.

Travis groaned and laughed, then rolled away. "Woman, you're killing me."

"I knew it. I finally give in to you, and after only a few weeks, you're already tired of me." She pouted and Travis laughed again.

"Never, my love. I'll never be tired of you." His voice was soft and low, sending shivers down her spine. "Do you have any idea how much I love you?".

"Maybe as much as I love you," she whispered.

Their lips met in a gentle, searching kiss before Travis pulled away. "Much as I'd love to stay and prove my devotion, I hear Pace crying for his breakfast. Lucinda will be bringing him in any moment, and you know how jealous he gets over his meals."

"That *is* Pace crying, but how did you know it wasn't Serena?"

"Because Serena is a sweet, patient, polite young lady. Pace is more like an angry young lion, especially at feeding time. And in case I haven't said it lately, I love them both very much."

Daniella's heart swelled with love and gratitude for this man who had changed her life so much and given her the will to live. She honestly believed now that even without the adoption papers, Travis would have loved the twins, just as he'd promised in the beginning, just as if he'd sired them himself.

Lucinda brought Pace for his morning feeding, and as the boy suckled greedily at his mother's breast, Travis dressed and kissed mother and son good-bye for the day.

He was headed out with the other men from the ranch, including Matt, to join Natzili-Chee and Jorge, who were several miles south with a small herd of wild mustangs they'd cornered in a narrow box canyon. He would have a long, hard day, but at least the weather was mild and clear.

"Lucinda, why don't we bundle these two kids up and go to the valley?" Daniella suggested once Serena was fed. "I've been promising you a visit to your grandmother for weeks. Let's do it today."

"Oh, *Señora,* I would very much like to see my grandmother. But the men are all gone. Who will take us?"

"I will," Daniella answered. "We'll take the wagon. If we leave right away, we can have plenty of time to visit and still be back before dark."

"Is . . . is it safe?"

"Of course it's safe. What can possibly happen to us between here and the valley?"

In less than an hour they were off. Pace and Serena were strapped securely in the *ts'al* and snuggled into a quilt-lined box beneath the wagon seat. They slept peacefully, undisturbed by the jolting of the wagon over the rough ground.

The sun was bright and the sky was crystal blue, dotted with an occasional light fluffy cloud drifting northward on the gentle southerly breeze. Daniella let her shawl fall back over the wagon seat, not needing its warmth. She smiled to herself, remembering the blistering cold and blowing snow that usually covered Boston this time of year. She was glad to spend this January at home.

Home. Home was Travis. Home was Pace and Serena, Matt and Jason. It was all the people of the Triple C. It was this land itself. But most of all, it was Travis.

Daniella had never felt such a sense of peace, of belonging, as she felt whenever Travis wrapped his arms around her and held her to his broad, sturdy chest. She hadn't known it was possible for a woman to feel so cherished, so loved, so happy.

Lucinda twisted in the seat and leaned over the back to check on the twins.

Bless Travis for finding Lucinda.

"You miss your grandmother, don't you," Daniella asked as she and Lucinda swayed and bounced side by side on the high seat.

"Sí, Señora. She is my only family, and she is getting old. I worry about her."

"Would you like to stay a few days with her?"

"Oh, no. Not unless she is ill. I would miss the little ones too much," she replied. "Besides, Grandmother would accuse me of hovering over her."

Daniella felt lucky to have someone so devoted to the twins as Lucinda was. The girl had a good sense of responsibility, despite her young age.

"Well, I can't say I wouldn't miss you if you stayed away for more than an hour," Daniella said with a laugh. "But I don't want you to feel like you're trapped at the ranch. Any time you want to visit the valley, you just say so."

"Muchas gracias, Señora." Lucinda looked as if someone had just given her the moon. Admiration and adoration glowed in her dark eyes. Daniella felt humbled by the tribute.

"We're halfway there," Daniella said. She pointed ahead to the huge boulder and the small stand of mesquite that marked the midpoint of the trip.

When they came next to the boulder, the horses suddenly shied. A lone rider burst directly in front of them from the cover of the rock. Daniella struggled to bring her frantic team under control. The rider grabbed the harness of the nearest horse and kept the team from bolting.

Daniella stared open-mouthed at Billy Joe Crane. Her hands froze on the reins. This couldn't be happening. This was ridiculous! What was he doing here?

Crane pointed his six-shooter at her, making her realize the dangerousness of the situation. Her heart lurched. This was no time to lose her head. She prayed briefly for the twins to stay asleep. If Crane had been prepared to hang two young boys, no telling what he might do to helpless babies.

A vision of Travis crossed her mind, but she knew he was too far away to save her this time. White hot anger gripped her when she thought of what this man could cost her — Travis, her babies, her life. *That's right,* she told herself. *Don't get scared — get mad! How dare he accost us this way!*

"What do you want, Crane?"

He grinned an evil, oily grin and said, "Just you, sugar."

"Well, isn't that just too bad," she shot back.

"Could be bad," he answered easily, leaning back in the saddle, "if you cause trouble. Behave yourself, and it'll be a hell of a lot easier on you."

Daniella glared at him, wondering what her team would do if she slapped the reins against their backs while Crane sat mounted directly in front of them.

As if reading her thoughts, Crane waved his pistol at her and ordered her to get down.

"The hell I will," she answered, amazed at the calmness in her voice.

"You will, or I'll shoot that there greaser bitch next to you. Now!"

One swift glance told her Lucinda was terrified out of her wits. Any second the girl might start screaming, and then Crane *would* shoot her. Daniella gave Lucinda what she hoped was a reassuring pat on the arm, then, with trembling knees, climbed down from the wagon.

If she could keep Crane calm, not anger him, she might have a chance to reason with him.

She nearly balked when he ordered her to climb up behind him. She *would* have balked, except he kept his gun trained on poor Lucinda.

If he'd only leave the girl alone, leave her here, Pace and Serena would be safe and Lucinda could go for help.

Somehow Daniella managed to get her shaking body onto the rump of Crane's horse. An instant later, he grabbed her arms, dragged them around his bulging stomach, and tied her hands together in front of him.

Daniella's anger threatened to desert her as fear clawed at her throat. From the wagon seat, Lucinda whimpered. Daniella forced back her own fear and turned to reassure the girl.

Before she could speak, Crane's gun barked. The bullet struck Lucinda in the left temple. The Mexican girl crumpled to her side, blood gushing brightly across the seat.

Chapter Thirty-two

"I wish those two boys hadn't taken a chance like that, starting this herd home without waiting for us," Travis said as the last wild mustang entered the corral.

"What are you complaining about? It got us back in half the time. It's barely past noon. Don't try to tell me you weren't eager to get home." Jason wore a teasing grin, knowing full well Travis hadn't wanted to go out after the horses in the first place. The older man had noticed in the weeks since Christmas his son hadn't strayed ten feet from Dani unless necessary.

As soon as they'd seen to their horses, Travis lived up to Jason's expectations and remained true to form—he went to find his wife.

The sun moved just far enough to send its rays past the boulder directly into Lucinda's closed eyes. She came to with a groan and pushed herself into an upright position. The pain in her head was excruciating. She touched her fingers to her throbbing temple and nearly fainted at the sight of blood on her hand. It was everywhere! On her dress, the wagon seat, her face, her hair. Then she remembered.

¡La Señora! ¡Los niños! Lucinda turned slowly on the bloody seat, feeling like her head might explode, and found the twins still sound asleep. There was blood on their blanket. Her blood.

¡El hombre! ¡He took la Señora!" She had to get help! Wha

388

should she do? How long had she lain there in the pool of her own blood?

The feverish activity in her brain could not necessarily be called thought, but she decided she couldn't have been unconscious too long, or the babies would be crying to be fed. And the sun—it wasn't even noon yet.

La Señora said this was the halfway point between the ranch and the valley. But Lucinda wasn't sure exactly how to get to either place. Looking back the way they'd come, she saw the wagon tracks they'd left in their wake.

I must go back for help. Someone must tell Señor Travis. Lucinda bent down, ever so slowly, carefully, and picked up the reins from where *la Señora* had dropped them, then reminded herself not to bend down like that again—the pain was blinding. She waited for her vision to clear, then grasped the reins as firmly as her shaking hands allowed.

But the horses were facing the wrong direction.

Lucinda had never driven a team before, and had only a vague idea of what to do. She just assumed the horses did most of the work. It took her over ten minutes to get the wagon headed in the right direction.

Each movement of the bumpy ride shot bright lights behind her eyes and sent tears of pain streaming down her bloody cheeks. The contents of her stomach repeatedly heaved to her throat, then dropped; heaved, and dropped; heaved, dropped. Her mind ceased to center on anything other than keeping her breakfast down, and keeping her body from toppling over.

She wanted to pray, but all she could think of was, *Ave Maria gratia plena . . . Hail Mary, full of grace.*

The bedroom and nursery were both empty, but before Travis could ask where Dani and the twins were, he heard high, excited, female voices shouting from in front of the house. When he went to investigate, the sight of a blood-covered Lucinda driving his wagon filled him with cold dread. He could hear the twins crying, but saw no sign of Dani.

Panicked, he raced to the wagon and looked inside the bed. Except for the box containing the twins, it was empty.

Several pair of eager hands reached to lift Lucinda to the ground. She swayed on her feet. Travis picked her up and carried her inside.

"Señor Travis," the young girl cried. "He took *la Señora*. He took her!"

"Who, Lucinda? Who took her?"

"A man. I don't know . . ." The girl's eyes almost drifted shut.

"Where did he take her, Lucinda? Did he say anything? Think, Lucinda!"

"I . . . she . . . called him . . . Crane . . . I think."

Travis felt his blood turn cold. "Tell me everything you remember."

A few minutes after Lucinda related everything her tortured mind could remember, Travis flung his saddle on his horse and headed for the area Lucinda said the abduction took place without stopping to tell Jason or the others. They could follow if they wanted, but he wouldn't waste even a few seconds waiting for them.

He covered the distance much faster than the two women had. From the spot where the wagon turned back toward the ranch, one horse, heavily laden, left a plain trail toward the east. Travis followed.

The buckskin's hooves beat out a steady rhythm. Travis's mind cried out in time with the beat, *I'm coming, Dani. I'm coming.*

He rode hard and fast, until his horse could go no farther, then rested the beast for as short a time as possible once again pushing the animal to its limit. Travis wanted to close as much distance as possible between himself and Dani before the light failed. Even with the full moon due tonight, it was all too easy to lose a trail in the darkness.

He tried to blot out the images of what Crane might b

doing to Dani, but the vision kept returning, torturing him in his present frustration and helplessness.

He stopped once to study some horse droppings, estimating they were less than two hours old. If Crane was smart he'd spot Travis's dust and head for the foothills. Travis had already spotted dust along his own backtrail. Triple C riders, coming to help.

The sun was going down. He'd lose the light soon.

Dani!

His eyes burned from straining to catch some glimpse of movement in the hills up ahead, but he knew the distance was too great.

There! What was that? Again. A flash. Sunlight reflecting off metal. A gun? A harness?

Chapter Thirty-three

Daniella's mind and body were numb with fear and fatigue. They'd been riding at a moderate but steady pace, nonstop, for hours. The vision of Lucinda crumpling to the wagon seat, blood pouring from her head, would not leave her. Dear, sweet Lucinda. She was just a child. She'd never harmed a living soul, and this bastard, this murderer, killed her for no reason—killed her in cold blood.

Daniella blinked back tears and tried to concentrate. She needed to know what he was planning, where he was taking her. So she asked him.

"Shut up," Crane snapped.

Daniella clamped her lips shut, deciding against any further questions. No point in antagonizing him. She shifted her weight on the rump of the horse, trying to find some small measure of comfort.

Before long she was surprised to realize her fear had all but disappeared. She was nervous, wary, but the actual fear had subsided. For now. Even though he was armed and she wasn't, he was still just one man.

Maybe later she'd be scared again. Right now she was preoccupied with trying to breathe past the sorrow and sheer, unadulterated rage over Lucinda's death.

After a long, hard struggle, she finally managed to clear her mind somewhat. She couldn't afford rage or sorrow right now. She had to think. Plan. Escape. Could she manage it? And if she could, what then? Could she make it home?

Yes, came the answer.

Her only chance for escape would seem to be during the chaos and confusion of setting up camp. He'd have to untie her hands before he could dismount. After that, it would probably be too late. He'd surely tie her up again. So she'd have to try it as soon as they stopped for the night. If they stopped.

The sun was sinking low behind them as they climbed into the foothills. The Santa Catalina Mountains loomed ahead, looking menacing to Daniella's frightened brain. Frightened. Yes. Her fear was growing again.

When they stopped, she glanced quickly around the small clearing. Crane's pack mule, the same one she'd seen him beat, stood tethered on the north edge of the clearing. Crane had obviously been camped here for a while. The blackened remains of a small campfire marred the center of the clearing.

Daniella concentrated on keeping her body relaxed. She wanted to give no warning of her intentions. Let him think she would meekly go along with whatever he planned.

Crane tossed his reins down and let them trail on the ground. Her mouth went dry. Would she be able to get to them when her chance came?

She felt a tug on her numbed hands as he untied them. When her blood flowed into her dead, swollen fingers, she wanted to scream with pain. She'd never be able to grasp the reins with her hands in such bad shape. But she had no choice. She had to do it when she got the chance—if she got the chance.

She didn't get the chance. Crane grabbed her by one arm and practically tossed her from the saddle. It had been too long since she'd ridden. After the past several hours astride, her legs refused to hold her. If Crane let go, she would fall.

But he didn't let go, not even while he swung to the ground. Before she could get her feet and legs to work, he dragged her to a scrub oak at the edge of the clearing and tied her hands to an overhead branch.

393

Panic threatened to overwhelm her. The branch was so high her hands couldn't reach it. Crane had looped the rough, abrasive rope tightly around one wrist, then over the branch a full foot beyond her reach, then around the other wrist. He pulled it so taut her feet barely reached the ground. Her arms felt like they were about to pull loose from their sockets. And if the physical pain and discomfort weren't enough, she'd just lost any chance of escaping.

Crane ignored her while he started a fire. Daniella shifted her weight, trying to get her legs to hold her. The rope scraped along the tree branch. Loose bits of bark trickled down onto her head. She stiffened. The rope had moved along the branch!

She waited, holding her breath until Crane turned his back toward her, then looked up at the branch. How far could she move? Her heart sank at once. Two feet in one direction was the trunk. Six inches the other way, the branch took a sharp upward turn toward the sky. So much for being able to scoot clear off the end of the branch to freedom. Although the limb was dead, it was about four inches thick and solid oak. It wasn't about to snap in two from her meager weight.

But she wouldn't give up. If she could maneuver without Crane becoming aware of what she was doing, she could pull the rope back and forth across the branch. With enough effort, and enough time—something she had no idea if she had much of—the rope or the branch might break. Maybe.

It was a slim chance, but right now it was her only chance. She shifted her weight around several times to get Crane used to her movements, so he wouldn't watch too closely. He didn't seem to notice her at all.

A loud crashing in the underbrush brought Crane upright, gun drawn.

Daniella held her breath, hope and fear mingling in her veins. The hope was useless. She knew it wasn't Travis coming to save her. He'd never come crashing into camp that way, announcing his presence minutes before his arrival. He was too trailwise for that.

When the rider broke through the last line of trees and emerged into the clearing, Daniella was stunned. Carmen! Crane grimaced and holstered his gun. Foreboding prickled along Daniella's spine. What was Carmen doing here?

The woman dismounted and brushed daintily at the dust on her skirt. She looked up then at Daniella and smiled brilliantly. Dark, deadly malice sparkled in her eyes. Daniella shivered, her fear growing by leaps and bounds.

"Well, I see you finally got her," Carmen said. "And it's about time, I must say, after your last bumbling attempt. I'm glad I came. Kill her now. I want to watch."

Daniella gasped.

Carmen sauntered toward her. When she stood but inches away, that smile still on her face, she raised a hand and slapped Daniella so hard her head snapped back.

Daniella straightened her head slowly, a cold numbness spreading through her limbs.

"But before you kill her," Carmen said, turning to Crane, "I want her to know why. I want her to know what's going to happen." She whirled back to Daniella. "I warned you. I did. I told you to leave the territory. But you didn't listen, and for that you will pay. With your life, *puta*.

"Until you came along, Travis was mine. Mine! You took him from me. Now I take him back. When he finds the broken, lifeless body of his wife, he will be filled with grief. I will be there to comfort him. You, who are afraid of a man's touch—oh yes, I know you fear him—you can't possibly give a man like Travis what he needs. I can. And I will."

While Carmen raved, Daniella grew sicker by the moment. She had to force herself to met Carmen's gaze. "So you hired Crane to do your dirty work, is that it?"

Carmen laughed. "*Señor* Crane and I, we have struck a bargain. For his part, I will see he gets that little valley you're so fond of. Then he and I will split the gold he finds there."

Daniella knew her only chance was to keep them talking, delay whatever they had planned for her as long as possible. Travis would come. Surely Travis would come!

She tried to swallow, but her mouth was too dry. "How can you give him the valley, when it's not yours?"

"When I marry Travis, it will be the same as mine. I will convince him to sell."

Daniella forced a tight smile to her lips. "I think you'll have trouble convincing Travis to sell something he doesn't own."

Crane growled and came forward. "What're you talking about, girl? If it was yours, with you gone it'll be his."

"That's true, under normal circumstances," she said. "But you see, I only own half of it. My partners won't be too eager to sell. And if anything happens to me, my half of the ranch goes to them, not Travis. I'm afraid Carmen has made you promises she won't be able to keep."

"Don't listen to her," Carmen cried. "It's a trick. She lies. We'll find a way, *mi amigo*. We'll get that gold."

"What gold is that?" Daniella asked.

Crane smiled at her. "You never knew, did you? That little valley of yours is full of gold."

"Of course it isn't. What ever gave you that idea?"

"This!" Crane dug in his pocket and came up with a shiny gold nugget. "This came from that valley."

Daniella quailed. Oh Lord! It looked like . . . but that was absurd. There must be thousands of nuggets shaped like a small fist. But yet . . . "Where did you get that?" she asked, her voice barely a whisper.

Crane gave her a strange, guarded look. "Like I said, I found it in that valley."

"When?"

Again, that guarded look. "Last summer."

Daniella threw her head back and cried out in rage. "You bastard! You lying, stinking, murdering bastard! I know exactly where you got that nugget!" She struggled uselessly against her bonds, chest heaving with effort, eyes wide

396

and glaring. "You didn't *find* it, Crane, you *took* it."

Crane took a step back from her look of pure hatred.

"You took it from my uncle's pocket, and the only way you could have done that was if he was dead. You killed him! You killed my uncle! You bastard."

"Now hold on!" Crane protested. "I might have taken it from his pocket, and he might have been dead at the time, but by God, I didn't kill him. You hear me? I didn't kill him. I didn't kill nobody! Not ever!"

"Liar," she hissed. "I saw you kill Lucinda today with my own eyes."

Crane flushed. "Well that don't mean I killed your uncle. He was already dead when I found him. I don't know how he died, but there weren't a mark on him. He was just dead, there on the porch. I fished through his pockets trying to find out who he was. That's when I found this." He waved the nugget in the air.

Daniella suspected he was telling the truth, in spite of her desire to believe the worst of him. Her father's letter had said Uncle John died of a heart attack. His heart had been bad for years. Crane was probably telling the truth. She nodded at him.

"All right—maybe you didn't kill him. But if you think you're going to find gold in that valley, you're wrong."

"Ha! Your uncle found this, and nuggets this size don't come alone. This little hunk has got lots of little friends laying around somewhere in that valley, and I intend to find 'em."

A wry grin formed on Daniella's lips. "Not in that valley you won't. It's a shame my uncle was dead when you found him. It's a shame you didn't get the chance to ask him where that came from."

"Don't listen to her," Carmen warned. "She's trying to trick you."

"Trick him?"

"*Sí*, trick him. But it won't work, *puta*. Even if you tell us exactly where to find the gold, you aren't stupid enough to think we will let you live. It's too late for that now. Travis will come after Crane no matter what."

Daniella hung there from the tree branch wishing desperately Carmen hadn't realized that. Now that it had been voiced, she knew they'd never let her go, no matter what she said.

"So why should I try to trick anyone?" she said finally. "*If* you get the valley, *if* you get a chance to look for gold, *if* you search for the next *forty years,* you still won't find anything. But you go ahead and look. I know all about gold fever, and you must have it bad to go to this much trouble.

"You see, Uncle John had gold fever, too, for a while, a long time ago. He went to California back in forty-nine. Sold everything he owned and went. He was smart enough, though, to put some money back, in case he didn't strike it rich. Just enough to give him a new start somewhere."

"Don't listen to her," Carmen urged.

Daniella kept on. "Uncle John spent three years in the California mountains, sleeping in a leaky tent, never enough food to eat. When he finally gave up, all he had left was that one nugget. He carried it in his pocket from then on to remind himself how foolish a man can be. He used to take it out and rub his fingers over it all the time, just like you're doing now," she said to Crane. "And he'd laugh at himself and his crazy, foolish dream."

Billy Joe Crane looked deep into the girl's eyes and knew. He knew without a doubt in his soul she spoke the truth. There was no gold in that valley. *Damnation!* What was he supposed to do now?

Carmen was right about one thing. If they let the girl go free, Colton would come after him. But Colton didn't know who had her! Crane could still stick to his original plan and sell her down in Mexico. He wasn't about to kill her. Hell, he wasn't no murderer.

He hadn't meant to kill that greaser girl earlier. It was an accident. But how could he explain that when Daniella Colton climbed up behind him in his saddle and he'd felt those firm, full breasts of hers press into his back, his whole body had tightened. He hadn't even realized he'd pulled the trigger until he saw the girl fall over.

Damnation. How had he got himself in this mess?

The answer to that question stood next to him and spoke in a cold voice. "It doesn't matter what she says. It's time to kill her now. I want to watch her die. I want to watch."

Crane glared at Carmen in impotent rage. "If anyone gets killed around here, it oughta be you, for getting us into this mess." He took a step toward Carmen, and she backed away. He grinned. Good. The bitch was afraid of him. Good.

"You've had your say from the beginning," he said, a low growl in his voice. "Telling me what to do, when to do it, and I've kept my mouth shut. But now it's time you know I got no intention of killin' her. I *never* had no intention of killin' her."

"Why you—"

"Shut up! I'll get rid of her, all right, and that husband of hers'll think she's dead, but I ain't gonna kill her. I'm gonna take her down below the border. Get a good price for her down there, with that pale skin of hers. That'll give me a grub stake. You, I don't care what you do. Me, I'm gonna sell her. After I get through with her," he added with a grin. "You still wanna watch?"

Carmen glared back at him, the buttons on the front of her blouse threatening to pop loose over her heaving chest. Whoowee! She sure was mad.

He didn't care.

Crane turned his back on Carmen and faced Daniella with a grin. "Now," he said rubbing his hands together, "I've been waitin' for this a long time, sugar."

Daniella felt her skin shrinking from his touch as bile rose to her throat. No! This couldn't be happening! She'd rather he killed her than this! She wanted to beg, scream, cry. But she couldn't. She couldn't make her voice work. She couldn't tear her eyes away from those huge, brutal hands. Hands that reached for her.

Fat, sausage-like fingers clamped over one breast. Daniella screamed. Crane cursed and clapped a hand over her mouth. She screamed behind his hand.

From the corner of her eye, she saw Carmen moving in behind Crane. An instant later Crane freed her and whirled to face his partner. Carmen had his gun! She waved it around wildly.

"Get away from her! She has to die, I tell you! If you won't do it, I will!"

Crane lunged for Carmen, trying to knock the gun from her grasp. The two struggled, the gun caught between their bodies. All Daniella could see were flailing arms and legs.

Frantically, while they were occupied with each other, she sawed the rope back and forth over the branch above her. She didn't take her eyes off the struggling couple, but knew if she looked up she'd see blood on her wrists.

A sharp explosion ripped through the clearing. Daniella froze. Crane and Carmen stared into each other's eyes. Daniella couldn't breathe, couldn't think. She didn't know what to hope for. If Crane won, he'd rape her; if Carmen won, Daniella would die in a matter of minutes.

She didn't want to die! Dear God, she didn't want to die! But neither did she believe she could endure what Crane had planned for her.

She stared, waiting, then watched with a sick feeling as Carmen slowly slid to the ground. The woman fell back, revealing a gaping hole in her stomach, blood gushing, spreading rapidly across her clothes.

"Goddamn," Crane whispered. "Goddamn!" He looked down at the gun in his hand, then threw it away in disgust. Another woman, dead. He, who'd never thought to harm anyone all the years of his life, had killed two women in one day.

Goddamn.

His eyes darted around the tiny clearing, trying to light on something that would help him make sense out of all this. Then he spotted Daniella, still hanging where he'd tied her.

What now? he asked himself.

Carmen had made several prominent friends in Tucson. She would be missed. And he'd been seen with her more than once. Someone would look for her. If they found her, no, *when* they found her—bodies always had a way of getting themselves found—there'd be questions.

He'd have to leave, that was certain. But he might still be suspected. Mexico would be a good place to go. He'd been headed there anyway, to sell Daniella.

That was too dangerous now, selling the woman. One woman he knew was dead, another woman he knew missing. No. Too dangerous.

Then he had it. Carmen had told him she couldn't be anywhere near when Daniella was killed, because everyone at the Triple C knew how much she hated the girl. If both women—he shook at the thought of killing Daniella, for he wouldn't be able to tell himself it was an accident—but if both women were found dead, next to each other, with signs of struggle, people would think they'd killed each other!

Daniella kept her eyes on Crane and sawed at the branch. She watched him look around, realizing he had something new on his mind. When the big bull of a man finally straightened and turned toward her, her hands fell still. Her heart thundered in her chest.

His gray eyes held a new light, different from before when he'd reached for her. Different. Harder. Colder. And there was something else there, too. Something that terrified her more than anything yet this day. An apology.

He was going to kill her. Right now. And he was sorry.

"Don't do this, Crane," she whispered. "Don't." It was the closest she could come to begging for her life. Then her tongue stuck to the roof of her mouth and she couldn't speak at all.

When he turned back toward Carmen and squatted next to the woman's body, Daniella didn't relax. He was still going to kill her, she knew. She had no earthly idea why he was ripping Carmen's clothes and scratching up her face and hands, but she knew he was going to kill her.

Then he stood and gave a slow nod to his work and came toward Daniella. She sawed at the rope again, too terrified to worry about whether or not he understood she was trying to get free. He didn't seem to notice her efforts. He reached out and yanked the braid wrapped around her head loose from its pins.

She was too scared to even cry out at the sharp pain. She started squirming, kicking, anything to keep his hands away from her. Her breath came in harsh, painful gasps. He grabbed hold of the front of her dress. She jerked backward. The buttons slipped from their holes, opening the dress clear to her waist.

Crane stared at the sight of her pale skin barely concealed by her thin chemise. He grabbed a breast and stared, seeming mesmerized as she felt warm milk ooze from her engorged nipple. Tender and swollen from not being able to nurse the twins all day, Daniella moaned against the pain.

His tongue came out and swiped at his lips, barely visibly through his grisly red beard. Daniella wanted to die. She nearly strangled on the revulsion rising in her chest. He squeezed her breast again. More milk leaked. He lowered his head slowly, tongue out. Daniella screamed.

He swiped at her nipple through her chemise and she flinched. When he raised his head, his gray eyes darkened like storm clouds. He held on to her breast and grabbed her hair with his free hand. Wet, slobbering lips covered her mouth, and his tongue forced its way past the barrier of her teeth.

Daniella gagged and squirmed against him, trying to free herself. Bile rose in her throat. As he pressed closer she felt him harden against her stomach. Almost of their own accord, her teeth clamped down on his tongue. He tried to jerk away. She clenched her jaws and bit down even harder. The coppery taste of blood flooded her mouth.

His hand in her hair yanked hard, breaking her hold on his tongue and jerking her away. "Thit!" he screamed. "Oo gaw-amn bith!" Blood spurted from his mouth. Teeth and lips gleamed red and hideous in the waning afternoon light, a different, darker shade of red from his beard. He swung at her. His beefy fist caught her squarely between the breasts, knocking the wind from her.

Daniella swung limply by her bleeding wrists, trying to suck air into her tortured lungs.

A hoarse bellow of rage echoed through the trees.

Travis!

In the next instant, all hell broke loose. Travis erupted into the clearing, going for Billy Joe Crane like a maddened beast. His pistol was still holstered, his knife still sheathed. He went after Crane with his bare hands, seemingly oblivious to the flashing steel blade Crane pulled from his boot.

Crane lunged with the knife. Daniella didn't even have enough air in her lungs to scream. Travis deflected the blow with his left arm and smashed his right fist into Crane's face.

Again and again the knife came at Travis, and each time he managed to block the blade and keep his skin intact.

Of the two men, Crane was by far the larger, but Travis was harder, leaner, faster.

Eventually Crane got lucky and managed to lay open a thin slit along Travis's upper arm. Travis drew his own knife then. They circled each other, dodging and feinting, lunging and parrying.

Having finally regained her breath, Daniella clamped her lips shut to keep from screaming as she watched her husband's blood trail down his arm. Time after time, the two men slashed and jabbed at each other. Several lightning-swift thrusts from Travis sent rivulets of red pouring down Crane's chest.

With a roar of desperate rage, Crane lunged at Travis with his whole body, knocking Travis's knife aside. The momentum of the rush sent Travis crashing backward toward

Daniella with a grunt. Crane had him in a fierce bear hug. Both men's faces turned red with effort.

They were only a couple of feet in front of Daniella now. She tried to swing out of their stumbling path.

Crane's grip held Travis's arms immobile, crushed as they were against his sides. Daniella held her breath, willing Travis whatever strength she had to break loose. Then Crane wrapped his foot around Travis's. She watched, horrified, as Travis's knee buckled. Crane leaned into him. Both men, wrapped together in their deadly struggle, crashed fully into her.

She would have cried out at the impact, but the breath once again rushed from her lungs. With the weight of two large men against her, the rope bit into her wrists until she thought sure they would snap in two.

In the next instant the thick dead branch holding her prisoner snapped like a twig, sending Daniella, with the two men on top of her, crashing to the ground.

Pain exploded in her head, her lungs, her wrists. Then everything went black.

When she came to, she had no idea how long she'd been out. Not long, she guessed, rolling to her side with a groan and pushing herself up, for she couldn't see any new wounds on either man. Travis was breathing hard, but Crane was gasping, clawing for each breath.

When she realized Travis's dangerous position, she felt a sickening lurch in the region of her stomach. He was about to back into the pack mule. She bit down on her bottom lip to keep from crying out. To distract him now would mean his certain death. Thanks to the height of the limb she'd been tied to, there was over two feet of rope between her bound wrists. Without taking her eyes off Travis, she fumbled with the knots, only to realize her fingers were so swollen and numb they were all but useless.

Travis jumped back to avoid Crane's vicious jab at his stomach. He shook his head, trying to cool his raging temper enough to think. There was something he'd overlooked

404

Something he should be aware of. Wary, he watched Crane's look grow more self-confident by the second.

A sound behind him, a shuffling—too late he remembered the mule.

The screeching bray came simultaneously with what felt like a locomotive ramming him below the ribs. He landed on his back, stunned.

Crane loomed over him and gave a triumphant shout. He raised the knife in his beefy fist, directly over Travis's head.

Travis, still stunned, realized his danger and rolled away as swiftly as he could, but Crane followed him. The gleaming knife poised, and Travis knew he couldn't move fast enough to get clear. He couldn't even breathe.

The bark of the pistol didn't register in his brain until he saw Crane's fist open, saw the knife fall to the dirt, and saw Crane stagger forward, stumble, and collapse to the ground, dead.

Travis raised his eyes slowly and stared at a sight he would never forget as long as he lived.

Chapter Thirty-four

Daniella stood across the clearing, on the other side of the small fire, feet spread, both arms stretched out in front of her, a smoking pistol wavering in her shaking hands.

She'd seen Travis fall beneath the hooves of the mule, seen Crane raise his knife for the kill. Frantically, she'd searched the ground for Crane's discarded revolver, finding it with no time left to think about what she was doing.

But what was there to think about, after all? Crane had kidnapped her; he'd tried to rape her; he'd killed Carmen; he'd killed Lucinda; and he was going to kill Travis. No, there was no point in thinking. She clutched the gun in both hands, ignoring the rope connecting her wrists, aimed at Crane's back, and pulled the trigger a mere second before he would have plunged his knife into Travis.

She stared blankly at Billy Joe Crane's body for a long, stunned moment, then began to shake violently from head to toe. The pistol fell from her trembling fingers.

Travis rose stiffly to his feet and gave one last look at the glazed, dead eyes that stared sightlessly at the darkening sky. In seconds he was across the clearing, taking Dani in his arms. The heat of battle still rushed through his veins. He was unaware of how tightly he held her until she whimpered in pain. He eased his hold at once.

"You're hurt. Where, Dani?" he questioned frantically running his hands over her, checking for injuries.

"No," she answered quickly. "Only bruises."

"Did he —"

406

"No!" Then, more calmly, "No. I'm all right. Really. But you're not." She tugged at his shirt in an effort to get at his wounds, every bit as frantic as he had just been.

"They're just scratches, nothing to worry about."

Jason, Luis, and Benito burst into the clearing all shouting, pistols drawn. Travis pulled Dani to his chest, gently this time, buttoned up her dress and untied her hands.

During the next hour the men carried the bodies from the clearing and set the camp to rights. Dani told what happened and explained Carmen's part in the plot. Travis never left her side. Jason and the others took the bodies and started home in spite of the dark. They wouldn't get far, but they wanted to give the couple some privacy. Travis was grateful. He needed Dani to himself for a while. He needed to hold her, to reassure them both that she was all right.

But she wasn't all right, he knew. He'd been watching the way she moved, slowly, carefully, the way she hunched her shoulders. The way she tried to hide the wet spots on the front of her dress with her arms.

"Dani?" She'd been keeping her head lowered, and he reached a finger to her chin, forcing her to look at him. Her eyes were dark and glazed with pain. "What's wrong? Where do you hurt?"

"I — I'm all right," she said, lowering her gaze.

Travis glanced once more to the damp circles on her dress. He'd seen them before, when her breasts were full and it was time to feed the twins.

Good God, he thought. She'd been away from Pace and Serena all day. She hadn't nursed them since early this morning.

"You're too full, aren't you?" he asked, raising his gaze to hers. She nodded mutely in response. "And it hurts like hell, doesn't it?" Again she nodded.

Then she took a slow, deep breath and insisted on cleaning his wounds.

"But you're in worse shape than I am," he argued.

"Maybe, but nothing can be done about my problem, unless you happen to have the twins tucked away in your saddlebags."

Relenting, Travis pulled off his torn, blood-stained shirt and let Dani clean his few cuts and gashes with a piece of her petticoat dampened from the canteen. She kept dabbing at his wounds, even as her own tears of pain splashed down her cheeks.

"That's enough, Dani." He stood away from her and spread out the blankets Jason had left, then led Dani to them and sat her down, pushing her back against his saddle. "Now we'll take care of you."

He tore a fresh strip from her petticoat, wet it from the canteen as Dani had done earlier, then proceeded to gently wash her face, then her wrists. After unbuttoning her dress and lowering the straps of her chemise, he bathed her neck and breasts. He felt her tense when he reached those painfully swollen mounds.

Daniella laid her head back on the saddle, closed her eyes against the pain, and tried to will herself to relax. The cool cloth did help, a little. Her eyes flew open in surprise when she felt his warm lips tasting her overflowing milk. Then his mouth enveloped the nipple and he began to suckle. She moaned at the fresh flow of pain.

Travis raised his lips and searched her eyes. "I'm sorry. I know it hurts, but it's the only way. I can't leave you like this." He lowered his mouth again and drained the warm, sweet liquid from her breasts with his own mouth to ease her pain. She laid her head back down.

His suckling both hurt and relieved. She felt the pressure begin to ease, and eventually the breast he nursed became visibly smaller than its mate. He moved his lips to the other nipple, and as that pressure, too, began to ease, the feel and sight of his warm mouth against her skin sent desire stirring in the pit of her being. He must have felt the same, for the smaller the second breast became, the larger and harder the bulge of his manhood grew as he pressed against her thigh.

When his lips finally traveled from her nipple to her

408

mouth, Daniella and Travis were both trembling with want and need.

"Better?" he murmured against her lips.

"Mmm," she moaned as his mouth took hers in a tender kiss. Her arms slid around his neck and she buried her hands in the curls at the back of his head. "Yes," she whispered with a smile. "But now I think you have something swollen that needs relief."

He groaned and laughed, and the rest of their clothes disappeared as if by magic. His gaze swept her body and nearly scorched her with its intensity. A chill wind swept through the clearing, but neither noticed as he pressed his hot body against the length of her. He spread kisses from her head to her toes, from her white streak of hair to the soles of her feet, while her hands roamed over him with increasing frenzy. He kissed away her lingering fears, kissed away the touch of her abductor, leaving a burning trail of flame as he went. They touched, stroked, clung, frantic at having lost an entire day of each other, desperate to forget they had nearly lost so much more.

Travis cupped his hand on the center of her womanhood, and his fingers slid inside, finding her hot, wet, and ready for him. With a deep groan, he settled between her open thighs and thrust into the depths of her velvet softness, branding her with the flames of his desire.

Only recently had he found her, and today he'd nearly lost her. Frantically, desperately, he thrust into her again and again, and she met him with a ferocity of her own. They came together, cried out together in release that was sweet, yet violent, as raw emotions seared them, binding them together in a tie that could never be broken.

Chapter Thirty-five

Travis leaned back against the mound of pillows propped up behind him on the bed and watched as Dani slowly pulled the brush through her hair. His thoughts ran over the events of the past few days.

Their trip home from the hills had been exhausting for Dani. When they arrived she'd been so relieved to find Lucinda recovering, and equally relieved that the twins were hungry.

Jason had picked up the mail in Tucson, and there was a letter from Tom Jeffords. That there was mail to pick up at all meant Jeffords had been at least somewhat successful in his talk with Cochise. The post office said mail was a regular thing again these days.

But the news was even better than that. It seemed Cochise took an instant liking to Jeffords, even giving his new friend an Apache name, Taglito—Redbeard. Dani and Travis were both gratified to learn that their instincts to trust Jeffords had been right. The man's friendship with Cochise could conceivably, someday, help bring about peace between the Apaches and the Americans.

And somewhere up in the hills—Travis hadn't asked Jason for specifics—there were two fresh graves where Billy Joe Crane and Carmen Martinez rested, side by side.

"What are you thinking?" Travis asked his wife as he took the brush from her fingers and finished the task of smoothing her hair himself. He buried his face in the silken tresses and breathed in the fragrance he loved so well.

"Just that I love you very much," she answered softly.

"You looked so serious just then."

She smiled at him over her shoulder. "I seriously love you."

Travis laughed easily and pulled her back into his arms. "And I seriously love you, too. Did you know I've loved you from our first meeting?"

"I don't believe you." She looked at him with suspicion, remembering their first meeting vividly.

"Well, it's true. When you walked into the dining room that morning I knew you were someone special. Your eyes . . . I wanted to drown myself in your eyes. But when you took off your hat, that's when I knew I loved you." He kissed the streak in her hair, then her eyes, her nose, and finally her soft, pliant lips. "The Chiricahua call you Woman of Magic, and they're right. You cast a spell on me that day."

She smiled up at him with eyes full of love. "I loved you long before then."

"How could you? We hadn't even met."

"I'd met you, you just hadn't met me. You forget, I saw you get this." She traced a finger over the scar on his cheek and followed her finger with her lips. "Oh, Travis, is the trouble over? Can we live a normal life now?"

"Yes, love, the trouble's over. We can raise our children here on this ranch and tell the rest of the world to go to hell." He pushed back the thought of the country tearing itself apart in war—a war between the North and South, and even closer to home, a war between the Apaches and whites. Now was not the time to remember those things. Not for them. Now was the time for a little peace, some hope for the future, and love.

Daniella was fully aware of what he left unsaid, but she, too, pushed it to the back of her mind. She took Travis's face in her hands and gazed softly into the depths of his dark eyes. "Whatever comes our way, we can handle it, as long as we're together. I love you, Travis."

"Yes, together," he whispered. His lips touched hers. "Always together." His mouth captured hers in a fierce, demanding kiss. "God, how I love you, Dani."

"Show me," she whispered against his lips.

And he showed her.

Author's Note

In researching southeastern Arizona of the 1860's, I ran across a dismaying number of conflicting reports. Many sources described incidents as happening in the same way, with the same people involved, but on entirely different dates; sometimes even in different years. The dates, locations, and people involved in the incidents I have used were confirmed by more than one source.

Cochise's war against the white man stemmed from an event which took place on February 2, 1861. He accepted an invitation from Second Lieutenant George N. Bascom to come to Apache Pass and talk. Cochise took several people with him, including women and children, and entered the officer's tent, which bore a white flag of truce. He was promptly arrested and slapped in irons.

He was accused of stealing cattle and kidnapping a young boy from the ranch of Mr. John Ward. Cochise flatly denied the charges, but offered to find the boy and arrange for his release. Bascom refused the offer.

Cochise escaped by cutting a hole in the back of the tent. (The soldiers had failed to take his knife.) The people with him, one of whom was his brother, did not escape. Cochise took three white men hostage and offered to exchange them for Bascom's Apache prisoners. Again, Bascom refused. Cochise tortured the white men to death. Bascom hung Cochise's brother and two nephews.

This incident was the spark that set Cochise on an eleven-year rampage. (Sources agree that Cochise probably would

413

have gone to war eventually anyway, due to the ever increasing white population.) History has exonerated Cochise of the crime of which he was accused that day in February, 1861. (It was February 2, 3, 4, or 10, depending on which source you read. If you read enough different sources, you can also place this event in 1862 or 1860.) The kidnapped boy escaped from his captors, the Pinalero Apaches, in February, 1862. In a few years, he became known as Mickey Free, one of the best scouts and fiercest manhunters the U. S. Army ever employed.

If you plan to read up on this period and location, keep in mind that the area (then officially part of the Territory of New Mexico) was sparsely populated and totally ungoverned, except for an occasional military presence. Eyewitness accounts, and later historical writings, do not always, or even often, agree on much. Many times you will be left to decide for yourself just what did happen, where, when, and to whom.

Many of the people in this story lived and breathed in the time and place I have described. Among them are Cochise, Dee-O-Det, Mon-ache (Mangas Coloradas), Golthlay (Geronimo), Nana (Nanay), Tahza, Naiche (Natchez), Lt. Lord, Pete Kitchen, and Tom Jeffords. Their physical descriptions are, for the most part, accurate; their personalities are based on research.

It is my understanding that the old-time Apaches did not call out the names of those departed, except in emergency, for fear of angering the spirit by calling it away from some pleasant pastime in the Spirit World. I hope that, since I am not an Apache, those in the Spirit World will not hear my voice. If I am wrong, and have offended anyone by using the real names of those long-ago leaders, I sincerely apologize. I meant no harm. I only meant to show that these people had names of their own, in their own language. The white man took away everything else. Let us at least leave them their own names.

I have also attempted, to a small degree, to indicate that

the Chiricahua, like all Native Americans, spoke (and some still speak) their own language. The words and phrases I have used are from the Chiricahua dialect. Until recent years, it was never a written language, and even now, spelling varies, according to each source. With the help of Leland Michael Darrow, Tribal Historian of the Fort Sill Apaches (the Chiricahua who remained in Oklahoma after their release in 1924 from prisoner of war status) I have used the Fort Sill Apache tribal spellings for the Chiricahua words in this book. Mr. Darrow generously gave of his time and talents to ensure my accuracy. Thank you, Michael. Any mistakes are mine, not his.

And then there's the dress, the ceremonial beaded buckskin in which Daniella was married. I have been privileged to wear such a dress myself. The dress in the book, lent to Daniella by Cochise's wives, was patterned after a Chiricahua ceremonial dress lent to me in 1989 by Mildred Cleghorn, Chairman of the Fort Sill Apache Tribe. The real dress (Mrs. Cleghorn's personal clothing) was not made by one of Cochise's wives, but the top half was made by his granddaughter, Dorothy Naiche Kawaykla, more than 50 years ago. The skirt was made by Mr. Talbot Gooday, Sr.

I am in awe of the talent, skill, and time these two people invested in such a beautiful garment. I am humbled and honored to have been allowed to wear it. Thank you, Mildred, from the bottom of my heart.

A few months after the almost spiritual experience of wearing Chiricahua ceremonial clothing, I was privileged to attend the ceremony inducting Cochise into the National Hall of Fame for Famous American Indians on August 6, 1989, in Anadarko, Oklahoma. After the unveiling of the bronze bust of Cochise, the attendees were treated to Apache songs, a war dance, and a social dance. I can still feel the beat of Apache drums in my veins.

As for the members of the Colton family and their friends, they are entirely fictitious, except in my mind. To me, they are very real. I hope they are to you, too.

Before long, Matt Colton will grow to manhood on the Triple C. Among the hordes of people streaming from the East looking for a new life will be a young woman named Angela. As a promise is extracted from her, the fate of an entire nation will rest on her slender shoulders. Angela and Matt will—

Ah, but that's another story. Someday soon, on some dark, lonely night, perhaps you and I will share a cozy campfire, and I will tell you of Angela's promise—a promise of love and passion, of loyalty and courage. An APACHE PROMISE.

Sincerely,

Janis Reams Hudson
Oklahoma City, Oklahoma